Fossil Island

Fossil Island

A NOVEL

Barbara Sjoholm

Cedar Street Editions

LIBRARY OF CONGRESS CATALOGING-INPUBLICATION

Sjoholm, Barbara, 1950–
Fossil Island : a novel / Barbara Sjoholm.
pages cm
LCCN 2015906167
ISBN 978-0-9883567-4-0 (paper)
ISBN 978-0-9883567-2-6 (e-book)

1. Nielsen, Carl, 1865–1931—Fiction. 2. Demant Hatt, Emilie, 1873–1958—Fiction. 3. Composers—Denmark—Fiction. 4. Ethnologists—Denmark—Fiction. 5. Women's rights—Denmark—Fiction. 6. Denmark—Fiction. 7. Historical fiction. I. Sequel: Sjoholm, Barbara, 1950– Former world. II. Title.

PS3573.I45678F677 2015
813'.54

QBI15-600093

This is a work of fiction. Names, characters, places, and incidents either are products of the author's imagination or are used fictitiously.

Cover painting: Detail from *A Stroll on the Beach*, by Michael Ancher, 1896.

Cover and text design: VJB/Scribe

CONTENTS

The Telephone

1887

1.

SHE FOLLOWED THE LOVESICK CRIES AND DARK-HEARTED groans into the parlor. A boy was half inside their old Marschall piano, his backside sticking out, rounded and muscular, in blue flannel trousers.

Mama and Aunt Marie, eyes riveted on the trousers, sat side by side on the green silk sofa with the curvy padded back. They held their ears tight and grimaced, but almost in pleasure. When they saw Nik, Aunt Marie shouted, "My foster son Carl is tuning your piano."

The horrid twanging and groaning stopped briefly, then resumed with a sporadic tunefulness, as if a baby were banging on a little tin pot. The windows of the parlor were open and dust from the country road blew in through the muslin drapes. Nik's mother took her hands from her ears and smoothed the dark bundles of curls at her perspiring temples. "Dearest, tell Mrs. Jespersen to bring more coffee."

When she came back into the parlor, the boy was out of the piano and sitting on the bench in front of the keyboard. A rubbery sort of face; blue-eyed curiosity; lips red for a boy. His thick light hair stuck up on top, like a hedge.

"My youngest daughter, Emilie," said her mother. "We call her Nik."

"The tomboy," said Aunt Marie, fanning herself. "Come here, sweet girl, and give me a kiss." It was mid-June and sultry but Aunt Marie was corseted as tightly as usual, stuffed into a maroon and poison-green plaid traveling dress. Her cheeks were flushed and she wore little rubies in her soft fat ears.

Nik had on a battered riding coat over an old dress that didn't reach her ankles. She'd just come from Marienlyst, a farm ten miles away that belonged to her godparents. When Old Franz appeared with the message to return home right away—Aunt Marie had arrived from Copenhagen with Carl—Nik had been leaping out of a barn loft into hay with the neighbor boy Jens. A few bits of straw still stuck to her electric hair and itched her legs. She went over to her aunt and mother and tried not to muss their dresses as she pressed her sun-browned face against theirs. Then she turned to the boy, who rose from the bench to shake her hand.

"Miss Nik. Good day!" He was on the short side, but well-proportioned. Springy. How nice his hand felt, how warm and alive. The fingernails were square-cut and clean, unlike her own.

"I'm quite embarrassed," said her mother cheerfully. "We so wanted to have a piano for Carl to play on. The Marschall has been out of tune for weeks and we've been waiting for Mr. Zangenberg. But in the end I had to ask the blacksmith to forge a tuning fork—as you can hear, with lamentable results."

Aunt Marie stroked her little ruby earring, glittering next to the loops of fading chestnut hair. "What do you think, Carl, is it possible to play on this old thing?"

"Let's try it out again, now that I've made some adjustments." He seated himself, then turned and bowed, sticking out his red lower lip and furrowing his brow: "Ladies. I give you—the Fifth!" He ran his fingers over the keys and then crashed down with the big Beethoven opening, before switching suddenly to a Bach gavotte. Even though a few keys were off, the piano sounded better than it had in months.

"I remember seeing my first piano," the boy said, twisting around to face Nik. "My mama had a half brother, the blind organist of Dalum Church in Odense. One day, when I was quite young, Mama and I walked all the way to town, seven miles each way. Mama brought him a sausage. How pleased the old fellow was! He sniffed it and rolled it in his hands before putting it carefully in a cupboard. Then he opened up his piano and invited me to sit next to him. For the first time I saw notes made visible, black and white, a long row of keys. Before then, notes were just something you hunted for on a fiddle string."

"I'm sorry your mama and papa are dead," said Nik. She thought it romantic, that her uncle and aunt had adopted this boy. She didn't know how old he was; he looked about sixteen or seventeen, two or three years older than she was.

"Nik!" said her mother, waving to Mrs. Jespersen to put the tray down. "Of course Carl has parents. It's not a real adoption."

"Though we think of Carl as quite our son." Aunt Marie took a cup of coffee from Mama and a large slice of cream cake. "Quite part of our family, and now your family too."

"Don't you worry about my parents, little one!" Carl said. "They're as hale and hearty as ever in Black Bog. Papa still plays his fiddle and Mama misses her children who've traveled out into the world. My brother Anders and sister Julie live in Chicago and another brother went to Australia, can you imagine? It's just coincidence I have the same last name as your aunt and uncle." He bowed slightly to Aunt Marie. "The kind Nielsens have taken me in hand and helped put me through the Conservatory."

"Carl brought his violin," said Aunt Marie. "Oh, we'll have some lovely musical evenings, you'll see. Carl, please continue. I adore Bach! How warm it is." She fanned like mad then took up her plate of cake again.

Why did Aunt Marie call this boy her foster son if he had parents and brothers and sisters? Why had her aunt and uncle sold their house in Odense and moved to Copenhagen for him? A fragment of a whispered story came back to her: something to do with an unsuitable attachment.

Nik couldn't keep her eyes off his fingers, how they skipped over the keys. That light quick touch of his fingers was something she felt in her own hand, where the warmth of his skin had surprised her.

~

Nik was fourteen that summer. She'd been confirmed in April. Now her schooling was at an end and no one knew precisely what to do with her. She wasn't studious like her sister Maj, who was enrolled at the women teachers' college in Odense, and she was too young to be married. Nineteen-year-old Maj had an admirer, the son of a nearby pastor and a steady sort of fellow, said Papa approvingly, with a future in his uncle's peat works near Viborg. Frederik Brandt was currently a lieutenant in the Royal Army; he wore a handsome uniform and a significant moustache. Behind his back Nik called him the Tin Soldier, because he was so tall and straight that he made the walls of their old house look crooked when he was in the room. Last Christmas Frederik had paid a great deal of attention to Maj, and Mama expected him to propose when Maj came home for a visit this summer.

As for Nik, she had few housekeeping talents and was still oddly childish, her mother sighed, for such a tall, well-formed girl. She still played with her toy circus, read adventure stories, and went out shooting with her father. Although she refused to carry a gun, she liked getting up at dawn and tromping through the marshes.

When she was small Nik often used to help measure sugar and wrap soft soap in her family's store. The Hansens were the main innkeepers and merchants in the village of Selde; her father sold everything from fresh eggs and pickled herring to lengths of fabric and hardware. Nik had liked wrapping cambric and iron nails in paper and tying them up tightly with string and strong knots. She was a fine packager, said the clerk, Mr. Svendsen. Sometimes he'd let her wear his striped canvas apron, knowing how she coveted it.

But for the last year Mama hadn't let her help in the shop; it wasn't suitable for a young lady to serve behind a counter, now she had a figure that could be observed and commented on by men who were drinking beer and brandy. Now it was time to learn to embroider and to help Mrs. Jespersen make her special meatballs. Now it was time to practice the piano and to lower her voice and read more serious books, not just stories about cowboys in America and nomads in Lapland.

Mama was kind-hearted and too fond of a good time to be very severe, but she was also conscious of their social position. Next to the pastor and his wife, the Hansens were the most prominent family in the village, on good terms with the local squires and even one or two of the aristocratic manor owners nearby. And that was as it should be, because even though she had married a man in trade, Emma Demant was born to a family of standing. Her father had been a lawyer in Odense. Her brother Hans Demant owned a large factory that produced sewing machines and velocipedes. Her sister Marie had married Jens Nielsen, a merchant, now retired, with a passion for music. Aunt Marie was much younger than her husband, and they had never had children.

The morning after the arrival of the guests, Nik got up very early, with a sense of expectation that felt like the buzzing of bees at a white clover patch. She washed her face quickly and screwed her dark curls into a knot, pulled on a dress, and jammed on a straw hat. No one was awake in the house except Jutta, the maid; they wouldn't miss her if she went for a walk. It was just a week or so after the solstice and the sun was up at four. It lit the fields as if the barley grasses were a million waving candles, each tipped with a feather of gold. The thrushes and song sparrows were singing in the hawthorn and the marsh hawks soared over the heather.

The land around Selde had once been heather and hardy oak but more and more of it was cultivated now into fields of barley, hay, and yellow rapeseed, separated by windbreaks of poplar and hawthorn and stands of beech and oak. In the winter strong winds howled straight from the North Sea across the Limfjord and twisted the poplars practically to earth, but in summer you forgot the lashing rain and ice storms. The landscape held traces of all the people who had lived here in ancient times, the burial mounds of the Old People, the harbors of the Vikings, the moated houses of the King's men from the Middle Ages. But Selde was an ordinary hamlet, with just a white-plastered church with a tower and a windmill on the rise behind her family's house.

Nik walked along the rutted country road for a time, the one that led to the ferry landing in one direction and to the market town of Skive in the other, then she struck off across a smaller path. She had been paying attention to a family of wood ducks on a reedy marsh nearby, watching the fluffy ducklings scuttle in an anxious procession behind their mother. Today the ducklings were fewer by one; a fox or stoat must have discovered a straggler. She explored the banks of cattails and sedges and the hem of her dress grew thoroughly muddy, in spite of hiking it up into her belt.

By the time she returned, farmers and laborers were weeding and hoeing in the fields and a few horses and wagons rattled along the road. Nik could see her family's timbered brick-and-wattle house, plastered ochre yellow, with the thatched roof and row of small upstairs windows. The house sprawled along the main road, with the general store at one end and the inn in a separate wing. Ranged around the cobblestoned square behind the house, forming a rectangular series of buildings, were the laundry and storage rooms, horse stables, a cow barn and dairy parlor. In the center of the square was a water pump and through an arched gate in the brick wall flourished a large vegetable patch. Beyond the garden was her mother's carefully tended apple orchard.

Christian Hansen's establishment was the main concern in Selde. Next door to the house and store, on the main road, was the schoolhouse and then the blacksmith; after that came a cluster of cottages and then the parsonage, pale red brick and trimmed in green and covered in hops, clematis, and pink ramblers. Schoolmaster Strandgaard and his four children lived in a manor house about a mile away, while other cottages in the village were rented by those who worked for Nik's father at the lumberyard or by widows, one or two of whom would have married the schoolmaster if it weren't for all the children or the fact that he was known to be a freethinker.

2.

"WHERE'S THE YOUNG GENTLEMAN?" PAPA ASKED AT breakfast that day.

In spite of the morning heat he had on his usual short loden jacket and underneath it a vest held his round silver pocket watch. His reading glasses sat at the end of his long nose as he took out the watch and peered at it: "Five minutes after eight! Can he still be sleeping?" Sunlight poured into the dining room, exactly at the head of the table where Papa sat, his thinning hair now more white than blond, his short neat beard entirely white.

Her father had taken coffee earlier in his office, but he always made a habit of joining the ladies for breakfast. He looked approvingly at the pewter tray of bacon and the basket of boiled eggs, and the bowls of churned yellow butter. Mama had brought out an earthenware pot of red currant jam and Mrs. Jespersen had made cardamom rolls. Papa cut one open and a waft of cardamom and yeast flew into Nik's nose. She reached for one too and let butter melt into its soft center.

Mama said, "Christian, the boy is on holiday. He's been working hard in Copenhagen and he and Sister Marie had a long journey yesterday. Nik—what is that in your hair? Is it a duck feather? Where have you been this morning so early?"

"Carl is used to late nights," said Aunt Marie, knocking the top off her boiled egg and salting its bright gold yolk. "The life of a musician is a late-night life. Besides, that's when he composes. We can hear him in our apartment half the night."

Her aunt wore a lace cap this morning and had more than the usual amount of lace around her neck, which hid her rippling chin. Her earrings were pearls. She was six years older than Mama, Nik knew, forty-seven. Mama was prettier but Aunt Marie had more lavish clothes and jewelry.

"I thought I heard piano music last night," said Papa. "But, does he want to be a composer? Are you and Jens encouraging him in this, Sister?"

"Carl Nielsen is a genius," said Aunt Marie. She had a dab of sticky yolk at the corner of her mouth. "Jens is no fool. He may be tight with his purse but he's always invested wisely. Even the decision to sell the business and our home in Odense and buy an apartment in Copenhagen—Jens turned that into a profit. We have more money than we know what to do with. Though unfortunately Jens won't let me spend much of it."

Mama's lips tightened slightly, then she laughed. After all, who would want to be married to an old man who carried his deeds and investment papers everywhere he went, in a bag with a little lock, and who picked up coal off the streets to save money?

"The boy must be clever, I'll grant you that," said Papa. "Whether or not he's a genius, I can't tell. But to go from being the son of poor nobodies to being taken up by rich folk in Odense and sent to the Royal Conservatory, he must have some talent. Still, you shouldn't spoil him, Marie. Let him get up with the rest of us and take breakfast like ordinary folk. I had thought to take him hunting. But you need to wake up at four a.m. for that."

"I don't imagine Carl likes hunting," said Aunt Marie with a little toss of her lace cap. She helped herself to another cardamom roll.

"Not like hunting!" Papa shook his head. "I thought the boy had been in the Army."

"He was only a bugler in the Odense Regiment," said Aunt Marie. "A darling little bugler and piccolo player. That's when my husband discovered him. Playing his piccolo one day in the yard at Nørregade. Jens told the servant to go down and bring the little fellow upstairs so we could meet him."

They had all heard this story before—it made a nice picture.

Still, Mama had said she wasn't sure if Aunt Marie might be exaggerating a little. After all, the boy played the alto trombone in the military band and was a fiddler in his spare time, not a piccolo player. Uncle Hans had told Mama that this Carl Nielsen had somehow gained the attention of various prominent people in Odense, not just Jens and Marie. There was a politician who had managed to get him an introduction to Mr. Gade at the Royal Conservatory of Music in Copenhagen. And once the boy had been accepted, many contributed to his expenses, including Uncle Hans. Hans Demant was just as wealthy as Jens, and probably more so, said Mama.

"That's right, a bugler," said Papa with a wink. "He used to take his turn sounding reveille, didn't he? Well, that was long ago! Thank goodness Maj comes back soon for a visit. Frederik will be here too, I imagine, and then we'll see some hunting. Now I'm off and will meet you ladies at noon. The boy too. If he's awake."

As her father rose, Nik got up too. "Where are you going, Papa? Can I come too, Papa?"

He waved her to follow.

As they left the room, she heard her mother whisper to her aunt a name that seemed familiar from another confidential conversation she'd overheard recently, between her parents: "And Karen Marie?"

When they were out in the yard, Nik said to her father, "Who is Karen Marie?"

Papa coughed. "Where did you? Bad mistake, bad mistake. A fellow needs to be able to control himself. Or else . . . well, never mind."

"But—Papa?"

"Ask your mother. Women can explain these sorts of things better."

They went into the general store, through the back door. The large room smelled of dark wooden floors, scattered with fresh sawdust; it smelled of barrels of salt herring and slippery wooden tubs of soap. There were other smells too: the sweetness of wheat berries, the sour tang of rye, the tins of West Indian tobacco, dark-roasted coffee beans from India, ginger and cardamom. Bald Mr. Svendsen in his striped apron and collarless white shirt stood behind the mahogany counter with its scales and ledgers, its cone of brown wax string for wrapping parcels. Glass jars of molasses candy and peppermints sat on the counter and Nik thought nothing of opening up the jar and taking one. The minty bite of the pink and white lump was part of the taste of the store, just like the sawdust on the floor gave everything a woodsy freshness that knitted the smells together.

Already there were customers: Farmer Jakobsen's strapping young son buying nails and bullets; Ingrid, the parsonage housemaid, who took a long time over some sewing needles; and the usual assortment of small children, not in school nor required yet in the harvests, who hung about the counter knowing if they looked long enough at the glass jar of molasses candy, Mr. Svendsen might give them a broken piece. A few men were drinking around a battered wooden table on the other side of the room.

Nik and her father went out the front door of the shop into the main road and began walking down to the lumberyard. Yesterday a ship had anchored offshore, a Norwegian ship with a cargo of spruce. The undressed logs were offloaded from the ship into the water and then pulled onshore. Afterwards came the slow process of hitching horses to the logs and dragging the logs to the lumberyard. Although Papa talked about building a sawmill and milling the wood using a steam engine, for now the de-barking and shaping of the logs was done with axes and planes. Just as Papa's right-hand man at the shop was Mr. Svendsen, he depended on Ole Dahl to run the lumberyard. Ole Dahl, tall as a tree, had a pure clear singsong voice. His beard was shaggy and his eyes a melancholy blue. He was from the south of Norway and like many Norwegians he didn't stand on ceremony: no one called him Mr. Dahl, only Ole Dahl or Dahl.

Nik usually found the lumberyard boring after a while, but she liked to walk down to the Limfjord and gaze across the water to the island of Fur. Fur was a fossil island, with a particular sort of cementstone that had hardened around plants and shells, and the bones of birds and animals that no longer lived on earth. The island was a memory of times before History began, before God created Man. At least that's what the schoolmaster said, even when most of the children well knew that the world was created in six days in a particular order with naked Adam and Eve at the end. Schoolmaster Strandgaard believed in Mr. Charles Darwin's theories as well as a lot of other notions about the age of the earth; those beliefs had cost him his job at the cathedral school in Viborg many years ago. Now, said Papa, many people believed in evolution and enormous time spans, not just educated citizens in Copenhagen. But Nik knew Mama was a little uneasy about natural selection and the possibility that humans were once chimpanzees and that woolly mammoths had roamed free around Denmark's farmland. Her mother agreed that the fossils Nik collected on Fur along with her schoolmaster and his children could well have been a few thousand years old (that was old enough) and that elsewhere in the world it was possible there had been dinosaurs and other hideous beasts. After making such mistakes with Creation, there had been a Catastrophe and God had to begin again. With more pleasing animals, such as cats and dogs and parakeets.

The kitchen was busy when she arrived home again. Mrs. Jespersen and Mama were preparing a large midday meal. Pastor and Mrs. Wellenborg and their niece Mette Bohm from Copenhagen would be there too, and the squire's son Henrik. It was well-known that the Wellenborgs once had hopes that the Tin Soldier might marry russet-haired Mette, but instead Frederik had been swept off his feet by Maj at Squire Christiansen's Christmas ball. Now it was Henrik who was considered the best catch for Mette, though Henrik was only twenty-one and Mette twenty-four, quite an old maid. Mette and Henrik had known each other as children, back when Mette's parents owned property in the district. They both died of influenza after her brother had gone off to make his fortune in the West Indies, leaving her alone in the world at nineteen. Mette was taken in by relatives in Copenhagen, but she returned to Selde every summer, which made her still a member of the parish. According to Mama, age mattered less than compatibility. "We don't live in a city like Odense where eligible suitors hang on every tree and a girl can pick and choose."

Lively warm-up scales on the violin buzzed at the front of the house. Then came a quick Danish folk tune followed by Mozart's *Eine Kleine Nachtmusik*, which Nik knew from her sister playing it over and over last Christmas. She tip-toed through the dining room to the parlor. Aunt Marie was nowhere in sight and the boy was silhouetted by the open window that faced the street. Nik hid behind the green silk sofa and observed him. He wore the same blue flannel trousers and a white and blue striped shirt. His hair was stiff but soft like the fur of an ash-blond hedgehog. He didn't stand rigidly as he ran his bow over the strings, but moved his hips slightly and nodded his head in time to the music. She remembered hearing he'd learned to play the fiddle at dances—it was clear he felt the music through and through.

Carl faced the window. Nik couldn't see his expression. Mama said this morning he was twenty-two, not sixteen as she'd first thought. But he didn't look fully grown. He reminded her of one of the figures in her toy circus, the acrobat she called Jacques. Jacques was two and a half inches tall, with muscled shoulders and narrow hips. His cunning Harlequin suit was plastered to his body. His head was topped by a painted square of yellow. Nik bounced Jacques on the trampoline she'd made from a bit of rubber and a tin; she urged him to dance on a tightrope made of waxed string from the shop. His arms moved, so she could make him walk on his hands too.

Again that tingly sense, like bees buzzing over a patch of white clover, came over her. She felt it in her stomach and all along the inside skin of her arms, right down to the tips of her fingers where the feel of Carl's hand still lingered from yesterday. She licked her lips, which still tasted of peppermint, sweet and bold.

Aunt Marie came in, her corset tightly laced so her bosom was high and full. Her face flushed with pleasure and she had a lace handkerchief in her hand. Nik could smell its delicious flowery scent across the room. "My dear! That's lovely. Chopin, my favorite."

Carl smiled at Aunt Marie, with a flash of impatience at being interrupted. Then he caught a glimpse of Nik crouched behind the sofa. He let out a peal of laughter when he saw her mouthing, "Mozart."

Their secret understanding began right then.

3.

BEFORE SHE MET CARL, NIK HAD ONLY THOUGHT FORWARD, into an adventurous future, long on daring, short on details. She rarely shared any of her dreams with her family; they only smiled or, like her sister, scoffed gently. "And how, exactly," asked Maj last summer, "will you get to Western Australia to find your gold mine?"

"In Australia, girls can do pretty much anything," said Nik. "I would first sail to Sydney by way of South America, then take a train, or maybe a wagon across the Outback. I suppose I could also sail down the coast of Africa and around Cape Hope, then directly to Western Australia."

It was surprising what could turn up in the local paper. One week it was news of gold fields in Australia, another day it was explorations of the North Pole or overland expeditions to Mongolia. Nik read about Danish people who were converting to a strange new religion, sailing to America, and making an arduous overland trek to Salt Lake City. The Swedes went to farms in Wisconsin and Illinois; the Norwegians to Minnesota and North Dakota. Danes, always much cleverer, took the train to Chicago, opened businesses, and became rich. Every Sunday there were advertisements for steamships to America, and they always made Mama sigh. "Will there be anyone left if they all go to America? It's all right for the Norwegians, they don't have much up there except fish and trees, but little Denmark! Why would anyone like to leave home?"

Who would want to live in Denmark their whole lives when they could travel the globe? Nik never thought that she'd like to go to Africa—it seemed very hot there—but Australia beckoned and so did North America. She dreamed of Canada and the Rockies of Colorado or the Sierras of California. If the servant girls that Nik read about in the *Skive Folkeblad* could sail to New York City by themselves to seek their fortunes, why couldn't Nik?

Carl and Nik rested under a hawthorn tree on the rise above the village, having walked back from the Limfjord. Mama believed in the health benefits of a morning swim, and by the third day of his visit Carl was no longer sleeping in. Mama marched everyone off to the beach immediately after breakfast. The general rule was that the females of the sex swam vigorously for twenty minutes. The men then had their twenty minutes. For reasons unclear to Nik the ladies were able to sit on the sand observing the men splashing about in their bathing costumes while the men were not allowed to watch the ladies. However, today Mama had relented. Papa was busy and there were no other men to swim with Carl. She had allowed the boy to join her and Aunt Marie and Nik in the water.

In his navy-blue sleeveless bathing costume, tight and wet against his chest, with his blond brush of hair flattened like a seal's, Carl looked to Nik even more like Jacques the Acrobat, diving and turning somersaults in the water. His arms were pale and muscular; golden hairs lay flat and wet along his forearms and his calves, but his chest, in the V of the suit, was smooth as a boy's. Nik and the women had to wear serge bloomers and tunics, and stockings and slippers as well as little caps. Aunt Marie tended to float like a large blue jellyfish on the surface, her plump white face continually turned to Carl's antics.

Today Aunt Marie and Mama had returned home early to prepare to receive friends from a nearby town. Their departure had left Carl and Nik to wander, damp-haired and fresh, along the road homewards. The hawthorn was out of sight of the village and Nik felt a shiver of wrong-doing as Carl suggested they sit down in the shade for a moment. It was around ten and the day's heat was just beginning to fire the grass and wildflowers. The birds, still flying, suddenly had nothing to sing about anymore.

"Ah, Nik, do you know, sweet girl, how I envy you?" Carl said, after a few moments of staring up into the tree.

"Envy me? How can that be?" Nik was pleasantly aware of the wet curls at her nape and the dampness between her breasts from the swim. "You live in Copenhagen. You will soon take up a post with the Tivoli Symphony Orchestra. What do I get to do? Darning and embroidery . . ."

"I always envy people younger than me." He looked up into the thorny green mass of the hawthorn where a pair of goldfinches rustled about. "Especially children of about eight." Carl chewed on a piece of grass and looked up at the faultlessly blue sky. "Eight! Isn't that the perfect age?"

"But I'm not eight."

"You're closer to eight than I am." Carl began playing with her fingers, which for once were not grubby. The touch of his hands went all the way up into her moist armpits.

"Imagine, Nik. If your first memory is from when you were four or five, it's not so long ago you began remembering. How fresh those memories must be for you! As much as I try to hang on to my early memories, something about them always seems to be softening or floating away. I can lie here thinking about the warm summer grass in our yard at home in Black Bog. I can remember how the grass prickled my bare feet, not sharply but softly, and how the green stalks poked up between my small toes. I see those small feet, feel the grass, really *feel* it. Then it vanishes." He looked at his shoes. "Oh, the joy of being bare-footed!" Slowly he began moving his fingers against her palm and the sensation of his fingers combined with the words "bare-footed" so that there was something silky and naked about the touch, as if he were also stroking her toes or her calves.

Then he dropped her hand and lay back, laughing. "When I was just a little chap, seven or eight, I was given the job of watching geese for a local farmer. It was boring work, you can believe, and lonely out among the ponds, but once, I heard trumpeting in the sky. A flock of wild geese was flying above. At once the farmer's geese began to screech and stretch their necks and begin to fly. *Herregud!* I didn't know that ordinary geese could even get that high off the ground! But they vanished over a hedge. I had an awful time getting them back to the pond. Hours and hours, and at the end the gander had fouled my shirt and I was in tears with exhaustion and rage. Yet why, when I look back, does it seem that the life I led that summer, lonely and bored, with only wretched geese for company, can still seem like a kind of heaven?"

To hear Aunt Marie on the subject of Carl's early years was to hear stories of poverty and hunger, of a mother who'd married beneath her and ended up with twelve children, of a father who couldn't provide for the large family, a day laborer who liked his tipple. But Carl's own stories of his childhood were different. He told about his mother's singing and his sisters' many kindnesses to him, how his father Niels the Painter was a tireless fiddler and an even better cornet player, much in demand at all the local dances. A sort of golden light lay over Carl's childhood, and a constant stream of dance music flowed through the stories—polkas, waltzes, schottisches, and mazurkas. When Carl told stories of playing for country dances until long after midnight and walking home with his brother in the light nights of summer or under the moon on frozen winter evenings, you envied him, you didn't pity the twelve-year-old who had to work for a living.

Nik had never thought of herself as having a past. When she daydreamed, she always saw herself fully grown, a daring young woman of eighteen, never as the child she'd once been. Life now was as it always had been, serene and safe with a few unexpected dramas: a horse that had to be put down; Sven Nyborg slipping off the end of the fishing boat and drowning; Helga Larsen dying from tuberculosis a week before her wedding to a Skive merchant. Saddest of all was the servant girl from a Roslev farm who was rumored to be a little easy with her favors, her swelling stomach and the loss of her position, the tiny baby found out on the moor, dead beside the bleeding mother. They all remembered that terrible story the same way they remembered the winter of '84, with ice storms that knocked down trees and heavy snowfalls that buried houses. When people talked about the past, it was those dramatic events, deaths and heavy snowfalls, that stood out.

Nik never thought about her own memories as anything to be especially cherished, even though she liked to hear Mama talk about her big family in Odense and all the fun they used to get up to. It was amusing to picture Mama as a baby being pushed in a pram, pushed by Aunt Marie into the pond at the park and the pram floating off like a ship while the nursemaid stood screaming and two young gentlemen plunged in and rescued the baby. Mama was the youngest. She lost her father when she was only three and as a result had been much coddled by her mother and older sisters.

"When I was in Odense in the regiment," said Carl, stretching and getting to his feet, "I still played and heard the music of the country people of Fyn. But ever since I went to Copenhagen I've had to fight to keep my simple memories from being swallowed up by the thousand new impressions of the city and the city's music."

"I want to live in a city," Nik said. "Or in the Rocky Mountains."

"The Rocky Mountains!"

"For the view."

"Don't be too quick to leave this behind, my sweet little girl," Carl said, taking her hand and pulling her up to stand next to him.

They were the same height. No, she was a bit taller, not a little girl. In only six months she would be fifteen.

Widow Poulsen, who had been to Berlin and Dresden in her youth, gave her verdict: The young musician with his charming combination of earthy humor and cultivated taste was a valuable contribution to village life. Pastor Wellenborg was not so sure. He had heard that the boy was setting the poems of J. P. Jacobsen to music—Jacobsen, the botanist and poet who had translated Darwin's *On the Origin of Species* into Danish and then had gone on to write the novel *Fru Marie Grubbe*, with its story too degrading to be mentioned in mixed company.

Nik asked her mother about *Fru Marie Grubbe*; Mama said the novel told about a seventeenth-century woman with an unhappy marriage who fell in love with a servant and sank from a high social position to his level from her own lust. "Not that I've read it, of course," she added hastily. "It is meant to be well-written. Darwin, of course, should not have been translated into Danish. Darwin is wrong and a bad influence. Just remember what happened to the schoolmaster."

Jacobsen had died young two years ago, leaving behind, in addition to the shocking *Fru Marie Grubbe*, a posthumous book of poetry. Nik borrowed Carl's copy one evening. The next day she folded sheets of paper together to make a little book and carefully calligraphed "Poetry" on the cover. After some thought she wrote a poem, "Wanderlust," which began:

I long to go out into the great world.
To follow the road wherever it goes.

The house resounded with music much of the day now, and not only did visitors to the general store linger outside the parlor windows to hear Carl practicing the piano in the morning, their horses seemed to like the music too. One of the horses, left to graze on the grass across the road, made its way to the open parlor window and stuck its head inside. Carl laughed and said that it was a musical horse, and with good taste too, because it seemed to particularly enjoy Liszt.

In the evenings local people and guests crowded into the house to hear Carl play country dances and popular short pieces. The galops and mazurkas of the composer Hans Christian Lumbye, "the Strauss of Denmark," were always a hit, particularly the *Champagne Galop*, which began with the pop of a champagne cork and was a great tradition at Tivoli. Carl made the pop himself with a thumb in his mouth. To listen to it made you giddy and more than one couple danced in the adjacent dining room and hallway and out into the garden.

Ole Dahl from Norway was known locally for his fiddling. On Carl's invitation, Ole Dahl brought his fiddle, made in Telemark and brightly painted with blue and red designs. The fiddle sat in his lap as Carl played Mozart. At the end, Ole Dahl said in his clear sharp Norwegian, "Oh, but you have a fine instrument. I could never get those sounds out of my violin. It's too old and battered."

But Carl lifted Ole Dahl's fiddle from his lap, admired it respectfully, tuned it a little differently, and played the same piece of Mozart.

Ole Dahl had tears in his eyes when Carl finished.

After the guests had departed in the evenings and the family had gone to bed, you could still hear Carl playing softly. These were his own compositions and they were not waltzes and galops or country dances, but something else, more tentative, heartfelt, and fine. They wrapped the sleeping house in harmonies.

During Carl's visit everyone said they slept very well and Mama remarked later it must have been the music.

But Carl wasn't always at the piano or with his violin up under his chin. Eagerly he joined into the life of the household, swimming every morning, walking and riding, drawing caricatures of everyone, writing a so-called novel about his adventures in Selde, which he would read aloud at dinner. He was a mimic and a storyteller who created all kinds of roles for himself: the genial drunkard, the foolishly fanning lady in love, the general, the professor, even a Russian Idiot.

He egged Nik on to the most absurd capers. He'd heard that her godfather, Mr. Gjeddes, was looking for a new maidservant for the farm at Marienlyst and when the old fellow came to call, Carl got Nik to bring a dress and bonnet to his room. Later he emerged as a simpering girl Nik introduced into the parlor: "This is Christina Engel—she is looking for work and heard that Godpapa and Godmama needed a good maidservant with references."

Godpapa Gjeddes, whose eyesight was failing, bowed and began in his deep, kind voice to question Christina. Aunt Marie burst out giggling and Mama, after a minute, did too. The girl in the bonnet roared heartily and rushed out the door.

"Pretty girl," said Godpapa. "Quite a loud voice for a female though. Could she be all right in the head?"

One day at a picnic Carl got them singing rounds of invented songs. One of the oddest was "Cheese and sausage and herring salad and pig's feet and fruit compote and beef with egg and jellied eel—that's delicious." Yet it sounded delightful in four-part harmony.

A few days after Carl's arrival, Schoolmaster Harald Strandgaard paid a visit to the Hansens with his two youngest children, Sophie and Anne. The two older boys were visiting their grandparents at their farm near Jebjerg.

The schoolmaster was a few years over forty, thin and brown and muscular, with a well-trimmed ginger beard and a bald head that he generally kept covered outdoors with a wide-brimmed hat. His glasses were strong and magnified his eyes. For all that the schoolmaster had once seemed to Nik like a particularly large sort of water bug, with his long brown limbs, bald head, and big jeweled gold-green eyes, Schoolmaster Strandgaard was nice-looking. His face creased with two dimples when he smiled and he had strong white teeth, which all his children had inherited.

He'd been Nik's teacher ever since she started school and his eldest son Joachim, now fifteen, had been a close companion all her life. Joachim had been living with his grandparents much of the last year and attending the new high school in Jebjerg.

"Joachim and Tom will be home again in a few days and I'd hoped to organize a natural history expedition to Knudeklinterne on Fur," said the schoolmaster. "We'd be pleased if Miss Emilie and Mr. Carl Nielsen could join us. We'll take a picnic and enjoy ourselves."

"Knudeklinterne are the western cliffs on Fur Island," Nik explained to Carl. "They're packed with fossils. Can we, Mama?" she asked, as her mother brought Sophie and Anne into the parlor. She had washed and brushed them up a little.

"Of course. But Sophie must wear her hat all day, Nik."

The Strandgaards all tanned in the sun, with attractive freckles across their noses. Anne was small for eight, with straight brown bangs and round cornflower-blue eyes. She was said to look most like her mother. Eleven-year-old Sophie had light green-gray eyes and dark lashes. Her pale ginger hair was usually in two thick braids. Nik couldn't recall her nose ever being childishly soft and snub; it was sharp and triangular as a tiny sail. Her mouth was wide and her ears were big. She had more freckles than the rest. Sometimes she talked too much; sometimes she was utterly silent. Joachim and Nik thought of her as quite pesky when she was small—did a child ever ask so many questions or seem less satisfied with the answers she was given?—but everyone had to admit that when it came to finding fossils, Sophie's eyes were the best.

The date for the expedition was set for the following week.

Joachim! Nik realized later that she hadn't thought about him for a minute since Carl's arrival. In fact she and Joachim had lost their footing from the time he went off to high school last autumn. He had become stuck-up with his knowledge; she'd noticed it during the Christmas holidays when he went on and on about mathematics and other boring subjects. "Now, Nik, *now* I am finally understanding geometry!"

Jebjerg High School was only for boys. For a girl to study after finishing grammar school she would have to travel to a larger city, like Aarhus or Odense, as Maj had done. But Nik was finished with studying. She had been bad at school anyway, and it was only her parents' insistence that kept her from leaving sooner than fourteen.

Yet compared to Carl, Joachim was ignorant. You could talk with Carl about religion or history, ask him questions and he would answer everything. He knew so much. First of all, he knew lots about the Army, from having been a bugler, and then he knew many things regarding Odense and all the villages around it. He knew everything about Copenhagen, and about all the concert halls and theaters and art exhibitions you could visit. He'd read masses of poetry—Byron and Shelley—and dozens of novels, even the Russians, Dostoyevsky and Tolstoy. He kept a copy of Plato's *Republic* on his bedstand. He had come to his own understanding of life through books and experience. He no longer believed in God. (Her mother didn't care for that; religion was bedrock and should never be questioned.) But most of all he knew about music. And when he played the violin for them in the evening, it was as if the joking boy disappeared and was replaced by someone else. Even Papa, who still thought Aunt Marie was exaggerating when she called Carl a genius, could be seen in the evenings smoking his pipe and tapping his toes in time to the *Champagne Galop*.

When Carl talked with Nik, she didn't feel stupid the way she sometimes now did with Joachim and his geometry. All she had to do was listen to Carl and she grew more educated and cultured. He rarely laughed at her, no matter what she asked. Mostly Nik listened—what a talker he was! How many plans he had for himself, what ambitions he nurtured, what dreams.

He was giving her piano lessons as well.

4.

"PAPA SAYS THE SCHOOLMASTER IS THE MOST INTERESTING man for miles around," Nik told Carl as they walked to the ferry landing to meet the Strandgaards for the promised excursion.

Harald Strandgaard's father was the skipper of a merchant ship out of Aarhus that called regularly at the port of Edinburgh. His mother was a young schoolteacher from a liberal Scottish family. They had met one stormy day in Edinburgh when Jesper Strandgaard gave her a hand over a large mud puddle. Then they eloped to Aarhus and had two children.

"That's why the schoolmaster speaks English and has advanced ideas. He and his sister used to spend summers in the Highlands with their grandparents and cousins. The schoolmaster almost studied in Edinburgh but instead he decided to read Zoology and Geology at the university in Copenhagen."

"But how did such a man come to be in Selde?" asked Carl, taking Nik's hand and swinging it a little. They were alone on the road that morning, with their arms free—the Strandgaards were bringing the picnic.

"He married a girl from near here and they moved to Viborg where he had a post teaching the physical sciences at the Cathedral School. A scandal took place a few years later."

"What happened—did his wife run off to Italy with a lover, leaving him and four children behind?"

"Oh Carl, don't be silly. It's a sad story—his wife died. But that wasn't the scandal. It was all about Darwin!"

"Darwin?"

"He wrote a letter defending Mr. Darwin to the newspapers when the book *On the Origin of Species* was translated into Danish.

And then it came out that the schoolmaster had been teaching evolution to his students. The bishop of Viborg Cathedral made a big fuss in his sermon about atheists and the sacredness of God's Creation and so on, but Schoolmaster Strandgaard said he wouldn't stop teaching evolution, and so he lost his job. Then nobody else would hire him, because of his views, and he and his family had to move in with his wife's parents, on the big estate in Jebjerg. And his wife wasn't well, and she had Sophie, and then Anne, and that was what killed her.

"So Papa asked the schoolmaster to be our grammar school teacher. I remember when they all arrived. I was about seven, and we hadn't had a teacher in the village for a while, since the schoolmistress had left to marry. I had to learn my ABCs at home. Maj and some other children read Latin with the pastor until the schoolmaster came. The Strandgaards have a wonderful house here, it's all filled with fossils and rocks and stuffed birds. And now the schoolmaster can do all the natural history he wants and no one bothers him."

"And yet," Carl said, "I suppose there are some in Selde who haven't approved of him either."

"Yes, almost everyone except Papa, I think," said Nik with a laugh. "But then, he and Papa think alike in many matters. They believe in education reform and social change. They're for progress and against Germans."

"If Strandgaard is half Scottish I suppose it's natural he dislikes the Germans. But your father?"

"We were at war with Germany," Nik reminded him. "They took our land. They occupied us!"

"But that was twenty-five years ago. I can't imagine that happening now."

"My papa doesn't think so. He fought in that war. He remembers."

~

The journey to Fur wasn't far, just thirty minutes across the narrow passage. But with seven of them making the expedition, with baskets, tools, boxes, and a picnic hamper packed by the Strandgaards' housekeeper, the ferryman had to make two trips. The usual procedure with the ferryman, if he didn't happen to be on your side of the water, was to hoist a flag. He would then row over and anchor his boat off the shallow shelf and wade to shore in his tall rubber boots to help carry supplies and females of all ages, who had to cling to his back. Schoolmaster Strandgaard and the boys walked out to the boat themselves; they didn't mind getting a little wet. On the Fur side the water was deeper and there was a wharf to tie up to.

Dozens and dozens of fishing boats—skiffs and single-masted schooners—were always to be seen off the coast of Fur. Along the shore women set hooks and cleaned fish and children played among the rocks. Most fishermen had small holdings as well, with a cow and geese, but there were also farmers with more land who had cattle and horses. Strandgaard had arranged with a farmer friend for the loan of a horse and cart for the overland trip to the western headlands. They'd set off early enough in the morning they were at the cliffs on the other side of the island from the harbor by eleven.

The massive bluffs here were layered black and white, with volcanic ash and a clay called *moler*. The cliffs were half a kilometer long; below them the shore was littered with chunks of bean-shaped cementstone that could hold fossils. While Sophie and Anne rushed around happily with their chisels and hammers, banging on rocks and just splashing their feet in the water, Joachim, Tom, and their father staked out areas they thought promising and methodically began to search and tap among the rocks. Tom was lucky and discovered a fragment of a fish skeleton. Joachim climbed up the cliff and disappeared from sight, though they heard his hammer ringing above. Schoolmaster Strandgaard found nothing. It was often that way with fossil hunting; you could look and look and look and day after day have little to show for it. Other times you merely tapped open a small cementstone concretion and the rock split cleanly to reveal a delicate dragonfly.

Carl and Nik were given hammers and chisels, and Nik tried to teach Carl the techniques she had learned from the Strandgaards. He wasn't an apt pupil; he preferred to sit on a large rock in the sun, humming to himself and looking out at the sea. Eventually he took off his shoes and put his hat over his face for a nap.

Nik and Sophie found themselves together at the far end of the beach below the folded black and white strata of the formation above. Many millions of years ago, Sophie's father had taught his pupils, when the climate was warmer and the seas were higher and what was now Denmark was covered by a subtropical ocean, a kind of plankton lived on the surface of the sea, and these bits of algae drifted down through the water to the sea floor, creating thick layers of sediment. From time to time volcanoes to the northwest sent clouds of ash up into the sky and over toward Denmark to fall and form another layer on top of the clay.

During this long period, twigs and leaves and ferns from land blew into the shallow warm sea: bamboo and laurel, sequoia and monkey puzzle trees. Fish, attracted by the plankton, lived in the upper waters. Some were still known—tuna, cod, smelt, herring, mackerel, and eel—others were more primitive. Insects with heavy wings that couldn't change direction quickly—cicadas, crane flies, caddis flies, flies, beetles, lacewings, and long-horned grasshoppers—sailed into the sea. Birds too, those with thicker bodies, were blown out to sea in storms: kingfishers, hornbills, bee-eaters, rollers, and hoopoes.

All these animals drowned in the water and fell to the sea bed and they did not disintegrate. There was no oxygen in those waters. The flora and fauna fossilized instead, preserved intact. The seas dried up, the land was exposed, the Ice Age froze the world, and the glaciers pushed the old sea beds up into folds and furrows. Horizontal bands of black ash and white moler were now zig-zagged cliffs on Fur. Within those clay layers and inside the cementstone beans at the base of the cliff were fossils from ancient times: leaves, fish, birds, and insects.

To Strandgaard, fossils were not just beautiful, they were chronometers of the geologic eras—clocks that kept ticking silently in their different layers, telling the same time always, buried beneath the seas and forgotten, or under the earth where cities grew and fell, where cathedrals were built and roads constructed. Fossils were the key to separating one layer of the earth's geologic history from the next, for the same fossils could be found, predictably, in the same strata of rocks over many miles of terrain—even in different countries separated by channels and seas.

The fossils, whether trilobites or dinosaurs, made up the fossil record of the earth. Nik sometimes imagined the strata like pages of a book, the fossils the letters on the pages.

Nik and Joachim, in years past, would sometimes lose themselves in contemplation of the notion of Denmark sunk under warm shallow seas, while off in what was now the deep cold Atlantic Ocean, volcanoes blasted ash into the sky and red lava poured into the steaming sea. Like his father, Joachim seemed to see the entire planet in three dimensions: continents rising from the sea and subsiding again. He and Nik had held many exciting conversations on this theme, illustrated by arm-waving and volcanic reenactments with booming shouts.

In those days they excluded Sophie from their rambles and philosophical discussions or tried to make her play with Tom and Anne. Of course Sophie was the best at finding fossils, she always had been, but she was peculiar, stubborn, and single-minded. Joachim had his father's fondness for constructing grand schemes. Sophie was better at observing and drawing conclusions from what she saw. Sophie had little use for the larger principles and no interest in speculating on vast time scales: a year or a million years or a thousand million—it was all the same to her. But she could spot a fragment of leg bone and suggest that not only was it a bird but that it was a kingfisher.

Although the sweep of time didn't stir Sophie as it did Joachim and Nik, that's not to say she didn't have an imagination. She particularly enjoyed being other people. It amused her to dress up in her father's old top hat and cast-off dinner jacket and take the glass from one of her father's old pairs of spectacles and put it in her eye as a monocle and pretend to be an English lord. She didn't know the parts of speech in English as well as her older brothers did, but she was a funny mimic and would say, "Hip ho, ladies and men, anyone for a spot of fox-hunting?" with her nose in the air. "To the hounds, what?"

She called Nik "Miss Emilie" as was proper but otherwise didn't bother to show her much respect. Now, as the two girls sat in the shade of the cliff above, she was frank.

"Are you sweet on this little chap? The musical snoozer?"

"Certainly not. He's just visiting with my aunt this summer. He's kind of a cousin. Besides, he's quite old. Twenty-two."

"He looks about sixteen. Because he's so short."

"He's a brilliant musician. My aunt says he'll be famous someday." Nik tried to change the subject. "How is your musical education coming along?" Sophie refused to play the piano like a proper girl. Instead she'd found out that the local blacksmith was an accordion player and she'd taken up the squeezebox. She was bad at it, but enthusiastic. Her father made her play outdoors.

Sophie was undeterred. "Joachim doesn't like him. He's jealous."

"Joachim has nothing to worry about," Nik said. And that was true, as far it went. But the touch of Carl's hand was imprinted on her palm. His voice was now so familiar it caught at her heart a little.

A stone or two fell from above where they were sitting. They heard Joachim's shout: "I've found something good!" A few minutes later he was scrambling down the cliff with a lump of cement-stone in one hand. She hoped he hadn't overheard her conversation with Sophie. He looked happy, but that was probably because he had found the complete skeleton of a *knogletunge*, a bony-tongued fish, when he broke open an ordinary but promising lump of stone.

By the time they returned to Fur's harbor and were ferried across it was eight in the evening, though still quite light. The group walked along for a little, then the Strandgaards split off for their house and Carl and Nik continued along the road. Carl had come to life later in the day and had amused them with songs made up on the spot about bony-tongued fish fossils and girls with ginger braids and straight brown bangs. Only Joachim didn't sing along.

"It's clear that Joachim doesn't like me, even though I tried like mad to win him over. I expect he's dreadfully in love with you," Carl said now, taking her hand.

"Don't say such ridiculous things." Nik pulled away. She had of course noticed throughout the day the irritable glances Joachim kept throwing Carl. By the time they set off for the ferry home in the farmer's cart, Joachim was sullen and silent and didn't meet Nik's eyes, not once. Why that should gratify her—that her closest childhood friend should ignore her—she didn't know.

"But Nik, my dearest little girl!" Carl's mobile face took on a lovelorn expression that she knew was play-acting but still made her insides soften. "Don't you realize what a glorious girl you are? In a year or two, suitors will be begging you to marry them. Naturally Joachim will be first in line. You'll marry in the Selde church and go to live in a little cottage somewhere near your families, and he'll be a schoolteacher and you'll raise rutabagas and children."

"Joachim is going to be a geologist," Nik said primly. "And I don't like rutabagas. Now I'll ask you to change the subject, please. You have nothing to worry about when it comes to Joachim. And Papa would not like to hear you going on like this. You're supposed to be my cousin."

Carl laughed and his lovelorn expression dissolved. She liked the feeling of having power over him, so much that when a little while later he tried to take her hand again, she let him.

The feel of his palm against hers was like the soft skin of a calf, newly born.

They dawdled, looking at the green fields of barley and hay, scattered with wildflowers, the barn swallows, the early bats, the line of pollarded beeches against a sky flushing with rose and orange and a darkening blue. At home, Carl went immediately to the piano while Nik lay on the green silk sofa with her head in her mother's lap, thinking about Joachim (was he really jealous?) and the nature of geologic time, which had a beginning and would probably have an end, but might as well be eternal for all that humans could grasp it. She found it hard to grasp that even this moment, this lovely moment, with music and summer light and her mother stroking her hair, would end and never be repeated, at least not in quite the same way.

5.

NIK HAD BEEN RIDING HORSES SINCE SHE WAS A SMALL girl, at the stables of a local baroness. The baroness had taken a liking to the Hansens' younger daughter, and recently she had given Nik her own complete ladies' riding habit with a sweeping skirt that had to be held up and a silk top hat. She said that now that Nik was confirmed it was time to learn to ride like a lady. Nik had been practicing at the manor, sidesaddle with her favorite horse, a lovely small mare.

The baroness, a small elegant woman in her thirties, had dark hair in an elaborate chignon; her brows and lashes were just as sooty. Her teeth were bad, with one or two missing, and when she spoke she had a tendency to hold her hand up to her mouth, as if she were holding back a secret. She looked older than she was because of her bad teeth, even though her face was quite unlined.

"She was such a charming young thing when she first came to the estate," Papa remembered. "Fresh as a peach and such a spirited horsewoman. Just eighteen, I recall. Her family was aristocratic; she had studied in France. But they were poor. They married her off to the baron, who was at least twenty years older, without her knowing anything about his reputation."

The baron was something of a rogue. He'd been married before and had driven his first wife to an early grave. Now he spent much of the year at the spas in Baden because of his health. He left the running of the estate to the baroness. They had no children and rumor had it that the baroness consoled herself with the estate manager. Mama didn't believe it; she thought that local people only envied the baroness her wealth and standing. Mama knew for a fact that the baroness was quite devout. She didn't come often to the church in Selde because she had her own chapel, but she gave generously to the parish, just ask Pastor Wellenborg. Mama had been quite pleased when the lady took an interest in Nik.

Since everyone in the district now knew about Carl Nielsen, the baroness had heard of him too. She sent a note to Mama asking if Carl and Nik would like to come for tea at the manor. Perhaps they would enjoy taking a ride first, on the sandy coast near the estate. Afterwards Carl might consent to play for her.

That morning Nik dressed in her riding costume. In the tea samovar, which always stood on the buffet in the dining room and which Nik had used as a mirror since childhood, she thought she looked quite ridiculous. But when she met Carl out in the yard, his expression showed he approved of the way the waist nipped in and how tightly the black dress buttoned over her chest. The baroness had sent a carriage for them and they rode to the manor in style, with Nik pretending to be a titled lady and Carl her ardent suitor. He was so silly with his calf eyes and bowing that she laughed all the way. He too had a riding hat, lent him by Papa.

Before Carl and Nik set off on their ride, the groom gave them specific instructions. The beach near the manor was not the beach nearer Selde. They must be careful and ride quite near the water line and not get close to the boggier regions around Risum Moor. For there was quicksand in places there, hard to see before you were being pulled down into it.

The day was warm. Nik sweltered inside her long dark riding dress and worried that the top hat, even though secured by pins and an elastic band around her chin, might sail off into the breeze. They rode side by side along the shore.

"When you come to Copenhagen to visit your Aunt Marie, we'll hire horses and ride through the parks and streets around Amalienborg. Perhaps we'll see the King riding and we'll lift our hats to him. Won't that be amusing?"

Riding along the sand, Carl lifted his hat to her, laughing. She was afraid to lift hers for fear she could never get it back on. The white wavelets of the fjord splashed around the horses' hooves and the sun beat down. Fur was across the water, close enough so that she could see the island's southern headland, Lille Knudshoved.

Carl rode quite well, just as he did everything physical with ease. He was of course not so imposing as Maj's young man Frederik, whose seat on his dark gelding Sultan was princely and straight. Carl began to tell her how he had hired a horse once in Copenhagen and had ridden up to the home of his friends the Rosenbergs, then stopped under the windows and hallooed them until they all came to the window to look at him on a horse. The Rosenbergs were a musical family who had made him welcome in the big city. Mr. Rosenberg was a history professor at the university, a widower; at his house were a number of children and a free and easy spirit. Carl was especially close to one of the daughters, Margrethe, who played the violin.

"I was once quite smitten with her but she just laughed at me. Still, we've remained the best of friends. She understands music like no other person I've known. It's a shame she's a girl. Otherwise she might go on to play in one of the orchestras. It's quite unfair."

Nik had heard of several flirtations in Carl's life—a childhood sweetheart, a married lady in Odense with too much time on her hands, a Gerda snatched away by a leather manufacturer. She didn't mind listening to these stories, he told them so amusingly. But she didn't like to hear the accomplishments of Margrethe Rosenberg extolled at length. It made her aware of her own meager education. All she knew was Selde and Skive. She had been to Viborg a few times and to Odense just twice, and in Odense she hadn't gone to a concert or a theater. She had played in the park. She was only nine and ten then, of course.

There was no sign of quicksand, though Nik had half hoped to encounter a small safe patch of it. She imagined being rescued by Carl—how he would have to take her in his arms and pull her to safety from the sucking warm wet sand.

The baroness gave them tea in the garden and was rewarded by

Chopin and Liszt. She held her hand up to her mouth in pleasure and her dark eyes never left Carl's face. Nik was glad to see that the lady took a liking to him. She'd noticed that most women did.

In addition to the green silk sofa in the parlor, firm enough so that ladies could sit and rise without toppling into it, the large dining room had a sofa along one wall, a sofa that Carl had christened "the soul's depths," because it was so vast and soft you could get lost in it and because that was where he and Nik conducted some of their serious chats in the drowsy afternoons when Aunt Marie and Mama were having their naps. Sometimes Carl told her stories, marvelous stories, from his childhood on Fyn, and sometimes he plotted out her future. Like Maj he was skeptical about her becoming an explorer, but otherwise he was encouraging. She could travel—she *should* travel! She could learn Italian and French, live in Florence and Paris. She must practice her drawing and music and become as cultivated as possible.

She soaked in everything that Carl had to tell her and resolved to read more novels and poetry and to practice the piano daily.

Many of the things Carl tried to teach her about music Nik didn't understand at all. He talked about his dislike of program music, of music tethered to ideas. "Music can't be like pictorial art or like literature. The tones themselves arouse feeling, but there shouldn't be ideas attached to those feelings. For instance," said Carl, sitting beside Nik at the piano bench, where a sheet of Bach was open before them, "when I play this"—his fingers touched a dark chord—"what do you feel?"

"I don't know. Something . . . a sort of sad feeling?"

"But there is no *idea* of sadness, is there? The emotion wells up purely from the tone itself. It's not like hearing a sad story about a horse that had to be put down, or looking at a painting of a poor little match girl in the snow, is it?"

"No," said Nik. "It's just sad sounding." Carl's arm touched hers and she smelled his shirt, a little like grass and soap. She did not feel sad at all. Her own arms tingled and she wanted to smile. She pressed her lips together.

She did not wish to be stupid; still, sometimes her head ached from trying to play the music Carl set before her and from trying to understand his complicated ideas about counterpoint. She struggled to follow him. She had always liked Mozart; she could listen to Mozart by the hour. But she couldn't understand how a theme changed into another theme and back again, or two opposing themes danced with each other. She certainly could not play Mozart in that way and she was self-conscious about her plinking tones and dissonant chords, at the awkward pauses as she read the music and tried to find the keys. It mortified her when she hit a wrong note, and she hit many.

He told her that to improve her playing she would need to develop not just her finger muscles but her memory. "Music is the art closest to memory," he said one day. "Perhaps that's why I love it so. It's not like a painting or a poem that you can stare and stare at or read over and over. As each note vanishes the next comes to replace it, yet you must hold the memory of the notes before in your mind. To really listen to music you have to hear the musical phrases sequentially, as they're occurring, yet have a memory of what came before. To compose music you have to hear it before it exists."

"I hope you don't expect me to *compose* something," said Nik irritably.

"Little Nik! Every time you remember something that happened you're composing one of an infinite variation on real events. The way you *tell* your memory of what happened is a kind of composition." He placed his hand on hers and returned it to the piano keys, arching her fingers slightly. "You do have a nice wide hand span."

His touch always made her mind go blank. How delicious it would be if he could simply move her fingers with his own fingers resting on top, over the keys, just like this.

~

Once, as everyone was retiring for the night, she returned to the parlor to get a book and he was there at the piano. His brush of light hair was bent over the keyboard, as if he were listening for something that his fingers knew first. He had his jacket off. His collar was unbuttoned. Candlelight was all that illuminated the piano, and a little last lingering daylight through the open window. She'd watched him for a few minutes before he seemed to be conscious of her.

"Come here," he said. "Don't be frightened. You're not disturbing me."

She sat down next to him on the bench. "What are you composing?"

"Am I composing? There's something I'm looking for. Composing makes it sound as though it's coming from me. But sometimes I believe it's coming from somewhere else. Through me. I merely have to listen for it and note it down."

"A sound?"

"Many sounds. Just before you arrived, I heard a full complement of strings—six violins and two cellos. And then three French horns echoing. Nothing to do with the piano at all. But here I was, sitting at the piano, listening to violins and French horns. Was I composing? Perhaps. It sounds a bit spiritual, doesn't it?"

"But you're not the least bit religious," Nik said. "You won't go to church with us even to please Mama."

"Music is the religion I believe in. Or perhaps I should say, if there were a god of music, I could believe in him."

"Nik!" called her mother from upstairs. "Come to bed, dear. Leave Carl in peace."

As she left the room obediently, she glanced back, expecting him to be bent over the keyboard again. But he was looking at her.

"Good-night, sweet Nik."

She lay in bed for a long time afterwards, listening to the soft notes of the piano fill the house. She did believe in God. When Carl said his music seemed to be coming from somewhere else, wasn't that *somewhere else* Heaven?

He wasn't always happy. He could be melancholy. Not all his brothers and sisters had emigrated or gone on to happy lives. One of his brothers, a better violinist than Carl, had had his hand partially crushed in the brick works. Three sisters had died, including his beloved eldest sister, Karoline. How were humans to understand that life was so up and down, so unfair and yet so joyful? Reading Plato brought out the philosopher in him. He sat on the grass with her talking about finding a balance in life, between tension and release. "Music must express the constant contrasts of life, its continual transformation, the will to keep living. I am not just speaking of harmony, but of moments of musical equilibrium that come hot on the heels of unpredictable shifts of tempo and key."

She didn't understand much of this, but she loved to hear him talk. His hair stood on end when he spoke of music, from running his fingers through his scalp.

Nik overheard her aunt and mother one day in the parlor. Mama said, "Something of a weather vane, isn't he? Compared to Maj's young man, Frederik, who has such a firm core."

Aunt Marie said, "He does have a center, but you mustn't think of it as a hard center, like wood. Carl's center is molten, like a volcano."

And then, oddly, the two women burst out giggling.

Carl *was* changeable, though when he was in good spirits no one was more sparkling. But even his bouts of despair passed quickly—not so much like wrong notes corrected but like dissonant chords that contested life's harmonies and couldn't be resolved, only absorbed into the vaster symphonic shape. That was how *he* explained it to her, anyway.

One day, after the morning swim, Nik and Carl were allowed to take the trap to Skive. Nik drove. She liked to drive quickly; she'd learned that from her mother. They made some purchases for Aunt Marie and strolled around the cobbled streets. Nik was proud of Skive. The railway had come to Skive twenty years ago and now there were factories and forges and machine shops, along with bakeries and butchers, clothing stores, tailors, shoemakers, a watchmaker, a goldsmith. The Skive Theater was built five years ago; it could hold five hundred people.

At noon, they had dinner with a friend of her mother's. Afterwards Mrs. Pedersen offered Carl schnapps and then they made their way over to the new telephone exchange so that he could call an acquaintance in Viborg. Carl had used the telephone several times before in Copenhagen, but it was new to Nik.

After much fishing around in his pockets, Carl came up with a name and a few numbers on a piece of paper and gave it to the woman at the large oak desk. Off to the side was a table with an upright wall of plugs and wires. Two young ladies sat in front of it, pulling out some plugs and putting in others. Carl and Nik were directed to a booth across the room, which held a large wooden box and something that turned out to be a speaking horn attached by a wire to the side. From across the room they heard one of the young ladies say, "Carl Nielsen wishes to speak to you."

The wooden box had two bells, which suddenly began to vibrate. Carl picked up the speaking horn and put it to his ear. He then spoke into the round opening at the top of the box: "Georg? Georg? Can you hear me? Can you hear that I've had a glass of schnapps? Yes, I'm in Skive, with my cousin, Miss Hansen."

Back and forth Carl and Georg went for a minute or two. It was unbelievable to Nik that Carl could actually be talking to someone as far away as Viborg, twenty miles away, just through a wire. But when he put Georg on, that was proof.

Georg said, "Hello, Miss Hansen!" He wasn't shouting, like Carl, but his voice sounded like it was in the middle of her head.

The curious thing was that there was really nothing to say. It was the mere fact of talking into a receiver to a person somewhere else in Denmark that was the fascination. It was also odd to her that everyone in the room could hear what Carl was saying, but no one could hear what the person in Viborg, Georg, said to Carl. You had to guess.

A day or two later, back in Selde, Carl suggested that they install a telephone connection between their two rooms. The phone line came from Papa's store—it was a length of sail cord and it made a complicated journey from Carl's room in the guest wing out back to Nik's bedroom on the street side of the house. The cord passed over a water trough where it slipped and got wet, then swung above the gate into the courtyard, where it was attached to a series of window latches all along the front of the house, until it reached Nik's window, the last in the row. Only in the evening, when the yard was quiet, could they speak. Carl sat in his windowsill and Nik stretched her head out. They held their hands to their ears and mouths and waited for the faint vibration that told them someone unseen was speaking to them.

6.

NIK HAD FORGOTTEN HOW WELL MAJ PLAYED THE PIANO. As soon as her sister arrived from Odense, Maj and Carl renewed their acquaintance. They had first met five years ago, when Maj was fourteen and came to live with Aunt Marie and Uncle Jens in their large house on Nørregade while she attended the girls' high school. At seventeen, Carl was just beginning to be a visitor to the Nielsens' home and Maj remembered how even then, before he went off to Copenhagen to study, people regarded him as especially talented. Now Maj, who had taken piano lessons all her years in Odense, could accompany Carl. Her ear was good enough that she could even follow him when he moved into variations on one theme or another.

Maj understood counterpoint, harmony, and, simply, how two instruments could complement each other. She also had the irritating habit of looking at Carl's face as she was playing the piano—searching his eyes for the musical tempo. And her pink lips would purse in concentration, as for a kiss. Worse was when they played pieces for four hands. They sat next to each other on the bench, shoulders touching, their fingers flying in unison up and down the keyboard.

Nik stopped practicing.

What was the point? To have a sister five years older means you'll never catch up.

Maj always did everything first, or had done it, long before Nik came to try. The worst of it was that Maj didn't even notice half the time that Nik gave up, since much of what Maj did well she didn't particularly value. Performing on the piano for guests came with being a young lady, just like embroidering and making cakes that didn't fall flat, and understanding what to do when people put a baby in your arms. But Maj wasn't interested in being an accomplished young lady.

If she'd been a boy, she told the family, she would have studied chemistry or become an engineer. "What a grand thing it would be to design and build a bridge," she once said unexpectedly at dinner when she was twelve, astonishing them all.

"You're exact with your figures," said Papa kindly. "Perhaps you'll find an engineer to marry, and you can check his additions as you do mine."

"A pretty girl like you will have more than enough suitors to choose from," said Mama.

For Maj *was* pretty, small-waisted and light on her feet. You never heard her coming; she simply appeared, around a corner, at the top of the stairs. Her eyebrows were gently arched over clear blue eyes and her lips were rose-petal pink. Her loose blond curls she wore in the style of the day in a coil or knot, but curls always escaped and they were sweet little curls at the nape of her neck, at her forehead; they softened her squarish face. Maj didn't have the bumpy long Hansen nose. It was short and straight and now a pair of small round spectacles perched on the bridge, making her look terribly clever.

Her given name was Marie but they had always called her Maj for the month that had been named after Holy Mother Marie. Maj was far from holy—she was less devout than either Mama or Nik—but in other ways she was just like the month of May, blooming and fresh, but changeable in her weather. Nik's temper tantrums were violent; her passions deep-seated; Maj blew up and forgot things quickly. Or so it seemed. She could be quite stubborn and secretive when she wished and just as easily, when it suited her, confiding and sympathetic.

Maj never mentioned bridge-building again, but went off to Odense to study. She had been there five years, living with Aunt Marie and Uncle Jens during the school year, and when they moved to Copenhagen in January, she began to room in the dormitory of the teachers' college with a Swedish girl named Eva Sandström. The family had been hearing about Eva in letters for some time. Aunt Marie said vaguely that the girl came from a good family originally from Göteborg. Mr. Sandström was an architect who'd gone to Brooklyn on a commission and had taken his wife and two younger boys. Eva had decided not to go to America but to study in Odense, where she had an aunt.

"Eva is rather a *loud*, *big* girl," said Aunt Marie. "But all the Swedes are rather loud and tall, I find. She has quite a lot of ideas for someone so young. I don't believe girls should have quite so many ideas. She dresses well, however. Her aunt is quite respectable."

Eva was a member of the Frederika Bremer Society in Sweden and Maj had joined too. Maj already belonged to the Danish Women's League.

"Who is Frederika Bremer?" Nik asked.

"Only one of the most important women writers of the past," said Maj. They were in Maj's room the first night of her return and Nik was rummaging through Maj's trunk, looking at her chemises and newspapers: one stack of the Danish paper *Women and Society* and another pile of *Dagny* from Sweden. Among the books was a novel in Swedish with the blunt title *Money*, by Ernst Ahlgren. But Ernst Ahlgren was really a woman, said Maj: Victoria Benedictsson.

Maj went to the dressing table and removed her glasses. "Frederika Bremer wrote novels about women, she traveled to America and Cuba, she never married, and she worked to advance the cause of women's emancipation and suffrage." Maj pulled the pins out of her knot and began brushing her hair vigorously, so that it flamed out pale yellow with darker streaks of gold. Nik had longed for such hair all her life.

"Voting?" Nik asked. "You know Mama doesn't believe in such things. It's the sphere of men, she says. Women are powerful in their own sphere." Even as she said it, it sounded unconvincing.

What sphere was that? Cooking and darning and making applesauce. She had already unloosened her own hair and plaited the curls in a braid. In her white nightgown, her body felt soft and new, as it so often did these days.

"Nonsense," said Maj, brushing hard. "We can do everything, almost everything, men can do. And more: bear children for instance. Why shouldn't we be able to choose our own lives?" Without her spectacles her blue eyes were dreamy. "The Frederika Bremer Society was founded a few years ago for the express purpose of helping women achieve all they can. In unity we'll find strength."

It was strange but her sister's voice seemed to get a Swedish accent as she said this.

"I don't really like girls that much," said Nik, to be contrary. "I prefer the company of boys. Girls are too silly."

"Eva isn't silly. She has a hundred plans. I never knew a person like her. She's learning English and wants to join her parents, at least for a visit, next year. Maybe she'll stay. What would you think of that, Nik, if I went to America and Eva and I set up a school in Brooklyn?"

"I would think you had forgotten about poor Frederik, for one thing. And I'd remember that you told me I was childish for dreaming of Australia."

Her sister began laughing. "Ah, Nik. You've caught me out in my own contradictions! In fact you must be a braver girl than I am. Because you thought up Australia all on your own as a possibility for yourself. Whereas I never imagined such a thing for myself until I met Eva."

She didn't say anything about poor Frederik.

Now that Maj was home the Tin Soldier began turning up many afternoons for dinner and often staying through the evening. His father was the pastor of the nearby parish of Thorum, a long ride back and forth to Selde. Still, Frederik never spent the night, even though there was plenty of room. Once he would have stayed at Pastor Wellenborg's home, but now, with Mette Bohm visiting, that would be indelicate.

Frederik's strong jaw was cloudy blue. His moustache sprang from his upper lip and, with the aid of a light coating of wax, drooped down into two curlicues of glossy black at either side of his mouth. A rectangle of hair two inches wide fell onto his forehead, stopping just above his straight dark brows. At first Nik had thought this was natural. But after much observation she determined that it must have been cut in this particular way, perhaps to go with his soldier's hat. Frederik was a man made for a uniform and even his normal clothes had a military cut to them: tight jackets and breeches and crisply pressed shirts. He danced well, had a firm handshake and a solid stride forward, but just sitting or standing, particularly in small rooms on delicate chairs, he seemed top-heavy, his shoulders so much wider than his hips. His skin was swarthy and pitted with old acne scars; that gave him a rakish look at odds with his Army bearing, booming voice, and responsibly conservative views.

Frederik was the younger of two sons. His brother Morten was in Copenhagen studying theology, but rumor had it he wasn't really suited for the Church. Morten wrote poetry, it was said, when he wasn't drinking or gambling his father's money away.

It was really Frederik, most people thought, who should be a pastor. Frederik believed in cautious, incremental reform: A ten-hour day for factory workers was long enough, though of course sometimes field hands had to work twelve or more during the harvest; everyone understood that. Moreover, children under ten should not be working a full day. He was proud that he had convinced his uncle to limit the hours of children picking up the bricks of peat their parents cut. The children must go home, even when their parents begged for them to stay and help. Everyone should have Sunday off.

Maj admired moral stances; part of the reason she'd accepted Frederik's attentions at Christmas was that he was so firm in his convictions. Or at least that was what she'd told her younger sister. "I like a man who knows his mind."

But Nik remembered it differently. Squire Christiansen had held Julefest at his manor and invited gentry and tradesfolk from miles around. The Christmas party was something everyone looked forward to each year, and both Nik and Maj had new dresses. Nik's white muslin gown, while modest, reflected her new height and shape. She wore stays for the first time, and though they weren't laced tight, they still gave her the sense of having a waist, accentuated by a large green bow with trailing streamers.

Maj looked like a fairy princess; her gown was blue velvet with ivory lace at the neck and pearl buttons at the back. The blond curls had tiny pearls threaded through them, and Mama had let her wear some pearl earrings as well.

Frederik Brandt, whom everyone thought would soon be proposing to Mette Bohm, hadn't had eyes for anyone but Maj. The two of them—Frederik so rakishly dark and tall, masterful on the dance floor; eighteen-year-old Maj so light on her feet, so delicate and blond in his arms—had captured everyone's attention. And Mette Bohm, twenty-three, with hair the color of a dark red beet and gentle chocolate-brown eyes, in a plain yellow taffeta dress with a high collar, sat with her aunt and uncle much of the evening, only dancing now and again with Henrik, the squire's son, just a boy with a rather plump backside and short legs, who seemed pleased to try a polka or schottische with every girl at the party.

After that evening, Frederik had called upon Papa, asking if he might pay court to Maj, and Papa had gladly agreed. He liked Frederik for his combination of riding and hunting skills, and of course the fact that he came from a well-to-do pastor's family pleased Mama no end. For the last week of Maj's visit, they'd all had great fun. They packed themselves in a sleigh and drove through the snowy evenings to one house or another, or entertained in their own home with cakes and punch. Maj played the piano and Frederik sat stroking his dark moustache in approval. On

New Year's Day, uncharacteristically bright with a crisp blue sky, everyone made snowmen outside and had a snowball fight with the Strandgaards, and Frederik wiped snow off Maj's face with great gentleness as she laughed—a laugh Nik had never heard before, a girlish trill of delight and power.

Mama said later, "If only there had been a little more time, I'm sure Frederik would have proposed that week."

But Maj left for Odense and the teachers' college just after New Year's Day, and Frederik returned to his Army posting near the border of Denmark and Germany. Mette Bohm went back to Copenhagen, where she was studying at an art school for women who would eventually be hired to paint designs on china at the Royal Porcelain Factory. One or two people speculated about the impression she'd made on Henrik Christiansen, but most people just said, "Poor Mette Bohm." Since her parents had died, it had become a habit to pity her, and Frederik's change of heart seemed merely the latest in Mette's misfortunes.

Yet Frederik didn't propose at Christmas, and he didn't propose at Easter either, when Maj came home for ten days from Odense and he took leave for a visit at the same time. The two greeted each other cautiously, even though they'd written regularly during the last few months. Maj had spectacles by then, and she had moved into the dormitory with Eva Sandström, who believed in women's rights.

This summer Mama was hoping that the two could finally have the time together they needed for things to progress as they should. It was probably for that reason that Mama agreed the four young people could travel one day soon to Nykøbing. Aunt Marie had said she wanted to go to Nykøbing as well, but then she changed her mind when she heard what a long day it would be with the train and ferry. She said, to no one in particular, "I suppose you wouldn't want to have to take care of me all day, and I find that my nervous headaches can come on quite dreadfully in the heat."

If she expected someone to contradict her, no one did. Her nervous headaches were well-known.

Aunt Marie had changed over the last weeks. She'd been quite happy when she and Carl arrived in Selde, and had exclaimed over and over about how much good it would do them both to rest up from the last exhausting months. A soft tenderness enveloped the two of them at times, when Carl would fan her or fetch her knitting or a book. But he was a restless body, always in movement, and he was much in demand from all sides.

Aunt Marie grew querulous, especially in the evenings when there was youthful merriment in the house and the guests were clustered around the piano in the parlor. Mama said wisely that Aunt Marie was having problems with the change of life. It was why she could abruptly turn red and then pale, and put her handkerchief to her eyes, a little teary at a popular waltz.

When that happened, Nik sometimes crept to her side on the green silk sofa. She too could feel neglected when Maj and Carl were playing music together. She noticed that Frederik felt the same, even though he pretended that it didn't bother him at all.

"Bravo," he said in his deep voice, which conferred authority so easily. "Well done."

"Come up to my room and let's rest together a while," said Maj after they returned, hot and dusty, from a picnic at the beach. It had been a large, rather tiring event, with all the Strandgaards, Frederik, and Henrik. Henrik talked guns and hunting with Frederik and Papa. Carl had been there of course, but he'd paid less attention to Nik than usual and more to Aunt Marie, who brightened and called him "dear boy" and "my own son" when he smoothed the sand for her and set up her chair and adjusted the umbrella above her head.

In years past Nik might have hitched up her skirts and raced along the sand with the Strandgaard boys or made sand castles with Sophie and Anne, but today she'd steadfastly ignored their pleas. When Joachim came after her as she strolled up and down the shore with her new parasol and asked her, rather roughly, whether she thought she was too good for the rest of them, she looked out over the waves in the direction of Fur and then back at him.

"I'm not a child anymore, Joachim."

He wore a cotton shirt and his trousers were rolled up. His white-blond hair was like salt spray against his brown face. Last summer he'd kissed her and they had made plans. Joachim would be an explorer and geologist; she would be his assistant. But suddenly at fifteen, though already taller than Carl, Joachim was far too young.

"I thought you were different, Nik. I didn't think you were going to turn out a coquette."

She turned and walked away down the beach, staring out over the fjord, hoping Carl might be jealous or that he might come after her. But Carl spent much of the day with the older ladies, hovering over Aunt Marie, listening to her mild complaints, and reading poetry aloud.

No, she wasn't a child anymore, but did Carl see that? At times he treated her like a cherished cousin, at times like a favorite puppy. In the last few days, since Maj had arrived, he'd seemed abstracted and more absorbed in his music than before. The way he looked down at Maj when she accompanied him on the piano was uncomfortably close to the way Frederik had looked at Maj when they'd danced at Christmas, with deep intensity, as if he were trying to read her thoughts.

Upstairs the sisters removed their dresses and their stays and washed their faces in the china basin. Maj wet a handkerchief and sprinkled on a few drops of cologne. Then they lay down side by side on the double bed with its sagging wool-stuffed mattress that had once belonged to a Demant great-aunt. Maj's bedroom faced the back courtyard and a beech tree had grown thick and close to the window. The green leaves shivered in a wind that had risen on the fjord. The breeze was dry but with a slight flavor of rain at the back of its throat.

"Do you remember when we used to lie outdoors on those long

summer evenings and watch the clouds and dream of adventures?" said Maj. She'd put the handkerchief at the top of her chemise and the scrap of damp linen rose and fell with her breath.

Of course Nik remembered. They were not big and little sister then, but mountain climbers in the cloud peaks. They sailed their cloud ships to China and Japan and brought them home loaded with wisps of ivory and pale jade.

"It's so amusing to see the little children in the school where we help out, pretending things, just like we used to." A drop or two of rain hit the leaves of the tree and Maj sighed. "I suppose as we get older, most of us lose our imaginations. But Eva hasn't. She always sees the possibilities."

"I still pretend things," admitted Nik. It was only a few months ago, after re-reading one of her favorite children's stories about the little Lapp Sampo, that she had gone out with the horse and sledge on a day when the spring sun beat down on the snowy fields nearby and pretended that she was a nomad girl driving her reindeer fast as blazes over the barren wastes of Finnish Lapland, with a howling gray wolf at her heels.

The rain pattered down.

"Don't let's close the window." Maj stroked her own arms, as if she were embracing herself. "It smells so sweet and fresh." She sighed again, more heavily, and said, "I suppose we won't go to the squire's tomorrow for our picnic if it's like this. Then Frederik will hang about here all day. He doesn't seem to like me playing the piano, have you noticed? Or sitting and reading. He thinks we should talk. Or that I should listen. But really, I can't talk about the Army for hours at a time. And the peat works are, if possible, even less interesting."

Nik was silent. Some floaty, discomfited sense of time passing had come over her and she seemed to see herself and Maj from above. As if she were in the clouds looking down at the two of them: Maj, small-boned, modestly breasted, her blond hair in hot curls at her temples, spectacles laid on the table, rose-pink mouth relaxed; and Nik herself with her dark hair fanned out on the pillow, her limbs long and gangly like a child's, but also now with rounded hips and breasts and tufts of dark hair under her arms. They looked nothing like sisters: Maj took after the fair-complected Hansens and Nik after the Demants (Spanish nobility, from Seville, washed up on the shores of Fyn, said Aunt Marie, repeating the old story). But they *were* sisters and no one would ever look like them or be exactly like them again the way they were right now.

And further: It would never be this exact day in July of 1887 again.

She was self-consciously astonished at this strange adult thought, how it seemed to change her even as she was formulating it. And what a *sad* thought it was. Almost as if she had already died and was on her way to Heaven and had been given one last look down to earth. And this is what she saw: two sisters lying side by side in chemises on a sagging woolen mattress with the wind picking up outside and spatters of rain jumping through the window onto the carpet. Why was the thought so melancholy?

Because the moment was over even as she noticed it.

It wasn't that her life was over and she was dead—the thought of being truly dead made her queasy but not unhappy. No, the sadness came from the fact that this moment was over and would never come again.

Her throat pulsed with the ache of it and she touched her sister's arm for comfort.

"Mama says Carl has been very attentive to you," Maj said quietly.

"We're friends."

"But you're friends in a different way from how you've been friends with boys before. You have been close to Joachim, over the years. And Jens at Marienlyst."

"Did Mama say something? Everything has been perfectly proper!"

"Nik, no one doubts your modesty and sense of what's proper.

Mama and Aunt Marie have only been a little surprised at how Carl has taken to you. Personally I haven't seen much evidence of it. Why, today he spent all his time with Aunt Marie." Maj put the handkerchief to her forehead. "He *is* charming, just the way he was in Odense. And what an extraordinary musician he's become—such utter joy to play with him."

Nik bit her lips. If this was going to be a lecture on how she should practice the piano more, she didn't want to hear it. Her mother had suggested she could handle her feelings better if she counted to ten before she spoke. Or better yet, learn not to speak at all when she was angered.

"Girls do get married young, of course," said Maj. "But not at fourteen."

"Marriage." Nik sat up in surprise. "Who said anything about marriage!"

"So—he hasn't pressed you, Nik . . . in any way?"

"Oh, Maj, don't be so stupid. We have conversations about . . . about Darwin and God and poetry if you must know."

Maj burst out laughing. "Darwin and God and poetry!"

"And besides, what about you and Frederik? Mama was married at nineteen. Don't you love him?" Nik settled back down on the pillow and glared at her sister.

"I don't *not* love him. He's admirable . . . and quite handsome of course. But he hasn't proposed. We're not engaged. To be truthful, I don't feel quite ready to give up my freedom. I have my practical teaching to get through. And I would like to travel too. Perhaps not to America immediately, but to Sweden . . . I had a letter from Eva today. She's staying with some friends near Göteborg. In their seventeenth-century Swedish manor! On a lake. With swans. She said the family would be happy to have me there as well. There's a boat to Göteborg from Aarhus, and then a train. I *could* if Mama and Papa didn't mind that I cut my time at home a little short. I could spend two weeks there and then return with Eva to Odense. What do you think, Nik?"

"You should really ask the lieutenant. He hardly sees you and now you want to go off to Sweden. It must be frustrating for him, the thought of delaying marriage for years while you study and teach. Maybe that's why he hasn't proposed yet," Nik added a little spitefully. In fact, the thought of traveling to Sweden and staying in a manor on a lake seemed terribly pleasant.

"Frederik is a sensible fellow. He doesn't yet have the position to support a family; he's still only a lieutenant, though I suppose he'll leave the Army for the peat works at some point soon." Maj squeezed a little more dampness from the handkerchief onto her forehead. "I don't see why, though, that women should always be the ones to bend. If I'm going to all the trouble of studying education, shouldn't I have the chance to teach?"

"And does he press *you*?"

"Of course not. We are always chaperoned, even if it's just you. There could never be the opportunity nor would Frederik take advantage of one should it arise. I'm sure Frederik shares my view that an unmarried man must restrain himself, just as an unmarried woman does."

"How dull that sounds, Maj!"

"Nik," began Maj again, in her kindly older-sister voice. "You and I have been lucky to have been raised in a decent home with strong moral values. Girls like us are never even tempted to go down unfortunate paths. Other girls are not so lucky."

"What about men?" asked Nik.

"Many of them find it hard to resist temptation," Maj said. "They look for release outside of marriage . . . in one way or another. It's objectionable, this double standard. I could never marry a man who had been with others."

Did she mean, a man who had loved other women?

"You make it sound like it's only men who have such feelings. And how would you know if your husband had loved anybody else before? Would you ask him? Would you ask Frederik?"

"I can't really be bothered with all these questions, Nik.

Frederik is a pastor's son. I'm sure he understands the importance of self-control. Of purity before marriage. As do I." She closed her eyes, and almost immediately soft kitten snores began, followed soon by real ones.

It was almost impossible for Nik to imagine her older sister removing her small spectacles and allowing Frederik to kiss her pursed pink lips. Almost as impossible as imagining her parents' mouths pressing passionately together. As for Aunt Marie and Uncle Jens—what a horrid thought. Ah, but if Carl were to bend his face towards her and put his arms about her waist and draw her close, now that . . . now that . . . How could she say no to that?

7.

NIK'S BEDROOM, AT THE CORNER OF THE HOUSE, ABOVE the parlor, had its disadvantages. She heard everything that happened on the main road through the two windows at the front, and that occasionally included the voices of drunken or quarrelsome carriers or seamen emerging from the inn. Her side window was above the one-story kitchen and scullery, so she also heard the sound of pots and pans and Mrs. Jespersen bossing Jutta dreadfully when Mama wasn't around.

In the summers, dust blew in when the windows were open. In the winter, wind from the northwest dashed snow and sleet against the glass panes. Still, the three windows made the room bright, when other rooms in the house were shadowed and cool, and Nik liked being able to look out easily to see who was passing in the road.

For the last week the telephone cord Carl had strung up with such effort from his room in the back to her room had not been in use. It had come to seem like an alien thing in the room, a reminder of an ease that was no longer there since Maj had come home. Yet she still could not help looking at the sail cord wound in a coil on the floor, as if hoping at some point it would begin to speak to her again.

Aside from that cord, everything in the room was Nik's and arranged to her satisfaction. Walls papered in yellow and white and a yellow and blue rag rug on the wooden floor. A narrow bed, painted white, with a drawer underneath, and a wardrobe. A small claw-foot table and a shabby armchair, a narrow bookcase, and a large trunk, which held her treasures, some of which her mother had suggested go to the attic now she was confirmed.

Nik had resisted. She still liked to pull out her toy circus and spin Flor the Ballerina like a top. She made the Indian Princess (in a red sari with a red dot on her forehead) encourage her small tiger to jump through a flaming ring. In addition to the tiger, an elephant, and a white horse, the circus box also contained a wooden reindeer carved by Ole Dahl. The reindeer was on loan to the circus from a separate story, which was *The Snow Queen*.

Now that she was fourteen, Nik was naturally given no more toys as presents, yet that didn't stop her from arranging the figures from the circus on her windowsills. She called what she did storytelling, not playing. She imagined herself on the horse (in summer) or the reindeer (in winter), trekking through the Rockies or Lapland. She had overheard her Aunt Marie telling her mother that she was planning to help the mysterious girl Karen Marie buy a steamship ticket to New York "when this is all over." Perhaps her aunt—if she was rich enough to throw money away on a practically unknown girl—could be persuaded to buy Nik a ticket as well.

One warm and breezeless afternoon, Nik was upstairs in her room. The midday meal was over—her mother and aunt were resting and Papa was down at the lumberyard.

The kitchen was quiet but from the parlor came the sound of the piano.

Schubert, she thought. The Hansens had a bound book of his scores for four hands.

One hand was more assured: Carl. The other, more businesslike but equally faultless: her sister.

Nik did not know the piece. Her sister, when home, was more likely to play Chopin and sometimes Mendelssohn.

A vivid series of chords was followed by a lyrical, almost plaintive passage played by Carl alone; it somehow reminded Nik of his story about the death of his eldest sister

The beautiful Karoline was engaged to the local blacksmith, a handsome and engaging boy. She went off to work as a maid for two old sisters in Copenhagen and developed a cough. She was sent home to recover her health. Meanwhile Karoline had received a letter from the blacksmith telling her his affections had changed. Carl was only a small boy of six or seven, yet sometimes he used to accompany her on walks in the woods. Later he would understand that they went to a particular log bench where she used to meet her fiancé in the past. She sent him letters; he responded kindly. She still hoped. But he was in love with another. And she had consumption. She faded away and then she was gone.

"She lay in bed with her face turned to the wall, crying."

That was all in Carl's playing of this heartbreaking passage. Maj didn't understand a thing about love, and you could hear that too in her brisker notes as she joined him.

Nik had a story now about Flor the Ballerina and told it to herself as she hopped the little figure in the pink tutu along the windowsill (sadly Flor could not walk properly since her legs were fused together, ending in two *en pointe* pink slippers):

Flor was only fourteen when she fell in love for the first time. It was with Jacques the Acrobat, who captivated her with his blond brush of hair and athletic build. Nik jumped him over to Flor and mashed them together in an embrace, feeling the blood rush to her lips and the inside of her thighs. But Jacques said no, Flor was too young, they must wait. The Indian Princess arrived on the sill and performed the Dance of the Seven Veils. Jacques and the Indian Princess went off together. A little time passed, with Flor prostrate on the sill. At first everyone thought she would die. She coughed and cried. But eventually she noticed that the tiger cage was unlocked; with a small push of her pink *en pointe* toe she opened it more.

The tiger was out. It was only a matter of time before the Indian Princess and Jacques reappeared. But it was too late. The tiger reared up on his hind legs with a terrifying roar. Flor had hoped the tiger would eat only the Indian Princess, but it was Jacques, sweet Jacques in his tight bathing costume, who was clawed to death first.

"I am so sorry," said the Indian Princess, before she was reduced to one of her seven veils. "I know he loved you best."

Jacques died in Flor's arms. And in that final mashing together, Nik felt raw excitement. And a shadow of grief.

From the open window Nik heard the hooves of a horse trotting along the main road, from the direction of Skive. She looked down and saw the Tin Soldier seated on handsome black Sultan. Frederik had come to spend the night in one of the guest rooms at the inn and tomorrow the four young people would go to Nykøbing.

Nik rushed downstairs and into the parlor. Maj was no longer playing, but perched on the green silk sofa, restlessly paging through an album of photographs. Carl continued to play the duet by himself. Nik wondered fleetingly if Maj had moved away from him when she heard the horse's hooves.

"Maj, Maj! Frederik is here. I just saw him out the window. He's on Sultan."

A week ago Maj would have jumped up and gone out to greet him, but today she merely sat listlessly, looking at Demants and other relatives.

"We should have more photographs of ourselves in these albums," Maj said. "These are just a lot of pictures of Mama and her sisters and brothers. How handsome Aunt Marie was then, before she married."

"I tell you what," said Carl. "There's a photography studio in Nykøbing. Henrik had a photograph taken there, he told me. We should all do the same tomorrow."

Frederik came in, looking as he so often did, larger than everything in the room. He was offered a cup of coffee and sat down on the sofa next to Maj, who gave him a small but warm smile. Carl closed the keyboard.

Frederik had been in Thorum for two days and related various bits of news. His father had given a sermon on drink and his mother was in a state of worry about Morten, the poet brother who had written asking for more money. He wanted to travel to Italy for the winter because his lungs weren't strong. "It's easy enough to claim your health is bad," said Frederik. "My father should really go to Copenhagen and have it out with him. Morten has now been studying for five years and is still no closer to a degree. Now he says he needs money to publish his book of poetry."

Nik was quite fascinated by Morten Brandt. What did a poet do? She could not imagine his daily life. Did he sit in a chair with a pen in his hand waiting for the right line to come to him? At least with Carl you knew he was composing when you heard something on the piano. Did a poet mutter aloud? Walk from one end of the room to the next, weeping with his hand on his breast, and then shouting a single word: "Crossroads. Yes, that's it. Rhymes with toads."

But the subject of Morten was soon dropped in favor of the Army. Frederik had heard Carl was once a lance corporal in the Ninth Regiment in Odense. At the Viborg garrison earlier this summer Frederik had come to know certain officers from Odense on joint maneuvers. He mentioned a few names and immediately Carl's face brightened.

"Ah, those were happy days in Odense," he said. "I remember how worried my mother was, sending me off at only fourteen to the regiment. What terrible things she'd heard of soldiers and their goings-on. She made me promise a dozen times to be sober and chaste. But she couldn't have imagined the warm-hearted welcome I got and the good friends I made among the soldiers." Carl sighed. "I sometimes think I would have been happier staying in Odense and continuing to play in the Army band."

"Nonsense," put in Maj. "You have a splendid career ahead of you!"

"Oh, but for warm-hearted and true friendship," said Frederik, "you can't improve on the Royal Army. My mother was the same way, worried about how the son of a pastor might fit in among the troops. Certainly there were a few times I wouldn't have wanted my mother by my side, but when all's said and done . . ."

And from there Frederik and Carl fell easily into talk while Nik and Maj sat silent. Nik felt her sister's body next to her on the sofa, so much smaller and neater than hers. Maj was all of a piece, cut out of a single piece of strong white linen, while Nik was composed from the ragbin. Maj listened to the Army stories for a while then put down the photo album and picked up the novel *Money* by Ernst Ahlgren, or rather, Victoria Benedictsson, which she was reading for the second time. Maj had told Nik that its heroine Selma Berg reminded her a little of Nik because Selma was boyish and an excellent rider, and yes, Nik *could* read it, she *should* read it, but not yet, not until she'd grown up a bit. Besides *her* copy was in Swedish, a loan from Eva, who would expect it back. Without ever having met Eva, Nik was already tired of hearing about her.

Frederik could have probably gone on talking about the pleasures of the Army all afternoon, but Carl finally noticed that Maj and Nik were quiet.

"How are you getting on with your novel?" Carl asked Maj.

"I finished it and now I'm reading it again. I think it's splendid, especially at the end when Selma simply leaves her husband and starts over."

"Have you read it, Frederik?" asked Carl.

He shook his head. Although he was a clever-enough man, he didn't go in for novels.

"I didn't care for *Money*," Carl said. "Though not for the reasons you might think—that the men don't come off particularly well in the novel. No, it was something else that irritated me." He had been sitting on the piano bench during the discussion with Frederik, but now he jumped up as if on a stage.

"We meet the heroine, tall, ugly, but also strangely attractive Selma Berg, at seventeen. Selma wants to learn to paint. She's eager to go to the Academy of Art in Stockholm but her father and uncle are against it. She has no means to finance her studies herself. Her uncle tells her that a wealthy squire has made an offer for her hand. And Selma forges a desperate bargain with herself. She will marry herself off to the squire in order to have money. But then—and this is the part that mystifies me—Selma doesn't use her wealth and leisure to become a painter. She simply gives it up in a rage. What was the point then of sacrificing herself to the fat old squire?"

"It's meant to be a gesture of renunciation, don't you see?" said Maj. "She's lost all self-respect by marrying. She knows she went against her own nature. She bargained away her freedom in exchange for financial security."

"All the same, I don't really see why it's so noble a gesture to give up your art. I found it rather stupid, to be honest, in a naïve sort of way. The fact is, very few artists, not just women, have the possibility of making art that feeds them, much less a family. Composers, painters, writers. Poets like Morten. Aren't we all in some ways forced to sell ourselves? Live off our families? Find benefactors? Accept patronage?"

Frederik shifted uneasily in his small chair. "Come now, old fellow. To accept wages is hardly selling oneself. It's the spirit of the age. The farm laborers are all leaving the countryside to work in the factories of Copenhagen. And you yourself—don't your students pay you? And what about that orchestra work of yours? That's only payment for services. Hardly selling yourself, I think. If my brother Morten were to become a professor of Greek and write a little poetry on the side, we wouldn't think him quite so hopeless."

"I don't mind teaching music. I feel grateful to be taking a post in the Tivoli Orchestra in September, even though it's only as a substitute player," said Carl. "I don't mind hard work. But I've also had to rely on my benefactors for my education and a great many things. I have no well-off family to support me."

"You have Uncle Jens," said Nik. "And Uncle Hans."

"The Demants and Nielsens are not my family. I'm a charity case and must sing for my supper." But he smiled at her.

"It's different for women," said Maj, tapping the book in her lap. "We don't have the opportunities. And in the novel, Selma felt she had sold herself to her husband." Maj blushed. "That's the crux of it. She had to sell her body like any common prostitute."

Frederik looked down at the fragile cup in his large-knuckled hand. "I hardly think marriage could be compared—"

"What do you think about all this, Nik?" interrupted Carl.

"It's not easy for a girl to get money except to marry it or have it given to her by fathers and uncles and brothers, is it?" It was the first time she had considered the question in that light. "I suppose she can try to find work, but there aren't so many things she can do, can she? In America and Australia I think it's different," she added. "You could work on a ranch."

"You could work as a teacher, Nik," said Maj. She had put her book away and sat with her hands in her lap. "But you would have to study."

"I'd rather marry," said Nik, to be perverse. "Though I suppose that's a lot of work too."

Frederik nodded. "Noble work, Miss Emilie. Marriage and children—they're a woman's work. And it's the job of the husband to provide for the family. Yet it's not a base financial transaction and if you call it that you make it sound like something far less noble and holy."

Carl said, "But Nik, don't you imagine more for yourself than to be a wife and mother? Wouldn't you like to be an artist of some sort? Perhaps a poet?"

"Carl, Nik is only fourteen. *Fourteen.* How can she know what she wants yet? Though, really," Maj added irritably, "I support her doing anything she wants as long as she does something mildly useful. Mama doesn't want to let go of her yet, that's the problem."

The atmosphere in the parlor had changed, as if a thundercloud had come in through the open window and taken up residence in the corners by the ceiling. There was no way around Maj in such a mood—just as you could not avoid a rainstorm out on the moors if it chose to rain on you. For Carl it was just playfulness to tease Maj perhaps, but it wasn't fair to let Frederik see this side of Maj before they married. Even Nik knew that.

A wicked spirit had taken hold of Carl. He continued teasing Maj, now about the views he'd heard she'd developed in Odense. "Your Aunt Marie says you've become quite the fervent supporter of the Vote for Women."

"All sensible people are," she said. "I'm hardly alone in my feeling that women deserve the same legal rights as men. Frederik, I think, agrees."

"Yes, of course," said Frederik unhappily. He looked very tall, tanned and swarthy, an outdoors man with ramrod posture on a tiny chair.

"I suppose, Maj, you're familiar with John Stuart Mill?" Carl said.

"I've read him in Danish," Maj said, "the translation by Georg Brandes." She smoothed her blond curls away from her face. "Though I'm not convinced Brandes is the supporter of women's rights many think he is, the way he attacked the Danish Women's League and its founder Elizabeth Grundtvig this spring."

"Brandes?" Frederik said. "Isn't he the Jew whose brother is the editor of *Politiken*? Very clever, those two brothers, about literature anyway. But they should stay away from moral and social issues. Those are best decided by the majority of Danish Christians, guided by the Church and the Bible. Voting, yes, of course, women should vote, but let's not act rashly. I don't think the country is ready for suffrage yet, because of the simple fact that most women are not educated citizens. First education reform, then voting rights. Isn't that right, Maj?"

"So then, Frederik, you're not convinced by the arguments in Mill's *The Subjection of Women*?" Carl's face was smooth on the surface but his mouth had a satiric twist. Nik felt sorry for Frederik.

"Haven't read it yet, I confess. But women are hardly oppressed these days, are they? I mean," Frederik stumbled, "compared to the past. These days women do all sorts of things. Why, Maj is studying to be a schoolmistress. The fact is, women have always done many things much better than men!"

"For instance?" asked Carl.

"Well, needlework. Ladies have the small fingers for it. And anything to do with children. Teaching, of course. And why shouldn't they be nurses?" he added. "And everything to do with family and the fine arts. Women have an excellent sense of how a home should be decorated, I find."

Maj ignored him and addressed Carl. "And are *you* such a great supporter of women's rights? Don't you think women are suited for some things and not others? And that *you*, as a man, are entitled to decide what those things are?"

"We don't know what women are capable of," said Carl. Suddenly he seemed not to be joking. His eyes were earnest. "Because we never let them attempt anything serious. Isn't that what John Stuart Mill says, more or less, Maj? Personally I would never choose a woman for a wife who didn't have the passion and talent to match mine. My wife must have a vocation. Ideally one that complements mine."

"She should be a musician, then?" asked Maj. Her cheeks were quite flushed. "She should play the piano to your violin? Though not to upstage you of course. Merely to accompany you and perhaps look attractive?"

"It's a given that my wife-to-be must be lovely to look at. But perhaps a painter or poet would be a better choice for me? What do you think, Nik?"

"I know nothing about your lovely wife-to-be," Nik said sulkily. She had never heard of Brandes or Mill or their books and speeches either.

"But it is unlikely that in most instances a woman can have the same vocation as her husband," said Frederik. "What if you were still in the Royal Army, eh, Carl? You must realize that women can never be soldiers. No more can they play in a public orchestra.

Of course your wife could play the piano from time to time. But a woman's place is in the home. Because who else could raise the children?"

"Perhaps men should take a hand," said Carl.

"And then how would you do your composing, if you had two or three children and your wife was a composer or an artist?" Maj tossed her head. "It's all words, isn't it, with you and even the great Brandes. When it comes down to it, the present order suits you well."

"Exactly," said Frederik, apparently under the impression Maj agreed with him. "Men and women have different spheres. The present order suits us."

"No," said Carl. "I don't believe that. Though I do agree with Brandes on many things. I think his criticisms of the Danish Women's League are sound. Those ladies are far too puritanical. In fact you could say they are far less radical than Brandes."

"Because he believes in free love? That's not radical." Maj's voice was hot with contempt. "The radical thing would be for men to learn to restrain themselves."

"Maj!" Frederik said. "You forget yourself, my dear. That is, it's not the sort of thing that's talked about in mixed company."

She looked at him in surprise. Frederik's voice had risen, in a firm and manly way that seemed to put an end to the discussion right there.

Carl, having done his mischief, opened the keyboard again and began to play a piece by Bach, measured and orderly, with his back towards all of them.

The evening passed well enough in the usual high-spirited way of the family dinners. Nik saw Mama glancing anxiously from Maj to Frederik but Maj looked as pretty as ever and did not draw attention to herself. She ate little but made conversation with her aunt about Odense and all its citizens, most of whom were behaving just as unpredictably and badly as when Aunt Marie lived there. Aunt Marie said she thought Copenhagen had its share of eccentrics as well (she did not mention Uncle Jens). Carl was then inspired to perform a long tale about the Siamese princes, two of them, who had bought a flat on Slagelsegade, at the top of Uncle and Aunt's apartment building. It was a complete mystery why they had come to Denmark, but they had a carriage and two manservants, and were handsomely dressed. If you met them on the stairs they did not bow properly—because they were royal—but gave shy smiles and said *god morgen*, even when it was afternoon, in lisping musical voices.

The only really sensible conversation went on at one end of the table where Frederik and Papa were talking about the many peat factories that had sprung up along the railway line between Langaa and Struer. From April to September hundreds of men, women, and children worked in the peat bogs. Frederik's uncle had bought up land at Sparkær outside of Viborg and was going into large-scale production, using steam engines and cutting machines. Frederik suggested that Papa ride over sometime to see the operation. Perhaps Mr. Hansen was looking for an investment opportunity.

"I don't believe in investments," said Papa. "Except for the ones that my wife's brother Jens makes for me. I'm better off doing what I do best, selling lumber in the district and providing the village with merchandise. But I would still like to see what goes on at your uncle's factory. The craze for digging up peat is certainly making fortunes for some."

After dinner the men stayed behind at the table to have a brandy, and the ladies retired to the parlor. That was when Maj whispered to her mother that she had a headache and thought that she would just rest upstairs for a little and come down later.

But half an hour later Maj still hadn't returned. Mama whispered to Nik to go up and see if her sister was all right. "Tell her I need her help with the cake. Mrs. Jespersen doesn't have the talent for icing cakes that Maj has."

Maj was lying on her bed, doing nothing, staring at the beech tree out the window. The air was so still that the leaves didn't rustle and the room had a shadowy green evening light.

Her sister was in her chemise and her arms and legs were splayed out, like a doll's. A large pile of letters with Swedish stamps was on the white coverlet, next to some issues of *Dagny* and *Women and Society*. She had been crying.

Nik stood awkwardly at the door and tried to explain about the cake needing to be iced. She made a joke about Mrs. Jespersen being in one of her moods. Maj just turned her face away.

The room smelled of Maj, floral and clean, and Nik thought about all the times she'd slept next to her sister as a little girl and all the games they'd played, with Maj patient and smiling. She had lived for her sister's smile. What had come between them? Why had Maj become so difficult? What did she want?

Cautiously Nik lay down alongside her sister. "Shall I talk to Papa, Maj? About Sweden? I know you want to go, ever so much. And he does sometimes have a bit of a soft spot for me."

"It's no use, Nik, they'll never say yes. They don't care about me. They just want me to get *married*. They want me to marry a man who doesn't read novels or care about music. A man who raises his voice to me and tells me how to think. And the worst thing is, I think I should marry him; it makes so much sense. But if I get engaged, I'll never get to visit Eva this summer." The word *Eva* came out in a wail and Maj reached blindly for Nik, sniffling into her chest.

"Then you should go to Sweden, don't you think? If we can persuade them. And then you can come back and marry Frederik. If you still want to."

She spooned up against her sister and put her arms around her and let Maj cry until she fell asleep. Mama looked in once, but Nik shook her head slightly. She heard Frederik's military step on the stairs and outside the room as he went into one of the rooms down the hall, and the voices of Mama and Papa closing up the house downstairs. Then the piano music began, softly.

For a long time Nik just lay next to her sister, the way she had back when they were small and slept in the same room. Finally Nik moved away, dislodging a pile of *Women and Society* from the bed. The broadsheets were dense with type. Many articles about women's education of course and voting and all sorts of boring things. She was about to put the newspapers on a table when she saw an article from a few months ago: "The Erotic and Women," by Elizabeth Grundtvig.

Nik sat on the edge of the bed, hoping for instruction, but finding none. It was a treatise on chastity. She read until she came to the questions at the end: "Shall women be like men? Or shall men be like women? Either or. It's up to us to choose."

She would like to be more like a man—to ride a horse like Sultan and sleep in the outdoors in a bedroll and look at the stars all night. But she didn't think Elizabeth Grundtvig meant that.

8.

THE NEXT MORNING DAWNED BRIGHT AND CLEAR, PERfect weather for the excursion to Nykøbing.

Frederik rode Sultan and Old Franz drove the girls and Carl in the hay cart to Roslev, where they could catch the train for Glyngøre and from there the steam ferry across the sound to Nykøbing. As it was six miles from Selde to Roslev, Old Franz had decided to wait with the horses and the cart for their return later that afternoon; he had a nephew in the neighborhood and would be perfectly comfortable.

Carl had on a red felt bowler. Aunt Marie had given the same sort of hat, one in white and one in blue, to each of her nieces, claiming they were quite popular in Copenhagen. "I rather suspect," Maj said, "that someone has been playing a joke on poor Aunt." Nik thought otherwise: Carl was as dashing as Jacques the Acrobat.

Nik wore a striped taffeta dress and a small hat with three feathers and a tiny veil. In her reticule was a bit of pocket money from Papa, with instructions to buy herself a handkerchief or some other bit of feminine mischief. It was the first time she'd ever traveled like this without one or both of her parents. Such a shame they had to rattle around in the inelegant hay cart because the trap was too small for all of them.

The whole way to Roslev Carl sang songs and clowned, making Nik laugh with his imitations of sheep and chickens. Maj said little; she looked as if her mind were far away. It was the spectacles, Nik decided, that gave her such a stern, distant air. Over her blond curls she wore a simple straw bonnet, refreshed with silk roses; she traveled in a plain blue dress with white cuffs and collar. Above the starched white of the collar her skin was clear, untroubled pink. She showed no signs of the sobbing fit of last night.

When they arrived at Roslev they found the small station full. Since the North Salling railway had opened three years before, towns had sprung up along the route, and Roslev was one of them. On the platform were farming folk with baskets of fruit and vegetables at their feet, bound for Skive. Some gangly high-spirited youths could well be students; they had the look of owning the world. There were those who might be businessmen and their wives, with interests in shipbuilding or bog-draining around the Limfjord: substantial people in summer suits and hats, with a servant or two carrying wicker hampers of food for the journey.

There were a few others whose reasons for travel Nik couldn't place. A girl of twenty in a straw boater, a carpetbag at her feet and a ticket she kept checking, as if she couldn't believe what it told her about her final destination. A man with a scholarly gray goatee and a monocle but shabby clothes and tired shoes, and a leather case with big brass locks.

Nik turned to tell Carl that the sight of the passengers made her long to go with them, to be off on a journey to some distant city. But she found herself standing next to a woman holding a shallow willow basket of ruby-red cherries. Carl and Maj stood a little ways off, engaged in a low conversation; Frederik wasn't there at all.

Maj leaned closer to Carl and he bent to listen to her. His face was attentive and then disturbed, which made him look much older. Lines appeared in his forehead; his chin weakened. He stepped back and shook his head. He seemed to be disputing Maj. Her sister's face was hidden from Nik but she was clearly speaking with emotion. Carl put a hand on her sister's arm and to Nik's shock, Maj covered his hand with her own.

All this took only a moment; the hands dropped almost immediately to their proper places. Frederik came up next to Nik.

"I went to ask the stationmaster if our train would be delayed.

He said no, it's only the Skive train that is ten minutes behind. Once it's out of the station I believe that ours can pull in."

His voice was deep and firm and everyone around fell back, at ease. The pocket watches were put away and people stopped staring anxiously at the tracks. The Tin Soldier had a reassuring air of authority.

"Maj. Carl," called Frederik. "Our train will be here shortly."

Carl remained standing there, slightly turned away, his pose unnaturally stiff, but Maj strolled calmly over to Nik and Frederik. Her face was composed. "Thank you for going to find out."

Had she sent Frederik off so she could snatch a few words with Carl? A bitter black wave washed over Nik, such a familiar feeling from years ago, when Maj would coolly pick up something dear to Nik and put it in her pocket "for safe-keeping."

The carriage wasn't full and they had their choice of seats. Carl and Frederik faced forward, while Nik and Maj looked backwards. Frederik and Nik were both by the window, so that although Frederik looked out, Nik could see his expressions reflected on the surface of the moving scenery, once the hot steam from the engine blew past. He made a number of general remarks at first, about the weather, the farmland, the speed of the train, and the small peat bogs here and there, where peasants cut bricks of turf without the aid of the machines like his uncle owned in Sparkær. When no one seemed inclined to do anything but nod agreement or murmur "Yes, that's true," he fell into silence. Although Frederik's posture was upright as always, his eyes looked troubled in the moving mirror of the window. Nik recalled her mother advising Maj to be careful with her future fiancé—he had a proud and suspicious streak. Mama knew that from Mrs. Wellenborg, the pastor's wife, who had been irate that Frederik preferred Maj over Mette.

"Oh Mama," said Maj, laughing gaily, as if she'd had long experience with the opposite sex, "I can certainly manage a man like Frederik."

Carl also stared out the window, humming a little. His bowler sat on his knees like a round red cat. He hadn't met Nik's eyes since the conversation with Maj and seemed out of sorts.

The landscape went backwards while the train roared forward, at several times the speed of the fastest horse. Flakes of soot blew in some of the open windows, as well as the wild hot scent of morning grass. For Maj of course this was nothing; she'd been on trains many times. But Nik found it strange, especially facing backwards. It was as if everything that had just happened was disappearing more quickly than it should.

At Glyngøre they boarded the steam ferry for Nykøbing. Out on the fjord the air was fresh and the water dark blue and so sparkling you wanted to jump in and swim away. Nykøbing was larger than Skive; it had all the same sorts of businesses and shops, but more of them, and all the red-brick and yellow-ochre buildings were arranged differently. The harbor and the fish market, eels in baskets, mackerel and trout in glistening piles, gave a fishy smell to the town.

They wandered up and down the cobbled streets, peering into the windows. Carl's red bowler hat brought stares. Frederik purchased a paperweight for his mother, and Carl some sheet music and a book of poetry. Heinrich Heine—in German.

Maj said to Nik, "Shall we bring back presents? Something for Aunt Marie at any rate." They stopped in several shops and finally Maj purchased a length of lace for their aunt and a long hat pin for Mama. Nik bought herself a handkerchief, then her money was gone.

They found Samuelsen's Photography Atelier on a side street, attached to a brick house; after a short wait, Mr. Samuelsen showed them into an elegant parlor with several walnut and velvet chairs.

First they had their photograph taken as a group. Nik in her striped taffeta dress posed in profile, while Frederik stood and Maj sat facing the camera. None of them smiled; it wasn't done to show one's teeth. Carl, however, seated in the middle of the photograph—placed there by the photographer who didn't want him to look too short next to Frederik—lounged and screwed up his boyish face into clownish expressions. After the group portrait, Carl arranged with the photographer to take a whole series of him acting out many of his famous roles: the Copenhagen Bohemian, the Russian Idiot, the Army General, Beethoven, simpering Christina Engel, the Man in Love. When he put on the exaggerated lovelorn face of the Man in Love, he looked for just a moment at Nik. She stared back coldly. Frederik said little during the session; he seemed embarrassed by Carl's antics. They did not go away with the prints, for they had to be developed from the glass plates. Mr. Samuelsen said he could arrange to send them by post to Selde.

By that time everyone was hungry.

They found a café on the main street where they ordered a large plate of open-faced sandwiches with egg and herring and shrimp, followed by coffee and apple cake drenched in thick vanilla sauce. Frederik, as usual top-heavy in the café chair, grew more relaxed. They all did. The talk turned to the merits of rail and steamship travel, and from there to European tours, with Frederik mentioning that Morten had visited Paris often, each time returning with a string of debts. His father had been angry; his mother, as always, forgiving. "Poets, apparently, must live in Montmartre and run up bills at the tailors and hatmakers of Paris."

"For a musician, Germany must be the great destination," said Carl. "Berlin, Dresden, Weimar! But for beauty and art and general gaiety, I've always imagined myself in Paris, surrounded by writers and painters and drinking champagne all night!" He made the cork-popping sound of the *Champagne Galop* and several people in the café looked over, startled.

"Just like Morten," said Frederik. Unlike Carl, he didn't enjoy public attention. "Let's hope you don't get into as much trouble as he does with the ladies."

Carl said nothing.

Maj laughed in an irritatingly airy way. "I agree with you, Carl. Paris is a place I've always longed to go."

"I thought you were hoping to go to Sweden next week, Maj?" Nik said. "If Papa would agree. Shall I ask him if you can go to Paris instead with Eva?"

"What's this, Maj? A trip to Sweden next week? Or Paris? And who, may I ask, is Eva?" Frederik's eyes had gone dark as a winter night.

"Miss Sandström, another student at the college. My roommate," said Maj, without emotion. "I'm sure I've mentioned her. Eva merely wrote that I might come to visit her where she's staying with friends outside Göteborg. But Papa and Mama said it was too far to go, so I thought little more about it. There was certainly no talk of Paris! Simply one of Emilie's fanciful ideas."

When her sister called her Emilie, Nik knew she was in trouble. The five years between them became fifty. Nik didn't defend herself, even though what Maj was saying was a bold-faced lie. She knew from looking at Frederik's tight jaw and black eyes that something dreadful had happened, almost worse than if Frederik had caught Maj covering Carl's hand with her own.

"You are of course quite at liberty to go to Sweden or Paris or anywhere else you'd like," Frederik said coldly. "I would only request that you tender me the courtesy of informing me in advance of your plans to make a foreign journey. And I shall do the same, shall I, if I decide to set off for Rome tomorrow?"

"Yes, Frederik," murmured Maj. "It wasn't really a plan, just a thought. About Sweden, I mean. There was no talk of Paris." How timid she sounded compared to last night when she had wept so passionately.

Nik's eyes caught Carl's. He saw the pleading in her eyes. He could have saved the situation by spouting nonsense about Paris and making more champagne pops with his cheek; but he merely began humming and said, "Shall we go?"

~

When they came out of the café, the air was no longer as breezy and fresh as earlier in the day; it hung heavy over the fjord. The four walked slowly back to the harbor. Frederik went off to buy a newspaper at the kiosk nearby and Maj sat down on a bench and pulled out a letter to read, pointedly ignoring Carl and Nik. They dawdled along the harbor front, then strolled out onto the dock where the ferry would come in, saying little. The blue and red smacks lay in their dozens offshore and the air reeked of fish, as women and children stood on shore re-baiting the lines. Nik felt tired and upset; the herring she had eaten for lunch refused to go down—her stays were too tight—and the oily taste of the fish seemed to fight in her throat with the vanilla sauce.

From the dock, they saw Frederik return to Maj's side and bend down to say something. Maj gestured to her letter and they saw her mouth move rapidly. Was she trying to explain about Sweden?

Frederik took a few steps away and stroked his moustache, and turned back to Maj. His complexion seemed to have grown darker, though perhaps it was just the shadow of a cloud passing overhead. He raised his hand, as if to explain something or remonstrate, but from a distance it almost looked as if Frederik might be ready to strike her. And Nik remembered that men were allowed to hit their wives. Mama had explained that, when certain women came into the shop with blackened eyes or cuts on their faces. There was nothing to be done about it.

Maj no longer looked frightened or apologetic. She waved the letter up and down. With her spectacles she looked every inch the schoolteacher, lecturing a student. She stood up, tiny next to Frederik. If he hits her, Nik thought, she will not back down.

Then suddenly both Maj and Frederik became aware they were being watched, not just by the fishermen and a few passengers waiting for the ferry, but by Carl and Nik from the ferry dock.

Uncertainly, Frederik walked a few steps away and stood staring out at the harbor. His jaw worked but he gradually unclenched his hands.

"It *is* warm," began Carl, removing and waving his red bowler hat over his head. "The clouds are gathering. It's quite oppressive."

"It's no use talking to me about the weather," said Nik. "You must choose a different subject."

"Gossip then? About the argument we're witnessing? It seems to be a melodrama, doesn't it, or perhaps a play by Ibsen? Maj is showing him a letter. Perhaps it says that Frederik has embezzled money or is the father of an illegitimate child. Which would be worse?"

"How can you say such things?" Nik scowled at him. "I recognize the letter; it's from Eva Sandström. And you shouldn't joke about my sister. Everyone wants Maj to marry Frederik. Maj wants it too."

"But would that be the best thing—for either of them? Your sister is pretty and intelligent. She could do better. Or not marry at all—just devote her life to the great cause of women. She is delightfully severe on the subject, isn't she?"

"Frederik loves her!"

"Love is brief. Marriage is slightly longer. Well, perhaps they'll simply agree to disagree about women's rights and everything else important to your sister. If that's the case, then in twenty years we'll see Maj with five children and a thick waist, reading novels in the parlor. And Frederik with a long white beard and that lovely moustache, gone all white, reminiscing about his days in the Army."

"Stop this, Carl. You're unkind now. Love and marriage are serious matters, at least in these parts."

"A love affair is also a highly fascinating spectator sport, in these parts as in all parts. And idle flirting as well as serious romancing makes the world go round."

"Idle flirting can be a hurtful thing."

"You speak as if you've experienced idle flirting. I can assure you, I don't flirt with you out of idleness."

He twirled his red bowler on his finger, put it on his head, and made a little bow. He looked like a music hall comedian. She almost laughed but then remembered her anger.

"I suppose you're not flirting with Maj then either?"

"Maj! Whatever are you talking about?"

"The way you look at each other when you're playing music! And at the Roslev station—I saw you. Touching hands!"

Carl hesitated. He walked a few steps away, and then back to her as if he had made a decision. Now he didn't look clownish at all. He said quietly, "Maj took it upon herself this morning to tell me what your aunt and mother have been discussing. It was the same thing Aunt Marie has mentioned to me. Maj was disturbed on your behalf. She's protective of you."

"What do you mean?"

"Aunt Marie is concerned about my attentions to you. Dear Nik, *you* have done nothing wrong. It's merely that Aunt Marie knows I enjoy female company; she knows things about me that I wish she didn't. I expect she's told your mother and perhaps your sister knows as well. Very rightly, I suppose, they're worried about your reputation."

"What could you have done that is so very dreadful?"

"To be a man is to be tempted. It's unrealistic to think otherwise. Still, if I were your aunt and mother, I'd be worried about you as well. You're innocent of the world, Nik, at the same time you're curiously wise and open-minded. Sometimes you seem like a little girl to me and sometimes you could be my older sister, you're so sagacious."

Nik didn't know what to say—like most praise that came from Carl it was entwined with levity. But *had* he done something dreadful? Something to do with a girl, perhaps the Karen Marie he never mentioned? And did Maj know?

She looked at her sister and Frederik, who were now talking quietly together. Maj seemed subdued after her outburst. She was often that way after an argument: penitent and cajoling. Frederik unbent and, though there was still some anger and certainly confusion on his face, he nodded and tried to smile. Nik remembered again their faces on New Year's Day, when they had looked at each other with such delight and discovery. Love is brief, said Carl. Was that true?

"Come now, Nik, we're on our holiday. And *we* shouldn't quarrel. We have nothing to quarrel about. Won't you be kind to me and laugh at my jokes—as in the old days?" He had on his silly, supplicating face now and the red hat was bent out of shape in his hands.

"The old days!" Nik smiled slightly. "But it was just a week ago that we were friends. Before Maj came and you began to prefer her to me."

"How could you imagine I could prefer Maj to you? With those spectacles she's so severe. Didn't I just tell you she was severe?"

"You said she was *delightfully* severe. As if you liked it! And you and Maj have so much to talk about—books and music and things I know nothing of."

"Ah, but Maj is terribly opinionated, don't you think? I believe—I believe you're more liberal in your judgments. No, you wouldn't judge a man. You'd try to understand."

They both looked at Frederik and Maj, who were now seated next to each other on the bench, but silent. The Tin Soldier continued to stare off into the distance, occasionally checking his pocket watch. Maj had put the letter away. They exchanged a few words and then Frederik waved at Carl and Nik, gesturing to his watch.

Carl smiled. "Frederik is used to authority. I was awfully bad at it, in the regiment. Once I overslept and missed reveille. Can you imagine? I was practically drummed out of the Army. If I hadn't been such a cheerful little soul, I'm sure they would have gotten rid of me. But I promised on my honor never to do it again and my superior relented."

"And did you do it again?"

"Oh my little girl," Carl sighed. "If I could take you in my arms now, I would. But the fact is, I must show you less affection now than before. And you mustn't tempt me. Can you do that? We must pretend indifference—at least for a time."

With that, he began to walk towards Maj and Frederik. Nik couldn't see his face. He had not asked her what she thought of this plan. He'd said she tempted him. Had she?

When they returned to Selde, dusty and hot from the hay cart and with specks of soot in their hair from the train, Mama and Aunt Marie were in the shady garden. Papa was with them, smoking his favorite meerschaum pipe, the one with the bowl in the shape of a man's head. The bowl had been dipped in golden beeswax and polished to topaz shine; the stem was real amber.

Jutta brought cool buttermilk from the cellar, Havarti cheese and rye bread, and a plate of gingersnaps. Nik sat close to her father, under the thick branches of a beech tree, and had no appetite, but drank a little buttermilk from a battered tin mug that had been hers as a child. She was tired of being a young lady all day. The stays bit into her breasts. Her feet were pinched in the boots. She unlaced them and under her long skirt, where no one could see, she gradually inched the boots off and dug her toes into the thick soft grass.

Carl and her sister were relating the story of the trip: what they'd seen, what they'd eaten, what they'd purchased—all the things that were of interest to the family. In the train, on the way back to Roslev, Carl had made a special effort to talk to Frederik about the Army, and gradually the Tin Soldier seemed to relax, though from time to time he looked uncertainly at Maj, who had her eyes closed most of the way with a headache. But now that she was home, there was no trace of a headache. She and Carl sat next to each other on a garden bench and Carl looked at Maj often as she described the photography studio and café, without saying a word about the quarrel. Once or twice the two of them laughed together. Maj had said nothing to Nik since the café. She hadn't looked at her sister in the train and had pulled away from even allowing their arms to touch.

Sadness washed over Nik. She'd looked forward to the trip to Nykøbing for days. Now she had been on the train and the ferry and had eaten herring and egg and apple cake with vanilla sauce. She didn't feel any different than she had this morning, except that her stomach hurt.

Frederik sat stiffly in a hard chair, with a distant frown on his face. After a while he took his leave, saying it had been a long day.

"But you will be here for dinner tomorrow, dear Frederik," said Mama. "We hope to see you every day while Maj is here. Please don't stand on ceremony, but consider this your home as well."

Frederik smiled but looked even stiffer, if that were possible, and made a polite bow in the general direction of Maj.

"I'm afraid I must be away in Viborg for a few days. A change of plans. My uncle would like me to go over some business matters connected with the peat works."

Maj met his eyes and said cheerfully, "Then we will see you again when you return, Frederik. Until then!"

Nik wished she were still small enough to sit in her father's lap and sob against his chest. Instead, Nik pushed her chair closer to Papa's and simply inhaled his cloud of tobacco smoke, a spicy English blend with deep notes, "particularly good against the mosquitoes" as he liked to say.

9.

"I BEGIN WITH A FEW SKETCHES," EXPLAINED METTE to Nik. "First I make a small drawing that only shows the dark and lights of my picture. The cliffs to the right, for instance, are quite light in value, and so is the sand. They're blindingly bright in the sun. Fur Sound is rather dark, with lights where the sun sparkles on the surface. The darkest of all is the shadow cast by the rocks, especially where the shadow's edge touches the underside of the rock."

Nik hung over her shoulder. Mette had brought her sketchbooks to the afternoon picnic, and a cunning wooden box of pens and pencils. They were on Fur Island, in a cove protected from the western breezes. The two of them perched on a slab of cement-stone, the sort of stone in which you could find fossils embedded. Mette's wide hat and veil shielded her dark red hair and fair skin. Her long gloved fingers grasped a thick pencil. Nik had asked Mette to show her how to draw.

The party had arrived on Fur after sailing around the Limfjord on Henrik's newly acquired sloop. How different, Nik, thought, than being rowed across the passage by the ferryman and then having to make your way by foot or cart across the island to these coves and cliffs. She missed the Strandgaards, but they'd all gone in another direction today. Schoolmaster Strandgaard had arranged an expedition to West Himmerland to investigate the remains of prehistoric stone circles. Nearby was a marsh where they expected to see goshawks and add to their collection of butterflies, insects, and plants.

Nik wished she could have gone with them, even though things were awkward with Joachim. But adventures with the Strandgaards were always active with little attention paid to social niceties or received ideas about what girls should do or not. Sophie was proof of that. Nik could imagine her leaping barefoot from stone to stone with her braid flying and a stick in her hand that she pretended was a Viking sword.

Nik, meanwhile, was stuck as the youngest in a group of dull old people—today she counted Carl and Henrik as old as well, for all the fun you could have with either of them—and relegated to being a nice, well-brought-up girl who couldn't even take her shoes off in the sand, no matter how hot it was. That was why she'd gravitated to Mette and her sketchbooks.

The men—Papa, Pastor Wellenborg, the squire, Henrik, and Carl—had gone off down the beach after the picnic lunch, to smoke and have a brandy, and to swim where they could disrobe unobserved. Most of the ladies had spread out below two large umbrellas. The pastor's wife and her sister, Widow Poulsen, were napping under one of them. Under the other, a striped green umbrella, Mama read, while Aunt Marie, who never picked up a book, crocheted. Aunt Marie seemed restless. She kept glancing down the shore to where the men had gathered, as if she couldn't help herself. It was a little indecent the way she stared, thought Nik, even though she too was curious. But all she could see were flashes of white and brown skin in the blue water, too distant to even make out who was who.

"And after I've done my value study and decided how to balance the lights and the darks," said Mette, "I begin my serious drawing. This way I know what is important before I begin." She picked up a second journal, with pages of heavy buff paper, and began to draw the same scene, faintly, in pencil, and then to go over it with pen and ink.

"Here," she said to Nik and handed her the first sketchbook and a couple of pencils. "Why don't you try? Remember, make the darks several shades of gray and don't be afraid to go quite black. It's a sunny day after all. The shadows are strong."

Nik opened the sketchbook to Mette's value rendering of the

sea and cliff and sand, with a few rocks in the foreground. She liked the boldness of the rough sketch with its deep darks and strong lines. Yet how little the sketch resembled the colors of the day: the glancing light on the marine-blue water; the fizzy bubbling blue-green of the wavelets rolling onshore; the white and green embroidery of the broken wave, slipping back over the pebbles with a glittery wet rattle and roll. Color had sound and smell and movement to it and a summer day like today was all mixed up with the seagulls mewling and the salty breeze, with the flash of tanned skin from down the beach as the men dashed back and forth in the white spray.

Mette's value drawing wasn't like life, but it had a life of its own on the page, and it was strangely more vibrant in its scribbled boldness than the delicate, detailed picture Mette was now creating in pen and ink in her "good" sketchbook. Nik picked up the pencil and hesitated. She rarely tried to draw. Generally she considered it mere girlish rubbish, like embroidery and what otherwise passed for accomplishments in the feminine sphere. She felt clumsy with pencils—her handwriting had always been messy—and bored with her mother's suggestions of what to depict: flowers in a vase, a landscape with the Selde church.

Like most young ladies, Maj sketched and painted watercolors, tight and controlled. Maj could barely stand to wet the page and her colors had a dry, feathery look. When Nik tried to paint, her colors all ran into each other, splotchy and blurred. Sometimes she liked the way they looked. In Maj's eyes, Nik's watercolors were always wrong, or what a child would do.

Nik glanced at her sister, sitting above the cove under a gnarled pine tree. Maj wore a wide straw hat and a veil to tie it down against the wind. She was reading a novel in Swedish, sent to her by Eva. Maj had been in her room or in the garden reading novels for several days now, since the trip to Nykøbing and the departure of Frederik. There had only been one letter from him to Maj, from Viborg, though the post had brought three letters from Eva and a package of books and journals. Maj said Frederik was delayed longer in town; the peat works were absorbing more of his time than he'd expected. It was a short note—Nik had fished it out, crumpled, from a waste bin—and was signed "Yours respectfully, Frederik Brandt." As if Maj had other Frederiks in her life.

Mama was reading *The Old Curiosity Shop* by Charles Dickens. The whole family was fond of Dickens, but Mama especially so. In summer when she wasn't gardening or putting up preserves or attending to the hundred other small duties of the household you could be sure to find her dreaming in her chair in the garden over Dickens. But today she seemed slightly distracted by Aunt Marie, whose crocheting kept falling from her hands. Under the green umbrella Aunt Marie's pale skin was greenish too and her chestnut hair more faded than ever. Sometimes her lips were the color of her ruby earrings, rouged and warm, but today they were dry pink with little wrinkles evident above the upper lip.

"I am so worried about Maj and Frederik," said Mama in a low voice, glancing around. But Maj was on the bluff above and Mette had walked to a more distant outcropping so that she could balance her sketchbook on it as she filled in the details of her drawing. Nik bent over her blank page, which glowed like a lamp under the sun's glare, and attempted to look absorbed. The rock was hard and hot against her back. They must have thought she was far enough away not to be able to hear.

"Do you think she could have sent Frederik away?" asked Aunt Marie.

"*Something* happened at Nykøbing," said Mama. "The next day I asked Maj about it—had they quarreled? She said no, of course not. But what would cause Frederik just to go off like that? He seemed cold to her when they parted. And I'm sure the peat works are absorbing, but this is the only time they have together and he *must* propose now if he's going to." Mama's soft voice trembled a little. "Girls have so few opportunities to marry well. Of course she says she wants to be a teacher. But that's not a *real* life for a girl—to rent a small room or live in a schoolhouse . . ."

"I suspect Maj would like a husband," sighed Aunt Marie. "Just not Frederik. He is not musical, I've noticed."

"What do you mean?"

"Only that Maj and Carl play beautifully together."

There was a slight pause and Nik felt the eyes of her aunt and mother rest on her. Her stomach tightened but she kept her head bent over the sketchbook and her hand moving.

Mama sighed and dropped her voice even more, so that Nik had to strain to hear. "He is a darling boy, of course, but not who I would choose for Maj. The life of a musician is so uncertain."

"He'll be a great man someday," Aunt Marie whispered back.

Mama did not disagree. She knew nothing much about the world of professional musicians but she rarely went against her older sister's opinion directly. "He would be a likeable addition to our family. Still I can't quite imagine Maj happy with that young man, though she'd probably put an end to his escapades. Marriage steadies a man. But Frederik seems so perfect. He won't be in the Army forever—he'll soon be leaving the regiment to go into business with his uncle. He could be quite wealthy someday." Mama rustled unhappily. "Maj wasn't a difficult girl growing up, but now—sometimes I don't know what to make of her. These books she reads, these women's societies she's joined . . . And in Viborg she would be so close to home."

"I agree that marriage would steady Carl. Of course that girl, that Karen Marie, would have only stood in his way. But our niece—don't you think Maj would be happier in Copenhagen or Odense than in Viborg? Jens and I would help, of course; they would always have a home with us, until the boy achieves his public success. Perhaps we could all move back to Odense." Aunt Marie sounded wistful but determined. "I'd like to keep him in the family. And the other one"—her voice dropped even further, she must mean Karen Marie—"well, she's simply too young."

With hardly a sound, Maj had made her way down the bluff to the sand and now shook out her skirts. "I must stretch my legs a moment. Don't worry—I'm going in the opposite direction from the men," she told her mother. She called sharply to her sister, "Come along, Nik."

"No. I'm drawing."

To her surprise, a picture had taken place on the page: a large rock and some rippled waves at its base. It didn't look like anything she'd ever drawn before. She hadn't started with an idea of a rock and waves. She had simply let her hand draw the darks and lights while she'd been listening to her aunt and mother. But now the rock stood before her. A real rock.

"I'll walk with you," Mette said to Maj. "I'm finished with my drawing." Her face was quite pink. Perhaps the wind had carried Mama and Aunt Marie's words after all.

The two of them strolled off, and after a moment, Mette linked her arm into Maj's.

Mama said, with a touch of guilt, "I suppose it's possible that Frederik and Mette would be married by now if Maj hadn't come along."

"That young man seems to show a great reluctance to commit," said Aunt Marie. "I've never trusted a soldier. And Mette will do well to accept young Henrik."

"Poor Mette Bohm," said Mama.

Mette gave Nik a small sketchbook and she continued drawing, but the drawings didn't turn out quite as well as the one she'd done at the beach, all unconscious. What was the difference? Nik tried looking at the world through narrowed eyes and upside down. She drew with her left hand and with her eyes closed. She produced some peculiar imagery from dreams. She drew the barn cat and the hens in the courtyard. She drew herself, wide-faced, with a huge nose, in the mirror of the samovar. Dreadfully amateurish, most of her sketches; still, at times she was pleased. She showed some of the drawings to Mette.

They began to meet daily at the parsonage. Mrs. Wellenborg

was glad to have Nik visit and never failed to say, in an encouraging tone, "My, Emilie, what a pretty dress," or "You begin to be quite the young lady, Emilie. I hope you will set an example now to little Sophie Strandgaard."

The first visit Mette produced several books of drawings by the Old Masters: Rubens, Rembrandt, and Dürer. They were different from most of the art Nik had seen before, the illustrations in newspapers and books and the sorts of genre paintings that hung on most people's walls: old women dozing by the fireplace; men on horses; familiar parish churches and manors and treeless moors. The Strandgaard home had painted ceilings of cupids, fat little bodies with wings, and maidens in diaphanous dresses. The figures were so cracked and faded and darkened by old smoke that they were judged to be either innocent or silly. On the walls of Henrik's manor were two dozen pale, bewigged ancestors, some with enormous feathered hats. They were framed in gilt and hung all along the staircase and upper corridor. Papa said that they couldn't possibly be Henrik's forbears; the old squire had bought them at auctions around the district when his fortunes began to prosper from fattening cattle for market.

The books that Mette showed her held engravings: figures, heads, torsos. Mette used them to point to the difference between line and mass. She talked about geometrical forms: columns, blocks, circles, and ovals. Many of the figures were nude. Of course Nik had seen naked people before—the men from a distance, swimming in the fjord; the women uncomfortably close, changing behind a blanket on shore. But she'd never thought of the body as a subject for art, had never dared to look closely at its fleshy swellings and saggings, its firm hard muscles and bony protuberances, its geometric shapes and the ways the limbs moved and were connected. Like all well-brought-up girls going into adulthood, her body had become increasingly protected by layers of muslin, whalebone, starched cotton, wool, and taffeta so that she could move only in particular ways. Less and less of her was meant to be visible to the outside world; her feet vanished and then her arms, finally her hair and ears under hats and veils, like a beekeeper.

"At the Drawing School we don't have nude models to work from," said Mette. "Consequently most of us have had to learn any notion of anatomy from books. In general, of course, we're not encouraged to think of bodies as having muscles and bones. If we draw figures they are always dressed and the clothing is our subject, as if the people wearing it were mannequins. Little men and women designed to fit on cups and plates." She sighed. "Never mind."

She set Nik to drawing her own hands—in contour outline first, and then with mass and shadow—and she suggested that Nik copy some of the drawings from the books. "Just the heads for now, or whatever would your Mama think!"

Nik had always thought she didn't like young ladies, but Mette was different. Not that Mette was a tomboy, not at all. She was always in fresh whites and pale greens; she always wore gloves and a hat outdoors because of her fair complexion. But around her Nik didn't feel awkward or too tall and dark as she did with Maj sometimes. She didn't feel stupid or silly or constantly reminded of her age. She simply felt at ease and as if Mette were genuinely interested in her thoughts and feelings. They were a decade apart, but it mattered little when they began to talk about things they cared about and things they disliked, so many of which were similar. Mette liked rising early and going out into the dawn. She hated cabbage and turnips. She liked strawberries. She was sincerely devout.

Most people practiced Christianity on Sundays. They might, the rest of the week, offer a few platitudes about being good to the poor, and some actually were charitable. But they did not pray. Mette enjoyed praying, she told Nik with a smile. It was the first thing she did every morning and the last thing at night. But Mette's true feelings of gratitude for God's Creation came over her in Nature, when she was walking on a hillside and the evening light struck a stone or a tree just so. It was the same for Nik, though she had never given words to it. Noticing the world was a form of prayer.

Whether Mette should marry Henrik—that was something they sometimes talked about, along with art and God. Maj thought Nik too young to discuss anything of importance most of the time, but Mette didn't. Henrik had not proposed, but he'd made his interest clear. Mette was sure he would speak to the pastor if Mette were to give him more encouragement. She wondered if she should; in September she would be returning to Copenhagen to continue her drawing studies. If she did nothing now, she and Henrik would not meet again until next summer.

They were in the garden of the parsonage when Mette told her this. Mette, in her wide-brimmed straw hat, with a shallow basket over her arm, was cutting back dahlias and deadheading roses. It had rained the night before, a light refreshing rain, and though it was sunny, droplets still sparkled underneath the petals and leaves.

"Henrik is young, but you can see he's already a good man. He and his father treat the farmers and laborers well; they don't squeeze the life out of their animals and servants to have a bit more for themselves. And it would please so many people. My uncle and aunt, who've been so kind to me. My relatives in Copenhagen who worry about my future. Henrik's father. And Henrik, of course. It seems to me that with very little effort—one word—I could make so many people happy."

Nik was struck by the simplicity of this notion—of choosing to make others happy. If Maj had put forth such an idea Nik wouldn't have believed her. Maj thought mainly of herself and it was clear, from the way she'd treated Frederik, that she didn't think of making him happy. Maj's idea of pleasing other people was to do what was expected of her—grudgingly.

When Mette spoke of pleasing other people, it was their well-being and happiness she meant to improve. What held her back then, from saying yes to Henrik?

"You don't love him, I suppose?" Nik asked.

"No, not yet," said Mette. "At least not in the way one should . . . the physical way. He seems a little boy to me still. But he'll grow up. And if I put my mind to it, I think I *could* learn to love him." Her straw hat hid her face and her voice sounded uncertain.

"Did you—did you love Frederik?"

"It would have been a suitable match," said Mette. "He's handsome, don't you think?"

She didn't have to say that Henrik cut a different figure from Frederik with his dashing black moustache and fine bearing. Henrik had thin brown hair and red downy cheeks. His backside was comfortably broad. He rode sturdy farm horses and didn't give himself airs, though in fact he would inherit a great deal of land in the district. With age, the old squire wasn't able to get around the countryside on horseback any longer, and although he was in charge of the farms and rents belonging to the estate, it was Henrik who was now handling the buying and selling of cattle. The meadows of their estate were judged particularly good for fattening up the animals, and Henrik had increased the size of the herd and managed to get good prices for them at auction. Such responsibilities gave him a solidity and fund of common sense. He was well-informed about what mattered locally, but he had few opinions about the larger cultural currents or faraway events. He'd never been to Copenhagen, only cattle fairs in southern Denmark and Germany, and he had no interest in traveling to the capital. He didn't read much, certainly never novels or poetry, and showed little regard for music or painting, though he always admired Mette's watercolors and had arranged to have several framed.

Maj would have never given him a second glance, in spite of his wealth and standing in the district.

Nik bent to pick up a freshly cut dahlia Mette had dropped. It had a sharp vegetable scent, hardly like a flower at all. She said, "My aunt and mother think Frederik's not coming back to Selde. That he and Maj had a quarrel. And that—maybe—Maj and Carl have fallen in love."

Nik relayed this gossip carelessly, as if it didn't matter to her.

But it mattered greatly what Mette thought. Especially about Carl and Maj. Ever since Nykøbing Carl had avoided being alone with Nik, but Nik was always coming across Carl and Maj together, usually at the piano but sometimes in the garden.

At first Nik had thought this was part of Carl's plan—to discourage Mama and Aunt Marie from thinking he was flirting with Nik. But now she wasn't sure.

"Perhaps," said Mette. "Maj and Carl don't seem to me to be in love. But then, I don't really know either of them well. I do know that falling in love isn't as easy as it is in novels. It happens less than you'd think and it's more precious than you can ever imagine." Mette clipped a bronze-orange dahlia the size of two fists. "I met a man once," she said quietly. "A friend of my brother's. Poul was his name. Claus and Poul went off to the West Indies together. Claus is still there, now married and with a family. Poul died of typhoid fever within six months of arriving. I had a few letters from him. I was eighteen. He asked me to marry him before he went, but my parents were afraid of losing me. They asked us to wait until he returned, to see what he'd made of himself. A year later Poul was dead and so were my parents, one after the next."

Tears rushed into Nik's eyes. "Oh, Mette."

"I thought I'd die too. To be only nineteen and lose three people you love. But the years pass and you find you can live after all. You find something else. Or someone else. I could be satisfied perhaps with painting flowers on china plates and teacups. Or"—she touched Nik on the cheek with one of the clipped, browning dahlias; the dry orange petals were soft on Nik's skin and fell to the ground—"I could get married to Henrik."

One afternoon, as Nik announced she was going to visit Mette, Maj said she'd like to accompany her to the pastor's house. Mette and Maj had never been close, between the age difference and living in Odense and Copenhagen most of the year. Triumphant last

Christmas about Frederik's attentions at the ball, her sister seemed now to take a different view of things.

At the parsonage Maj embraced Mette quite sincerely and reminded her that on their walk at the beach a week ago Mette had promised to show Maj some of her watercolors. When Maj put her mind to it, she could be quite charming, Nik thought irritably. Would Maj now take Mette away from her, as she had Carl?

"But these are lovely," said Maj. Quickly she paged through Mette's portfolio of scenes from Copenhagen streets and parks. Seen all together like this, the pictures formed a parade of pastel images: ladies with parasols and small dogs; men in carriages; flowers and weeping willows.

Where were the darkest darks and the flowing lines and geometric masses of Mette's sketches? These pictures had no weight or strength; they were merely decorative.

"I'll make a better wage at the porcelain factory if I design the patterns for the china than if I merely paint them. This is the kind of thing they like—small figures, bouquets, the weeping willows. If I go back to Copenhagen this fall, I'll work on these designs to present to the factory."

"If?" said Maj. "Why wouldn't you return to Copenhagen?"

Mette smiled vaguely. "Oh, Aunt is not very well at the moment."

Maj began talking about articles she'd read in *Women and Society* about women's attempts over the years to be admitted to the Royal Danish Academy of Art. "In Stockholm women have been studying at their Academy of Art since 1864. It's disgraceful how far we're behind in this country."

"But we've had the Drawing School for Women in Copenhagen for twelve years," said Mette in a quiet voice. "It was set up expressly by the Danish Women's League for the purpose of training women in the arts and crafts. And it's been quite successful. Many women now have work at the porcelain factories."

"Of course it's splendid that women are trained to work," said Maj, looking up from the portfolio. "Still, you can hardly make the case that it's the same education as you'd get at the Academy of Art. Of course it's not the same! Johanne Krebs writes in *Women and Society* that the teachers at your Drawing School are inferior to those at the Academy. There's no drawing from the model, no advanced art training. It's unfair that women who study art must pay for classes. Male art students study free at the Academy if they're accepted. They compete for travel stipends and can study in Paris and Rome. Most importantly, the men can take themselves seriously as *artists*. Have you read Johanne Krebs on this? If not, I can loan you a copy of the article."

Maj's cheeks began to flush in a way that had become familiar to Nik this summer. It was as if a wrathful pot in her stomach had begun to bubble, sending up heat to her face and causing her glasses to steam a little. Once again Nik was astonished by all that her sister seemed to know about life beyond Selde. What a great number of opinions Maj held on subjects of no immediate use.

How did Maj know, for instance, that the Drawing School for Women was considered to be inferior to the Royal Danish Academy of Art? What did that say about Mette and her art then? Looking at the pretty little watercolors, Nik realized they were well done but nothing special. Mette's quick charcoal drawings of the rocks at Fur Sound had more life than these finished pieces.

Mette was pink-cheeked too, but her tone was level. She closed the portfolio cover protectively over her work. "And what would most women do after graduating from the Academy, even assuming they could get in eventually? Most male artists have a difficult time financially unless they're brilliant and lucky or their families support them. Married women have no time for painting and single women need to make a living."

Maj looked a little abashed, but she stood her ground. "It's the principle of the thing, Mette. Nothing will change if we don't fight for it. Look at Sweden; they're much farther along in the struggle for women's rights than we are, because they don't back down. I am confident that if we women in Denmark had the courage to go against what our parents and husbands and politicians told us was proper for ladies, we would have at least as many rights as our Swedish sisters."

"You're quite right, Maj," said Mette. "But you have more optimism than I do. Women have been fighting to enter the Academy of Art for many years. If I'd spent my time doing battle instead of studying what I *could* study, which is illustration and design, I wouldn't be almost finished with my courses and able to find work. It's fine for Johanne Krebs—she's a real painter, a fine painter—but I don't make the mistake of assuming I have more than a modest talent for drawing. My goal has only been to support myself."

"That's what I want too," said Maj. "It's why I'm studying to be a schoolmistress."

"I thought you wanted to get married," said Nik. Really, she wished her sister would make up her mind. She must know that Frederik would never let her teach school after they married.

Maj stared coldly at her. "Really, Nik, you should think before you speak. There's no reason a married woman can't live a life of her own. Do you stop feeling and thinking because you put a ring on your finger? Every woman should have something she can do. You should think about that. Are you just going to sit in the parlor in Selde reading and writing poetry?"

Nik glowered. "I told you—I'm emigrating!"

"Not for a few years, miss. And perhaps you'll change your mind. Besides, that's not an occupation, emigration. It would be far better if you tried to study something. You could come to Odense and attend the high school there, just as I did. You could stay with Uncle Hans and Cousin Ottilie."

Ottilie! What a useless girl. Nik had met her cousin only a few times. Since losing her parents when young, Ottilie had lived with Uncle Hans, and she had become the lady of the house after Aunt Regine died. She was three years older than Nik. She had a long neck, like an ostrich, and an elegant nose, of which she was overly proud. When she preened in the mirror, she always turned to see her profile. From the front her cheeks were pillow-plump and her chin minuscule. She had a list of feminine accomplishments as long as Maj's, but unlike Maj, she thought they were valuable.

Mette had been looking with quiet surprise on this quarrel. She moved to the table and rang the bell for the servant and coffee. As if in passing, but perhaps in rebuke to Maj, she said in her kindest voice, "Emilie, have you ever thought that you might study art? I think you have a gift for it. If Johanne Krebs and the others are successful, perhaps the Academy will open its doors to women by the time you're ready to take classes there."

"Oh—perhaps," said Nik, turning her shining eyes away from her sister. She didn't want Maj to see the hope in them.

10.

SHE REMEMBERED HOW EARLIER IN THE SUMMER SHE used to come into the parlor after he'd gotten up from the bench and gone out or just picked up his violin instead. She would run her hands over the ivory keys to feel if they were still warm. And if they were, it was her secret thrill to stroke them lightly with a fingertip or make soft chords where his fingers had been.

Nik was never alone with Carl in the parlor now, nor did they go off by themselves riding in the afternoons or sit in the depths of the old soft sofa trading stories about childhood. In spite of their confidential talk in Nykøbing, it was hard for Nik to believe that Carl cared a fig for her. Indeed, it was as if the first weeks of his visit, before Maj arrived, had never happened. He seemed restless and less carefree and began to talk longingly of Copenhagen. He was just as amusing as before, making up songs and acting silly at the drop of a hat, but he had stopped writing his pretend novel and drawing caricatures. He sat reading Strindberg and Dostoyevsky and Heine's poems. He composed, often late into the night. Phrases from one particular adagio movement were so familiar to the family that they woke from quite different dreams all humming the same melancholy melody.

He liked to switch from piano to violin and repeat the same passages in different keys. When he played the violin he had Maj accompany him, and she was willing enough most afternoons to try variations and repetitions. It was strange, Nik thought, that Maj, so impatient in so many ways, didn't mind playing the same melodies in higher and lower keys and even offering her opinion, as if she could really hear the difference.

What was Maj up to? Every morning after swimming she wrote

a long letter to Eva in Sweden—what could she have to say at such length? Then she helped Mama with sewing and Aunt Marie with embroidery. She sat in the garden reading Swedish novels. She seemed not to have much appetite, but was pleasant to everyone at meals. She never mentioned Frederik and, as no word came from him after his first short note, Papa and Mama stopped mentioning him as well. Immediately after the midday meal Maj and Carl would usually drift off to the parlor for music, but sometimes, if Mama and Aunt Marie were not there, they fell into conversation and it was invariably the same: They would get into a heated argument that excluded Nik.

Back and forth they went about, echoing the sharp exchanges in the newspapers on the morality debate. July and August were evidently not too warm for arguments in *Politiken*. Georg Brandes mocked Elizabeth Grundtvig and her puritanical views about women and men. Then the great Norwegian writer Bjørnstjerne Bjørnson came to Miss Grundtvig's defense. Brandes then attacked Bjørnson. Was marriage bondage or love? Should the same moral rules apply to men and women and what should those rules consist of? Restraint for both or freedom for both? What was the nature of men and women? Was hypocrisy inevitable? Did women pay the price for men's indiscretions?

A few years ago Bjørnson had written a play, *A Gauntlet*, in which Svava broke off her engagement with Alf because he had once been involved with a married woman. Later Bjørnson wrote a novel on the same theme, about a girls' school in Norway where the students debated morality and struggled over purity. Maj had read this novel; Carl had not—but he knew all about it from reviews and parodies in the papers. He thought it ridiculous that Bjørnson, an old fellow with a checkered past himself, had taken as his subject a bunch of adolescent girls who went around pronouncing things only Bjørnson brooded about, such as, "The woman who marries a man who has had an immoral past makes herself an accomplice."

Brandes, on the other hand, said Carl, was honest about human desire. In a foreword to his translation of John Stuart Mill's *The Subjection of Women*, the great literary critic had argued that nothing natural for a human being should be suppressed. That went for women too. It was madness to demand abstinence from both sexes. It made both men and women sick and unhealthy.

Maj thought abstinence made the body strong. Elizabeth Grundtvig herself said so.

They never asked Nik's opinion, and if anyone else came into the room, such as Aunt Marie or even Jutta, they immediately stopped their discussion and began to bang on the piano keys.

Three times a week swollen envelopes arrived from Sweden. Clutching them, Maj would run back to her bedroom and read for an hour. Afterwards she seemed even more agitated than before the post arrived.

Nik now sought reasons to be out of the house as much as possible. Her mother wouldn't allow her to help out in the shop and she couldn't spend all her time with Mette, nor was it possible to ride out as often as she would have liked, as Papa's two workhorses were needed every day for hauling timber from the shore to the lumberyard. The baroness was at Lake Como with her husband and had left no open invitation to use her stables.

It wasn't just Maj and Carl that Nik was tired of listening to; it was other unsettling fragments of conversations. Overheard whispers between Mama and Aunt Marie about Karen Marie. A word or two between Papa and Mama about Frederik and whether Papa should drive over to Sparkær on the pretext of taking a look at the peat works and see what the young man was up to. Papa was to ask Frederik, nicely of course, when he was planning to return to Selde.

And then there was that peculiar business with Aunt Marie and Carl. The seamstress, Miss Humlegaard, had come from Skive to make a dress each for Maj, Nik, and Aunt Marie. Aunt Marie had not gone swimming that morning but had stayed behind to have a fitting. She asked Carl to stay behind too, to keep her company and give her advice about her dress. They waved the family good-bye and Carl went right to the piano, with Aunt Marie trailing behind.

Nik returned home earlier than the others; she'd run all the way. She had a foolish, childlike wish to creep up to the parlor window and listen to Carl playing without him knowing. But there was no music in the parlor, no one in the dining room, and only Mrs. Jespersen in the kitchen. The cook said Miss Humlegaard had come into the parlor and asked Aunt Marie to go upstairs for a fitting. She didn't know where the young man had gotten to. Nik caught a glimpse of herself in the shiny samovar as she went back through the dining room. As always the distorted look of her face made her laugh a little: what a big nose she had! What a broad forehead and tiny ears.

Upstairs she heard a murmur of voices from Aunt Marie's room and then the creak of footsteps as Miss Humlegaard went out and down the passage to the workroom. Quietly Nik crept upstairs; she could not have said what made her wish to be so secretive.

"What do you think, Carl?" said Aunt Marie. "I'm not certain about the neckline. Miss Humlegaard says it's fashionable, but then, she's only from Skive."

"I know you like the lace, Mrs. Marie, but sometimes—you wear too much lace, especially at the neck." Carl's voice was kind but different than usual—more commanding. And he called her Mrs. Marie, not Aunt Marie, how strange. "Try it without all that trimming. Let me help you with the pins."

There was an odd silence, and then came her aunt's voice, a little shaky. "There now, it's gone. Jens would not approve of course; he would find this too low-cut."

"Uncle Jens isn't the one you should be trying to please," said Carl, and from the sound of her aunt's suppressed laugh, Nik imagined Carl making an Uncle Jens face: long and somber, with a down-turned mouth. She almost went in, because she found Carl's imitations so amusing, but something made her hesitate, perhaps the odd little purr her aunt gave then, a purr of delight, like a cat being stroked.

"Oh, Miss Emilie," said Miss Humlegaard, coming up behind her on the landing. "Come with me. Your aunt's dress is almost finished and we're trying to decide on the trim. She's not sure if she wants lace or not at the neckline. I think lace suits an older woman. I've brought one or two more samples from my basket. Can you give your opinion?"

When they went in, Carl was at the window, looking carelessly out and tapping his fingers against the sill, and Aunt Marie bent over a box on the bed containing various bits of trim and lace. But there was nothing at the neckline of the evening dress. Strange that with her faded chestnut hair and with the lines around her mouth, her bosom could yet be so firm and unwrinkled. Perhaps because she'd never had children, the rosy skin matched the flush on her cheeks.

Harald Strandgaard's brick manor and adjoining lands, bought for him by his wife's parents, lay a short mile from the village. The large property had once belonged to the aristocracy and still had the remains of a moat. The bridge over the moat and the large beech grove gave the grounds a fairytale look. In these woods grew mushrooms in fall and snowdrops and bluebells in spring; it was the haunt of grouse and pheasants, foxes and hedgehogs. The house itself was old-fashioned and spacious, with high ceilings and an airy if somewhat ramshackle aspect. Some rooms hadn't been used for a century and the plaster walls had crumbled. One of the two wings had been closed off for safety. But the main part of the house was still quite grand, with the remains of painted ceilings and a chandelier or two. A massive oak staircase led from the entry hall upstairs to the bedrooms, while from the main salon tall glass doors opened onto a stone terrace and from there into a hedged garden and lawns with a view of the Limfjord. The Strandgaards used the grand salon, along with the adjoining dining room, as a workroom as well as a place for meals. From these two rooms the schoolmaster maintained a large correspondence with scientists in Copenhagen, Germany, and Scotland.

From early childhood, Nik had been part of the Strandgaard family's natural history expeditions around Selde and to Fur, and she was quite at home in the workroom with its many tall glass-fronted walnut cabinets. Here were to be found shelves of animal embryos in jars and a multitude of stuffed birds. Labeled boxes held bird skulls, nests, and eggs with the yolks blown out. Mounted on the walls were glass cases of moths and butterflies and beetles. She and Joachim had spent many dark winter evenings arranging and rearranging the collections and making up stories about the animals to tell the smaller children.

The schoolmaster made no mention of Nik's absence from the house for the last weeks when the housekeeper let her in one rainy afternoon. It was one of those thunderous summer storms that could sweep across the Limfjord and make August seem like a November with green leaves.

"Emilie, you've come at an excellent moment! Joachim and Sophie are cleaning and packing up some new fossils. We're sending them to Mr. James Geikie in Edinburgh, so that he can learn from our finds in the Limfjord. He is professor of Geology at the university there. Can you lend a hand?"

Joachim acknowledged her presence only with a little redness at the top of his ears, but Sophie said, "Miss Emilie, why haven't you been here for so long?"

"We've been busy at the house this summer with so many visitors," she mumbled. Strandgaard had organized his numerous fossils in wooden trays that pulled out from the tall cabinets. The most common fossils to be found in the moler cliffs of Fur were tiny salmon that once swam through the ancient seas that covered Denmark. But the family had also found the skeletons of various mackerels, tuna, and herring. He had a beautiful example of a snake mackerel, from snout to tail, as well as the well-preserved bony-tongued fish that Joachim had found a few weeks ago.

It was the starfish that Nik had always liked most, the way they left their imprint on the stone like a pattern of wallpaper, but of course she was impressed with the fish fossils, whose living structures had been replaced by minerals, creating hard and unyielding skeletons that could be revealed with patient chiseling: cement-stone memories of what was once swimming in the sea, living, moving.

Of course there were many other fossils too, some quite tiny: leaves, ferns, mosquitoes, dragonflies, cicadas. One of her favorite fossils was only an inch long; it was the wing of a cicada traced into the rock. She had admired it so longingly that last Christmas, Strandgaard made her a present of it.

Joachim had hammered together a few wooden boxes and Sophie had brought in a basket of hay in which to pack the fossils. Nik took a soft brush and picked up a stone with a tracery of tree needles. Strandgaard suspected it was a giant sequoia, from millions of years ago. If so, it would be a great find. He wanted confirmation from Mr. Geikie.

The Edinburgh professor was one of the many esteemed scientists who had sent the schoolmaster signed copies of their books in English, French, and German. Strandgaard also purchased books from antiquarian bookshops in Edinburgh and corresponded with book dealers in London, Paris, and Berlin. He had Buffon's *Histoire Naturelle* and Cuvier's beautiful volumes on fossils in sets bound alike in Morocco leather. A fine reproduction of Steno's seventeenth-century dissertation "Concerning a Solid Body Enclosed by a Process of Nature within a Solid" was given pride of place. From childhood Nik and Joachim had spent many rainy days looking through different illustrated books on the dining room table. One of their favorites was Playfair's *Illustrations of the Huttonian System of the Earth*. James Hutton, a Scottish chemist, was known for his theory that heat drove the creation of the world. Much like the steam engines his friend James Watt was building, the world was a dynamic machine: "The earth shows no vestiges of a beginning, no prospect of an end," said Hutton.

Nik and Joachim were especially taken with pictures that showed sequences of volcanic eruptions and sedimentary deposits. The layers, of different thicknesses, lay on top of each other like a cake assembled of various ingredients: gingerbread, crumbly oatcake, smooth buttercream; somewhat similar to the English trifles that the Strandgaard's housekeeper Mrs. Ekorn had learned to make for the family, created of sponge cake and jelly, preserved fruit and cream. Each earth layer suggested an entirely different planet. Countless seas had risen and dried up; whole oceans had shifted north to south and back again; entire continents had been flooded and thrust back up. Volcanoes exploded and mountain ranges eroded. Glaciers deepened valleys and shoved around huge erratic rocks as if they were pebbles. Jungles, deserts, alpine meadows, and swamps all came and went. Most of this happened slowly over millions of years but occasionally there was a cataclysm, though that too—that flood, that eruption—was often hardly bigger than a pencil mark on the long diagram of time.

Each layer of the trifle was a former world. Each new world was built on a forgotten world. The new strata didn't erase the old; it covered it. If you dug down far enough you would find all those former worlds. Some of Nik's favorite illustrations were panoramic views of men in shirtsleeves with shovels tunneling down through Time, layer after layer below the earth, to find fossils far below the surface.

For Sophie, the fossil itself was the thing of value. If she could have dropped a fossil skeleton in a glass of magic water and watched the animal come alive again, she would have been quite happy. Her favorite pictures in books weren't the stratified layers of rock—how boring!—they were fanciful imaginings, from De la Beche, of ichthyosaurs eating plesiosaurs and of pterodactyls flying through the sky. A fossil, even a small one, was a memory of a living being. For Joachim and Nik, fossilized remains were page markers, letters, and clocks. The layers themselves were what most interested them.

All afternoon they worked as the rain pelted down, Nik with Sophie and Joachim and their father on the fossils, and Anne and Tom on pressing flowers and organizing their butterfly collection. Their housekeeper brought in strong tea and milk with scones at four and Joachim began to seem more at ease with Nik working next to him. At six the rain stopped as suddenly as it had begun and sunshine poured in. The wooden boxes were hammered shut and carefully placed in a trunk with several pages of description and notes in Schoolmaster Strandgaard's careful hand. It gave them all a thrill to see the label on the trunk: "Mr. James Geikie, Royal Scottish Geographical Society, 10 Randolph Crescent, Edinburgh, Scotland."

The trunk would go by train to Esbjerg and then by ship across the North Sea. They all imagined the wooden boxes being opened in some august hall at the Geographical Society and men with gray beards and top hats exclaiming in Scottish accents just how amazed they were by the finds coming out of little Selde.

When Strandgaard suggested an expedition to the northwest knob of Fur the next day, to the fossil-rich cliffs of Knudeklinterne, she immediately agreed. Her mother helped her fish out her boots and the old bonnet that she always wore when prospecting for fossils.

"To learn to draw is to learn to see," Mette had said.

Nik hadn't been to this part of the island since she'd started her art lessons with Mette. It was deeply familiar, this shoved-up bluff, like a many-layered petticoat under a skewed green pannier of turf. She'd climbed up to the top of the headlands many times; she'd clambered over the rocks and slabs at the base of the bluff half her life. But she had never stood looking at the bluff from below and seen a landscape. She'd never noticed the pattern of darks and lights, the zig-zag of white clay and dark ash layered and folded, as something she could translate to the page with charcoal and pencil.

"Miss Emilie!" Sophie shook her arm. "What's wrong? Why are you standing there with your nose all wrinkled up?"

It was as if the heavy rains of yesterday had never happened. It was summer again, fresh and dry, with a blue breeze off the fjord. Nik picked her way partway up the slope after Joachim, who was turning over promising lumps of cementstone. He wore a soft brown felt hat that had seen many weathers and a red neckerchief that gave him the dashing air of an explorer. He heard her climbing over the rocks after him and he turned and held out his hand. She didn't need to take it—she was a strong and sturdy hiker and her old cotton dress was ruched up enough so that she could move freely—but she did. His hand was so different from Carl's. Joachim's palm was hard and slightly calloused and his knuckles were big. Carl's palm was warm and a little soft, his fingers agile and teasing.

Joachim's hand felt more trustworthy, and that was strange, because he was only fifteen and Carl twenty-two.

The sun grew higher and the sky blazed with that radiant blue of late summer above the moler, which baked white in summer. Sweat ran pleasantly down their faces under their hats. By noon, when they stopped to eat lunch, none of them had found a single fossil.

But this was as it had been many times. Strandgaard himself was happy enough to poke around the cracks and fissures of the formation and to measure the inclines. His mind was probably imagining sheets of land ice forming and retreating and pushing up the bluff. He'd once told Nik that geology was the pleasure it was to him because it made present losses seem tiny next to the eternal rising and falling of the earth. He said that epochs like his university studies or his teaching years in Viborg or his life with Mrs. Strandgaard were like former worlds that ended in cataclysm and then began again.

The schoolmaster had been a bit in his cups from holiday punch when he told Nik this last Christmas at a gathering at the Strandgaards. It was then he'd pulled open a cabinet drawer and given her the fossil cicada wing.

Joachim cut slices of his apple and fed them to Nik. The apple was a little sour and salty on the peel, from his fingers.

Joachim said to her, "I suppose you play the piano really well now. We always hear duets coming from the house when we're passing."

"That's my sister," Nik said. "Maj and Carl play beautifully together. I haven't improved much!" She laughed and it was the first time she'd laughed about her failures as a musician. It felt good to be away from the infernal parlor and that constant tinkling and string-sawing of Mozart and Brahms, the insidious melodies that got into your head and pounded through your veins.

"What a shame," said Joachim, "that so much of the summer has gone. I'm back at school in two weeks."

Schoolmaster Strandgaard said, "We must find a way to keep you occupied, Emilie."

"I'm studying drawing with Mette Bohm."

"An excellent occupation for a young lady," said Strandgaard. "But I had thought of teaching you more natural history. Would you like that?"

"Yes, of course."

"It's too bad the high school at Jebjerg is only for boys," said Strandgaard. "When I was part of the committee discussing its building I advocated strongly for making it open to girls. But of course I was voted down."

Tom said loyally, "Sophie is much smarter than me. The boys at Jebjerg would get a run for their money if Sophie went there."

"Sophie will have to go to Aarhus, to the girls' high school there, I'm afraid," said their father.

"Sophie is different from most girls," said Joachim. His smile patronized his sister, who was sitting with Anne on a rock. While Anne played with her doll, Sophie was using the edge of her chisel to scratch something into the surface of the stone. "Most girls couldn't do the work we do at Jebjerg, like Greek and Higher Mathematics."

"In America, girls can study as much as they want," Nik said, irritated. She didn't feel she could counter Joachim directly, she who had been so slow at mathematics and Latin, much less Greek.

"I suspect even in the United States, girls face difficulty trying to get the education they want," said Strandgaard, glancing benevolently at his daughters. "Still, what do you say, Sophie? Shall we move to America?"

"No," said Sophie, still scratching on the stone. "I'd rather go to Cambridge or Oxford to study. I plan to become a paleontologist, as you know."

"My sister would be proud of you," said Nik. "She's strongly in favor of women's education."

Joachim smiled at Nik, again with that patronizing flash of white teeth. "They say your sister supports the Vote for Women, Nik. I suppose we can expect the same from you?"

"Well why shouldn't we have the Vote and everything else?"

"She's right, Joachim," said Sophie. "And when we get the Vote I think all the women should vote the men out of Parliament and we should decide everything. And everything we decide will be good and best for women in Denmark."

"Then I'll have no choice but to move to Scotland," teased Joachim. "I don't want a pack of ladies making decisions about my life. No, thank you!"

Nik got up abruptly and went over to Sophie's rock. It was clearly fine with Joachim that ladies had to put up with men making decisions about *their* lives.

Sophie had scratched a picture of a dinosaur with wings.

They resumed fossil hunting, but a shadow had fallen over the day for Nik.

Nik remembered the year Strandgaard became their schoolmaster and she finally started in the classroom. Nik was placed at a desk with Joachim that first day. He was eight. She'd never sat next to a boy before, this close. She was surprised that Joachim smelled like soap. Most boys, the ones she played with anyway, smelled like frogs and pocket lint.

"Now, who can read?"

"I can!" Nik's hand shot up.

But she'd never done a lick of arithmetic before, even though she could count on her fingers and though she'd watched Papa and Mr. Svendsen add and subtract long columns in the store, so she knew that numbers were the same as coins that farmers placed on the counter.

Joachim already knew his times tables. He knew some English and some Latin already and quite a few dates. His spelling was perfect. He was learning penmanship.

He was a hero to Nik that first year of school. Later, as she caught up, she could read as well as he could and spell better. But she was uncertain with her sums; it was usually only a matter of luck when the numbers came out right. They were deskmates for several years and Joachim's hand and arm on the desk next to her were as familiar as her own. Then the schoolmaster moved them apart and Nik had to sit with Sophie, who tormented her with questions and occasional tickles.

At twelve Joachim tried to push her away and said he preferred to play with Tom. At fourteen he was just the opposite. He sought her out. He gave her a bouquet of wildflowers. All last summer they were outside and dreaming dreams. Then Joachim went to live in Jebjerg with his grandparents and attend the high school. When he came home on visits, he was not the same.

He was superior and scientific now. And even though he seemed just as fond of her as before, Nik felt left behind. He considered her merely a girl. That was enough for him. He could be in love with her without caring that she wasn't as clever as he was. In fact, he probably preferred her to be less educated. Even in matters of deep time and geology, where small matters of masculinity and femininity should count for naught, he considered himself her master.

Last summer she and Joachim had pretended they were explorers in the Andes Mountains of Peru. Or rather, Joachim had said, "Let's pretend I'm the Great Danish Explorer Strandgaard, discoverer of Inca ruins, and that you're my wife and assistant." He'd kissed her and she'd felt flattered. Just think, she had felt flattered to be along on his exploration, flattered he would *allow* her to be his assistant.

Now she didn't take his hand when he offered to pull her up the side of the cliff, and shortly after she struck off on her own in the opposite direction. *She* would be the adventurer. She stomped over the rocks and probed with a stick, turning over cementstone lumps as if they were turtles. Sophie came up beside her and the two of them walked down the beach.

"Sophie," said Nik. "Are you really going to be a paleontologist? And what do you mean by that, exactly?"

"A dinosaur-bone hunter! I'll go to look for buried skeletons and I'll be like Mary Anning at Lyme Regis. I'll find a lot of old crocs and megasaurs in China maybe or Wyoming, but I'll be a scientist, so I won't just sell them like she did. I'll send the fossils back to Europe and maybe work in a museum and I'll know everything!"

"Sophie, you're quite absurd, do you know that? And anyway, not all fossils are bones. So you could be a paleontologist and just study ammonites or trilobites or something."

"I'm a pterodactyl," Sophie shouted, taking off down the beach, flapping her arms. "See me fly with my giant wings!"

Nik lifted up her skirts and ran too, a little self-conscious that Joachim might be watching.

Sophie shrieked again, "I'm a pterodactyl. Catch me!" and Nik flew swiftly after her.

11.

ONE HUMID AFTERNOON WHEN NIK WAS IN THE GARDEN reading, swatting flies, and listening half-heartedly to the waltz tune coming from the parlor, the middle movement of what Carl was now calling his "little suite for strings," she heard the quick clop of horse hooves approaching on the Skive road.

She looked up, and through the trees that shielded the garden from the road she saw the Tin Soldier trotting along on Sultan.

Frederik had returned.

But to Nik's surprise, the horse hooves didn't turn in at their gate. She stood up and saw Sultan and Frederik disappear down the road, in the direction of the lumberyard. Perhaps—just perhaps—he was going to visit Papa and finally ask for Maj's hand in marriage. Papa would accept; Maj would be engaged; and Carl would have time for Nik again. Not that she cared a whit for him now.

Nik ran into the parlor. Maj was lying on the green silk sofa, restlessly paging through an illustrated newspaper. Carl continued to play his violin a moment or two longer; the waltz seemed to have a dancing life of its own.

"Maj, Maj! Frederik is back. I just saw him out the window. He's on Sultan."

Maj continued to leaf through the newspaper without saying anything. Carl finally put down the violin and looked questioningly at Maj.

"But he didn't stop here," said Maj. "Did he?"

"No, he didn't stop here. I think he must be going on to the lumberyard—to talk to Papa . . ." She paused. Maj's blue eyes had taken on a sharp look.

"Why would he do that? How would he know that Papa was at the lumberyard?"

Carl put his violin back in the case. As so often when he finished playing intently, his brush of hair was askew and his forehead damp. "Well, why don't we three go out for a walk and see if we can meet up with him? That is," he glanced at Maj, "if you would like to."

"Yes, of course," said Maj. "I suppose—at the very least he would like the photographs of himself." She picked up the brown envelope from Samuelsen's Photography Atelier, which had been on a table in the parlor for some time. When the package first came, Carl had been the only one happy with his picture. His set of nine shots, three to a row, showed a series of rubbery, ridiculous faces, with his Man in Love just as silly as his Russian Idiot. Even Aunt Marie said uncertainly, "Darling boy, now that you're twenty-two and about to make your mark on the world, I can't help but wonder if you should not try to look more *dignified* in your photographs."

The girls put on their hats and gloves and Maj took a parasol. Ten minutes later they stepped out into the road and began walking in the direction Nik had seen Frederik ride.

"Perhaps he went to the parsonage first, to pay his respects to the pastor and his wife," said Carl. For once he wasn't clowning. He walked on the other side of Maj; Nik couldn't see his face. He must be fearing the return of Frederik and the end of his flirtation with Maj.

"And Mette," said Maj. "The oh-so-patient Mette. Perhaps now she'll have her revenge."

For some reason Nik recalled Mette's face last Christmas at the ball, when Frederik and Maj flew by in a waltz, the first of many that evening, with Maj, her sister, so light-footed in her sky-blue velvet dress, her angelic curls tied up with pearls, and Frederik in his dress uniform, with epaulets and braid. And there sat Mette in the yellow taffeta dress with a defeated smile, unable to do anything about it. Had Mette really been waiting all this time for Frederik to tire of Maj?

It was the kind of stifling day where you began to perspire doing nothing; but then, Nik felt she easily broke out in a sweat these days, especially when she was having her monthlies as she was today. She could feel the circle of perspiration growing under her arms. That never used to happen.

When they came a little farther down the road they saw that Sultan was indeed tied up at the parsonage.

Carl glanced at Maj and he took her arm. Maj seemed not to notice. Nik was disgusted; had he ever taken Nik's arm? No, but he had held her hand. He had left his touch on her fingers. Now he went ahead, in the middle of the Skive road, clutching on to her sister, in front of Nik, not caring how that made her feel.

"Did I ever tell you two girls about my oldest brother Peter?" said Carl. "He was a terror to us all. I was so in awe that I hardly dared speak to him; he was ten or twelve years older and a frightfully big boy with a strange temper. One day, when I was perhaps four and he was sixteen or seventeen, he managed to get hold of a big black horse in the neighborhood and he rode it back to our little house. I was playing with my brothers and sisters in the yard when he came dashing up. He didn't stop when he saw us playing; in fact, he made straight for us. He was as tall as a house on that thundering black horse, and he shouted, 'Get down!' All of us flattened ourselves in the dirt, expecting to be kicked or crushed to death by the horse. Then there was a smell of slathering horse and a feeling of heat rushing above, and the horse flew over us. Peter was laughing the whole time."

"What a dreadful story," said Maj.

"Shall we turn around, my friend?" asked Carl in a low, calm voice.

"Why ever for?" said Maj.

But even turning around at this point would not have helped, for the garden was visible from the road and Frederik and Mette were in the garden. It made a winsome painting; the summer roses were in a last flush of color, blooming red and peach pink, while the dahlias flared tall and wild. A woman in a white dress with a wide sun hat tied under her chin in a bow and a basket over her arm. A man in a jacket and tight riding pants that showed his muscular thighs.

The three of them stopped in the road. Over the low stone wall, they saw Mette put a white handkerchief up to her eyes and Frederik nod his head. Then he made a quick pained bow to Mette and came out into the road in front of the parsonage.

There he saw all of them staring at him, and Nik called, "Hello, Frederik!" because really she had always liked him and he had such a handsome horse. "We have your photographs—from Nykøbing!"

Carl and Maj were still arm in arm. Frederik glared at the pair of them and his jaw worked as if he were about to say something. But he merely bowed, so politely it was disrespectful. Without even a word of greeting, he untied and mounted Sultan and rode off, past them, tall in the saddle, stone-faced, as fast as he could in the direction he had come.

Maj's face had gone from pink to white and then quite red. She looked down at Carl's arm as if it was something strange that had attached itself to her. She was still holding the envelope.

Mette came to the small wooden gate in the wall and they went towards her. Her face was damp. Nik had never noticed she had a few small freckles on her eyelids; they had darkened with tears. The basket over her arm held shriveled rusty dahlias and rose hips with a few petals clinging to the hairy knobs.

Maj said, with suppressed violence, "I suppose he proposed to you!"

"It didn't get that far," said Mette. "I told him I was going to marry Henrik."

In her hand Mette had a pair of flower scissors and had forgotten to close them, so their steel points glittered.

"You won't go back to Copenhagen!" said Nik. "You'll be staying here in Selde!" She went to Mette and kissed her cheek.

Carl said, "Congratulations, Miss Bohm. Henrik is a fine man."

"Yes, he is," said Maj, chastened. "Congratulations, Mette."

~

It was immediately agreed, the very same evening, that Maj could go to Sweden after all and that she should leave as soon as possible. The insult to Maj and the family was completely unexpected. It didn't matter that Frederik hadn't actually proposed to Mette—he clearly *would* have if it hadn't been that Henrik had gotten there first. There was no saying either whether Mette might not have accepted Frederik if she hadn't just become engaged.

Mama was furious at everyone—at Mette, at the pastor, even at poor Papa for not riding over to the peat works and having a talk with the young man. Frederik should never have been allowed to leave for Viborg after the trip to Nykøbing and whatever misunderstanding had arisen there; he should have been dragged back here by force. She was angry at Carl, whom she suspected of using his talents as a pianist to befuddle her poor daughter, just when Maj should have been spending time with Frederik. But most of all, she was angry with Maj, for being so difficult and driving away such a fine suitor with her ideas of suffrage and reform.

Still, Nik couldn't escape the feeling that her mother was oddly relieved not to have Frederik as a son-in-law. And after a day or so, when she had calmed down, it turned out she had had reservations about him all along. As for Papa, he claimed that a young man who courted a woman for over a half a year and then proposed to someone else right under her nose was a coward, "Though he was an excellent shot."

Maj never cried; in fact, the damage seemed more to her pride than her heart. "Of course if he had proposed, I would have asked him to wait another year," said Maj to Nik the morning after the unfortunate meeting. "But he should at least have proposed! Can you imagine? Mette has now had two offers and I've had none." Yet she said this almost merrily as she gave Jutta a letter to Eva Sandström, letting her know the time she would arrive in Göteborg and what train to expect her on.

A day later Maj's trunk stood open and all the journals, newspapers, and books had been packed away along with much of her clothing. This trunk would be sent on to the dormitory in Odense. A smaller valise and trunk would accompany her to Sweden.

"My only regret is that all this with Frederik didn't happen right after Nykøbing. I think we both knew then it was impossible. Just imagine, I could have spent most of August with Eva. Still, ten days is better than nothing."

Nik sat with her arms at her sides on her sister's bed. She knew better than to offer to help Maj finish packing. Her sister was very particular. She simply watched as Maj, in her dark blue traveling dress, darted from bureau to trunk, re-folding chemises and petticoats that Jutta had ironed and brought up to the room.

The bedroom window was open and a strong breeze blew the curtains almost horizontal, as if they were flags snapping on a ship's mast; the air today smelled of the North Sea, where most of their weather came from. Nik imagined her sister on the steamer to Göteborg, crossing the Skagerrak. She knew that Maj would forget all about the family as soon as she left Selde this afternoon. She wouldn't stand on the deck, the way Nik would, staring longingly back at the coast of Denmark. Maj would sit in the ladies' salon, reading a book.

She thought about the first time Maj went away at the end of a summer, when she was Nik's age, just fourteen, five years ago. The whole family had accompanied her to Odense. They stayed with Uncle Jens and Aunt Marie at the house on Nørregade. What a lot of people there were in Odense! The streets were thronged, day and night, and in the shops everyone was there to buy, not just to look. Papa bought Nik the toy circus and Flor the Ballerina and some new kid shoes with buttons. They went to a café with a gold-painted pretzel for a sign and had slices of a soft vanilla cake with raspberries and whipped cream between the layers. Because it was the first time she had traveled so far and because it was all like a holiday, Nik forgot that they were in Odense for a reason.

Only when it came time to say good-bye to Maj did Mama begin to cry, sympathetically joined by Aunt Marie. Papa's eyes were wet and even Uncle Jens began to cough and mutter about how they would be second parents to the little maid. Nik was frightened at their tears and she had suddenly howled with understanding. Maj would not be returning home with them.

Maj was the only one who didn't cry. She simply sat, self-possessed as always, wondering what all the fuss was about.

"But I'll be back at Christmas," she said to Mama. "Just think of all I'll be learning. History. Literature. Latin. Mathematics."

All of them had eventually calmed down, though Mama, on the long journey home, had occasionally wiped her eyes and hugged Nik to her, saying, "You won't be leaving me, my dearest. Not for a long, long time."

Maj wrote frequently and came home at Christmas to be made much of. The following August the family again traveled to Odense. This time Nik was given a pair of white horses for her toy circus and a little elephant, the Indian Princess, a silk sash, and a new pair of gloves. She was forced to spend more time than she wished with her cousin Ottilie, playing cards. Ottilie was rather simple-minded for a girl of thirteen; she could barely count and she cried far too easily if she lost at whist, as she always did. This time Nik's own tears were fewer when she said good-bye to Maj. The following year, only Papa accompanied Maj to Odense in August because Mama had badly sprained her ankle and she wanted Nik to stay with her. After that Maj traveled alone. She took the train from Skive to Fredericia and then a boat over the Little Belt and then the train to Odense. She seemed to think nothing of the journey.

This time was different. Maj wasn't just going to Odense, but to Sweden. She was not going to marry Frederik and live in Viborg. She was moving farther away. Perhaps she would marry Carl and live in Copenhagen. Carl would give Maj the freedom Frederik never would. Carl wouldn't complain that she was too reform-minded; he would be bossed by tough little Maj, so "delightfully severe." She'd make him take care of the children, and because he loved her, he would.

There were voices below and then Carl began playing the piano. He'd once told Nik he always played Mozart when he felt unsettled. He must be miserable that Maj was leaving, because there had been a veritable flood of Mozart since breakfast.

If only Nik had been able to play the piano! If only Nik had been older, prettier, more well-read and musical, Carl would have been in love with her. Now there was no chance, even though she grew older by the day. Maj was like an embroidered screen that had been placed in front of the fire that was Carl.

"Poor old Nik," said Maj. "What *will* you do this autumn when we all leave?"

Nik wasn't sure what to say. Her sister seemed to think none of them did anything interesting when she wasn't around. But that was far from the case. There would be one or two more trips to Fur to search for fossils before the Strandgaards were busy with school. The horses would have less to do as the lumberyard slowed for the cold season and she could ride again. Papa would take out his gun and hunt waterfowl. The inn would bustle and so would the general store as the harvest ended and men drank away their earnings and wives stocked up for winter. They would go to Skive and perhaps even to Viborg on the train. She and Mama and Mrs. Jespersen would put up currant jam and spiced applesauce. They would make apple cider in the big wooden press.

Still, she would miss Maj—how could she not? And now that Maj was leaving, Nik still had so many questions. Had she ever cared for Frederik? What did it mean that Carl took Maj's arm as the three of them walked up the road to the parsonage? What did her sister want? To look at her now, so elegant in her traveling dress, so light-hearted, fluttering around her trunks and getting ready to go to Sweden, you'd think it was Eva she was in love with. Why didn't she go downstairs and comfort Carl, who was suffering already at the thought of her absence?

"I hope you'll continue to learn something about drawing from Mette," Maj said. "If she has time with all the preparations. Do you know when the wedding will be?"

Nik shook her head. She'd kept it to herself, but Mette had confided, when Nik went to see her for a drawing lesson, that in fact she hadn't made up her mind to accept Henrik until Frederik appeared with his surprising proposal.

"It was as if he'd been thinking it over, without consulting me at all, and he'd decided I would be a better wife than your sister. He told me he was leaving the Army in October and settling in Viborg, to help manage the peat works. His uncle would buy him a house; his uncle wanted him to marry. He was so business-like with me; he went straight to the point. He could offer me a good home. We could be married as soon as I liked. He didn't say a thing about Maj. It was as if nothing had happened at the Christmas ball. As if he didn't know that Henrik had shown an interest. As if I had just been waiting all this time! That told me everything about how it would be to be married to Frederik. I should have just said no, but I felt I had to have a reason. And now—well, I had almost decided to marry Henrik anyway . . . Yes, I had. I sent a letter to him immediately after you all left, asking him to visit. That same afternoon he spoke to my uncle. He is an honorable man."

A large gust of wind swept through the room, and Maj shut the window. From below came the merry-sad counterpoint of Mozart. "I will miss playing duets with Carl," said Maj, standing still for a moment and listening with a slight smile on her face. "I agree with Aunt Marie—some day we will all say, 'Imagine! We knew Carl Nielsen as a young man.'"

Nik screwed up her courage. "Aunt Marie thinks you should marry Carl. That it would be good to keep him in the family."

"Yes, she would think that, wouldn't she?" said Maj. "But I can't imagine it's for my sake. He is a brilliant musician but as a husband . . ." She sighed and folded up some stockings and laid them in the valise and snapped it shut.

"Aunt Marie said she hoped you and Carl could live with her."

"Oh—what a delightful plan! No, thank you."

"She thought it would be better if it was you he married, and not the young one, that's what I heard her telling Mama. I suppose that was Karen Marie."

"Not at all likely. Aunt Marie would never allow Carl to marry a maidservant like Karen Marie, in spite of her condition." She looked closely at Nik. "You really don't know, do you? You know bits and pieces, perhaps. What you've overheard."

Stung, Nik said, "I did overhear things—with everybody whispering, of course I did. Karen Marie was a maid in the building where Carl used to live before he went to live with Uncle and Aunt. And they had an 'unsuitable attachment' and Uncle and Aunt moved to Copenhagen to break it off. And now Aunt Marie is going to buy her a ticket to New York. I wish she'd buy me a ticket."

"Of course Uncle Jens and Aunt Marie want the girl to disappear," said Maj. "Why else did they move in such a hurry to Copenhagen? Why else did Aunt Marie whisk Carl off to Selde this summer? Karen Marie had to be settled somewhere quiet, to wait out her confinement."

"Confinement?"

"Well, that's the price the poor girl had to pay. He got her pregnant. Now she has to slink off in shame while Carl can just waltz on as if nothing has happened. I'm sorry to be the one to tell you this, but it's better you should know why Mama and Aunt Marie were a little nervous about Carl's attentions to you when he first arrived. *You* are the 'young one' Aunt meant. I had to talk to him seriously about his flirting with you. At Roslev station when we were waiting for the train."

Maj had put her valise by the door and now sat at her dressing table, arranging her hair. In that superior tone that always set Nik's teeth on edge, she said to the mirror, "Carl and I have been arguing over his conduct for ages, haven't you heard us? Oh I know it may have seemed like we were discussing Brandes and Bjørnson, but of course it was really all about Carl. He wants to live in a world where men can be free to love and take no responsibility. Of course he says women should do the same. It's not healthy for people to repress their instincts; it results in neurasthenia, he claims. He gets his ideas from Strindberg and Brandes.

"It's quite convenient for men to say we should do away with the double standard and just pretend that women don't suffer the consequences. But *women* are the ones to bear the public shame if something happens. *We* are the ones who have children out of wedlock. If Aunt Marie weren't taking care of Karen Marie, the poor girl would be in dire straits. Carl certainly has no resources of his own. Yet he won't admit that his behavior changed her future. Just like that horrid Don Juan Georg Brandes! It's well-known that Brandes is a skirt-chaser who breaks up marriages and seduces women right and left."

Nik heard her sister pause, as if she were looking at Nik in the mirror to see the effect of her words, but Nik had already turned away and gone to the window to hide her feelings. The wind was blowing the trees in the orchard sideways and the heavy apples, still green, banged against the branches.

Fragments of the arguments between Maj and Carl about Bjørnson's plays and Brandes's editorials and all the letters in *Politiken* came back to Nik. She bit her tongue so hard it hurt. Below, Carl played Mozart like an angel. He couldn't be the Don Juan Maj had painted. Not Carl. You could know something about a person through his music, and Carl wasn't cruel. He'd never love a girl and then abandon her. It must have been the girl herself who created the problem. Who trapped him or duped him in some way. For Carl was kind-hearted, just a foolish boy who liked to make faces and play pranks. Still, he hadn't told her the full story at Nykøbing as they waited for the ferry. He had said—what had he said? That Nik wasn't the sort of girl to judge a man.

Nik remained silent; she heard Maj come up behind her at the window. “My dearest little sister,” Maj said, putting an arm around her. “You’ve gotten so tall. You’re growing up.”

Nik still said nothing. She was shaken by what she’d heard, but also hopeful. Maj didn’t love Carl. And he didn’t love Maj. He had taken Maj’s arm in the road as a brother—only to help her bear the sight of Frederik and Mette.

Maj said, softly, “I know I’m not an easy person. That some of my actions hardly make any sense. Everything with Frederik must have seemed a mystery. And I suppose my behavior with Carl has been confusing too. But if you knew how unhappy I was sometimes, you would forgive me. You must know I care for you, even though we quarrel. Don’t you?”

Hesitantly, Nik nodded.

“I’ll write you from Sweden, dearest Nik. Perhaps at Christmas Eva can come for a visit here. Or next summer we’ll all go to Copenhagen—would you like that? We could stay with Aunt Marie and go to lectures at the Women’s Reading Room. It’s a library, with all sorts of women’s books and newspapers.”

From downstairs, Papa called up, “Maj, it’s time we should be going.”

“Wait,” said Nik, and ran from the room.

She returned clutching a small stone that had been split in half. “For good luck in Sweden.”

It was the fossil of the cicada wing that Schoolmaster Strandgaard had given her and the most precious thing she owned. She pressed it into her sister’s hand.

12.

THE MORNING AFTER MAJ'S DEPARTURE THE CLOUDS vanished, and a week of heat followed, long enough for the farmers to cut their hay and dry it on long ricks in the fields. The golden air smelled of hay and cows and blackberries. The bathing was good again; the fjord had warmed up and Nik and Carl and Mama walked to the beach every morning straight after breakfast. Aunt Marie had developed a head cold and some palpitations of an inner organ. She wasn't able to accompany them and once or twice suggested that she needed Mama's company in the mornings.

Mama, however, seemed less inclined after a month-long visit to attend to her sister's wishes, and claimed she needed to worry about her own health, which was improved by daily bathing. The waters of the fjord were silky and fresh on the skin and Mama could become lively in Carl's company. He didn't have to exert himself much to make her laugh.

"My dear boy," Mama called him, and once, by mistake, "My dear son."

It was impossible to imagine Carl as a father.

Without Maj, the mood around the house relaxed. No one felt inclined to discuss problems found in novels or newspapers as the family sat together in the garden on the warm August evenings, perhaps joined by Ole Dahl or another neighbor. The talk was of the weather, the harvest, the well-being of cattle and the ripening of apples. Mette and Henrik came to dinner one evening, and Mrs. Wellenborg and the pastor with them. Frederik, of course, was never mentioned, and Henrik glowed with pride every time he so much as glanced at his fiancée. Nothing about Mette's face or bearing showed regret or even resignation.

The Strandgaards had gone off to Scotland, all in a rush of butterfly nets and hiking boots. They were to spend two weeks there visiting the grandparents and their cousins in the Highlands.

Late at night, after Aunt Marie and Mama had retired and only Papa and Nik were still in the garden, Papa with a last pipe glowing in the dark, Carl would slip into the parlor. Soon familiar phrases from the little suite for strings would begin to repeat and vary.

"I want to bring the adagio together with the minuet, so that the last movement contains them both," he told Nik. "But every combination sounds like cacophony, not the stirring resolution I'm trying for."

It did indeed sound like battle was going on in the parlor sometimes, between the merry three-time and the melancholy slow beat of the adagio, which also had three notes, but existed in another world and could not be coaxed to dance. Papa sometimes put his hands over his ears at the most experimental combinations.

Aunt Marie's cold had not lingered long; it was the wandering pain in one organ or another that kept her often bedridden. It didn't affect her appetite; still, the pains, sometimes sharp and sometimes "dull but very deep," forced a postponement of the trip back to Copenhagen. There was talk of Carl returning by himself, but he said he wouldn't hear of leaving Aunt Marie and that he could compose just as well for another week on the old Marschall. He did not have to take up his new position with the Tivoli Orchestra until September.

Piano lessons with Nik resumed and now she began to make a little progress. Carl seemed to enjoy the simplicity of her progressive chords. He said one day, "Your sister plays with more exactitude but you play with more feeling. And feeling is more important in the long run than always hitting the right notes." She chose to hear that as a compliment and it spurred her to pay more attention to reading music. She also had returned to sitting in the parlor when Carl played, but instead of reading she often drew in her sketchbook. She refused to show the pictures to Carl, however much he begged.

~

A perfumed letter with a crest arrived from the baroness, who had returned from Lake Como without the baron, asking if Nik and Carl would like to borrow her horses again and then stay for refreshment. Once again Nik donned the dark riding habit and top hat and the baroness's driver came to collect them in the carriage. Halfway there, Nik noticed that Carl didn't have his violin with him. He had not forgotten it, he said, it was merely that he wanted to ride a horse, not pay for the experience with his fiddling. He seemed a little unlike himself today, thought Nik, abrupt and restless. His mind was full of his suite; his eyes were cloudy with it.

As soon as they were mounted on the horses and had cantered to the shore, Carl asked her leave to go ahead. Racing the horse for a stretch along the sand might give him what he needed—he didn't explain what that was but flung an arm in the direction of the sky, oceanic blue with piles of billowy clouds. His horse was a handsome gray stallion, a favorite of the baron's on the infrequent occasions he was home. Nik nodded; she too wanted to gallop on her sturdy little mare, but she let Carl go ahead before she sped up. Just as she was feeling the breeze of movement the band on her infernal hat snapped and it sailed off into the fjord, where it sat on the surface like a small black chimney with a brim. There was no hope of rescuing it.

A little more sedately, Nik resumed cantering along the sand as it turned to hummocks of beach grass and tough succulents. Soon she came to a boggier stretch with rocks to be avoided. What a distance he was ahead of her. But at least Carl was waiting. Why was he waving so? Of course she saw him; did he think he was invisible? He seemed to be bucking up and down on his horse. Something must be wrong.

She quickened her pace until she was galloping towards him.

When she was about a hundred feet away she could see that the gray stallion was up to his hocks in wet mud and not able to pull his hooves free, though he was jerking and shaking. Carl wasn't foolish enough to jump off the horse into the quicksand, but he looked frightened, almost panicked, and of course the horse felt that and was panicking too.

"Don't come any closer," he shouted, but she ignored him.

She guided her little mare from tussock to tussock, avoiding the wet mud, until she was near enough to see that the stallion could easily, with some encouragement, step onto a firm grassy hillock to the side.

Nik said calmly, "When I say the word, slide the reins over the stallion's head so as not to spook him, and I'll use my riding crop to take them and guide the horse out."

"No, Nik, the reins will break or you'll fall in." His voice shook. "You must ride back to the manor or to the nearest farm where they might have horses and a cart. You'll need help."

"Nonsense," she said. "You're not in that far and the stallion is strong." She began talking to the horses, calming them both. "Don't say anything more," she told Carl. "Just throw me the reins—softly, softly."

He took a deep breath and did as she asked. Nik caught them with her crop. The stallion flinched at the reins as they went past his eyes, but he didn't start or buck. Only his big nostrils flared steamily.

"Now, young fellow," said Nik, wrapping the reins around the saddle horn. She wished she weren't in this silly long dress, sitting sidesaddle. "Walk on. Walk on." She and her mare began to move away, tugging at the reins. For a moment Nik was worried the reins would snap; they were of course not strong enough to actually pull the stallion free. But the horse heaved forward to follow, and the suction was broken. With a leap, the stallion staggered onto the hillock, and Nik continued to lead both horses back the way she'd come.

Only when they were on stable footing again, down by the water, did Nik hand the reins back to Carl. His boots were caked with clay mud and the hem of her trailing dress was damp with silt. They tried to wash off the sand and silt as best they could and continued walking the horses through the waves along shore, hoping to erase some of the evidence before returning to the manor house.

After a period of quiet, Carl said, "When I was a small boy, we lived near a brick works with deep clay pits. When it rained, the clay pits would fill with water to make ponds where ducks would sometimes splash. My youngest sister, who was only three or so, went too near the slippery edge to see the ducks and fell in. She couldn't swim and I couldn't save her—I was too small and didn't know how to swim myself. I screamed for my mother, as loud as I could. My sister was struggling, gargling water, and she sank and then came back up, her eyes already looked drowned. But my mother was suddenly there—she found a branch and shouted, 'Grab it!' She was calm, like you were, dear Nik. I remember the helplessness I felt. How it froze my limbs."

They continued walking the horses slowly. Carl laughed. "Can that possibly be your hat coming towards us?"

The black top hat, still upright, had veered inshore and was popping up and over the wavelets like a most peculiar vertical boat.

They began to laugh until their stomachs hurt. Carl swiped down and grabbed the hat, which was really only wet at the brim. They said nothing to the baroness about the mishap, but Carl, to make up for almost bringing her husband's favorite gray stallion to harm, played for an hour or more on her piano and was as delightful as he could be.

In the carriage ride home Carl made up a song about her hat and was in the liveliest of spirits. But Nik remembered the fear in his eyes in the quicksand. She *had* saved him, and now there was a new bond between them, not just the friendship that had sprung up again once Maj was gone.

The journey to Copenhagen was delayed once more, for Henrik's father was to host an engagement party for his son and Mette, and everyone in the district was invited. Aunt Marie wanted to wear her new ball gown. "After that, we *must* return to Jens!"

Nik's new dress was finished too, a peach silk with a scooped neck and three-quarter sleeves and a white satin ribbon around her waist. In a bag she carried a pair of dancing slippers Aunt Marie had ordered from Copenhagen. Mama had worked especially hard with her curly hair, to coil it up neatly and anchor the coil with plenty of pins so that in the heat of dancing it would not unravel. While Mama dressed her hair, she reminisced about her own dancing days with Papa in Odense. Imagine—Papa dancing a mazurka! But he had danced many, and polkas and schottisches as well.

Now he mainly waltzed, while Mama tended to sit out many dances in favor of gossiping with Aunt Marie and the other ladies of the district. They drank champagne punch and were merry among themselves while keeping a sharp eye on their daughters if they had them, and on other people's daughters if they didn't. Sometimes one or another was asked to dance and then returned to her seat flushed and panting. Aunt Marie didn't dance; her feet hurt her too much. But she followed Carl with her eyes and smiled sometimes to herself.

Carl was in great demand among the ladies—he was young and amiable and could dance as well as he did all things. By the middle of the evening Carl was easily the most popular person at the ball—aside from Mette, of course. Not only had he danced with almost every lady there, young, old, pretty, wrinkled, but he had talked the hired orchestra into allowing him to borrow a fiddle and lead them in some of the country dances he knew well from his Fyn days. He was like a spinning top that drew every eye.

Nik danced with her father and with Henrik, who even in the midst of a violent mazurka kept his eyes on Mette. His heavy face radiated pride whenever anyone congratulated him or said how lovely Mette was or how good a wife she would make. He had never wished to be with anyone else.

Aunt Marie said, "Oh my, even *watching* you, Emilie, makes me exhausted!" She and Mama sat fanning themselves near one of the open windows. Nik felt the breeze from the fjord. She had been allowed to have two glasses of champagne and she still felt its fizzy sparkle, just the way she still felt Carl's arm around her waist as he'd whirled her in a dizzy waltz an hour ago.

The family came home after midnight, Mama and Aunt Marie in the trap while Papa drove the cart and Nik and Carl sat in back, looking up at the falling stars. Stars always fell this time of year, on August nights just before the autumn began. The darkness smelled of horses and drying hay and the tang of the Limfjord, neither salt nor fresh, but both.

In her bedroom Nik could not sleep, and then she did, and then she was awake again.

Music came from the parlor below. She recognized the familiar phrases of the little suite. He was trying out fragments and variations on the piano keys, but tonight there was no sweet minuet. The music was slow and cautious, stepping carefully. Then came the short adagio phrase in A minor. And another familiar phrase, over and over, a long note and three short ones. What did those four notes mean? And if they didn't mean anything in words—Carl would say they didn't have a meaning—how could they give her such a sad feeling? It was like going hunting with her father and coming above the soft feathery body of a pheasant in the tall grass, realizing it was only stunned and might fly again, and then seeing her father lift his gun and take its life.

She put on a wrap over her nightgown and barefoot slipped downstairs, avoiding all the places on the stair boards that creaked.

A single lamp was lit in the parlor, directly over the piano keys. Carl was still in his clothes from the ball, but his shirt collar was off. The flush of champagne had left his cheeks and his hair stuck out in all directions, quills of light striped by shadow.

He looked up at her hopelessly, all the fire and spark of the evening gone.

"I apologize if I woke you with my plunking. I can't get the sounds out of my head. Sometimes if I've been playing the violin all evening, with the strings up against my ear, it's as if the music has moved into my head and won't leave me. And then I play the piano to get the music into my fingers and then back into the piano." He was making a joke, but looked miserable. He pulled the lid down over the keys.

This is when she felt she knew him best, when the joking covered misery. When he was serious, almost desperately somber. Everyone could love the Carl who was a clown, everyone wanted to bask in his humor and radiant talent. But when he was like this, he could belong to her alone. She didn't say anything but simply moved across the room and sat next to him on the bench.

The next moment he had buried his head in her neck and then he was kissing her.

It happened quickly and afterwards she knew it was her fault. She had come to him half dressed, of course she tempted him. How familiar to be caressed, and yet how wildly unfamiliar the feelings it roused in her. But when his hands touched her unloosed breasts under the wrap and nightgown she broke away and, breathing hard, retreated to the green silk sofa.

He seemed as shocked as she was and the look on his face was so guilty that she had to say something accusing.

"Why didn't you tell me the whole story about Karen Marie?"

"But I . . . I thought you knew everything." He looked as if he was about to come over to her, but thought better of it.

"I didn't know you were going to be a father." She felt her body deflating, like a balloon. She shivered.

"But I . . . ," he said again. And then he composed himself. "My darling Nik, how can I make you understand? It was a night like this one. I'd been playing for hours at a private party. Playing the violin and watching bourgeois women in their low-cut Paris dresses. The party was in a large and beautiful apartment in Frederiksberg; it was the home of a wealthy industrialist and his wife who had hired a group of musicians. They gave us champagne, of course, and they paid us well. The scent of French perfume—a roomful of women all perfumed—intoxicating. We were all tipsy when we left and two of the fellows said they were going straight to Vesterbro"—he looked at Nik but saw she didn't understand—"to the ladies there, you know. But I . . . I've never liked such encounters. A fellow never knows what he might catch. And it's bestial, bestial . . . Oh, how can I say such things to you and make you understand?"

He stood up and began pacing back and forth in front of the piano, while continuing to look at Nik. His hair was wild and his hands clenched and unclenched, as if they ached. She did not know the expression on his face; all his melancholy and despair was there, as well as yearning.

"It's only that, when I came back to where I lived then, as I went up the stairs and came to the floor where the consul lived and where Karen Marie had her room—she heard me on the stairs and came out. In her wrap, but with no nightgown underneath.

"She put a finger to her lips and led me into the room. It was just the once. But we were unlucky."

Nik continued to shiver in her wrap. Her feet were cold and her breasts almost painfully tender. "You didn't love her? Didn't want to marry her? Aunt Marie thought you did. That she wanted to marry you as well. Wasn't she beautiful enough? Good enough?"

Carl clenched and then opened his hands, with a helpless gesture. "Of course she was—is—nice-looking, and she is a very good sort of person. It's not as if I ever looked down on her for being a servant. Our backgrounds were not so dissimilar—I think my family in fact was much poorer than hers. But our futures? Already they had changed, thanks to the help of so many people who have believed in me. When I met her I was just finishing my studies at the Royal Conservatory and hoped to become a violinist. Now my dreams are even greater. I have the feeling—no, I'm certain—that given the opportunity, I could become a fine composer. But I must work at it. I couldn't tie myself to a girl like that. She would have held me back. Aunt Marie was right to see that. There was a moment when I could have made a fatal mistake, but I confessed everything to your aunt and she took it all in hand."

There was truth in what he said, and yet something was wrong about it too. It was the excuse of a bad boy, not a man. Nik didn't know what to say. Her heart was pounding. "And me?" she finally managed to whisper. "Would I be good enough for you? Would I hold you back?"

"Of course you are good enough for me, sweet Nik. You are far far better than me." He stopped pacing and dropped to his knees. "In four years, when you're eighteen, just think of how much more established I'll be. I will be able to marry. If we can wait that long, if you can wait. It won't be so long. We can write. I do have a future, my dearest treasure. I have a future."

Now he did come over to her, walking on his knees like a penitent, and sat on the green silk sofa and held her close.

In four years. When she was eighteen. Three and a half years really.

"I can wait," she said and kissed him back.

13.

THE LOVING LETTERS, FULL OF ENDEARMENTS, BEGAN immediately. Some of the letters—about the Tivoli Orchestra, about his friends and pupils, Nik could easily share with her parents. Other parts of Carl's letters were not at all suitable for the dinner table. He called her his "naughty, naughty girl" for making him lose sleep. He told her he loved her and would take on sorrows for both of them if they came. "No raging storm shall batter or even touch my darling little love." He sent her a thousand kisses. He gave her a thousand caresses. He was hers forever.

Without a blush Nik said to her parents, "Carl sends his best to you," and put the letters back in her pocket, then took them upstairs to her room and hid them in a cigar box under a pile of clothes in her drawer. She sat at her small desk at the window and tried to find the words that would keep him writing back to her, that would tell him how she felt. His sudden love had flooded over her life like some vast geological event. It seemed to come out of nowhere. It was huge and breathtaking. It demanded a response.

She couldn't call him "my dear little boy" as he called her "little girl." That would sound foolish, as would "naughty, naughty boy." Nor could she speak of love and losing sleep; she slept the same as she always had, long and well, especially as the days darkened and it was so tempting to lie in bed in the morning. Once or twice, in the week after he departed, she did wake in the middle of the night, and thought for a moment that she heard the faint caressing notes of the piano below. Then she realized it was the wind, an autumn wind off the Limfjord.

Unlike Carl she had no triumphs to report or ambitions to confide. The days were often full, but with nothing of great importance. Her letters described the events of the village and other people's lives: the Strandgaards' return from Scotland with boxes of natural history treasures to be sorted and labeled; the doings of the baroness and her wayward husband, who traveled all the way home from Lake Como and then was gone again two days later. She reported a visit with Pastor and Mrs. Wellenborg, who were not interesting in themselves but had news of Frederik and his brother Morten, the student and poet. Frederik had resigned from the Army and had become a director of the peat works outside Viborg. It was said he was courting a lady in that town whose father was a merchant in woolens. Morten Brandt had published his first book of poetry, for which he received not a penny; the reviews were mixed as well. Perhaps Carl had seen them?

The general store could take up several paragraphs with amusing descriptions of some of the customers, as could Papa's dealings with Ole Dahl, who tended to drink more as the days darkened and to sing ballads in Norwegian in the inn and sometimes in the road. Ole Dahl was playing his violin again, now that Carl was no longer among them to claim first rank. Mama and Mrs. Jespersen were putting up every bit of fruit in sight and Jutta bore the brunt of the cook's nervous temper. Even Mama had raised her voice to Jutta once or twice, and Jutta had wept until Mama apologized (Mrs. Jespersen, her hair in a tight knot, never apologized for anything).

In the evenings it was the custom of the family to gather in the parlor and read. Mama did not care for *Crime and Punishment*, which Carl had left behind for them, and she put down his favorite novel, *Anna Karenina*, after a hundred pages. It was as bad as *Fru Marie Grubbe*, she said. Did the upper classes have nothing to do but betray the vows of marriage? She went back to Dickens and reread *David Copperfield* that fall. Papa smoked his pipe and perused the liberal newspapers, interrupting Dickens occasionally to vent about Parliament or to approve of a progressive initiative (for the current government was not as bad as it could be). Nik would have liked to read *Anna Karenina*, but not in front of her mother. Instead she made her way through some of Mr. Darwin's book about evolution, hardly better in her mother's eyes than Tolstoy, but recommended by the schoolmaster. It made her drowsy.

In September and October, when the weather was still good, Nik ranged over the district with the younger Strandgaards, hunting mushrooms and watching the birds fly south. On rainy afternoons she helped organize the specimens and rocks they'd brought back from Scotland. Sometimes Sophie stopped by after school and the two of them walked together across the heath, pretending it was the Highlands. Sophie was a great pretender of things. She had returned from Scotland with a deerstalker's hat, which had belonged to one of her uncles, and which she clamped over her big ears and braids.

Nik's memories of Carl and what she had allowed Carl might have grown fainter, like a dream, if his letters had not come so often. He said he was in love with her. Was she in love with him? She must be, if she had let him cup her breasts in his hands and put his lips to her neck. When Nik thought of those hurried moments in the parlor that night and of the walk they took the next day through the Strandgaard manor woods, where she let him press her to a tall beech tree and kiss her from her lips to the unbuttoned top of her dress, she knew she must be in love, she felt so woozy, so flooded.

Before that day he had never said anything about adoring her. Did allowing him to caress her unleash all those feelings? He said he had been on the verge of allowing himself to fall in love with her all summer. He had never dared to show it. He didn't think she cared for him. He knew she was young—yet she did not *seem* young. She seemed so *knowing* in some way. So sure of what she wanted.

That afternoon, the leaves were still green, barely beginning to turn, but old leaves lay on the path, and rustled as they walked. He made to put his arm around her, pull her close; she wrested free and ran; he ran after, caught her, pinned her to the tree, arms behind her back. His kisses were fierce. She didn't remember him unbuttoning the top of her dress, he moved so quickly, just with one hand. His sweet salty mouth and the cotton flavor of his shirt. The clean young masculine scrape of his chin. The firm dry strength of his fingers, his hand stroking her neck and clavicle, cupping her breast through her dress. His moan, "I adore you. I love you." And up above the fluttering beech leaves, the blue sky of late August.

That afternoon day in the woods had been his last in Selde. He played a little concert for them that evening and looked at Nik longingly as she said good-night. Aunt Marie was ensconced in the green silk sofa and Mama sat beside her sister. The next morning Carl and her aunt left for Copenhagen.

One morning she went out shooting with Papa on the marshy lands west of the village, at Risum. The fog was dense and the ground crinkled a little with frost when they set out. They hadn't eaten yet; Nik was still half asleep. She pulled her heavy shawl around her shoulders. This was one of her favorite times of day and the time she had always shared with her father. Papa had on his felted loden jacket and a wool cap. His white beard was beaded with moisture. His gun was over his shoulder with a leather game bag swinging below.

His voice came out of the fog, God-like. "You seem to be regularly corresponding with Carl."

That could not be denied. "Yes, Papa."

"Mama and I have wondered a little at the long letters he sends. And you write him back. Long letters."

"Yes, Papa."

"Your mother and Aunt Marie thought he might have been interested in Maj. All the piano playing and so on. I suppose it was after Maj left that something happened."

"Yes, Papa. But we had always liked each other. It was just that . . . I don't know. He began to look at me in a new way."

"You're young still, Emilie," he said unhappily. "Your mother asked me to talk with you. She kept meaning to say something to you when Carl first arrived, but then it seemed he began to take an interest in your sister and there was no need. Your mother and I . . . well, there may be some things you don't know about this fellow."

They'd struck out across the marsh, keeping to the track. In the fog you could hear a subdued quacking, but the curtain of white was too thick to shoot. It helped to talk about Carl here, where she couldn't see her father's face closely and he couldn't see hers.

"I know everything," she said. "He told me."

"About the girl? He told you that? About the child coming?"

"I know it all. It doesn't make any difference to me. These things happen—don't they, Papa?"

"They don't just happen, my girl. You may not know everything there is to know about it all. I sincerely hope you don't. But after all, we do have farm animals."

Now he sounded more like himself.

"Papa! Can there be any harm in writing and receiving letters?"

"Your mother—your mother and I just don't want you to get hurt. You should have your childhood. And then, when the time is right, you'll find the right husband. Maybe Carl is the right one, but you are far too young to even be thinking about that sort of thing now. Maj never thought of such things at fourteen. All she wanted was to study mathematics."

They laughed a little. "Papa, haven't you always said I was a sensible girl? Underneath all my wild dreams and fancies? Then, please don't worry. These are just letters—delightful letters—about his music and the things that happen in Copenhagen. He makes my world bigger. But don't imagine that I'm going to run off with him. I know I'm young. And I don't plan to leave you and Mama for a long long time."

"How grown-up you sound, Emilie! Just a month or two ago all we heard about were your plans to emigrate to America."

"What makes you think I don't still dream of the Rocky

Mountains?" she teased him, but she thought to herself that she must find a better hiding place for those letters, and she must learn to hide more of herself from her parents as well.

In late October Mette and Henrik were married; that took several letters to describe in full to Carl. Before the wedding, the district was busy with preparations. The cake and puddings were baked in the large kitchens of the manor farm. Five pigs were roasted and twice as many grouse and ducks. Chocolates and champagne came from Paris and a whole new set of china arrived by train from the Royal Porcelain Factory, as well as silver flatware and boxes of wine and champagne glasses.

Mette's dress was made by a seamstress from Copenhagen and her veil was real lace. It lay like sea foam on her dark red hair. Henrik had given her diamond earrings and a bracelet. The old squire choked up at the ceremony, but Henrik's voice had a grave authority as he took Mette as his bride.

No one said "poor Mette Bohm." She was now Mrs. Christiansen and, after the baroness, the first lady of the district. Everyone remarked on how well things had turned out and only Widow Poulsen dared to say, "Still, Frederik Brandt was a fine-looking man."

After the wedding Mette and Henrik went to Belgium for their honeymoon. Nik felt sure that the trip could not have been Henrik's idea; he knew nothing of the paintings and architecture Mette longed to see. Yet he returned in good spirits; the monks brewed excellent ale, and in addition to visiting Bruges and Ghent and Brussels they had attended a horse sale and he had purchased two heavy Belgian horses for use on the farm. By the end of the year Mette was expecting their first child.

In early December Bjørnstjerne Bjørnson spoke at the theater in Skive. He had arrived in Denmark in the middle of November, as part of a tour that would take him all over Scandinavia. He was scheduled to give eighty lectures on "Monogamy and Polygamy," and his first stop was Copenhagen, to coincide with a meeting of the Danish Women's League on the subject of moral purity. In Copenhagen the students built him a triumphal arch and he spoke to hundreds in the Casino Theater. Since then he'd been lecturing in large towns and small all across Denmark. Maj and Eva had gone to hear him in Odense. He was brilliant, Maj wrote. A towering figure of moral clarity.

Nik went to Skive with her mother and father to hear Bjørnson. Schoolmaster Strandgaard brought Joachim and a handful of his fellow students from the high school, and the group sat near the Hansens. Nik and Joachim nodded awkwardly and then she ignored him.

What an imposing bear of a man Bjørnson was, a giant in his mid-fifties with gray mutton-chop whiskers and a wide intellectual forehead. Once he had written lovely and tragic stories about the peasants who lived in Norway's deep valleys, their loves and losses. But as he became greater and more important he wrote bigger novels, longer poems, many plays. He weighed in on every topic of the day. He had been a theater director. He had written Norway's national anthem. He had been exiled for treason. He had lived in Rome and Paris. He was more famous than Ibsen. He was said to be Scandinavia's greatest orator. He stood behind his podium on the gas-lit stage and his voice boomed into the corners of the theater, into every seat. He raised his arm, he slashed his hand across his chest, he lifted his eyes to heaven, then dropped them to the floor.

The lecture was long and convoluted, but delivered nimbly, with elegance and sometimes violence. He spoke of Human Progress—from bestiality to spirituality, from polygamy to monogamy. He spoke of harems and Mohammedans with many wives; he spoke of Mormons and Hottentots; of the reasons the American Civil War had been fought (so slaves could claim their right to be monogamous); of Darwin and his theories of race and heredity.

The higher animals—and of course people were the highest—

all took a great deal of time to mature. And the reason for that was so they could be at their peak when they reproduced. At maturity they were able to pass on their best traits, not only to preserve those traits, but to improve the race.

In humans, Bjørnson thundered with conviction, the age of maturity—for marriage and healthy reproduction—was twenty-five for men and twenty-one for women.

A kind of collective shudder went through the boys from Jebjerg high school at this, and Nik caught a glimpse of Joachim and his friends poking at each other before they were silenced by Strandgaard. Squeezed between her parents, Nik was hardly less agitated.

Twenty-one was eons away. The difference between fourteen and twenty-one was the difference between the Triassic and the Jurassic.

Having made this pronouncement Bjørnson went on to promote the benefits of abstinence, which—contrary to popular opinion—made no one ill. Look at the German nation, which valued chastity before marriage, as compared to the French, which was depravity itself. It was not abstinence that sickened men and women—it was promiscuity, which led to delusions of grandeur in men and created Don Juans in all classes. Women who were led down the slippery slope and gave into vile desires were almost equally culpable. Both sexes were punished by the most dreadful diseases, many of them given to wives by their unfaithful husbands. You could see the results in the streets of Copenhagen—missing limbs, gaping sores—as well as in the drawing rooms of Paris.

But the real misery of depravity was not what it could do to the body. It was the damage that giving rein to lust outside marriage could do to the soul. Could a man who was unchaste before wedlock simply wash away that stain? Could a woman? Were these traces of defilement to be simply brushed off as soon as you married? Was anyone foolish enough to believe that?

Carl's lips on hers, Carl's hand on her breast—they were

wrong. She'd known it at the time, even looking up through the green leaves to the blue sky. But they were still so delicious. She didn't want those memories taken away from her. She refused to think of Carl as defiled by his relations with Karen Marie, of herself as dragged through the mud.

Fervent applause and cheers erupted around them.

Mama sighed. "He is a fine, handsome man. And so right in everything he says."

Papa said, "It was well put except for his praising the Germans as models of restraint. Has the fellow never been to Berlin?"

Joachim avoided Nik's eyes as the high school boys, subdued, filed up the aisle. Nik remembered his sweet kisses when she was thirteen.

She had kissed two boys, not just one, and allowed Carl to take the greatest liberties. That would have to stop. They must vow to be faithful and to restrain themselves until marriage.

But how could she wait seven years?

At Christmas, Carl, accompanied by Uncle Jens and Aunt Marie, traveled back to Odense. He was with his own family for a few days around the holiday itself, in Black Bog; he played cards with his father, fiddled, and was happy, he wrote Nik, though he could not help recalling Karoline who had died, the brothers and sisters who had moved to America and Australia. Nik had sent him the present he'd requested: a new photograph of herself. Skive now had a photography studio of its own and she and Papa had made a special trip there by sleigh to pick up a train delivery of holiday orders.

She thought she looked well enough in the photograph, though she was no beauty. She was abashed when Carl wrote that he showed her picture to his mother, who kissed it. He said Nik's expression in the picture was just the same as the one she used to have when she came into the dining room at breakfast, stopped in the doorway, and said, "Good morning!"

After Christmas Day he went back to Odense to stay with Uncle Hans, whose birthday it was. There was a large dinner, which Maj and her friend Eva also attended. Carl said Eva was a striking tall girl with a massive amount of golden hair and a long stride. An Amazon. He and Maj had immediately begun to argue about women's rights—"just like old times in the summer." Nik wondered if Carl spoke of her to Maj. Her sister wrote only that Carl had come to the party at Uncle Hans's house and was as charming as ever. He'd made a special attempt to teach Ottilie a few tunes on the piano.

On January 8, 1888, just after the New Year, when the district was caked in heavy snow and all the birds looked dark and hungry, Karen Marie gave birth to a son, Carl August Hansen. Until then Nik hadn't realized that she and Karen Marie had the same last name. The family learned this news from Aunt Marie, who reported that the mother and baby were doing fine and back in Fyn, living with relatives. She would stay there a year and then sail to New York to make a fresh start. Mama read the paragraph aloud to Nik and after that nothing more was said about Karen Marie.

Carl did not mention the event in his letters to Nik, though two weeks later, he wrote to congratulate her on her fifteenth birthday:

> May nothing but sunshine and happiness ever come into your life. If I were a king, you would be my most delightful queen and I would kneel at the foot of your throne. Ah, talk! I don't want to be a king, except in the realm of sound; but then I wouldn't kneel at your feet. I would get up and take you by the throat and kiss you, kiss you properly.

The Strandgaards were invited to dinner. Joachim was back at school but all the others had presents for her. After the meal Sophie came upstairs with Nik and the two played with her toy circus. Outside the window the snow fell steadily.

Sophie made the tiger and elephant do tricks and then battle to the death while Nik bounced Jacques the Acrobat around. Flor the

Ballerina performed a *pas de deux* with him as the Indian Princess looked on longingly. She was still in love with Jacques.

Sophie asked, "What's that sail cord doing on the floor by the window?"

Nik said, "It's left over from the summer."

She remembered that, in spite of their best efforts, all they could get out of their telephone was a kind of vibration and no words at all.

Leopold's Hotel

1888

14.

UP WITH A SCREECHING LURCH OF GEARS AND RATTLING metal they rose, up through the wooden beer bottle constructed as an advertisement for the Tuborg Brewery, crammed together in the July warmth in an iron cage that was Denmark's first hydraulic elevator. They jerked to a stop at an observation platform shaped like the bottle's cap, where the fresh air blew. Nik was higher than she'd ever been before, higher than when she stood on the bluffs on Fur Island; she was perched on the peak of a Tuborg mountain, looking down at the grounds of the great Nordic Industrial, Agricultural, and Art Exposition and the city of Copenhagen spreading out in every direction around it.

If only the ladies wouldn't shriek so. Nik herself had felt a little dizzy when they made their stuffy, bone-shaking ascent, but she would die before admitting it to Carl. It was the first time she'd seen him since last summer in Selde; she wanted him to find her poised and adult.

Carl stood squeezed between Nik and Maj on the small deck, pointing out the long glass-roofed exhibition halls and the turreted wooden pavilions of the Exposition. Just below them sprayed rainbow showers from the electric fountain. In one direction: the agriculture displays—toy pink pigs and blurry chickens—and the dairy with its forty-six milk cows and the long low fishery buildings. Five aquariums inside, Carl told them, filled with swimming cod and halibut from northern waters. In another direction, the green hedges of the labyrinth and the small figures of children running through its convoluted maze. Over one boulevard, across an elaborately constructed "air bridge" with massive wooden towers on either side, lay Machine Land, the sports stadiums, and the

Army and Navy parade grounds. Across another boulevard, a specially built exhibition hall just for French paintings and sculpture.

And in the center of it all ranged the flower gardens and lime walks of Tivoli Gardens and all the amusement park's civilized delights: the Chinese-style outdoor theater with the mechanical curtain in the shape of a blue and purple peacock's tail, which took five men to unfurl; the large lake with a full-sized frigate anchored in the middle and smaller rowboats for hire criss-crossing the water; the beer gardens and the kiosks selling burnt-sugar almonds and buttery toffee. Yet up here, a hundred feet up, the salty sea breeze overpowered the faint smell of beer and sausage and burnt sugar and everything was as small as Nik's toy circus at home. You looked down at the tops of trees fluttering in the breeze, at striped awnings rippling, at women's silk parasols, moving circles of navy blue and ice green.

What about that magical white Oriental palace near the lake, which looked like something from *Arabian Nights* with its bulbous towers and latticed windows? "Does a sultan live there?" Nik asked Carl, half believing it. They'd seen a brown-skinned man in a turban at the entrance to the Exposition, along with a family dressed in Scotch plaid.

"It's the Tivoli Concert Hall, of course. And tonight you'll be sitting inside listening to the orchestra perform Niels Gade and Mozart, with me somewhere in the back of the strings. Never mind that I'm not first violin! My own little suite for strings will be premiered at the Glass Hall this September. 'Suite for String Orchestra, op. 1, by Carl Nielsen,' it will say in the program—if I manage to finish it in time. The building down there, with the glass roof and open sides."

Up here, high in the sky, Nik felt like a character in a fairytale by Hans Christian Andersen, a girl who'd flown across Denmark on a magic carpet into an enchanted tower. She gazed in wonder past Tivoli and the great expanse of the Nordic Exposition to the twisting cobbled streets and the sweeping new boulevards of the city proper, to the carriages and horse trams, to the narrow brick houses with iron balconies, to the church steeples and copper domes. Far off was a chain of lakes, and beyond that, the apartment on Slagelsegade, where they were staying with Aunt Marie and Uncle Jens. The tiny village of Selde could fit into the corner of this city; it would be as nothing from the observation platform of a giant beer bottle.

The military band struck up a march in a rotunda in the distance. Maj moved to the other side of the platform and Carl edged closer to Nik.

"Up here," said Carl. "I don't feel like a substitute player for the Tivoli Orchestra. I can feel that I own this city. It's mine." He looked over at Nik, who had taken off her hat so it wouldn't blow away. "And are you glad to be here with me, my treasure? Haven't you been longing for just *this*? A view of the city where we'll live together someday and your very own adoring Carl to see it with?"

"Oh *yes*."

Last night Nik had silently wept herself to sleep, missing her parents and her familiar bed. The sounds of the city were frightening to her; she longed for the wind off the Limfjord rustling the beeches and poplars, for the occasional hoot of an owl hunting voles in the fields. Even having Maj next to her wasn't enough; it only added to her loneliness to have a sister she'd not seen for months sleeping beside her, softly snoring and oblivious of Nik's homesickness, probably dreaming of meeting Eva Sandström again.

In March Eva had sailed across the Atlantic to visit her family in Brooklyn. She'd only just returned to Copenhagen. Eva's father had a friend who kept a hotel in a good part of the city, and Eva had taken a room there. Nik suspected that Maj would never have agreed to spend an entire month with their aunt and uncle if it hadn't been for the fact that Eva was in town for the Exposition and to attend a conference organized by the Danish Women's League. Maj had spent much of the train trip from Odense rereading Eva's letters and trying to understand, with the help of an English dictionary, a pile of newspaper clippings that Eva had sent from Washington, D.C. Eva had traveled there in early spring to an international women's congress; she would be lecturing on her experiences at the Women's Reading Room in Copenhagen. She was also volunteering at the Nordic Exposition, in the booth displaying Rational Dress.

Nik and Maj had pulled into the Central Station earlier that day in a cloud of steam, a long screech of brakes.

"What if Uncle Jens and Carl don't come to meet us?" Nik pressed her nose against the window of their compartment but saw only dim figures through the train fog.

"We'll find a hackney cab and drive to Uncle and Aunt's apartment."

"What if we don't recognize them? There are so many people. I've never seen so many people."

"We'll certainly recognize them," said her sister. "It hasn't been *that* long."

But people changed. Maj herself had lost some of the lightness once so characteristic of her movements. She was thicker around the waist and her cheeks had filled out. The small spectacles, which had perched on her nose so delightfully last summer, were now more a part of her face and hooked more firmly around her ears. And although blond curls still softened her face, her lips seemed less rosy to Nik and were more often than before set in what Carl had called her severe expression, especially before she made a point or stated a fact. Yet it was her clothes that had changed most markedly. Gone were the sprigged summer muslins with lace and flounces, tight at the waist to show off her figure. Under her travel duster, Maj's dress was a sedate dark blue draped poplin with a fitted bodice and a high starched collar.

"It's Carl!" He was jumping up and down on the platform and

waving his hat—not the red bowler from last summer, but an ordinary brown derby—as Nik and Maj stepped out of their compartment. Yet for all the talk in his letters of kissing her a thousand times when they met again, Carl could only take her hands and hold them an instant and then press them to his chest. Maj pretended not to notice. Nik pulled away and then smiled uncertainly. Maj and Carl then shook hands, and Uncle Jens appeared.

How could she have imagined she could forget Uncle Jens?

His face was pale and elongated as a halved vegetable marrow, and the sparse white mutton-chop whiskers on his cheeks made it look longer still. He had large melancholy eyes rimmed with suspicion. Uncle Jens always dressed in black, a black that was invariably shabby, like a faded rook. His collars shone with grease where his longish white hair curled down, and his broadcloth was none too fresh. He looked like an elderly relative dependent on the goodwill of the Nielsens instead of Mr. Nielsen himself, formerly a successful wholesale merchant in Odense and a wise investor in government bonds and railway and steamship stocks.

"Welcome to Copenhagen, my dear girls. I would hardly have recognized you, Emilie, you are so grown. Maj, you have spectacles! Take my arm, Maj. The porter will find us. Carl, look to Emilie. We mustn't lose her."

"You're growing up, my darling, it's true," whispered Carl into her ear as Maj went ahead with Uncle Jens, pushed forward by the jostle of arriving passengers. "But rather thinner, aren't you, underneath this huge travel duster? Are you well, my darling? Do you still love me? Tell me you haven't changed your mind. Haven't you been longing to see me as much as I've longed to see you? Has love made you pine away for me?"

A year had not aged him; he still looked sixteen or seventeen instead of twenty-three. He was as well-made and energetic in a summery suit and blue-striped cotton shirt as she remembered. And the expression in his blue eyes was the same: playful, teasing, hungry.

Nik felt she'd changed more than he had. Between the heels of the new boots Papa had bought her the other day in Odense and a narrow-brimmed feathered hat, she was taller than Carl. She was much thinner too. She'd had no appetite since the beginning of May, when Mama said yes to the invitation from Aunt Marie to come to Copenhagen for a month.

Ten months had passed since she'd waved good-bye to him on the platform at Roslev on a hot windy afternoon in late August. She'd dreamed often of this moment of meeting, and yet she'd also believed his love couldn't be real and that he could change his mind any moment.

"Are you happy, my Nik?" He pressed her against him as they followed Maj and Uncle Jens to the hackney cab.

"Of course!"

She wondered, as she lay in bed next to her sister that night and cried silently, why she did not feel happier. What kind of a world traveler would she make if she missed her parents like a little girl? And hadn't she been longing to see Carl just as much as he longed to see her? Yes, of course she had.

"And you *see* that *this* model dress I am wearing is meant for walking in the country or cycling. You *see* it is sturdily sewed and *modest*, but offers great *freedom* of movement." The velvety voice spoke Danish emphatically, with musical Swedish intonations. They heard her before they saw her, after making their way through the packed Hygienic Hall with its exhibits of clothing, toys, and surgical instruments. Fifty or sixty people stood around a raised platform under a sign reading:

DANISH WOMEN'S LEAGUE
Rational Dress for Women!

The crowd was listening to a statuesque young woman—it could only be Eva from the accent and the way Maj was flushed with pride—standing in front of four dressmaker's dummies, a sort of headless chorus to her lecture.

Eva had a massive amount of blond hair piled on her head like freshly-plaited straw, with a light blue, gilt-edged ribbon twining through the coils. She had such creamy skin it was almost pale yellow; a high, intellectual brow; and hazel eyes. She was like a delicious milkmaid carved of butter, a butter that did not melt.

The costume Eva was wearing wasn't what Nik had been expecting from her sister's descriptions. Nik had imagined something more along the lines of a man's suit—now *that* would be rational—with a jacket and skirt. Eva's "walking and cycling" dress was merely what a sensible farmer's wife might wear so she could nurse a baby with one hand and pluck a chicken with the other. Farmer's wives rarely wore stays, and their skirts were frequently hemmed up so they didn't drag in the muddy barnyards or out in the fields. Though Eva was far from being a farmer's wife; the shortened dress revealed a nice pair of ankles, and even without stays her bosom was high and rounded.

Carl said, "What a magnificent specimen of Modern Womanhood!"

"Hush, you silly boy," said Maj. "She *is* magnificent, isn't she?"

Eva twirled and moved her arms up and down, continuing in the sing-song accent that stressed words, enunciated consonants you didn't usually hear in Danish, and occasionally gave ordinary two-syllable words three syllables or more:

"The Rational Dress Society was founded in London in 1881 and now is part of the Danish Women's League's platform. Last winter the organization instituted a *competition* throughout Denmark, asking women to submit finished dresses from the four patterns available or from their own designs: a party dress, a dress for daily wear in the city, this walking-cycling costume that I wear now, and a dress that working women, particularly factory workers, might wear. The *criteria* for such clothing are these: the dresses should not *squeeze* the waist; they should not require any more *under*things than what is described in our pamphlet *On Health and Women's Dress*; they must not hinder the *movement* of the limbs; and they must be of the lightest fabric *possible*." Eva had been ticking off these requirements on her fingers. She looked at the audience with a serious expression, made delightful by the natural curve of her mouth. "And it is especially important, for the ordinary city dress and the walking-cycling dress, that they don't collect *dust* or *crumple* easily."

A fellow called out, "If all women were as pretty as you it wouldn't matter what they wore," but he was quickly drowned out by the sound of women clapping and pushing up to the dress displays and to buy patterns. Someone else was hawking issues of *Women and Society*. More than one woman touched Eva on the arm or back or made her turn around and stroked the dress's material. Maj pushed her way forward, but Carl pulled Nik away from the crowd.

"I want to be alone with you—just for a little while, darling girl. It's been agony these last hours, wanting to take you in my arms."

"You talk as if it had been days, Carl. We just arrived yesterday!"

"It has been months, Nik." He fingered her silk gloves. "Almost a full year. It was last August we kissed. Now it's July of 1888! All this time I've been waiting like the best of dogs to lick the hand of my mistress again, and here I find it completely covered by a silk glove!"

He was so intentionally ridiculous, imitating the woebegone expression of a faithful retriever as he tugged at her thumb as if to pull off the glove, that she had to laugh. But it was a nervous laugh. Behind all that clowning and face-pulling there was something more determined, as if he really were a dog tugging on a rag in her fingers. To tease him, she put her hands behind her back.

Carl laughed. "Can't we leave Maj here and go somewhere by ourselves? Or do you want to purchase a dress pattern that makes you look like a farmer's wife?"

"Nonsense. I quite like the look of Eva's dress. Perhaps I'll have Miss Humlegaard make me one of those walking costumes. How I'd love not to worry about tearing my clothes when I go fossilizing on Fur."

"You know I adore you as you are, sweet Nik, but we are in Copenhagen now, the Paris of the North. And you could look so beautiful in the right sort of clothes." His lips grazed the nape of her neck, and sent a hot buzz of excitement through her shoulders down her back. "I think it was when I danced with you at Mette and Henrik's engagement ball that I realized what a stunning creature you were. If I had my way, I'd see you dressed in lace and velvet that showed off your bosom and your small waist."

"Stop, Carl. Mama wouldn't like you talking like this. Much less Papa."

"You know how I adore your mama and papa!" he said, stepping back dutifully, but with his red lower lip pushed out a little. "But your parents aren't here." He sighed when he saw her expression. "I won't force you, darling. I'll behave myself. But after all those letters . . . if you knew how near I was to madness sometimes at night, thinking of you. No, now I'm frightening you. And on your second day in Copenhagen too! Forgive me. We have time. We have a month." He looked sober. "But only a month. Please tell me you love me. Please let me give you a kiss."

"I love you," she whispered. "Not here though."

Eva eventually disentangled herself from her admirers and the four of them had cream cakes and strawberry tarts in a café adjacent to the Japanese Exhibition. They sat at a table facing an eight-foot-tall statue of a fat man in draperies that showed his smooth chest; he was seated, with one foot on his thigh and a necklace of beads around his neck. It was an Oriental god, Maj told Nik, but Eva corrected her: "It's the Buddha from India. An ordinary man who became enlightened."

Carl tried a joke. "Is it enlightenment to wear very few clothes? Perhaps then the dress reform movement is heading in the same direction. First the corset goes, then the whole dress?"

Nik laughed, but Maj and Eva looked coldly at him. Or rather Maj looked coldly at Carl and Eva simply looked through him. She was like a glowing gas lamp that could suddenly go dark.

She said to Maj, "I saw Larsen yesterday. She came to the Rational Dress display while I was there."

"Larsen!"

"Yes, and Dyrberg too!"

"Not Dyrberg? I thought she always went to Faaborg in summer?"

These were girls from the Odense Seminary, who were always called by their last names. Nik only knew this from what Maj had told her. Several of them were apparently also in Copenhagen at the moment, for the Exposition and for the conference on women's rights in two weeks.

Nik pushed her cream cake away. Carl was staring at her so longingly that it made her lose her appetite.

"Not hungry?" said Maj. "Can I have yours then?"

"I just remembered that Andersen came by as well," Eva said. "She is simply *dying* to see you."

Norway's contribution to the Nordic Exposition led to the left and Sweden's to the right off the main exhibition entrance, and to Nik it was no contest: the Norwegian exhibits were far and away more splendid. Imagine, a whole three-story mountain cabin made of logs with a charming little balcony you could sit on and survey the wonders in the hall: fishing rods, skis, skates, hunting knives, and ice axes displayed all along the walls and in glass cabinets, along with stuffed animals and birds of the North: an arctic fox, a wolverine, ptarmigan, and a staring snowy owl. Nik was disappointed not to see a reindeer; but there was an enormous bear on his hind legs. And everywhere were photographs of fjords and mountains and throughout the hall people from the Norwegian Tourist Association dispensed brochures calling Norway "Tourism's Promised Land."

In contrast almost everything in the Swedish exhibit was industrial and dull. Their glass display cases were filled not with silver rings and pewter bowls but with cannon balls and knives, farming equipment and tools, all of iron and steel. It seemed, on the face of it, that Sweden was turning its forests to matchsticks and its mines to weapons and nails, and was proud of it.

Eva's Rational Dress fit in well with the Norwegian hall and had some visitors coming up to her to ask for information. She glided over to Nik, who stood gazing at some photographs of the Jotunheim Mountains. "What are your plans for yourself, Emilie? Maj says you are quite *interested* in travel. Maj says you think of being an explorer."

"I suppose I used to dream of riding horseback through the Rocky Mountains or driving a sled with reindeer in Lapland," Nik said. "But that was a year or two ago."

"What a shame," said Eva. "Driving *reindeer* in Lapland! I haven't known many girls who dreamed of that! Oh you must—or something equally as marvelous."

"I've been considering becoming an artist," Nik said, so as not to disappoint Eva. "I like to draw. A friend at home who's studied art in Copenhagen says I have a little talent."

"Splendid!" said Eva, clapping her hands together. "The Academy of Art has finally been *forced* to open its doors to women and the first sessions begin within a few months. Shall *you* be attending?"

"I think I would need more training first." In fact, Nik hadn't drawn anything for many months. Mette's honeymoon and tiring pregnancy had broken up their drawing lessons and Nik found it hard to continue on her own. She grew increasingly irritated whenever Mama said, "Well, what about our windmill? You could draw that, dear, couldn't you?"

"Certainly you must have the basic art training!" Eva radiated encouragement. "I've heard of two artists, Emilie Mundt and Marie Luplau, *fine* painters who had to study in Munich and Paris because the Academy of Art in Copenhagen *refused* to admit them ten years ago. Now they have opened their studio to women art students. Shall we visit them while you're here?"

"Oh! Oh yes," said Nik, her heart leaping with both fear and pleasure.

Maj came up with Carl and took Eva's arm. Eva stroked it enthusiastically. "Dearest Hansen!" she said. "Just *imagine*. Emilie is going to be an artist, and as soon as I can arrange it we'll all go visit the studio of the Misses Mundt and Luplau, who give art instruction to women students. *Shall* we? Won't it be fun? Miss Luplau's mother is the famous Line Luplau, who practically *invented* the women's movement in Denmark."

"What about men? Are they allowed to enter the studio?" said Carl.

"Oh no!" said Eva. "This is an excursion just for *us*."

Uncle Jens had bought the best of seats in the Tivoli Concert Hall, down near the front, so that they could see Carl plainly—clean-shaven and cherubic amidst the graying heads and beards of many of the other players. Carl winked at Nik once, when the orchestra was first tuning up, and chatted with some of the others on stage. How strange it was to see him sitting with his violin among so many other violins. Eva was no longer with them. She'd been introduced to Uncle Jens and then she'd gone back to the Hygienic Hall to change her clothes and to join the mysterious Andersen and Dyrberg for a play at the Casino Theater.

Uncle Jens turned around in his seat when the orchestra was finished tuning up and whispered, "Shhh," to the people behind them. "The maestro is coming!"

An energetic portly man in a dress suit bounced out on stage, took his bows, and lifted his baton. This was Baldouin Dahl, who thought highly enough of Carl to put his Suite for Strings on at

Tivoli this September. But tonight it was Hans Christian Lumbye's *Amelie Waltz* and Niels Gade's Symphony No. 2 on the first half of the program, to be followed after the interval by a symphony of Mozart's.

Carl had said Lumbye was on almost every program at Tivoli and that the audience protested when he wasn't. Niels Gade, Carl's former teacher at the Royal Conservatory, was another great favorite with the public. Gade's symphony was agreeable, by turns placid and stirring with a strong marching beat at the end. Nik tried to hear Carl's violin but it blended so well with the others that she could only look at his arm moving up and down and his concentrated expression and imagine his particular notes among the greater sawing away of the violins.

At the intermission, Carl came off the stage to find them. His face was flushed and his ash-blond hair stuck up. Nik stopped herself from smoothing it down.

"Well now, friends," he said, "what did you think of old Gade? He's a special favorite of mine, even though he's predictable as a farmer who always plants his crops in the usual rotations."

"I liked it," said Nik. "The slow parts made me think of pleasant things, as if I were back home sitting on the shore at Fur and watching the fishing boats in a bit of a breeze."

"Yes, it's rather music to doze by, isn't it? Never mind, the Mozart will wake you up." Carl turned to ask Uncle Jens about the tempo in the second movement. Uncle Jens, Nik had always heard, had a remarkable ear for music. She glanced at the two fleshy protuberances under his tall black hat, pinkish squash blossoms framing the pale marrow face.

Maj said to Nik, "Let's take a short turn around the hall." As soon as they were out of earshot, she went on, "Now, I'm dying to know what you thought of Eva. So handsome and yet unconscious of the figure she makes. The silly comments of men mean nothing to her; she's the perfect person to model the Reform Dresses. She makes them look so stylish."

Maj had never seemed so enthused about Frederik, yet there

were some similarities between Eva and the Tin Soldier, Nik thought. They both were tall and straight-backed. They both took up all the space around them. Nik thought that she'd like to see Eva on a horse. You could also imagine her standing at the helm of a Viking longboat, with a diadem around her flowing blond tresses.

"She's splendid," said Nik sincerely.

"Oh Nik, that's it *exactly*. She's splendid." Maj bounced a little on her toes and burst into a wide smile. "Eva told me our friend Dyrberg teased her today that she had an American glow about her. As if she were a 'spirited filly' in one of those novels about girls in America that Dyrberg's always reading! But I think—at least to me—Eva has always had that glow. America has nothing to do with it."

After the concert Carl joined them, carrying his violin case. It was not quite dark yet; the sky remained blue streaked with pink for a long time. The willows around the lake were wound in strands of colored electric lights and as the shadows deepened, their colors grew warmer, like glimmering candies. The pale green night moths, some with wings as large as sparrows' but thinner and almost transparent, circled around the red-paper lanterns and fizzing gas lamps.

"How are you, my darling?" whispered Carl, as Uncle Jens and Maj walked in front of them. "You look exhausted. It *has* been a long day for you, hasn't it, filled with so many new things."

She was so often tired these days, but she didn't want to tell him that, tell him that she'd fallen asleep during the Mozart and had only jolted awake again with the sound of the clapping. She felt as if she were in a long dream that had begun yesterday in the steam of the Central Station.

At eleven were fireworks, and in the shadows created by the blazing flowers and rockets above, Carl stripped off her silk glove and pressed his palm against hers, hot and hungry.

15.

SOMETIMES NIK WOKE WITH A LONGING FOR SELDE SO painful it seemed to split her heart. She missed the sweet green scent of the wet grass at dawn and the sawdust-cigar-herring-potato-peppermint smells of the general store and the warm apple and hay breezes of an afternoon in the garden. She missed riding and swimming and walking slowly in the cooling shadow of the elderberry and hawthorn windbreaks along the country roads, with a stalk of wild fennel in her mouth. She missed Mama and Papa the most, but also Mette, who was now so big with child she had to lie on a settee in the garden fanning herself. Nik missed Jutta and Mrs. Jespersen and Ole Dahl and Mr. Svendsen and the Strandgaards. She missed Sophie. Were she and her brothers and sister out with their jam jars and long-handled nets hunting for beetles and butterflies? Chiseling fossils from cement stone? Of course they were, as Nik had done last summer.

Mama wrote almost daily and she always began with the weather, which was generally fine and dry this summer, praise God. Papa's lumberyard was thriving and the barley was ripening well. The apples were abundant, the currants even better. And what else? The pastor's wife had been to Aarhus and bought a hideous new hat; Jutta had a new beau; and make sure you tell Maj, but gently, that Frederik is soon to marry the girl from Viborg. Nik pressed Mama's letters to her nose and could have sworn she smelled clover and honey.

Copenhagen had a warm rainy summer that year. The streets stank of soggy manure, tanneries, and brewing hops; the canals of fish and sewage. At night the windows in the bedroom she shared with Maj were closed to keep out the sounds of the city, with heavy velvet drapes drawn against the morning light. The bedroom, with its carpets and cushions and settees and potted ferns, its dark rose walls lined with family photographs, could seem suffocatingly small and fuggy, just as the apartment and even the city outside could feel constraining as a prison.

She hadn't realized how much freedom she'd had in Selde until she lost it. At home if she disappeared for two hours, up into her room or out into the orchard to read under a tree, no one thought anything much about it. Here in Copenhagen—impossible! She had never so much as been able to go down to the corner shop, a mere twenty steps from the main door, without her aunt having a fit and sending one of the maids after her. As for wandering about the city on her own, she was strictly warned that decently raised girls never did such a thing. Only servants and loose women went unaccompanied in the street, said Aunt Marie. "Men of the worst sort prowl the streets day and night."

"What about Eva?" Nik asked. "She often goes about alone."

"Miss Sandström is Swedish," said Aunt Marie. "I don't know how they raise their daughters in Sweden, but as far as I'm concerned, the behavior of a Swedish girl can never be a model for you or Maj."

In Selde no one, not even Aunt Marie, had shown much concern about her going for a stroll or ride with Carl or sitting alone with him in the parlor. Yet here in the apartment Nik felt awkward having even the most ordinary conversation with him. Everyone kept such a sharp eye on them; everyone eavesdropped or broke in with their own opinions on the weather or how nice the marmalade was. When she and Carl did manage to exchange a few private words, it was invariably in a hallway or in a corner, and it gave everything a furtive, tainted air.

The apartment lay north of the center in Østerbro, an elegant district of newly constructed five- and six-story buildings.

Slagelsegade 18 gleamed with white stone and plaster trim; the street door, carved and heavy with beveled glass, led into a foyer with a polished oak staircase up to the second floor. They didn't use a key to let themselves into the apartment; a smartly dressed maid with a narrow fox-like face and auburn hair under a stiff white cap opened the door. She was called Westberg—even Carl, breezing in, called her that. How lordly and cool that was, but after a time it felt natural to also say, "Thank you, Westberg."

Westberg and Ditlevsen were the housemaids, and Ditlevsen also helped Mrs. Zandt in the kitchen. Only Aunt Marie's personal maid was called by her first name, and this was strange, because Hanne was the oldest of the staff, the only one whose room was inside the apartment proper. The others had their small rooms up in the attic of the building, along with the servants from the rest of the building. In the apartment above the Nielsens resided a well-known Russian translator, and on the next floor was a friend of Uncle Jens. The Siamese princes lived on the fifth floor, but Nik waited in vain to meet them.

"My sweet girls," said Aunt Marie from a sofa where she lay with her feet up, fanning herself. "Come here, darlings, I can't get up. The doctor has forbidden me, my feet are so swollen."

"Aunt, you look fine," said Maj, smiling, coming and embracing her. "I hope you will rouse yourself. You haven't been outside the apartment since we arrived three days ago."

The two girls and their uncle had been out again to the Nordic Exposition. They had eaten lunch with Eva, who was once more demonstrating rational clothing at the Danish Women's League's booth, but they had been forced to spend much of the visit in Machine Land with Uncle Jens. Carl had been giving music lessons and had returned to the apartment earlier.

"My dear Maj! And disobey Dr. Marten? Perhaps in a day or two!" Aunt Marie's hair was covered with a long lace cap; jet earrings dangled from her ears. "Nik, come here, my dear. I look at you and think how you've changed since last summer. I must call you Emilie now. Look how tall and elegant you've become. *Charmante.* Oh, you make me feel a thousand years old, both you girls, with your fresh faces!"

"Nonsense, Aunt Marie," said Carl, coming into the parlor from the hallway, having heard their voices. "You look lovely as always and we depend on you to come out with us in a day or two when your feet are better."

Old people, once they got old, always looked the same and it was impolite to ever comment on it, Nik knew. Still, as Nik pressed her cheek to her aunt's and smelled the faint perfume of powder and creams, she thought, I hope when I'm forty-eight I can still walk. Aunt Marie was wrapped in a light wool shawl and a coverlet of satin, even though it was warm and close in the room. Her ankles and feet, peeping out at the end of the coverlet, were wrapped in bandages, with a pair of embroidered satin slippers tied on to the toes with pink ribbons.

"Tomorrow or very soon, I will take you to lunch to the Hotel d'Angleterre at Kongens Nytorv," decided Aunt Marie. "And perhaps to the ballet at the Royal Theater one evening—that is always restful. As for the Exposition, we'll have to see. I was there last week and the crush of people was astonishing. I'm sure that's what brought on the swelling—having to stand there with your Uncle Jens looking at the latest mechanical inventions for hours."

Uncle Jens had slipped into his favorite chair by the window where Westberg always kept a pile of newspapers. He read the financial pages assiduously, the better to follow his many investments.

"Yes," Aunt Marie continued, "I think a visit to Kongens Nytorv is something I can manage. And there are so many fascinating little shops nearby as well. One or two French merchants have opened the most charming boutiques on Bredgade, full of enchanting *bijoux*."

Uncle Jens, behind his newspaper, said, "I'm sure the girls haven't come to Copenhagen merely to shop, Marie. They are still rather young for such frippery and frivolity. They're here to be exposed to Denmark's advances in industry and agriculture. And their father, remember, is but a country merchant. Christian knows the value of money; he doesn't waste it on *bijoux*."

"We have money to spend, from Uncle Hans and Papa," said Nik.

"My dear husband," said Aunt Marie. "The girls are our guests, and more than that, they're my sister Emma's daughters. And didn't Christian and Emma treat Carl and me to a splendid holiday last summer? It's the least we can do, Jens—merely a few gloves, dancing shoes, and hats, of course. There is a delightful milliner's shop quite near here, and Mademoiselle Clarisse already knows all my tastes."

"Hats," said Uncle Jens. "Marie, you have twenty boxes of hats in your closet. What can a woman who hardly goes out for a walk do with so many hats?" But he sounded resigned.

With her trailing lace caps and little satin slippers, her pillows and sighs and sniffles, Aunt Marie had often seemed out of place in Selde. But here she lay royally on her brocade sofa swathed in shawls and coverlets and was mistress of a large apartment.

"Maj, I've missed our duets of last summer," said Carl, moving to the grand piano in a corner of the room and lifting up the face-board. It was a Bechstein, from Berlin.

Her sister followed him over to the piano but didn't sit down. "It is so beautiful that I feel quite intimidated to play it after our old Marschall. I'm afraid it's gotten out of tune again. Nik, I hear, hardly touches it anymore."

"But that can't be true," said Carl. "I've heard good reports from Nik about mastering some of Chopin's *études*."

"I haven't been playing much this summer," said Nik, glaring at her sister. "It's not easy to keep progressing without a teacher."

"We'll soon change that," said Carl. "The Bechstein has such a beautiful sound, it almost plays itself."

"I'd like a piano that did that," said Nik.

Uncle Jens looked up from his paper, all thoughts of hats forgotten, and stroked his sparse white whiskers. "Yes, a Bechstein, ordered especially for Carl. The top of the line."

"Clearly we spare no expense when it comes to music," murmured Aunt Marie.

"Of course I would have been content with a smaller Danish piano," said Carl. "This almost feels too grand for me."

"Nonsense, my boy," said Uncle Jens. "The piano is for us to enjoy your musicianship. Play them your composition for Tivoli this September," said Uncle Jens. He pulled his chair close to the piano, while Maj went over to the window and looked out.

Nik perched on an embroidered footstool next to her aunt and watched her sister. Would Carl forget all about her again and want to play the piano constantly with Maj?

The tall windows where Maj stood were draped in maroon velvet and swagged to the side with golden tassels. Heavy walnut cabinets and mahogany sideboards held leather books and curios. The room was papered in cream and maroon, the walls hung with paintings of cows grazing in meadows and schooners in quiet harbors. Every claw-footed table had an embroidered cloth and more objects on top: glass-domed displays of coral flowers or stuffed songbirds, bouquets of fresh flowers, small china bowls of dried rose petals. All this went together with the rich sonorous tones of the Bechstein.

Carl began in the middle of his Suite for Strings, with the swinging spin of the waltz she remembered so well from last summer, when she would sit in the garden listening to him inside the house. How gay and flirtatious the intermezzo was, but with some undercurrent of real longing. Nik couldn't tell if the longing was in the waltz itself, in the melody, or whether the longing was all in her imagination, in her memory of sitting with Mama in the garden one afternoon in the shade of the big beech and looking at the parlor window where she knew Maj lounged on the green sofa while Carl composed.

Maj turned away from the window and seemed lost in pleasure, swaying in time to the waltz as if she were dancing with the Tin Soldier that long-ago Christmas. Smiling, she walked over the piano and sat down next to Carl.

"Oh, my friend," she said warmly. "How happy your music makes me!"

Carl broke into a smile, and when he finished the movement, he jumped up and bowed, then took hold of his violin and began to play the opening movement, oh very slow and sad with that aching melody of four notes, first a long one, then three, the four notes building, and Nik heard now how the waltz was built on the prelude's ache and longing. But why not begin with the waltz in the first place? Why begin with the aching notes? And she remembered that Carl had told her once that his mother used to sing to him, and in her voice there was a sort of wistfulness.

His mother was the prelude; his father the fiddler was the lively waltz; and Carl himself would be the third movement that was both. But the finale did not come. Instead, when he came to the closing notes of his wistful first movement, he put the violin down. "I'm still not satisfied with the finale so I won't bore you with it," he said. "Perhaps when I hear it all played properly at Tivoli, I can stand back and see what is amiss."

"How can you stand back?" asked Nik. "If you're playing the violin during your own composition?"

"It is not quite there," agreed Uncle Jens. "You've developed your themes so well in the prelude and the intermezzo, but when it comes to the finale, you're almost stymied by your own inventiveness. Which themes will you choose to carry through? Which instruments will carry those themes? How many strings again, my boy?"

"At the moment, thirteen violins, six violas, five cellos, three bass cellos. Now I begin to wish I'd scored it for the full orchestra. I miss the percussion and the horns. I could use a drum and trumpets so splendidly in the finale to give everything a rousing flourish and be done with it."

Aunt Marie sighed. "I wish it could just be Carl playing at Tivoli. I get so muddled when I hear an orchestra, everybody tooting and sawing away at the same time. I'm a great music lover, as everyone knows, but what a cacophony an orchestra is, with all the instruments playing at once."

Carl laughed heartily at that, and after a moment they all did, even Aunt Marie. Carl bowed in three directions. "Tonight, ladies and gentlemen, we'll dispense with all the other players in the Tivoli Orchestra. The young genius Carl Nielsen, hitherto unknown, will astound us by performing his entire Suite for Strings himself. As the composer, he will also sit in the audience and clap for himself." And Carl, mugging as only he could, rushed from side to side, panting and taking up first an imaginary cello and a violin, right and left, before pretending to sit down with his chin in his hand and then clapping wildly.

Westberg had slipped in with a pot of coffee and pastries, and Carl bounced over to Nik's side and insisted on feeding her a small raspberry tart with his own hands. How beautiful his fingernails were—clean and square-cut—and his fingers seemed to buzz a little still with music. Those musical fingers touched her lips as the red sweet raspberries slid over her tongue.

"Do you see how thin Nik is, Aunt Marie? We must cram her with every delicacy we can and treat our little girl like a princess."

Aunt Marie sighed and said, "You are quite thin, Emilie. But it suits you. We will have the dressmaker make you a new dress while you're here. Isn't that a good idea, my boy? Something feminine for Emilie, with ruffles at her neck?" She leaned forward between the two of them and said, "And what about a taste for me, sweet boy? A little raspberry tart?"

Nik didn't eat more than a bite or two. The sensation of the red raspberry clots in her throat was unpleasant. This queasy feeling around food was familiar, as was the overall physical tiredness that had dogged her all summer. She couldn't ride over to the squire's to visit Mette; she had to drive with her mother. And as for walking all the way to the Limfjord, much less swimming, that had become unthinkable. When she went out with the Strandgaards she had to sit on a rock instead of climbing the bluffs. Sophie was disgusted: "Why a girl has to wear a corset and get the breath squeezed out of her picking up a pebble, that must be the stupidest thing in the world."

But it wasn't the corset. Sometimes Nik felt exhausted just walking up the stairs to her room.

Mama had been so worried at one point that she'd called in the doctor, fearing he would diagnose a case of consumption. Instead he shook his head and grumbled, "Fatten her up with calf's foot jelly and beef liver and potatoes and plenty of butter. The girl is too thin, probably anemic. Girls are always trying to fit into their new dresses."

Alone with Nik the doctor asked about her womanly troubles. Blushing horribly, Nik stammered out that yes, her monthlies came regularly, but since the spring she'd had painful cramping and yes, she did bleed strongly. She gushed with blood and some of it was clotted and thick. The doctor asked to examine her, advising that she think of something else, something pleasant, while he did so. Afterwards he said she was quite normal, and that some girls simply had heavy flows, particularly before they married and had children.

Papa's opinion was that Nik was simply tired from growing so much, and it was true that sometimes her legs ached and her neck hurt, as if the bones were being stretched on a rack. Her feet got huge and her hands seemed twice the size of the year before. She had to have new clothes. The worst was that so many people in the village commented on her new height and farmers who hadn't been to the general store for some time felt especially free to remark, "Miss Emilie, that's a strapping great girl you're getting to be."

Even Maj had been surprised when she saw Nik in Odense last week. "I suppose I can't call you my little sister anymore, since you're now about half a foot taller than I am."

And Ottilie had piped up, spitefully, "Yes, she's practically a giant, isn't she?"

"Nonsense," said Uncle Hans in his kind but business-like way and got a measuring stick. "Five six and a half. As long as she stops there, she'll be fine."

16.

IN THE BACK OF THE MUSTY HACKNEY CAB DRIVING away from Slagelsegade 18, Carl fell on Nik energetically, holding her face up in his hands and kissing her all over her cheeks, lips, and neck. It was a sticky day and their flesh clung together.

"You are mine, do you hear? Say you're mine and will never be anyone else's." He gave a kind of moan and buried his face in her neck, knocking off her hat. "Say you adore me as much as I adore you."

"Carl, be careful!" She pulled away. His ardor was too hot. The driver was outside and couldn't see them; no one could see them. Still, she was guilty of allowing even this much. "You don't want me to look a complete scarecrow when we arrive to meet Margrethe and Vilhelm, do you?" They were to have tea with Carl's great friends, the Rosenbergs, at their villa on Pile Allée in Frederiksberg.

"The Rosenbergs' villa is miles away. Oh, how I've longed to have you to myself, just for a short while." He pulled back and sat gazing at her, tracing her cheek with his finger. "You can't imagine what it's like to lie in my room at night and know you're just a few doors away. Or to endlessly sit in the parlor with Aunt Marie ready to pounce should I touch even your fingernail. Even when I give you your piano lessons, Uncle Jens is always hovering. The mere sound of the faceboard being folded back brings him like a shot. 'Are you working on the finale, my boy?'" Carl mimicked Uncle Jens's croak. "Bless the dear old fellow, he is far too interested in helping me resolve my themes."

"At least we can always hear him coming," said Nik. Uncle Jens clunked through the apartment in wooden shoes he'd brought from Odense, the better to save shoe leather indoors.

"Do you know, I think we were far better off in Selde than here? I thought it would be just the opposite. But now I dream of those beautiful days when we would ride and walk and swim. It was a kind of country paradise, the same as I recall from my childhood."

In Carl's memory, his childhood always seemed to be a paradise, however poor the family had been, but now that Nik was in Copenhagen she began to understand his yearning for fresh air and freedom. In Selde she could have driven them both in the trap through bright yellow fields of rapeseed with the sound of thrushes and robins all around. The hackney cab was dank and hot and rattled over bumps and holes and the noise from the streets around formed a clattering cloud.

Carl began caressing her again. "This may be our only chance alone, Nik. Shall we elope as in the novels? Drive to the Central Station and take the first train to Paris?"

"We have no money for Paris," she said nervously, trying to keep his hands from straying to her waist.

"Little Nik, don't be so practical! In Paris we could live as we like. You could model for artists and I'd play the piano at the Moulin Rouge." But he was laughing now. He picked up her hand, quite respectfully, and laid it against his cheek. "I adore you. I worship you. I'll do whatever you like. If you want to live in Selde, I'll happily move there. Of course I hope you'll want to live in Copenhagen. You do like it here, don't you?"

"Yes—what I've seen of it," she said. "Can't you show me some of the city out the window? I'm far more familiar with Machine Land than Copenhagen itself."

He allowed himself to be distracted for a while, pointing out the churches and cemeteries, the Botanical Gardens with the glass Palm House. He told her stories about friends he had in different buildings: musical friends, artists, writers. Here was a café he liked to frequent. There a bookshop. Around them swirled other cabs and riders, a few bicyclists, and hundreds of people on foot. From time to time he kissed her, but not so hungrily. Now it was pleasant, almost sweet, and she kept her hat on and felt grown-up, a young lady with her attentive, handsome fiancé.

They passed near the Central Station onto Vesterbrogade, where the population was dense and the streets smelled of horse dung and machine oil and cabbage. This was a district of factories, and tenements. It was where the masses of rural people flooding into Copenhagen came to find work and lodging—if they could. Down one or two side streets Nik saw women not properly dressed, in pantalettes and silk wrappers, lounging in doorways or leaning out windows, their breasts partly exposed. She had never seen such women before in such numbers. Here they were, red-faced in the muggy heat and with garters and corsets showing. Some were quite young, Nik's age. Vesterbro was where Carl said he'd refused to go the evening he'd spent with Karen Marie. Had he ever gone to Vesterbro, had he bought girls to sleep with, was he unclean? He'd told her last summer that what his mother most feared for him when he joined the regiment in Odense was the French disease, which smelled, she said, like rotten potatoes. Nik imagined she smelled that stench as they passed through Vesterbro; it permeated the cab and made it hard to breathe.

For either of them to turn their heads away from the sight of the women would be to acknowledge that they saw them. She felt his breathing quicken, while she flushed in shame. Her own breasts ached a little, the way they often did these days.

Neither of them said anything.

Nik had asked her mother, on the platform at Roslev when she and her father were departing for Odense to meet Maj, whether she could say she was eighteen when she arrived in Copenhagen. After all, no one would know. In every way, it would make things easier.

"Certainly not, Emilie!" said Mama, and then she smiled. "Some day you won't want to be older than you are. You'll want to be younger."

But standing in a crowded parlor of Rosenbergs—seeing Margrethe, twenty-three, and now a music teacher, standing next to Carl and teasing him about his shiny new shoes with the ease of long habit—Nik knew it wouldn't have made any difference whether she said she was eighteen. She was fifteen and a country girl and there was nothing more pathetic in the world than to be her. Margrethe wasn't beautiful, but she looked clever, rather skeptical. It was the way one side of her mouth moved more than the other, Nik decided. She had a low voice for a girl and a decided, self-assured way with Carl. She gave him a sisterly pat on the arm; he caught at her hand and squeezed it.

It was in his last year at the Conservatory that Carl had proposed to Margrethe.

"'Marry you?' she said. 'I'd sooner marry a street sweeper as a poor would-be composer. And anyway, I plan never to get married,'" Carl had told Nik in the hackney cab after they left Vesterbrogade for a more elegant street leading to Pile Allée. "I don't think Margrethe meant to hurt my feelings." He looked at Nik closely. "I thought I'd better tell you before you met her, but honestly, you must not worry about it.

"Of course she was right. I was far too young and unsettled then for any sort of engagement. But I think her real reason is that she's devoted to her brother and family and to music. She told me she hoped that we would stay the best of friends. That, we have. I always thought I might propose to her again sometime, but . . . the opportunity didn't come up."

Nik didn't feel she could hold her own with Margrethe, especially when the girl launched into a description of a chamber music concert she'd recently played and asked Carl's opinion of Edvard Grieg. Grieg's *Holberg Suite* and one of Johan Svendsen's *Norwegian Rhapsodies* were on the Tivoli Orchestra's program tonight. Nik couldn't hold her own with any of the older Rosenbergs, not with the professor, a stout family man with a big head of hair, or Vilhelm, the would-be composer with a fresh new moustache, both of whom insisted on asking her opinions about the Exposition and

Copenhagen and seemed surprised that she had so few.

She sat with a strained smile sipping tea and nibbling a biscuit with no appetite and wished she were a hundred miles away. How happy Carl was, joking and jumping around from piano to sofa, whirling young Thyra in a dance, producing sweets for some of the little ones. This family had meant so much to him during his student years, he'd often told Nik. Their dinner-table discussions, the books they loaned him, the concerts and lectures they took him to—all had shaped him. He'd spent three years at the Conservatory with Margrethe and Vilhelm; they had introduced him to musicians, artists, journalists. They'd turned him from a country bumpkin to someone who could pass in good society for cultured.

"How old are you?" Thyra squeezed next to her on a settee. "We all want to know."

"Fifteen."

"I'm a year younger. I wish I could put my hair up like you. Do you play music?"

"Not really . . . a little piano."

"What a shame. We all play here and we have the most marvelous trios and string quartets, just in our own little family. I'm going to the Conservatory in a few years like Margrethe and Vilhelm. I play the violin. Maybe if you practice more, you could go there too?"

One of her little brothers said, "Miss Hansen speaks different from us. It's funny."

"That's because our guest comes from Jylland," said Margrethe from across the room. "Miss Hansen, don't let them pester you. They're just curious about everyone who comes to the house. Your provincial accent is delightful, isn't it, Carl?"

"I never notice her accent. Only how charming she is."

Carl was playing the piano now, and he beamed over at her, imagining Nik as popular with the family as he was. Did she have such a strong accent as all that? Did it mark her as a provincial girl so distinctly?

Vilhelm picked up his violin and so did Margrethe, and then

Thyra ran over with her violin as well. It sounded like Mozart but Nik wasn't sure, it could be Haydn, and that filled her with despair: Not to be able to tell Mozart from Haydn, how pitiful. Worse was when the four of them agreed to play something by Beethoven and they launched into it without a score in sight. The three Rosenbergs all played the violin in the same way, as if they were connected by telephone wires, and at the piano Carl kept them to the right tempo with his nodding head as well as his fingers. The room was washed in afternoon light, pale gold. It fell on the jade-green carpet and the well-worn furniture.

They were all to accompany Carl to Tivoli that evening in a caravan composed of their own carriage and two cabs. Before they left the villa, Margrethe asked Nik if she would like to freshen up, and brought her up to her bedroom. While Margrethe went into her dressing room to change, Nik washed her face at the basin and then sat at the dressing table to try and puff up her curly hair, which seemed to be flattened on one side, perhaps from leaning against the side of the cab. When Nik looked at herself in the mirror, she couldn't believe that Carl really loved her. She could understand him loving someone like Maj, so small and blond and musical. She could understand him loving someone like Margrethe Rosenberg with her ironic smile and quick understanding.

Margrethe came back into the bedroom in a silk dress that far outshone Nik's striped taffeta, which was now crumpled and stained with the grubby hands of one of the young Rosenbergs. Margrethe glanced at herself in the mirror and patted her hair, which was already smooth. She said, "I'm so looking forward to hearing Carl play tonight. Tivoli isn't the Royal Orchestra, but it is a tremendously spirited group of players. They'll massacre the Grieg but will do splendidly with Svendsen. He's far less subtle—though immensely talented of course. Carl expects to audition for him at the Royal Orchestra. Svendsen's the conductor there, you know."

"We've heard Carl play twice at Tivoli," said Nik. In the mirror she watched Margrethe move over to the washbasin and run a cloth around her neck. Margrethe didn't have much of a bosom but her waist was small and her movements assured. She had that in common with Maj; her limbs all seemed in tune with her body, instead of awkward and disjointed like Nik's.

"I understand this is the first time you've been to Copenhagen," Margrethe said. "Thyra tells me you're just fifteen. That surprised me, I admit. Carl never mentioned your age. Fifteen, imagine! I was still such a baby at your age. The only things I cared about were my cat Blackie and my violin. I didn't give a fig for boys. All except my older brother."

"Vilhelm seems kind," said Nik uneasily.

"Oh, he and Carl are thick as thieves. Really, the three of us are. We met our first week at the Conservatory and have been together ever since. A trio." She returned to stand behind Nik at the dressing table. "But now perhaps a quartet if you'd wish to accompany us on the piano."

"I don't really play the piano all that well."

"No? How unusual." Margrethe picked up the crystal bottle of French perfume and sprayed herself once behind each ear, then she spritzed Nik's neck generously. Nik didn't like the smell.

At Tivoli, Nik didn't sit with the Rosenbergs, but with her uncle, who had bought her a ticket. Margrethe was not far away; from time to time she left off gazing at Carl in the orchestra to give Nik a quick sharp look, followed by a half smile. Margrethe might have refused Carl once, but that didn't mean she hadn't expected Carl to ask her again. Perhaps what came between them was Karen Marie. It shamed Nik to think that Margrethe might know the story of Karen Marie and the baby. It shamed Nik that she'd walked into the Rosenbergs' house half disheveled from being kissed in a musty hackney cab. It shamed her that Margrethe might have guessed why her hair was flattened on one side, might guess how she'd responded to Carl's kissing. Well-brought-up girls didn't let themselves be made love to in closed carriages.

Carl seemed so far away up there on the stage, playing Edvard Grieg with all his might. On the way to Tivoli he'd talked the whole time to Vilhelm and Margrethe about the difference between Edvard Grieg and Johan Svendsen, how the former was a brilliant miniaturist who worked intensively with few instruments, and the latter was so much more colorful. "How the man understands orchestration," Carl said. "If I could only work with Svendsen someday."

"But of course you will," said Margrethe. "Once your Suite for Strings has premiered at Tivoli, why shouldn't you get into the Royal Orchestra next year when they audition again? Mr. Svendsen is here tonight. We'll be especially friendly to him, won't we, Vilhelm, for your sake!"

"Svendsen," said Nik without thinking. "We have a Mr. Svendsen in our general store at home. He's the clerk."

Margrethe's lips twitched to one side as she glanced at her brother.

Carl said, "Bless you, Nik, and isn't your Mr. Svendsen the jolliest fellow in the world? Whenever I needed something from the store last summer, all I had to do was ask him." He patted Nik's hand.

As if she were a child. She was mortified.

"Johan Svendsen is Norwegian," said Vilhelm kindly. "His father was a bandmaster, and he studied in Leipzig and conducted in Norway before taking the position here at the Royal Theater. He's been here for about five years."

"He was a composer too, once, in his day," Margrethe added. "But romance seemed to take it out of him. He rushed off to America to marry an unsuitable woman and returned with her. She was jealous and unstable—one night she threw his newly completed Third Symphony in the fire. Ibsen used the story in one of his plays. But poor Mr. Svendsen never composed another symphony.

What you'll hear tonight is garden-variety Norwegian Romantic Nationalism, from ten or twelve years ago."

"Still," said Vilhelm, "you must admit, Margrethe, that the Second Rhapsody is an excellent piece for strings. And his music is so good-humored, you can't help but enjoy it."

"Yes, I for one enjoy him," said Carl. "You mustn't be too hard on the fellow for having a heart, Margrethe. Just because you don't believe in romance doesn't mean we mere mortals don't sometimes stumble into love."

Margrethe laughed, but it had a tight sound. "I never said I didn't like his music. It is terribly cheerful."

During the intermission Carl bounded down from the stage to talk briefly with Nik and Uncle Jens about the Grieg, but his eyes kept shifting to the group of Rosenbergs and their friends from the Royal Conservatory.

"Shall we go over to them, Uncle Jens? I see they're joined now by Maestro Svendsen. I've met him before but would be glad to shake his hand again."

"I'm well enough here in my seat," said Uncle Jens. "I don't like to go gadding about during the intervals. It disturbs my concentration, all that chitter-chatter."

"Will you come with me, Nik?" Carl said, but made the mistake of joking, "Shall we see how the real Mr. Svendsen compares to your clerk?"

As if *her* Mr. Svendsen were not as real.

"I'll stay here with Uncle and keep him company," she said in as level a voice as she could manage. "You'll have to get back up on stage in a minute anyway."

When she sat down again with Uncle Jens she looked hard at the program so as not to cry tears of humiliation. She was glad to be with Uncle Jens. He wasn't Papa; he was too eccentric. When they arrived home later this evening he would step to the right or the left of the center of the staircase, to save wear on the carpet. He would sit down to his usual late-night meal of cold rice pudding that the cook had left out on the kitchen table for him. No, he wasn't Papa, but like Papa, Uncle Jens still saw her as a little girl, still in the midst of her childhood, and did not expect her to be older or more cultured or more musical than she was.

Tonight that was very comforting.

17.

"AN ARTIST DESCRIBES THE WORLD," DECLAIMED EVA on the horse tram from the Central Station to the apartment and studio of the Misses Mundt and Luplau on Gammel Kongevej. "And we need women painters, sculptors, poets, and novelists to describe the world of women, not from the *outside*, as men do, but from the *inside*."

Eva wasn't dressed in her reform clothes, but her costume was plain, a light blue and green striped skirt with the merest hint of a bustle, the sole ornament a line of mother-of-pearl buttons down her blue bodice. Her bountiful straw-blond hair was neatly braided and knotted up behind a small hat with a tall crown that tilted forward. Her velvety voice and Swedish accent turned heads on the tram, something she paid no mind to and probably even enjoyed, for Eva was, as Carl said, "theatrical."

Eva had never seen a drawing by Nik nor asked to see one. All the same, she was quite eager that Nik embrace an artistic calling as soon as possible. For a woman to become an artist was necessary for the liberation of the female imagination. It was of *crucial* importance to have women artists, writers, and musicians. No longer should women just be muses and the *subjects* of novels and paintings written and painted by men.

Maj did not dare to say anything about Nik's lack of diligence or general want of intellectual curiosity in front of Eva. Privately she may have wondered to see her sister's casual interest in art elevated to a calling. But sometimes Nik felt that Maj didn't occupy herself much about Nik at all these days. And that was a relief.

~

Emilie Mundt herself opened the door to the apartment on the fifth floor of the large apartment building. Her graying blond hair was parted in the middle and pulled back into an efficient knot. She wore a voluminous paint-spattered smock over her thin frame. Plain, a little stern, and yet somehow exotic, with stains of indigo blue on her cheek and forehead and several fingers that gave her a tattooed look, like a woman captured by South Sea cannibals.

Nik breathed in the sharp turpentine scent of the stuffy room.

"How wonderful it smells in here," she said.

"Is this the girl who wants to be a painter?" came a voice from across the room, from behind an easel with a large horizontal painting. "It's a good sign if she likes turps and oil paint then."

A full-bodied woman of forty, a little younger than Miss Mundt, stepped out from behind the painting, and Nik drew in her breath. Marie Luplau's dark hair was cut just like Carl's, in a hedgehog brush about two inches long. It outlined a strong olive-toned face with sensuous lips and well-modeled cheekbones. Miss Luplau looked like a kind of man, except that her chest was rounded and she had big hips. She was wearing a plain old-fashioned black dress, not a smock, which didn't have a single streak of paint on it. She wore no shoes, only black wool slippers.

After introductions all around, the guests walked into the large studio with the row of tall windows facing the buildings across the street. On the dark green walls were rows of paintings, right up to the high ceiling: landscapes, portraits, figures, all in gilded frames.

"Johanne Meyer sends her greetings," said Eva. "I was just at the editorial office of her new newspaper yesterday. The first issue will be out next week, to coincide with our Nordic women's congress. Isn't it a brilliant name for a paper?"

"*What We Want*," whispered Maj to Nik. "Miss Meyer said she was first going to call it *The Women's Democrat*, and then had a better idea."

Marie Luplau laughed, a kind of warm rumbly laugh that Nik had never heard from a woman before. It was a good laugh.

"That firebrand! What are she and my mother up to now? I heard from Mother that she and Johanne want to start a whole new women's organization. They find the Danish Women's League far too conservative."

"Well of course it is," said Eva, drawing off her gloves with a snap. "We need an organization that is solely about getting the Vote, and doesn't *compromise* or settle for anything less. Your mother never loses her perspective or gets drawn into issues that distract from the real struggle. Just having come from America, it's clear to me that the Vote and of course more *education* for women are all that matter."

"That's right," said Marie Luplau, "You've just come back from America. And you're going to give a lecture about it soon, aren't you? Now you must sit down with me and tell me all about it over tea and cakes. And not just the worthy political facts you're going to put in your speech. The gossip. And then I'll tell you all the Copenhagen gossip in return." She took Eva by the arm and led her to a red brocade settee. Maj trailed after and sat down in an armchair opposite them.

"Come here and let's talk, just you and me," Emilie Mundt said to Nik, pointing to a worn horsehair divan by the green velvet draped windows. She took off her smock; underneath was a plain blue dress, also a bit paint-stained.

"Sit down, child," said Emilie Mundt. She seemed completely unconscious of the indigo stripes on her face. Pulling out a box of cigarettes, she lit one and said, "Have you heard of Line Luplau, Marie's mother? She first sent Marie to Copenhagen by herself at the age of twenty to study art, and then she came herself when Marie's father retired. She's never stopped battling for women's rights. She is a marvel to us all. Imagine, seventy years old and she only gets more fierce."

The maid brought over a tray with teacups and a small plate of rather dry-looking shortbread, and placed it on the table in front of them.

"Now," said Miss Mundt, drinking tea and puffing clouds of fragrant smoke. "Here's what I know about you from Miss Sandström's note. You are fifteen. You don't go to school. You live in a village in Jylland, far away from a city, and you've never studied art. And yet somehow you've gotten it into your head to become an artist."

"Yes," said Nik. "At least I want to try. I have a friend, Mette Bohm—Mrs. Christiansen now—who studied art here in Copenhagen. She gave me a few lessons and she thought perhaps I might have a little talent."

"Did you bring a portfolio of your sketches with you?"

A portfolio, what did she mean? Nik said, "I'm just visiting my aunt and uncle here for a month. It was Miss Sandström who—"

"Are you bright? Do you read?" Miss Mundt interrupted. Across the room Eva and Miss Luplau were laughing like old friends though they had just met. Maj was looking on, with that silly expression she sometimes got when she stared at Eva. You'd think Maj would be embarrassed to look at another girl like that, but sometimes Nik felt the same way about Eva. She was so shiny, like a just-polished silver vase. Miss Luplau seemed to think so too.

"Your sister, I believe, has gone to high school in Odense and is now studying to be a teacher. That's what I did too. I taught small children before I came to Copenhagen to take art classes. Haven't you thought of studying in a girls' school where you could learn Latin and German? You don't need a classical education to be an artist, but it helps discipline the mind to study languages. And of course you'll want to travel someday to Germany or France for further study with artists. Marie and I have lived in both Munich and Paris."

"I am not particularly educated," admitted Nik. "I don't know any languages. I know more than most girls about a few things, natural history and geology for example. I don't enjoy studying that much—except when I'm quite interested in a subject." She didn't mention that her favorite subjects had often been adventure stories. "I like to read. Jacobsen and Dostoyevsky. And Darwin."

"Darwin?" said Miss Mundt, looking her over. "So many girls are content to be ignoramuses. I hope that you don't think of just getting married at eighteen?"

"Well, I . . ."

"Vilhelm Kyhn, who ran a drawing school for young ladies where Marie and I first met fifteen years ago, used to say that marriage was the thing that stopped most women from becoming artists."

"And was he married?" asked Nik.

Miss Mundt ground her cigarette out in the tea saucer. "Well of course he was. But marriage doesn't stop men from doing anything. It makes their lives easier."

"But two artists could marry," said Nik.

"That is true. Mr. Kyhn told our fellow student Anna Brondum that if she married the painter Michael Ancher she might as well trundle her art supplies down to the sea in a wheelbarrow and throw them in the waves. But she didn't do that and she did marry Michael Ancher and now both of them paint and she only gets better and better. But Anna Ancher is the exception. Most women who marry soon find themselves with half a dozen children and no time at all to themselves to think, much less to make art."

"Still," said Nik, stubborn. "You and Miss Luplau live together and paint."

Miss Mundt's light blue eyes looked straight at her. Then she smiled. "You interest me, Miss Hansen. Now, here is what you will need to do if you want to be an artist."

She went to the window and pushed back the green velvet drapes and beckoned to Nik.

Nik stood next to her. What was she supposed to be looking at? There was nothing but another elegant apartment building across the way, not as tall as this one, and foot and horse traffic below.

"What color is the sky?" said Miss Mundt.

"Blue."

"Is it?"

"Well, I suppose it's rather gray," said Nik. "It's that wet gray-blue Copenhagen sky with soot in it and rain threatening."

"What about that building opposite, faced with stone. Is it a yellowish rosy brown or a brownish-red-beige or something else entirely?"

"It's yellow and pink towards the roof," said Nik, now interested. "Not brown at all where the sun strikes it. But by the time the light gets to the street the stone is more reddish—reddish gray. It's even more gray than brown. I know the facing is sandstone and sandstone is brownish, but there's nowhere on the building it really looks brown to me. I don't know why."

"You don't have to know why, right now anyway," said Miss Mundt, appearing satisfied. "You just have to learn to see shadows and light and how surfaces take on the colors of the sky and change throughout the day. And then you must learn the properties of paints. And how colors work together, the warms coming forward, the cools receding. You could spend a lifetime learning about blue. Or about the effect of sunshine and shade on stone."

"Weren't you going to tell me what I should do to be an artist?" Nik prompted her.

"I just did! You must learn to see." Miss Mundt stepped away from the window. "And then of course you must draw a great deal. It doesn't matter what. Just draw. You have only to begin. And in two or three years, whenever your parents allow it, come back to Copenhagen and we will teach you all you need to know to enter the Academy of Art. The important thing, you must promise me this—don't get married, at least before you find out who you are as an artist."

Did that mean Miss Mundt wouldn't teach her, if she married? That she couldn't become an artist and learn about color and light and shadow? Surely not.

"And you must learn at least one other language besides Danish. German, that's easy. French is beautiful. Take your pick."

"What about Italian?"

"*Molto bello*, but rather useless."

They joined the others. Miss Luplau was now smoking a small cigar and telling a story about their good friend Mary Steen, a photographer and wicked card player, who had opened her own photography studio at Amagertorv, near the Women's Reading Room. Mary Steen was younger than the Misses Luplau and Mundt, but already successful in her profession, the first photographer to take pictures of people in their own homes. Some of her photographs were displayed at the Nordic Exposition. "Mary's just been here recently to take our photograph in the studio."

"She admires Marie's sculptured head and profile," said Miss Mundt. "I, on the other hand, look terribly serious."

"You *are* terribly serious, Emilie," said Miss Luplau, blowing smoke from her cigar. She had dried perspiration stains under her arms. Neither of them, thought Nik, would be quite welcome in Slagelsegade.

"Miss Sandström, you must have your portrait taken by Mary Steen. She'll hang it in her photography studio, along with all the other remarkable women she has on her walls."

The conversation moved on to other women artists and writers, of whom the Misses Mundt and Luplau knew a great many in Copenhagen. Nik was surprised that Maj seemed to have so little to say. She herself didn't pay much attention to the talk; she was looking over the heads of Eva and Marie Luplau at the paintings, which ranged all the way up to the ceiling. She liked the ones of the sea washing on shore under lavender and sage tinted bluffs. They reminded her of Fur and of home. That was what she would want to paint, if she began to paint—the sky and sea. Not Selde's church tower or the windmill.

Nik drifted, was brought back when Eva mentioned that Victoria Benedictsson, who wrote under the name Ernst Ahlgren, was staying at Leopold's Hotel. Eva had learned this from a maid at the hotel, Ingeborg Larsen, who did the rooms for both of them. The Swedish writer, in fact, was just down the corridor, though Eva had not yet run into her.

"We haven't read Benedictsson's newest novel, *Fru Marianne*," said Miss Luplau, "but it hasn't received good press. Edvard Brandes was very critical of it in *Politiken*. An anonymous review, but everyone knew it was him."

"That's hardly a surprise," said Miss Mundt. "He and his brother Georg claim to be staunch supporters of the women's movement, but they don't either of them care much for women they're not sleeping with.

"But I don't think the new novel has been as popular with the ladies either," she continued. "It's all about the virtues of monogamy, in spite of the fact that Victoria Benedictsson stopped living with her husband years ago. Ragnhild Goldschmidt, our friend who directs the Women's Reading Room, says most readers feel it's old-fashioned. Nothing like *Money*."

"Well I heard something from the maid at Leopold's Hotel this morning that astonished me," said Eva. "Ingeborg said that Victoria Benedictsson had a *romance* here in Copenhagen with a well-known man who used to meet her often in her hotel room. She would come over from Sweden several times a year, sometimes for weeks at a time. But that's all *changed* now, at least on the man's side. Sometimes, Ingeborg told me, she comes to make up Victoria Benedictsson's room in the morning and it's clear she hasn't *slept* at all. She's been sitting by the window in her chair writing in a big fat journal all night. She's thin and pale and she walks around and around the statue in the center of Kongens Nytorv. Then she comes back to the hotel and calls for champagne and *brandy*, and fresh flowers, and sends a message to the man to come and see her. But he doesn't come often. Not like a year ago."

"Who is the man?" asked Marie Luplau. "We're in suspense."

"Georg Brandes," said Eva. "That's what Ingeborg told me. And I realized I'd passed him once or twice in the corridor or on the stairs when I first came to Copenhagen two weeks ago. You can't mistake him with those devilish eyes."

"Brandes—that horrid man!" said Maj. She stared at Eva in

shock. "How is that possible that Victoria Benedictsson of all women could . . . With *him*?"

"Well, she did stand behind him last year in the morality debates in the newspapers," said Emilie Mundt. "Well, well."

Marie Luplau ran her fingers through her short hair, just like Carl did, so it stood up askew. "So Mrs. Benedictsson is pining over the worst Don Juan in Copenhagen and yet writing a novel about the joys of marriage and monogamy. Emilie gets angry when I maintain that women can be inconsistent minxes, because *she* never is; still I have to say that Victoria Benedictsson seems to me more than unusually complicated. Is that because she's Swedish, do you think?" She smiled at Eva.

"Marie and I think differently about the morality issues," said Emilie Mundt calmly. "I pity Mrs. Benedictsson if she has really been in love with Georg Brandes. For him it's nothing. For her, it must be terribly painful."

"Oh how tired I am of the morality debates!" said Marie Luplau. "What a waste of ink all those letters and counter-letters were last summer. And then Bjørnson came here, invited to address the League by Elizabeth Grundtvig. Emilie and I went to hear him—such a lot of noise about Hottentots and Mormons. At least I thought so. Now if Bjørnson had something intelligent to say about women's economic issues, about legal equality or the Vote. But no, all he wanted to pontificate about was monogamy for both sexes, for purity before marriage, the reformed old lecher! My mother and I voted with Nielsine Nielsen last winter at one of our meetings that it was pointless to argue in the newspapers about sexual morality—people are going to do what they want to and damn the consequences. Nielsine is a gynecologist, she should know. Personally I don't like anyone telling me what to do—why should a man like it any better? We were voted down, of course."

"I couldn't agree with you more," said Eva. "In America the women's movement is focused on education and better living conditions for women. If women were educated they would have more opportunity and make better choices about their lives. As for men—they will always be the same."

Nik waited for her sister to jump into the argument. Hadn't Maj been a great supporter of purity for women and self-control for men? Hadn't she spouted Elizabeth Grundtvig and Bjørnstjerne Bjørnson at every possible opportunity, so that she drove off the man who wanted to marry her? Hadn't she lectured Nik about Carl and planted suspicions in her mind? And hadn't Maj written that she and Eva had gone to hear Bjørnson in Odense last autumn and thought him wonderful?

But Maj just sat there; clever Maj, who always had an opinion, just sat there, her eyes glued on Eva. Maj was breathing more heavily, in a way Nik recognized: the teakettle beginning to boil on the stove. She would keep her anger in for a while, then it would burst out. It always did.

Nik's palms were damp and there was a heaviness in her limbs that made her wonder if her period might be coming early. Her stays squeezed her lungs. She wished that they could open the window, just a little. The turpentine smell was very strong.

There had been some talk earlier of going to the zoological gardens nearby, but out on the street again, Maj announced she had a headache and was heading straight to Slagelsegade. She said this in a violent way and began marching off by herself down Gammel Kongevej. Eva tugged Nik's arm into hers and walked quickly after Maj.

"What's wrong with your sister?" Eva said under her breath. "We were having a perfectly lovely time with the ladies. Is it my fault that Miss Luplau was friendly to me?"

Nik looked at the sandstone facing of the buildings they passed; it was browner down here in the street and lighter above. The wet blue sky had gone gray and thick. She thought that Maj's temper should be no surprise to Eva, not if they had roomed together at

Odense Seminary. She must know too that Maj would get over it. Nik liked the feeling of being propelled along the sidewalk by Eva; her arm was firm and strong.

They caught up to Maj at the tram stop, just as it began to rain. Eva put up her umbrella. Nik did as well. In her fury, Maj simply stood there getting wet. She refused to look at either of them until the tram trundled up, and she got on first and pushed her way to a seat. Sighing, Eva followed her, leaving Nik to find a seat of her own. Nik was just far enough away that she could hear only small bursts of their conversation: "Bjørnson . . . photography studio . . . *portrait* . . . ignored . . . *humiliating*."

Nik stared out the open side of the tram, at shop windows, at doors, at columns and steps. She looked at hats, coats, and umbrellas, rounded and dripping. Her hand opened and closed, as if she held a pencil or a brush, and she felt her eye connecting to her hand. She seemed to still hear Miss Mundt's parting words: "You must learn to see. That's all. You will have problems continuing—everyone has problems continuing. But that is not your problem now. Learning to continue resolves itself, drawing by drawing, painting by painting. You have only one task now and that is the hardest. You have only to begin."

By the time they reached the Central Station it was pouring and they took a hackney cab instead of another tram in the direction of Kongens Nytorv and Leopold's Hotel, to drop Eva off. But now Maj felt better, she said. Her headache was gone and it was still early. Perhaps she would not go back yet to the apartment, but stay and visit with Eva a little longer.

"You'll be all right continuing in the cab to Slagelsegade," said Maj to Nik, less a question than a statement. "It's hardly fifteen minutes away. Aunt won't know that I didn't come with you the whole way."

One of the many things Papa had warned Nik against, when he brought her to Odense on the train, was taking a cab alone or a cab alone with Carl. He'd also said, "You must promise me never to go off on your own—no matter how tempting it may seem. Go out only with Maj or with your aunt and uncle. I know Maj can be trying sometimes, but remember, she only has your best interests at heart. I put my greatest trust in my little girl and her good sense." He had tried to smile, but his voice choked up and he hastily filled the golden bowl of his pipe and took a number of puffs in succession.

Papa hadn't accounted for Maj being so willing to bend the rules in order to spend time with Eva. The other day, for instance, Maj was supposed to accompany Carl and Nik to the Rosenbergs; they had all gone down to Østerbrogade together and the next thing Nik knew Maj was speaking quietly to Carl and then announcing to Nik that she'd told Eva she'd accompany her to a luncheon party with women friends. She'd somehow forgotten it until this instant.

Now Nik said to her sister, "I'll be fine by myself. Don't worry. I'm glad you're feeling better."

Maj looked at her gratefully. "It *was* a lovely day. I'm so glad you and Miss Mundt got on."

Eva too was buoyant again and gave Nik a kiss on the forehead before she alighted from the carriage. "I will see you soon, Emilie!"

Nik arrived at Slagelsegade without incident, as she expected, and felt very grown-up, paying the cab driver. She was tempted to use the opportunity to at least walk around the block; she felt giddy with her small quarter hour of independence. But it was more than that. She wanted to look at the buildings in the drizzle and practice *seeing*.

But instead she opened the street door with its beveled glass and went up the stairs.

Carl was just coming out of the apartment. He carried a sheaf of music.

He lit up to see her. "What good fortune, my darling. I was just about to go out for a practice session, but I'm early. Now you're here, I'll go back in. But—let's take advantage of this moment!" He pulled her over to the wall and embraced her, so intensely that she moved in his arms in protest. She couldn't breathe. Yet his lips tasted delicious, they were so firm. And his scraped chin smelled of the cologne Aunt Marie bought him.

The door opened and Westberg poked her white cap out, noticed them, and pulled her head back in without closing the door. "It's just Miss Emilie," she called back into the room. "And Mr. Carl is still here."

Was there something mocking in Westberg's voice? Nik hastily straightened her hat and slipped past her into the apartment. She thought Westberg gave her a sly glance; the girl was really just like a fox, with her auburn hair and narrow face.

"Thank you, Westberg," Carl said. He sounded irritated as he brushed past her after Nik.

"Madame asked if anyone was at the door. She sent me to look."

"Never mind," said Carl hastily. "It's fine."

Why would Westberg speak to Carl like that, so mockingly? It was quite impertinent. Nik liked her even less.

"Where is your sister?" asked Aunt Marie from her sofa.

"She dropped me here and then went back with Eva to the hotel," Nik said. "She had a little bit of a headache and they planned to have a quiet hour or two."

"But how can a hotel be quieter than our home?" Aunt Marie asked in annoyance. "Really, this is beginning to be too much, with Maj deciding for herself what she will and won't do and where she will go and what she will do with her time. She may be twenty but she is not married. And I don't care that Miss Sandström comes from a good family and the hotel is said to be reputable. It's not right that Maj spends hours there. Jens, you must tell Maj that. Perhaps you should go and fetch her."

"Now, Marie," said Uncle Jens behind his paper. "It's only three in the afternoon. And if Maj has a headache, it won't be soothed by a quarrel about what she should and shouldn't do. Why not ring Westberg to bring coffee and some of Mrs. Zandt's cardamom buns? Carl, can't you play us something? Surely you have time before you go out for your rehearsal?"

Aunt Marie calmed down and Carl went to the Bechstein and played Beethoven. He had been playing a great deal of Beethoven lately, especially when he should have been composing. The frosted cardamom and currant buns were much better than the dry cakes the Misses Mundt and Luplau had served. Without warning, Nik felt very tired. She sat on the sofa with her aunt and played with her rings, just as she had as a child, slipping them off and putting them on her own fingers. When she put the wedding ring on her finger she looked up to see Carl winking mischievously from the piano. She ignored him. Yes, she would like someday to marry him, of course she would! But wouldn't it be lovely to be an artist and have a painting studio and no one to bother her with sly, knowing looks and caresses? She took off the rings and leaned against her aunt, eyes half closed.

Aunt Marie had returned to the subject of Eva Sandström and the extreme *oddness* of Maj wishing to spend so much time with her. "She quite puts little Maj in the shade. I wonder if that's Miss Sandström's intention. Some girls like the company of a friend who is no competition. But I don't know how Maj will ever find a husband if she spends all her time with Eva. Eva simply makes Maj look short and dowdy. She should have married that lieutenant when she had the chance. I imagine Frederik is doing quite well with his interest in the peat works. Tell me, dear Emilie, is there a chance there still?"

"Mama said Frederik is engaged now, to a girl in Viborg, Aunt."

Carl said in the midst of his playing, "Maj reminds me of a girl I used to know in the music conservatory. She was naturally a mezzo, but she wanted to be a coloratura soprano. She had a lovely voice, very expressive in its lower registers, yet she was always trying to reach the high notes and strained her vocal chords terribly."

Aunt Marie took a large bite of her bun. "Oh, she should have married that lieutenant!"

18.

KING CHRISTIAN V'S GREAT STALLION WAS CRUSHING Envy underfoot; that was the meaning, said Carl, of the equestrian statue of gilded lead that occupied the center of the vast cobbled square of Kongens Nytorv. Their hired carriage had circled the statue twice and the second time swung much closer, jostled on every side by traps, cabs, and open barouches like theirs, along with horses, velocipedes, and flower carts.

At one edge of the great square was the narrow harbor of Nyhavn, where fishing smacks delivered their catches. On either side of the harbor were cellar restaurants with wooden signs creaking in the breeze. As the barouche circled for the second time past Nyhavn, Nik breathed in and was reminded of the Limfjord. The sea smelled stronger when rain threatened, as it did now. The sky surged with clouds and stray drops spattered on them.

"Oh if only Uncle Jens would allow us to keep a carriage and horses here in the city," said Aunt Marie, "I would never own a barouche, of course; the weather is far too uncertain in Copenhagen, not like our dear Odense. I believe it was far more often sunny there. A rainy summer like this would not have been endured in Odense."

"Shall we put up the hood then, Aunt Marie?" asked Maj.

"Certainly not," said their aunt. "Not after we've taken the trouble to dress so beautifully. We must pull up to the Hotel d'Angleterre in style."

The sweeping tour of the grand square, to be followed by a meal at the Hotel d'Angleterre, took place without Uncle Jens; he thought it frivolous and muttered about dinners and milliners and did his extravagant wife think he was made out of gold coins? He was a retired man now, on a fixed income, practically a pensioner. Aunt Marie ignored him, as usual. She wore a tightly laced rose-pink summer dress with a large bustle that made it difficult for her to sit comfortably without tilting to one side. She had propped herself up with a pink and white ruffled parasol. Nik and Maj wore simpler clothes, though they too of course had to manage their smaller padded bustles and draped skirts. Nik couldn't help thinking that sitting would be much easier if they were able to wear the Rational Dresses Eva had modeled. Better yet would be if she could ride the horse herself and not have to worry about getting in and out of an unstable carriage with a silly cushion strapped to her bottom.

Around the square they drove for a third time past the Royal Conservatory of Music, the Royal Theater, where Maestro Svendsen conducted the orchestra for the Royal Opera, past Charlottenborg Palace, which housed the Royal Academy of Art. She daydreamed of strolling through the palace gate into the courtyard, going upstairs to a light-filled studio to an easel like Miss Luplau's where her brushes and paints awaited her. She would pick up her brush and then . . .

Carl glanced at her and smiled. "Are you imagining something pleasant, Miss Emilie Hansen? Perhaps arriving at the Royal Theater to hear my First Symphony have its premiere?"

She smiled back, distracted. Emilie Hansen? What a dull name for an artist. And Emilie Nielsen was not much better. "Women artists should not get married before they know what they can do," Miss Mundt had said. Nik had no idea of what she could do yet. She had hardly begun to live.

It was pouring when they came out of the Hotel d'Angleterre's restaurant, and Aunt Marie announced that she was immediately going home and putting her feet up in front of a nice hot fire. She had eaten well: a plate of oysters and eel soup, followed by roast pork, potatoes, and a sweet soufflé. She regretted the oysters.

"With your permission, Aunt," said Carl, "I'd like to take Maj and Nik to a very respectable café on the square for a cup of chocolate."

He made it sound spontaneous, but in fact Carl had raised the idea of visiting the café yesterday with Maj. Carl said that he had often gone there in his days at the Royal Conservatory and that it shouldn't be missed. It was a gathering place for artists and musicians and writers. There they were to meet Eva, whose hotel was just around the corner on Hovedvagtsgade.

The warm gas lamps of the Café à Porta were welcome on this gloomy day. The intimate rooms seemed larger with so many topaz-tinted mirrors. At zinc tables businessmen nursed brandies and students in wide soft hats and cravats called for more wine. Some ladies accompanying the men reminded Nik of the girls in Vesterbro, with their plunging necklines, but their hats were plumed and they wore jewelry. Were they actresses or ballerinas? A few girls sat together, laughing comfortably over coffee and cake. At home in Selde there were few ways to be a woman; here in Copenhagen there seemed to be so many. Nik glimpsed herself in one of the mirrors and was surprised at how mysterious and adult she looked.

Carl greeted any number of people as they made their way to a table at the back of the front room. Musicians mostly, it seemed, for several young men said things like, "Carl, you old dog, is it true Maestro Dahl is really going to allow a piece of yours to be played at Tivoli? Should we come with our ear plugs?"

Carl mugged and joked that they should certainly bring their ear plugs. As for himself, he too would wear them at the performance, so he wouldn't have to hear the booing. Yet he whispered to Nik as he pulled out a chair for her, "How envious they are of me! They remember that my marks weren't the highest at the conservatory and that I've always been a very ordinary violinist. And they think to themselves, how is it possible that this boy from Black Bog could imagine himself a composer and even have persuaded Maestro Dahl to perform his Suite for Strings? If I fail, of course, and am hooted and jeered off the concert stage, I won't be able to return here, so we might as well enjoy it now."

"Don't be silly," said Maj, settling herself on a banquette along the wall with a mirror at her back. "You have many faults, but lack of talent isn't one of them. Perhaps you're even a genius. Nik, I hope you've been keeping all Carl's letters to you in a safe place. Carl, dear, you must write me a letter too, so I can sell it at auction in fifty years."

"I will write you one now, or as soon as the waiter brings me a napkin."

"Of course I save the letters," said Nik, though she recalled that she had them stuffed in a pillowcase under the mattress at home. Perhaps she should look for a box here in Copenhagen. Uncle Jens might help her. He was certain to know where you could find strong metal boxes with keys that could survive floods and fires and prying maids.

Eva appeared in the doorway in a blue cape that was vaguely military, with a rolled-up bunch of foolscap in her hand. One or two fellows tried to stop her and make conversation, including a man with a full head of dark hair parted in the middle and rising up in two waves on either side. His skin was darkish and he wore an expression of pride and curiosity. He and a friend were drinking red wine at a small table near the café's entrance.

"That's Georg Brandes," said Carl. "Does Miss Sandström know him?"

"Unlikely," said Maj. "I suppose he accosts every woman who walks by."

But Eva did know him, Nik remembered. She'd told the Misses Mundt and Luplau that she'd seen him in the corridor of Leopold's Hotel.

So that was the great mind and even greater sinner Dr. Georg Brandes. Nik gaped at him. He was a short fellow, but unmistakably Satanic with those waves of dark hair on either side of the center part; they looked as if they hid his horns. His eyes followed

Eva through the room and lit on Nik, who immediately dropped her gaze. There was something alarmingly practiced about those dark eyes.

"I don't like everything about the man, but surely you must admit that there's far more to admire in Brandes than to dislike," said Carl, standing up to pull out a chair for Eva. But she slid onto the banquette close to Maj and gave her a kiss on the cheek.

"What do you admire about Brandes?" Eva asked, taking off her cape and handing it to a waiter. Her abundant coils of yellow hair immediately took on the topaz sheen of the café.

"Brandes has been in the forefront of every important movement," Carl said. "Just this spring he lectured on Frederik Nietzsche at the university to hundreds of people. We sat there, rapt. It was as if a bomb had gone off at the hall in Studiestræde."

"Oh, Nietzsche," Eva groaned, drawing off her gloves. "Shall we have some coffee? I *must* have some stimulus if we're to talk about the Übermensch. Have you ordered? I want one of their divine slices of chocolate torte. Emilie, you must have one too; the café is known for its tortes. Maj, I have *finished* my talk." Eva pushed the roll of foolscap over to her. "You *must* read what I've written about the women's conference in Washington, D.C., and let me know if it's too *boring*. I'm terrified. But it must be done! I hope I can pronounce the English words correctly. And tell me, have you been practicing your English? Don't be shy—*How are you?*"

"*How. Are. You?*" Maj repeated, laughing.

Then Eva turned to Nik. "Emilie, say *I am very well. Thank you.*"

"I am wery vell. Tank du."

"I studied English once," said Carl. "I had a small book when I was a young man in Odense. Like my brothers and sisters, I thought of going to America and starting a new life. The book was called *English in One Hundred Hours*. But after twenty hours of hard labor I was still on chapter three."

"I think Emilie's accent is very good, don't you, Maj?" said Eva. "Don't you think your sister might like a trip to New York?"

"She's too young," said Carl and Maj in chorus, and Carl added, "It's so far."

"Nonsense," said Eva. "The steamship I traveled on, the dear old *Geiser*, only takes ten days. You hardly think about the fact that you're on the Atlantic Ocean, it all goes by so quickly in meals and games and dances. Why, many people travel to America and back again several times a year."

Nik loved the way that Eva said *nonsense*. It seemed to brush all obstacles out of the way.

"Really, Miss Sandström, I don't think you should be so dismissive of Brandes, at least if you'd heard his lectures on Nietzche," Carl said. "Nik, just imagine the huge hall and Dr. Brandes at the podium, speaking so brilliantly in a way that you felt was just to *you*. Nietzsche has been scorned and vilified. It's taken Brandes to interpret him for us in Denmark. Brandes has seen that Nietzsche's message is about liberation in every form. *Aristocratic radicals*, that's what Brandes encouraged us to be. Heroes of our own lives."

"And are there to be heroic women?" Eva inquired. "Personally I think too *much* in the world has been created by men, too *little* by women. I can see why Brandes would lecture on Nietzsche though; it's a vindication of everything Brandes believes about himself, the genius to whom all must bow."

"Brandes is a woman-hater at bottom," Maj said. "I can never forget how cruel he was to Miss Grundtvig in the newspapers. *Aristocratic radical* indeed."

Eva gave Carl a level look. "The message of Nietzsche, correct me if I'm wrong, is that there's room at the top for only a *few*, and those few are not women. That's not the way I see the world, as master and slave with women always the slaves. Why does the conversation always have to be about power, or that kind of power—the 'will to power'? The power I'm interested in is *social* change, dull things like education and suffrage."

"No one said women shouldn't have the Vote," Carl said. "No one said anything about masters and slaves. I have no desire to be anyone's master. But I do care about music and what music can do. I want to create bold and powerful symphonies. Maybe you don't think that's worthwhile, Miss Sandström. What *I* took away from Brandes's lectures is that my music could have the power to stir listeners now and in the future—if I could make it magnificent enough. But perhaps we should drop this quarrel. I don't think philosophy is my strong point, nor yours."

"I never pretended to be a philosopher," said Eva. "I don't care for people with Big Ideas. I respect men and women who *make* things and *do* things, like my father. He's building a church in Brooklyn, a large one. My mother wants to start a school. That I understand. I understand people who create schools and build useful buildings."

"Useful! I hate that word," said Carl. "Music is the least useful thing in the world—and the most important."

Maj sighed. "Carl, even you must realize that music can't be everything in life."

"Oh, let him be an Aristocratic Radical, Maj," said Eva. Her chocolate torte arrived and she took a bite and smiled. "You and I—we're off to America, where people build churches and schools. We're going to start a school and change the world while he sits here in Copenhagen at his piano creating beautiful music."

"It *is* beautiful, Eva," said Nik. "Carl's new composition is sublime!"

"My music is more beautiful than my attempts to argue," said Carl, smiling and touching Nik on the hand. "Still, that's what people come to the Café à Porta to do. To argue about the meaning of life."

All of them laughed, and Nik felt rather pleased with herself for interjecting herself into the conversation with the word *sublime*. She felt that Carl sometimes rubbed Eva the wrong way, but she wasn't sure why. Still, how fine to sit in a café in the middle of broad daylight, listening to an argument about Nietzsche and eating chocolate torte. At home, only carriers, sailors, and wastrels guzzled spirits in the middle of the day, sitting in the general store by the pot-bellied stove. If they got too loud, Mr. Svendsen made them go out into the courtyard in back. Once or twice a year he had to break up a fight. The fights were usually about ridiculous things, like whether Norwegians were stupid or only pretending to be stupid. But here, in the Café à Porta, at three in the afternoon, vigorous discussions on art, philosophy, and the meaning of life raged all about them, fueled by champagne and wine.

A tall woman, leaning on a cane, had now come into the Café à Porta. She was rather handsome, with a long neck and curled dark bangs across her noble forehead, above deep-set gray eyes. Her clothes, the blue poplin jacket and lacy jabot, the blue wool skirt, were soaked from the rain. She had no umbrella and her hat was especially bedraggled—the small stuffed bird on the brim was wet through, as if it had drowned in a puddle and been plucked out again.

The woman came directly to Brandes's table and held out a hand to him.

Astonishingly, he didn't rise to greet her or even hold out a hand in response. He acknowledged her but said nothing. The man at the table with Brandes had a romantic sweep of blond hair, spectacles, and a goatee. He stood and spoke a few words; he seemed to know the lady as well. Was he inviting her to sit or asking her to go? She took no notice of him but continued to stand in a bold and yet beseeching attitude in front of Georg Brandes, as if to say, "*You* shall ask me to sit, and only *you*."

Carl had his back to the scene, but Maj had followed Nik's eyes, and after a minute Eva noticed them looking at the table by the door.

"It's *her*," she said in a low voice. "Victoria Benedictsson. But how wet and terrible she looks. And why doesn't she sit down at the table? Why is he ignoring her? Oh, how dreadful to see her *begging* for his attention."

Carl twisted around to look, along with several others in the café, who seemed to be expecting a scene. Most people continued their conversations without pause.

The blond man had gotten Victoria Benedictsson into a chair, where she sat, shivering slightly. The waiter brought another bottle of red wine. She drank off a glass quickly, and then most of another. She hadn't spoken to either of the men.

Brandes had said nothing either, but after she had drunk her wine he suddenly gave her his full attention, and the change from indifference to intimacy was almost coarse. The woman didn't look at him directly but she showed in every particle of her being that she was aware of his scrutiny and that it both mortified her and excited her.

Brandes spoke finally, and as if in response, she took off the hat with its sodden bird and placed it on the table. She unbuttoned her jacket as well. He mopped at her face with his handkerchief. He almost seemed kind for a moment, or pitying, but then an ice-cold expression came into his eyes. With both hands, Brandes ran the handkerchief around her neck, as if he were drying the back of it, and then he used the cloth to pull her towards him over the small table. He said something, something that must have been cruel, judging from her shamed expression. She would have recoiled, that was clear, but she was unable to move; she had been partly lifted from her seat and was held, almost suspended, at an angle to the table top. It was like a peculiar stage trick of hypnosis, yet it wasn't; there was something too powerful and pitiless about it to be entertainment.

The blond man, frowning, put his hand up to free Mrs. Benedictsson, whose arms seemed paralyzed by her sides. Her eyes were fixed on Brandes, who continued to stare back like Mesmer himself. Smiling, he let go the handkerchief and the woman fell back into her chair and then, losing her balance, to her knees on the floor.

"But this is intolerable," said Eva, and was across the room. She helped up Mrs. Benedictsson, swept her hat off the table, and with a few choice Swedish words to Brandes, of which they heard only *swine*, escorted the lady out the door, leaving the cane hooked on the back of the chair.

Carl said, “What happened? Was she drunk?”

At the same time Maj said, “How brave Eva is. She never thinks. She does.”

The three of them went to Leopold’s Hotel shortly afterwards and the manager told them that yes, Miss Sandström had accompanied Mrs. Benedictsson up to her room. If they would like to wait here in the lobby, he could send a message.

“I have a rehearsal soon, but there’s time to accompany Nik back home,” said Carl. He looked at Nik the way he did these days, with a mixture of hope and frustration. They both knew that if he got her into a hackney cab he would kiss the breath out of her and run his hands all around her waist and a little higher. He thought of these rare moments alone as opportunities, while Nik thought of them as trials. She’d have to rearrange her clothes and her face before meeting her aunt, and a furtive shame would accompany her into the apartment. She cared so much for him; why was it then that she spent more time resisting Carl than enjoying his company? Was it his intent to pester her to death with kisses and caresses? He said it was because he was besotted by her and couldn’t help it. Didn’t she love him? Of course she did. Yet why must he always say, “You are mine, Nik. Say you are mine.” She did not want to be owned.

“I shouldn’t leave Maj,” said Nik. She added, “I’ll be all right here. We’ll come home later. Aunt Marie isn’t expecting us quite yet.”

Maj said, “Yes, stay with me, Nik.”

Carl seemed about to protest but then nodded and left quietly. As soon as he was gone, Maj asked for the key to Eva’s room and they went upstairs. Maj had been here several times before, but Nik had never been in a hotel.

Though Papa and Mama ran an inn, it was nothing like Leopold's Hotel. In Selde there were just four rooms, low-ceilinged, clean, but sparsely furnished with a bed, chair, and washstand. When family or friends stayed in the rooms, Mama instructed Jutta to bring in small comforts—rugs and cushions and flowered chamber pots. These were otherwise wasted on the Norwegian sea captains or traveling salesmen, who required only brass spittoons and coarse sheets and blankets. Leopold's Hotel had leather chairs and tables with the latest newspapers in the lobby. The stairs and corridors were carpeted and well-lit with gas lamps. The rows of doors on either side of the hall each had their brass keyhole, knob, and number plate.

Eva's room on the third floor faced the street. The carpet was thick and the curtains velvet, but it wasn't large and contained only a bed and armchair and desk, with a wardrobe and washstand in an alcove. The desk bore signs of great activity: sheets of scribbled foolscap, newspapers and journals in English and Danish.

Maj perched on the bed, looking quite at home, and unrolled Eva's lecture and began to read, while Nik wandered over to the desk to pick up a newspaper. Her attention was arrested by several framed photographs. This must be Eva's family in Brooklyn. The two brothers had light hair and strong features and already looked more American than Swedish, with their confident white smiles. Their parents faced the camera squarely and solidly. Eva's mother had rather a doughy face but a high full pompadour and her father was the very essence of high-collared professional competence.

Half hidden in the papers on the desk was another photograph, good-sized but unframed, mounted in a thick green cardboard folder and stamped "Mary Steen, photographer, 4 Amagertorv." The photo was of Eva and Maj. It unsettled Nik to see this picture, first because she realized that Eva and Maj must have had a sitting at Mary Steen's without mentioning it to anyone at Slagelsegade, but also because there was something unusual about the photograph. It took Nik a few seconds to realize that neither her sister nor Eva had their faces front, as was traditional. Instead they leaned towards each other on a small sofa. Maj had left off her spectacles and her cheeks were softly lit, her lips full and pretty. Eva's hair was different; some of it came down her back and made her appear younger. Her mouth curved a little, not quite in a smile, but as if she held back a secret, a pleasurable one. The oddest thing was that at the bottom of the photograph you could see that they were holding hands.

Nik didn't dare pick up the photograph or stare at it too long. Instead she took a newspaper, a recent *Politiken*, and went to the window. The rain splattered down on a steady parade of black umbrellas.

After about half an hour Eva came in. She didn't seem shocked to find them in her room. She sat down on the bed with Maj and kissed her cheek.

"Ah Maj, I knew you would remember my cape and things. Thank you, dearest."

"How is she?"

"Agitated at first. *Weeping* with shame and hurt. But she took a glass of brandy and that seemed to calm her. She became quite sensible in fact. She said she *knew* that he was bad for her, and that she would soon go back to Sweden and end it completely. She called him a *devil*—said that for all he claimed to despise her he *still* kept coming to visit with books and gossip to share. Sometimes he *begged* her forgiveness and kissed her hands and her face.

"She traveled to Copenhagen two weeks ago only to discuss the production of her play *The Telephone*, but as soon as she arrived, he came *crawling* around and trying to break her spirit as usual. She said this time she would fight it. She said she was writing down everything he said and did to her and the world would know it someday and then he would not be such a great man in their eyes. He would be *punished* in the public eye for his cruelty. She said she had seen him as a great man once, but no longer."

Eva began to quiver a little and Maj stroked her hair, unloosening one of the coils, and again Nik didn't know what to make of any of this. She had always thought of Eva as so strong and bright. Eva was always the brightest in the room. Now her buttery oval face had crumpled and her hair was unraveling in Maj's fingers.

"Today Brandes had promised to come visit her in the morning for a serious talk," Eva said, "but as so often he didn't show up and she grew angrier and more upset, stuck in her room waiting—and the room is full of *expensive* flowers, four or five vases of them, like a hothouse—and unable to concentrate on her writing. And finally at two she went out without an umbrella and began walking around Kongens Nytorv until she realized that it was raining and she was *talking* to herself and people were staring. And then she thought of the warmth of the Café à Porta and thought too that perhaps he was there and was possessed by the desire to see him, to look into his eyes and make him realize how intolerable he had made her life. But she felt *paralyzed* when she did see him, and completely foolish, and she couldn't make herself go out the door again into the cold. He called her a pathetic old woman when he had her by the neck. She is only thirty-eight!"

"Are you sure she should be left alone?" asked Maj.

"She's not alone now," said Eva, whisking away her tears. "No, the blond man in the café turns out to be a friend of both of theirs, but especially of Mrs. Benedictsson. He's a young Swedish writer, Axel Lundgård, and he knew her in Sweden. I think he introduced her to Brandes a few years ago. He brought her cane and apologized for Brandes and told me he would stay with her. So I left them."

Eva sat up straight and began to pin up her hair again, as if trying to pull herself together.

"Shall I stay with you this evening, dearest?" asked Maj.

"No, you must go." Eva stood up, and reluctantly Maj followed. "I know you're planning to attend the ballet this evening, and I must leave shortly myself. I have to talk over the arrangements for the lecture with Ragnhild at the Reading Room. But to end on a more cheerful subject, did you read my lecture?"

"Yes, and it is wonderful." Maj's face lit up. "How clever you are, that was all I could think. I can't see a single thing I would change."

Nik could not help but see them now so differently; as they were in the photograph so they had been together on the bed a minute ago, intimate and loving, Eva's braid in Maj's fingers. It gave her a queer feeling, yes it did, as if they were the sisters and she the outsider.

At the bottom of the stairs, almost in the lobby, Nik and Maj met Georg Brandes coming up. He had a bunch of dark red roses in one hand and a bottle of brandy in the other. Drops of rain clung to his dark beard. Maj hesitated, as if to speak, but she couldn't manage more than a glare at him. With a glance at Nik, a quick, curious glance of appreciation, Dr. Brandes nodded and passed by them and continued up the stairs.

19.

IN A FORM-FITTING NAVY-BLUE DRESS AND WITH HER yellow hair plaited and coiled at the back of her head, Eva stood gleaming in front of forty people packed into the Women's Reading Room one afternoon. A few of the tall windows were open because of the warmth, and the noise from the square at Amagertorv below came up and into the room, but Eva's voice was strong and confident, the velvet stiffened with starch.

"Ladies! I am here today to give you my first-hand impressions of the *great* International Council of Women, which was held this past spring at Albaugh's Opera House, in the capital of the United States of America. It was an un*pre*cedented gathering of women from all over the world, and you will be glad to hear that Denmark was well-represented among delegates from all over America, from Europe, even from India. Denmark was the subject of not just one, but *three* talks.

"You have read about the conference in Washington, D.C., in *Women and Society* and have doubtless already learned *much* about what went on there: what intelligent, brave, and *generous* women said on the subjects of temperance and moral purity, of education for women, of careers and professions. I am here today only to provide a sense of what the gathering felt like. As you know, I am not Danish, but Swedish, yet I have spent two years in Odense and have many *strong* friendships among Danish women. I also have ties to America. My father and mother are now resident in Brooklyn, along with my younger brothers. They went for a year in order that my father might design a building in New York, but they find themselves so happy there, so at home, that they think of staying permanently.

"I can assure you that there are great things afoot in America when it comes to women's rights. They are *blessed* to have powerful vibrant leaders and a clear program of advancement for women. If I were an American, you *might* be excused for putting my admiration down to simple bullishness—for Americans are well-known for their self-regard! Yet I believe, in the case of suffrage, education, and the strength of their movement, American women are *correct* in regarding themselves as the vanguard. And now I propose to tell you a little of what I saw, heard, and understood at the conference. What *better* place to begin than with a quote from the great Susan B. Anthony as she convened the opening ceremony? 'Much is said of universal brotherhood, but for weal or woe, more subtle and more binding is universal *sisterhood*.'"

Eva had found Maj and Nik seats in the front row, but at the last minute Nik escaped to the back of the library, telling her sister she needed to be near the windows in case she felt faint. From here she had a good view of the people in the room. Most of them were women, though a few had brought husbands and there was at least one male journalist in the room, scribbling madly. The ladies were of all ages (though none as young as Nik) and many were in sober brown or subdued plaid, while others were more elaborately kitted out in plumy hats, parasols, and reticules. The room smelled of perfume and feminine perspiration.

When they first came upstairs Maj had pointed out all the important women in the room in somewhat awestruck tones. "That's Johanne Meyer, the editor of the new paper, *What We Want*. She's a socialist as well. Imagine, all her own babies died, and then she and her husband went ahead and adopted five needy children and have been raising them like their own. And over by the window is Johanne Krebs. She's the painter who stood up for women's right to enter the Academy of Art and she didn't rest until she'd convinced Parliament to force the issue." Miss Krebs was calm and beautiful, not at all the firebrand Nik had imagined. Ragnhild Goldschmidt, the director of the Reading Room, was lean and witty and white-haired. She had introduced Eva.

Elizabeth Grundtvig Nik had expected to be hoary and moss-covered. Everything Georg Brandes had written about her made her sound like a puritanical old spinster. Spinster she might be, but she was only thirty, fresh and mild, though with a determined set to her mouth. She was surrounded by supporters, while the women who disagreed with her stood a little way apart. One of them was Denmark's first woman medical doctor, Maj said. Nielsine Nielsen, who had returned for the summer from Birmingham, where she had been studying with a gynecologist with a plan to practice that specialty in Denmark. Not only was she a doctor, she had been in fact one of the first in Copenhagen to enter the university at all, when classes were opened to women.

The Danish Women's League's conference on women's rights had finished yesterday with many resolutions and calls for change. Eva and Maj had attended every session, while Nik spent the days of the conference with her aunt, who had a sick headache in addition to swollen ankles. She wanted someone to read to her and keep her amused—wasn't that what a niece was good for? Aunt Marie thought the whole question of women's rights subversive and alarming. How could women compete with men in the spheres of finance and education? Women were far better suited to keeping house and maintaining a civil tone in society. Aunt Marie couldn't stop Maj from attending the conference, but she could prevent Nik from participating on the grounds that her mind was still too unformed and she might pick up immoral ideas. Today Aunt Marie and Uncle Jens had gone up the coast to Charlottenlund to visit friends and had given Nik permission to accompany her sister to hear Eva's "travel lecture."

"I will tell you the *enthusiasm* with which the Americans and international delegates greeted the lecture on the work of the Danish Women's League," Eva went on. "In every country women have been working to secure the rights of married women to retain their own income from property, inheritance, and work. Our association in Denmark has been instrumental in bringing a bill before the lower house to give married women more rights over the money they earn after marriage. This year the Danish Women's League, as you heard at the conference yesterday, is working with some members of Parliament on issues regarding *natural* children. What is wanted is to procure for the child admission to inheritance, the right to an education, and the right to the name of the father. The Americans applauded greatly at this, for it is an issue of *extreme* consequence at a time when so many men seduce and *abandon* young servant girls, leaving them to fend for themselves, often forced to raise a child with no support from the father."

Eva looked up from her notes and straight at Nik, then away. She must know about Carl and Karen Marie—of course, Maj must have told her! That accounted for Eva being so cool to Carl every time they met. Eva saw him as a seducer who had abandoned a housemaid. She believed the fatherless baby and the unwed mother were now stamped forever with the stigma Carl avoided. And now the stigma fell on Nik as well, for wasn't she in love with this young man who took no responsibility for his child because the law didn't force him to own that he was the father? Nik looked around the room, at all the stately older women, morals intact. She edged closer to the window, overheated and ashamed, but also angry at her sister and Eva. Why must they always be so superior and so *right*?

For that they were right, and Carl wrong, there was no doubt.

"Well, what do you want to do now?" Maj tapped the tip of her parasol on the ground in the street below the Reading Room. When they left, Eva was surrounded by admirers, including the Misses Mundt and Luplau and another woman with brown standup hair and a masculine shirt. This was the photographer Mary Steen. "Did you see I have your portrait in my shop window?" Mary Steen asked Eva. "I shall soon be getting orders from your admirers."

Maj had said to Nik upstairs, "I suppose we should go and not just hang about waiting for Eva to take notice of us," but as soon as she was away from Eva she wanted to return. What would it be like, Nik thought, to be so enamored of a person that you gasped like a fish when you were out of their waters?

"You don't have to worry about me," said Nik, impatiently. "You can go back upstairs to Eva."

"Aunt Marie would never forgive me if I let you go roaming off by yourself."

"I wouldn't go *roaming* off by myself," said Nik. "I'd walk up Strøget to Kongens Nytorv, where we've been half a dozen times, and then take the horse tram up Bredgade to Østerbrogade. Aunt Marie and Uncle are gone all afternoon. Westberg will let me in and no one will be the wiser if you get home by five o'clock. You've said yourself that I look at least eighteen, and I'm tall and strong enough to fight off any would-be abductors."

"Well . . . if you promise not to tell Mama or Aunt Marie . . ." Maj smiled. "Oh Nik, it's just that I want to hear what everyone is saying about the speech. She talked so well, didn't she?"

"I know," said Nik. "Now go ahead, while everyone is still there."

Nik began walking up Strøget with a determined step, just in case her sister was watching, but after a block or two she thought it safe enough to duck into a side street in the direction of Nikolaj Plads. Flooded with relief and excitement at being alone at last, she felt like running but forced herself to a purposeful and ladylike pace. She glanced in at one or two shops around the dark red brick church and found a ring she thought Mama would like and some English tobacco for Papa. Just across from the church was a shop selling pens, papers, and artists' supplies. In the bow windows of the shop were displays of artists' easels and paintboxes.

"You must learn to see," Miss Mundt had said. But Nik also had to learn about the materials to make art. The smell inside the shop was like that of the ladies' studio—linseed oil and turpentine—but there were also other smells she recognized from the general store in Selde: sawdust and charcoal and glue sizing. And the round-shouldered man standing at the dark counter with cabinets behind him reminded her so much of Mr. Svendsen that she felt right at home.

"May I help you, miss?"

"I had thought to buy some pencils," she said, "and perhaps a sketching pad or two."

From under the counter he pulled out a selection of drawing instruments and sketchbooks. She chose several soft-lead pencils, an India rubber for erasing, and a small sketchbook. But her eyes were drawn to the glass bottles of powdered and flaked pure color in the wooden cabinets. The nearest memory she had of such concentrated color was of waving fields of yellow rapeseed in summer. If you walked straight into one of those fields you smelled the slightly bitter color of the yellow and almost blinded yourself, it was so like the sun. That was the color of the warm yellow powder in the glass bottles. It made her want to taste it.

"Most artists now buy their oils in tubes, but some painters still prepare their own colors, miss. That's why we have the bottles of pure pigment. I sell lapis lazuli by the ounce and the artist grinds it in a mortar and mixes it with linseed oil."

"But where do these colors come from?"

"Some pigments come from stones, like lapis or viridian. Some colors originally come from metals, changed through a chemical process. Lead white. Cadmium yellow or red. Some are plant-based, like madder blossoms, which make the loveliest rose. Most colors these days are permanent, meaning they don't fade. Some pigments, especially the watercolors, are more delicate. They're sometimes called fugitive colors. Some yellows are particularly prone to fading."

"Fugitive," she repeated, memorizing the word.

"Are you an art student, miss? Are you looking to buy paints?"

"No, not an art student. Not really. I mean, not yet. I hope someday soon to study art. I would like to buy some paints though, to . . . look at them properly. To get to know them . . . I don't really know where to start." She would have liked to take a bottle of the yellow pigment home with her to Selde and put it on the windowsill of her bedroom.

He nodded as if he knew exactly what she meant. "We have a new shipment of watercolor paints from England. The Winsor & Newton line is popular with people who paint outdoors and who travel. They come in boxes that are quite portable, in tubes or pans."

From under the counter the clerk pulled out two flat wooden boxes and opened one. Inside were twenty-four cunning little lead tubes with paper labels. "For watercolors, the color men grind up the powders and mix them with glycerine so that when they're wetted, the colors flow onto the paper."

Nik bent over them, trying to read the English names: Cerulean Blue, French Ultramarine, Cadmium Yellow, Viridian, Rose Madder.

The clerk opened the other box. Here were small squares, dried up like color fossils.

He dampened a brush on the counter and rubbed on a cake, then stroked a line of French Ultramarine across the first page of Nik's new sketchbook. How rich it was and concentrated.

It wasn't that Nik had never seen watercolors before. She'd watched Mette Bohm dip her brush into small bowls of watery color and fill in green leaves and blue sky in a pen-and-ink drawing. But Mette was tidy and careful with her colors. The green was leafy, the brown was earthy, and the blue was always thin. Mette had no Cobalt Violet in her palette, no Venetian Red, no Prussian Blue.

Nik remembered looking at the sky with Emilie Mundt, and the stone facing of the building across the street, and trying to identify the colors she saw with boring words like yellowish. If you knew all these pigments by name you could look at the world differently. You could say: the sky is Cerulean and Payne's Grey and the building across the street Burnt Ochre with a touch of Rose Madder. You could do more than call out the colors of a landscape; you could make that landscape again, on a white canvas, with a brush and a palette of paints.

Nik bought the Winsor & Newton box with the tubes of paint and two sable brushes, along with the pencils and sketchbook. The clerk wrapped her purchases beautifully; Mr. Svendsen could not have done it better.

She walked quickly the few blocks to Kongens Nytorv and began to cross it in the direction of the Academy of Art. What if she *could* study here someday, not too far in the future? Her mind was busy with a picture of herself in a studio surrounded by other girls when something made her stop.

In the middle of the square, right at the statue, was a figure she recognized from the rainy afternoon at Café à Porta. It was Victoria Benedictsson, dressed in black like a widow, but without a hat or veil. With a cane in one hand she was marching around and around the statue of the King on his horse. Nik wanted to go up to her, but was afraid. The lady's expression was so remote; her eyes were dark but hot, like coals. She was muttering nervously under her breath. In the summer sunshine she looked like a crooked old crow.

Nik hadn't yet gotten around to reading *Money*, but she remembered all the talk of it last summer. *Money*'s heroine Selma had wanted to attend art school in Stockholm, but had allowed herself to be married off to a fat old squire. Then, instead of using her new fortune to hire an art teacher, she spent the rest of the novel brooding until she finally decided to go to Germany and study to become a physical therapist. A physical therapist instead of an artist. To Carl's mind that was the real tragedy of the novel. But Victoria Benedictsson herself was no failure. She'd become an author whom everyone read and talked about.

If Nik had been Eva, she would have gone up and taken the

lady firmly by the arm and brought her back to Leopold's Hotel. But Nik was only fifteen. She remembered the scene in the café, the beseeching look on Victoria Benedictsson's face as she stood before Georg Brandes, the degradation of her scrambling fall to the floor. There was something morbid and self-willed about the lady that frightened Nik. Why did she stay here in Copenhagen to be mistreated by a man who didn't love her? Could such a love drive you mad? Why hadn't she allowed Selma to go to art school and become an artist?

Nik clutched her parcel of art supplies and headed across the square in the direction of the Academy of Art, but found it closed for the summer. Instead she walked up Bredgade and turned off into Sankt Annæ Plads, where tourist bureaus, ticket agencies, cheap hotels, and rooming houses had sprung up for Denmark's emigrants. Soon she could see an enormous steamship, three times bigger than anything on the Limfjord, tied up at the wharf at Larsen's Plads. The hull was all of iron, with a broad main deck fitted all around with a high railing. Three tall masts, in case the steam engines failed. Eight lifeboats on deck and several steam winches that were in the process of hauling up crates and trunks into the hold. Seamen swarmed all over the ship and up and down the gangplank, shouting cheerfully to each other.

On a posted schedule Nik read that the ship was the S/S *Geiser*; she had stopped in Copenhagen from the German port of Stettin to pick up passengers and would be embarking this evening for Christiania in Norway before crossing the Atlantic. Leaving Christiania on July 19, the *Geiser* would reach New York on August 3. Imagine that! Hardly two weeks to sail to America. Nik was caught up in the excitement. Clots of families in traveling clothes, children clutching beloved dolls and toys, started up the gangplank. Eager young lads and teenage girls hardly older than Nik stood on the wharf with valises and food hampers, stood there unafraid, seeing only possibilities. A man played the accordion. Several women snuffled into their shawls. Seagulls cried overhead.

Nik thought about Eva crossing the Atlantic back and forth on this very ship and hardly thinking anything about it. Nik wondered how she'd feel if Maj were going to America. And what about herself? To throw over this life, to go to another country where English was the language? Suddenly the adventure and the loss seemed real. She glimpsed a young woman with a baby in her arms. She seemed to be quite alone. A tremor went through Nik's body. What if, by some awful coincidence, this was Karen Marie, fleeing Denmark for a new life in America with Carl's son? But as Nik stood there watching her a man carting a toddler in one arm and holding a little girl by the hand came up and the five of them started up the gangplank.

Out in the harbor the blue water sparkled. It was the same as the line of color the clerk had brushed into her sketchbook: French Ultramarine.

Westberg, surprised, let her in. She thought the maid looked less well-turned-out than usual. The cap that usually sat so stiffly on her glossy auburn hair was askew and her narrow face was slightly flushed.

"Is your sister with you, miss?"

"Miss Maj will be along directly. I suppose Uncle and Aunt are still out."

"Yes, miss." Westberg paused slightly. "Mr. Carl is in the parlor."

Nik burst into the parlor where Carl was seated at the Bechstein. She was eager to show him her new purchases.

"Carl, I'm so glad to find you alone! You'll never guess what fun I've had. I've been out and about in Copenhagen on my own. I walked all the way here from Amagertorv."

"What's this, Nik?" he said, and if she hadn't known him so well, she would have almost thought he was displeased with her. "Alone in the city? You didn't have a falling out with Maj and run away, did you?"

"No, of course not. We went to hear Eva talk on the subject of women's rights in America and Maj wanted to stay on a little longer. I said I'd take a horse tram home but then I thought about how amusing it would be just to walk. It's not as far as I imagined it would be. *You* walk all over the city. Why shouldn't I? I thought you'd be interested to hear my adventures. I went by Larsen's Plads. I saw the ship, the *Geiser*, loading up to sail tonight for Christiania. Oh it was so exciting."

Now he got up and came towards her and made as if to take her in his arms.

She stepped back. "Should we ring Westberg and ask for coffee? Then I'll tell you all about the art store I found and about all the colors and paints and everything. Carl, there was the nicest man at the store. He treated me like a real artist."

"Don't ring. I don't want any coffee," he muttered, retreating. He plunged down on the sofa where Aunt Marie usually lay with her feet up. "Oh Nik," he said, "If you only knew how bottomlessly unhappy I've felt today."

"What's happened? Has anything happened?"

"No. But I had an awkward conversation with your uncle this morning before they left."

"Oh. Was it about money?" Often they had laughed about Uncle Jens and his niggardly ways, but today Carl seemed genuinely troubled. She perched beside him on the sofa. He had a different smell than usual, and his hair was disheveled.

"I want to be grateful. I *am* grateful. Last year when they sold up and moved from Odense to provide me with a home, I was astonished at their generosity. But these days I can't help but feel how they keep me on a leash. Of course I make a little money of my own teaching and substituting at Tivoli, but until I manage to get a place with the orchestra at the Royal Theater I have no steady income of my own. I'm horribly dependent. Yes, I have a room and food and a small allowance that is usually gone before the end of the month. But I feel like a trained monkey. That piano! Having bought it, Uncle Jens expects me to play it, and when I'm trying to compose he seats himself in the chair by the window. 'Don't mind me, old chap. Just go ahead and make whatever sounds you like.' But after an hour, he'll say, 'Can't we have a little Beethoven for a change?' Or your aunt will come in and start talking to me, because it looks like I'm doing nothing but staring at the piano keys! How the devil I'm going to polish the finale to this wretched suite I have no idea."

What a black mood he was in. Nik felt her joy fade. He put his head in his hands and then raised it again to stare despondently at her.

"I invent music lessons so I have a reason to leave the house, but then Uncle Jens says, 'With so many music lessons you must have extra money. It's a question of saving, my boy!' In reality what I do is go to the Conservatory and beg to use a piano there to bang out variations of the finale. Or I visit my old teacher Orla Rosenhof and work with him on a composition. Or I go to the Rosenbergs and play trios with Margrethe and Vilhelm. I'm not earning money, Nik!"

He moved closer to her and grabbed at her hands. Too hard.

"But in future, you'll make money," she said. "I have faith in you. And you must be so pleased, to have the Suite for Strings being performed." She was thinking of him playing trios with Margrethe and Vilhelm. Had he escaped to the Rosenbergs during Nik's visit? When he said he had pupils, was he fibbing then? He must have fibbed.

"Yes, and then what? After Tivoli has played it once, then what?" Carl interrupted. "What I really need is time abroad to study and learn from other composers and musicians. I need to hear more concerts and orchestras. Uncle Jens could so easily send me to Germany for six months, if he wanted. But he doesn't want to lose his grip on me. As for your aunt—she used to be so lovely to me. Now she treats me like a servant. 'Fetch me my shawl, Carl. Read to me.'"

"Carl, please!" she said. "They have done so much for you!" She pulled her hands away and put them behind her back.

"Don't let's quarrel, Nik. I didn't mean to sound so angry," Carl said. "Don't be disapproving, my darling girl. Of all people you must not be disapproving. I couldn't bear it! Come, sit on my lap. Tell me about your adventures. Show me what's in that parcel. Is it a present—for me?"

But she felt rattled now and uneasy. She didn't want to sit on his lap. What if Westberg came in? He hadn't heard anything she'd said about the art store, or Larsen's Plads. He thought her precious new paints and brushes and sketchbooks were a present. For him! He was talking about playing music with Margrethe. He was talking about going to Germany for six months. What else did he do and think that she knew nothing about?

"Will you excuse me for a moment?" she said, getting up and hugging her parcel to her. "I should wash my face and rest a little. I'm *très fatiguée*, as Aunt would say."

He had that grimace of frustration she'd come to find so irritating, as if she were depriving him of something that was rightfully his. But he stopped trying to grab her hands and allowed her to slip away without even trying to kiss her for once. She didn't come back into the parlor until she heard her aunt and uncle return an hour later, and by that time he was gone, having left a note that he would be dining at the Rosenbergs.

That night the bedroom felt particularly hot and muggy to Nik. She said to her sister, "I don't care, I want to open the window. The maids open it during the day, so we know that the sashes move."

For once Maj didn't oppose her. "I'm quite warm too," she admitted. She sat up in bed reading the latest issue of *What We Want*.

Nik raised the window and stuck her head out. The breeze felt so good on her skin that she hung outside for a minute or two, until she heard footsteps below in the street and remembered she was in her nightgown. But she was still restless. She lit a candle and walked around the room, staring at the framed photographs of the Demant family. There was Aunt Marie in her youth. Her half smile showed two dimples in a much thinner face. What had made her marry a miserly bachelor sixteen years her senior? It could only have been money. He was old, but she herself had been almost past her prime, at twenty-five when he proposed. With their father dead, all the Demant children had had to make their way in the world as best they could. Only Mama, the youngest girl, had been allowed to marry for love.

"I saw Victoria Benedictsson at Kongens Nytorv today," she said. "She was walking around the statue, muttering to herself. When I was on the way to the horse tram," she added, getting back into bed but sitting up.

Maj put down the newspaper. "Eva has knocked on her door at the hotel several times. Once or twice Mrs. Benedictsson invited her in. She always tells Eva the same story: she's planning to leave in the next day or two for Stockholm. But she doesn't leave for Stockholm." Maj's voice lowered. "Eva invited her to come hear her lecture today but she didn't come. Once, when Eva knocked, Georg Brandes was there and they were drinking brandy. At ten in the morning. And I'll tell you something else, Nik, but only if you promise never ever to tell Aunt Marie."

"I promise."

"Last night, as Eva was getting ready for bed and was just wearing her wrapper, there was a knock at the door. She thought it was Ingeborg, the maid, bringing her hot water. But it was Georg Brandes! And he wanted to talk about Mrs. Benedictsson and her 'sad situation' to Eva, because Eva seemed so sympathetic. But all the time he was looking at Eva in her wrapper."

"Oh!"

"Eva closed the door on him and locked it and even put a chair against it. But she told me today she now feels a little uneasy being there in the hotel by herself. She . . . asked me if I might consider staying with her for a night or two, just for company."

"At Leopold's Hotel? You know Aunt would never allow that."

"It's a perfectly safe place, at least during the day. Eva likes it there. And you know Eva and I have been roommates at college. We've spent many nights together in the same room. In fact, it feels unnatural to be separated."

Jealousy jabbed Nik: Maj was *her* sister, not Eva's. Yet it was so clear this visit that Maj preferred Eva's company all day, and now even wanted to move into the hotel with her. Trying not to sound too childish, Nik said, "But soon you'll both be back in Odense and you can spend all the time you want together."

Maj said nothing for a moment. Out the window were the night-time sounds of Copenhagen: carriage wheels and the clop of hooves from Østerbrogade a block away, and occasional footsteps and bursts of talk in the street below.

"Eva is thinking of not going back to Odense, at least not to study. She wouldn't graduate from the seminary next spring with me in that case."

"But why not?"

"She says she sees more of a future for herself in America. Her father wants to buy a house in Brooklyn. He has more work in the Swedish community than he could have imagined. Her mother is quite happy and one of her brothers is planning to attend Yale University. Eva says she could study English and find a teaching job. She wants to work with immigrant girls just arriving from Scandinavia."

Maj paused. "She plans to make a decision soon about her future. Just imagine, she asked me if I'd like to return with her if and when she sails back to New York. At least just for a visit to see if I like it and to meet her family. You heard her today, she *loves* America. She says it's everything Denmark is not—freshly minted, democratic, exciting, free of our old superstitions and ways. She makes it sound appealing, don't you think?"

"Maj, you can't be serious. How can you think of sailing off to Brooklyn! What if you never returned?"

Nik expected her sister to say that yes, it was an impossible notion, not to be considered. After all, she was a serious student and had long planned to graduate from Odense Seminary next spring. Nik sat down next to her sister on the bed and looked accusingly at her.

"They'll have you at home," Maj said. "And it's not that I really live in Selde anymore. I've been gone since I was fourteen, and once I begin teaching I won't come home to Selde except for visits. They'll have you," she repeated.

Nik burst out, "But I don't want to live in Selde my whole life. Why would you think that I want to live in Selde forever? I have my own dreams, thank you very much."

Maj hesitated. "I know you do, of course you do. We all do. My dream is to be useful. To teach children. And . . . to be with Eva."

"Then we must persuade her to stay in Denmark," decided Nik. "At least to finish her degree in Odense. Then, if you both want to, you can go to America. In a year, everybody will be more used to the idea. As much as we could get used to losing you to Brooklyn."

Maj wrapped an arm around Nik. "Dear Nik, do you really think so?" They stayed like this for a while, then Maj said, in a kind voice, "And your dreams, Nik? What are your dreams, tell me. Not to go to the Rocky Mountains anymore?"

"Perhaps I'll move to Copenhagen in the next year or two and study art with the Misses Mundt and Luplau, and then attend the Academy of Art. And Carl and I . . . I suppose we will marry."

"That won't happen for a long time." Maj's tone was cautious, but there was something in it that infuriated Nik.

"Not that long. I can wait. Anyway, you met Frederik when you were eighteen. You almost got engaged."

"Carl is only at the beginning of his career as a musician. How can he support a wife? Frederik was much different. He was already a lieutenant in the Army and was going into business with his uncle. With Carl you'd both have to be dependent on Uncle Jens and Aunt Marie for years. Do you imagine they would fund your art education and take care of you? Perhaps they will, ask them! Meanwhile you and Carl would have to live here, yes, in this very bedroom perhaps, with Aunt Marie just across the hall. Would you like that?"

"Why do you always have to be so mean?" Nik jerked away from her sister. "You always make things sound so hopeless."

"Someone must talk sense to you, Nik. Carl is the most charming fellow in the world. He's talented, he's sociable, he's passionate and warm. But you can't rely on him. At least not yet. Someday, perhaps, he'll settle down."

"What do you mean, settle down?"

"Learned self-control. Nik, don't forget about Karen Marie. That was only last year. Can you trust him not to do the same thing again? And even if Aunt Marie has taken care of things with Karen Marie and the baby, what about Carl's responsibility? He's a father. As far as I can tell, he's pretending to everyone it never happened. Do you trust him? Can you trust him?"

"Karen Marie was a one-time mistake. He'd been drinking champagne and she invited him in. She was just as guilty. She took advantage of him to get him into her bed. Why is the baby his responsibility? And why did you tell Eva all about it?"

"I tell Eva everything."

"Now Eva thinks I'm awful for wanting to marry Carl. Well I don't care what she thinks. I don't care what anyone thinks. Especially you."

Maj was silent a moment, and then she said softly, "Let me ask you again, Nik. Do you trust him? Do you trust him around other girls?"

And before she could answer "Yes, of course," indignantly, the memory of Westberg's cap when she let Nik into the apartment today flashed into her mind.

Turned just slightly, as if someone had pushed it away while kissing her.

20.

UNCLE JENS LOVED COMBUSTION ENGINES AND ANYTHING with working parts. He loved boilers, valves, and pistons. He admired steam pumps, pressure gauges, and smoke boxes; he paid close attention to gear shafts, cogs, belts, and coupling rods. If there was something you could grasp, like a crank or fly wheel or a hand brake or lever of any sort, he would test it. He was a man of the steam age, with all its iron and copper and boiling mist and coal-fired smoke. Naturally there was no place he was happier at the Nordic Exposition than Machine Land.

In Machine Land an enormous windmill spun above a diving pool, where a man with a big, round, goggle-eyed metal helmet submerged himself for minutes at a time. Part of the vast exhibition hall was given over to the machines that had something to do with the Exposition—dynamos to create electricity, a steam-fired press where flyers and labels and signs were printed. Elsewhere, for display, were locomotive and steamship engines, screw propellers, stamp presses, industrial sewing machines, even a small chocolate factory with eleven separate machines that smelled of chocolate, not grease and oil. The ceilings of this hall were tremendously high and the din of the machines echoed all around.

Uncle Jens's father had made his fortune in trade, but had died when Uncle Jens was still a young man. Uncle Jens had been forced to take on family and business responsibilities sooner than he might have; it was to his credit that he'd become a wealthy and respected member of society who supported his widowed mother and four sisters. He had not been able to enjoy his bachelor years. He had deferred marriage until his forties, and had denied himself many other pleasures during that time, until denying had become a way of life. But in his sixties his passions for music and steam engines grew.

He envied his brother-in-law Hans Demant. "Think how you could walk among the factory hands, all day long, listening to the rattle and chuff of steam engines!" Perhaps it was that money quietly moving around in banks did not have quite the satisfying sound as money produced with a lot of noise. At any rate, if left to himself, Uncle Jens would spend every day in Machine Land, having long discussions with the engineers and technicians about combustion points and buffers. It was why Aunt Marie didn't like to come to the Exposition with him alone. It was also what made him an excellent companion for Nik and Carl. All they had to do was lead him into one of the aisles of the machine hall and up to a man stoking a steam-driven stamping press, for instance, and Uncle Jens was a lost man for the afternoon.

Although in theory Uncle Jens believed his youngest niece should be chaperoned at all times once she left the apartment, today he'd allowed himself to be convinced that Nik was quite safe in the Exposition grounds with Carl. What was the harm, indeed, if the two of them visited the art exhibit at the French Pavilion or even had an ice together at one of the cafés? They would all meet again for dinner. Carl was playing in the Tivoli Orchestra that evening and Uncle Jens and Nik would of course be in the audience.

Aunt Marie had been suffering from intermittent and unlocalized aches and pains, and Maj had angelically agreed to stay home with her all day. This was in return for permission to attend an evening party of ladies at the home of Ragnhild Goldschmidt. Astonishingly, Aunt Marie had even agreed that Maj could spend the night at Leopold's Hotel with Eva. Carl had assured Aunt Marie that Leopold's was refinement itself; even so, Uncle Jens stopped by the hotel. After a brief look around and a conversation with Mr. Leopold, Uncle Jens agreed to the plan. Still, Aunt Marie found it odd that Maj would prefer a hotel bed over the comfortable one at Slagelsegade. "I don't mind telling you, Emilie, that it would be a very good thing if Miss Sandström considered returning to America to live with her parents. She is too Swedish and free and big to fit in well here in Denmark. Many of her ideas are far too advanced. Young ladies alone in hotels!"

The first thing Carl and Nik did when they found themselves on their own was to eat a large sausage each, washed down by cider, followed by a great slice of cake. Afterwards they strolled through the grounds of the Exposition until they came to the French Pavilion, one of the grandest of the exhibition halls. Here there were no aisles, just palms and a high glass ceiling and two hundred sculptures mingled among the three hundred paintings.

"Admirable, but old-fashioned," Carl pronounced the art on the walls. "Imagine, not a single painting by Monet or Renoir. Only Édouard Manet at his dullest, and then canvas after canvas of Salon-approved historical scenes without a speck of life in them, framed in gold leaf. The cream of the Académie des Beaux-Arts, or the dregs, depending on your point of view. The French clearly didn't see fit to ship off the Impressionists to represent their country. *C'est dommage!*"

What could he find to criticize in these paintings? Nik couldn't imagine having the ability to blend colors so beautifully and render clothing and furniture so exactly, never mind the astonishing verisimilitude of the horses and dogs. Even the nude women—pearly-skinned or fleshy pink—looked real, embarrassingly so. These paintings were so finely executed that she was dying of envy. Could she paint two regiments of soldiers facing each other on the field of battle? Oh, not in a hundred years. Could she paint a woman crouching by the seashore, the froth of the wave as perfectly rendered as the flowing hair over her shoulders and breasts? Nik could barely draw a flower or a pebble on the sand.

Carl liked the sculptures much better. They were nearer to music, he said. "Classic in form but full of movement and life." He came near to one marble maiden lolling on her side, her big thighs tensed, her buttocks silky hard. "Sculpture has no story. It's just the beauty of the human body and soul. And that's what music should be too. Essence and variation, shape and pleasure in the shape, and sublime emotions that can't quite be named. Why don't you become a sculptress, Nik? Wouldn't that suit us both? I'd compose all day and you'd tease out the essence of human longing and grandeur from a block of stone."

Nik looked at the frozen marble bodies lounging on pedestals all around. They were so white they looked like they had been left out in the snow.

"I'd rather work with color," she said, remembering the studio on Gammel Kongevej. "I'd rather smell paint and turpentine and make a mess on my palette. But, oh, what a long way I have to go."

Then he was a kind teacher, the way only Carl could be, and led her from painting to painting, pointing out things he'd noticed and making her notice them too: a color combination, the juxtaposition of shadow and light, the expression in a man's eyes. She hung on his arm, and imagined a life with him. Sometimes, like now, it didn't seem so far off.

"You know so much about these paintings," she said finally, full of admiration.

"Vilhelm and Margrethe and I all came here in May, when the Exposition first opened," said Carl. "Margrethe was the one who noticed the lack of Impressionists. She's been to Paris, of course, and attended a Salon des Refusés half a dozen years ago with her father."

Of course Margrethe had been to Paris. Of course.

They hired a boat out on the lake and Carl paddled and sang a song about ducks and geese. It was a warm day, and humid. The sweetish smell of the lily-padded lake edged by willows gave Nik a languid, heavy sensation. She lay back in the boat, looking at Carl. He wore a straw hat with a ribbon and his expression was by turns dreamy and comic. She knew him well enough to understand that somewhere deep inside he was anxious about drowning, about saying good-bye to her in less than a week, about their future, about how on earth he would make a living as a musician. But he continued to sing his funny song about the geese and ducks and blow her kisses from time to time as they paddled safely around the little lake.

After boating, they watched an "acrobatic potpourri" by the Wartenberg family at the island pavilion. The five Wartenbergs were circus performers of astonishing flexibility: three boys, an older man, and a girl. The males wore blue and red tights and striped undershirts that showed their muscular arms. The girl had on a striped black and red dress and tights; she looked about thirteen or fourteen and her black hair was pinned tightly back. She wore color on her lips and two red circles on her cheeks. The boys stood on each other's shoulders, threw the girl back and forth, put her on top of a pyramid.

All their antics were accompanied by drum rolls and frantic tapping by another member of the family, a man who may have been their father. He had a hunchback, which he disguised as well as he could in a jacket with epaulets. His arms were strong; his hands very fast on the drums. Carl watched him as much as he watched the young acrobats.

Like spiders, the boys now climbed up ladders to the high wire strung between two sturdy poles and walked back and forth. They were more thrilling and heroic than Jacques the Acrobat, who relied on Nik's hand for balance. Then the girl came up the ladder and was tossed a parasol. The drum rolls were a soft, thrumming ostinato to her deliberately timid steps around the platform, her slow unfurling of the parasol. She put one slipper on the tautly strung line as if uncertain that it would hold her and pulled it back. Some in the crowd yelled encouragement but others fell silent. The boys had bounced so quickly back and forth across that you didn't notice they had no net. But with the girl you saw how badly she would hurt herself were she to trip and fall.

Nik said, "I have to cover my eyes," but she didn't. She wanted to see the girl *not* fall, but make it to the other side.

The drum rolls increased in intensity. One boy stood on either platform; another was stationed below. The girl started across, hesitant, then a little more confident, then hesitant again as she stopped midway, and then, with a rush, she was confident again and stepped quickly, twirling the parasol, over to the opposite platform, where one of the boys reached out his hand to her.

Afterwards Nik and Carl were hungry again and ate some toffee and Carl drank a glass of beer. They watched ten minutes of a pantomime at the outdoors stage of the Chinese theater. They looked at stalls with trinkets for sale. Finally they went into the labyrinth. The maze was a box hedge, trimmed square at the top, just too high to see over and rather thick. Children's voices could be heard coming closer and then farther away. Other sweethearts had sought out the maze as well, so at times there were the sounds of kisses and sighs along with the birdsong. Nik, succumbing to the green privacy, let Carl hold her hand. As always she was struck by the dry firmness of his palm and his beautiful fingers.

"What are you thinking, my darling?"

"I was thinking about being fifteen," she admitted. "And how strange it would seem if an older girl, like Eva or someone, went around with a boy eight years younger, like Joachim or someone. Everybody would be shocked."

"Too much is made of age," Carl sighed, "Equality of taste and of spirit is far more important. I would be happy to marry someone older than me if I loved her . . . Not that you need worry about that."

"What about that married woman you said you flirted with in Odense?"

Carl started slightly. "You mean Gerda, who waltzed off with the leather merchant? But Gerda was my age. That's where age is important, my dearest Nik. *She* was old enough to marry but *I* was not. The man should be able to provide for a family. That's why we see marriages of such age disparity in society."

What had Carl said last summer? A married woman with too much time on her hands? Now he couldn't even remember the woman's name. If it wasn't Gerda, who was it?

"If one of the two is older," Nik said, "the younger one is always the pupil!"

"I've been taught a thing or two by women older than me," Carl laughed. "Why shouldn't I teach you? And besides, you are perfectly wise and clear-headed at fifteen. When I was your age I hardly had a reasonable thought in my head. I'd spent a year among the men at the regiment but I still went home every chance I could and let Mama coddle me. Yes, you're more suited to teach and guide *me*. Haven't you brought me through the labyrinth to the center?"

"I don't think this is the center. This is probably a dead end."

"All the better, because the center will be crowded." He took her in his arms. "I prefer to think of it as a cozy corner of the maze." He brought his face close to hers and would have kissed her, but out of perversity she turned her lips away.

"Oh Nik, Nik, why do you always resist me now? You weren't that way in Selde last summer."

"I don't know," she said. "I do care for you. I care so much! It's just that . . . everything is more confusing here."

"Confusing, how?"

"We're at Uncle and Aunt's. We're watched!"

"No one is watching us now."

"Still, everybody disapproves. Aunt, Eva, Maj. I feel that! And, I see your life. Your friends. I feel so . . . I can't help but feel so wrong for you sometimes."

"How could you think that? Who could be better?"

"Margrethe Rosenberg," she said, trying to keep her voice from quivering. "Always it's Margrethe and her exquisitely cultured taste. She's your friend, she's a musician, she's been to Paris, she's a year or two older than you! She's perfect. Why don't you marry her? Why don't you ask her again? She might say yes this time."

"Nik, look at me." He held her chin in his hand and regarded her with dismay. "Is this why you've been so distant? Because of Margrethe? Did she say something to you when we visited them?"

"You were the one who told me that you proposed to her." Tears gathered behind her eyes.

"But that was ages ago. And she wisely said no. She knew, better than I did, that she was wrong for me and that she didn't love me that way."

"She's so clever though. She can play the violin."

"Now you're just being silly. Haven't I told you a hundred times that you're the one I care for? And yet you don't believe me. Why is that?"

"Because . . . because I think you care easily for girls. And they like you back. Of course they do. Everyone thinks you're wonderful. Women anyway."

"There are two kinds of women who like me," said Carl after a moment. He no longer looked serious, but almost amused. "The first sort have something motherly in their affection. They see me as a wayward boy, like your aunt. Margrethe is like that too, though she's my age. She and Vilhelm brought me home with them the first week of classes at the Conservatory. They knew I was living in rented lodgings and had no friends in the city, that I'd been little more than an Army bandsman in Odense with impossible dreams of composing music. The Rosenbergs took me in, fed me, and educated me. Margrethe in particular took it upon herself to turn me into a more cultivated person."

"What other sort of girls like you?"

"The frivolous coquettes who like to flirt with anybody," said Carl, smiling and stroking her cheek. "But you don't need to worry about them either. For you're different, Nik. You don't flirt and you don't mother. You're my dearest friend, but also I hope, someday not too far in the future, my wife."

This time when he kissed her she did not resist at all. But it seemed as if the labyrinth was crowded with them, the mothers, the aunts, the Gerdas, the Margrethes, and the frivolous coquettes. How could she completely believe him, even though she longed to?

~

They went afterwards to the outdoor restaurant to wait for Uncle Jens, and each had a tall glass of cool ale. This was more than Nik usually drank and it made her gay and took away the worry and heaviness she'd been feeling. Carl looked unusually handsome to her and it was easy to pretend that they were regular sweethearts, just like the other couples around them, and to look into each other's eyes. His were so blue sometimes, such a warm lively blue, unlike her sister's, which went from cool to hot with little in between.

He took a program for the events of July 21, 1888, at Tivoli from the ground where someone had dropped it. It was on newsprint, in a large format with ads for corsets, hats, hairdressers, shirt stores, shoes, and pianos.

"Let's take a look at the orchestra schedule," he said. "It's a long and full evening for me. Even more for the audience if they manage to sit through the entire program. At seven we have the usual crowd-pleasers, the *Queen Olga March* and lots of mazurkas and polkas for the masses, all directed with great gusto by Mr. Baldouin Dahl. Then at eight thirty the real music. Beethoven's Sixth, but first—how appropriate!—Mendelssohn's *Wedding March*."

She thought he was joking, and snatched the program. He'd only told her they were playing the *Pastoral Symphony* tonight. But there it stood, Mendelssohn's *Wedding March*.

"Carl, you devil!"

"I had nothing to do with the choice, dear Nik. But you must admit, it is a great stroke of luck. Shall I ask the maestro to dedicate it to us?"

"You wouldn't dare. Remember, Uncle Jens will be right next to me."

"Dreaming of the marriage of valves and pistons, no doubt."

She took the program and folded it. "I'll keep this for my

strongbox," she said. "Uncle Jens found me a metal chest for important documents."

"Oh Nik, you amuse me! What will you put in it?"

"Your letters, of course."

"My silly letters—do you think they're worth saving?"

"Don't you save mine?"

He looked taken aback. "Certainly. Certainly I do. Now what else will you keep in this strongbox of yours?"

"Important things. Photographs. Things like this program. It will be a sort of fossil record. And then when I'm old, I'll take everything out and look at it, and I'll laugh at how young and foolish I was."

"Do you really think about getting old? I don't. I don't want to be an old man and sit in a chair and drool on my clothes." He made a hideous drooling face.

"You can't decide how old you're going to be when you die," said Nik. "Anymore than you can decide if you're going to be born a girl or a boy or how rich or how poor. It's one of those things that are out of your hands."

"Listen to the wise Miss Hansen! Do you imagine yourself an old lady of eighty, lying in bed listening to the birds outside?"

"I would like to live to be eighty," she said. "To see what happens in the world. Just imagine, we could live long into the twentieth century. What a strange thought. Will everything be electrified then? Will we still have war? I don't think so. And I think that women will have the same rights as men."

"You make the future sound bright," he said. "Too bad we'll be so ancient when all these good things happen."

"Our grandchildren will enjoy them."

"Ah yes, our grandchildren," he said. "But if you are eighty, just think, I'll be eighty-eight. I suppose that the age difference between us won't matter so much then."

They began laughing. No one made Nik as happy as Carl, and no one ever could.

Later that evening, when Nik sat next to Uncle Jens in the concert hall and listened to Carl play Mendelssohn's *Wedding March*, she couldn't help giggling a little. After the piece ended, Uncle Jens said, "I'm glad you still think the idea of marriage is amusing, my dear."

Uncle Jens and Carl had discussed Beethoven's *Pastoral Symphony* over their meal; it was a favorite of theirs both and they undertook to explain to Nik what she must listen for: how certain musical phrases in the first movement, the allegro, would be repeated by different instruments. These phrases would be variations on the essential themes running through the symphony. The variations would grow more and more elaborate through the symphony.

"You can always enjoy the music for what it is, of course," Uncle Jens had said, "but how much more valuable it is when you can recollect the measures played earlier in the symphony and see how the variations in tempo and volume and the changes of key are layered over and through the essential structure of the music."

"Here's all you need to know," said Carl, scribbling on her program. "There are five movements—think of it as five chapters in a novel. The first chapter is called, 'Awakening of Cheerful Feelings upon Arrival in the Country.' Just how I felt when I came to Selde and was so glad to be in the countryside again and away from all the noise and smoke of Copenhagen. In Chapter Two we have a delightful babbling brook; in Chapter Three we sway in time to a cheerful country dance. Then comes the excitement in Chapter Four, a summer thunderstorm that scatters the dancers, and finally a long last chapter: shepherds giving thanks. I never play the Sixth but I recall my childhood summers."

After Mendelssohn, the audience rustled in anticipation of the *Pastoral*. A general burst of coughing had flared just before Maestro Dahl walked back on stage, but as soon as he raised his baton, silence. Uncle Jens closed his eyes; his hands were firmly planted on his knees, his feet rooted to the ground. Nik had noticed before her uncle's ability to still himself body and soul when listening to music. Unlike most people he didn't sway a little to the rhythm or tap his feet or his fingers, however danceable the music. The notes went through his ears right into his head, which must be more spacious than it looked, the gears and cogs all locked away in a closet to give room for the notes to flow around the empty space and to make patterns. His breathing slowed; the most emotion he showed was occasionally the faintest of smiles.

Nik tried to close her eyes too. She tried to hear what Uncle Jens heard, what Carl might hear as he played his violin: the repeated short motifs of the gay dance-like first movement. Seven motifs, Carl had said. She counted three. It was like grasping at leaves as they fell from a tree in autumn. It wasn't hard to hear the short repeated melody on the flute that was taken up in turn by the clarinet, oboes, and strings; she captured it and held it close. But there was something else beneath that little melody, a thrumming, a bodily sense of being rushed along, a leaf on the stream.

Her body felt pleasurably swollen with the music, as if the notes were falling on her skin like rain. Her own childhood returned: Running, when she used to run every day, and was allowed to run. The delicious speed of pumping her legs and seeing the leafy world slide past her eyes. How the music brought back her childhood in Selde, now vanished. Running up a hill to see what was on the other side. Stopping only to look around a moment and then running down again.

The second movement, "Scene by the Brook," was flowing and stately. She heard the clarinet and oboe and flute. They were the birds: the cuckoo, the quail, the nightingale. She caught her leaf again, it turned into a nightingale, a series of flying notes, and then she lost it. She preferred it free rather than in her hands. There it was again, but different, the clarinet had taken it up. She opened her eyes. How well they were all playing tonight and so many instruments, so many! The stage was abundant with music, you could almost see a cloud forming over the players and then, like a fountain or a waterfall, flowing into the audience.

Then came the third movement, the country dancing, strings

and horns, everything much faster than the first two movements. The woman next to Nik tapped her toe unconsciously. Nik breathed more quickly and marveled that Uncle Jens didn't feel the urge to dance. Nik squeezed her hands together and kept her eyes fixed on Carl's moving arm. The mystery of it all, of playing in time, in unison with the other string players, of keeping one eye on the music stand, one eye on the conductor, and yet listening intently the whole time; no, she couldn't fathom how Carl, how any of them managed it. But then, Carl had been playing country dances since he was a boy. She thought about his father, Niels the Painter, and how Carl always spoke of him so lovingly. He took Carl and his brother often to accompany him at one dance or another around the district. Once he let Carl play a polka of his own devising, full of syncopation. "Too many notes," his father said. "No one will ever be able to dance to this!"

His father should be here to see Carl play at Tivoli. Why couldn't Uncle Jens and Aunt Marie bring Carl's parents for a visit to Copenhagen? Were they ashamed of them? Carl wasn't ashamed, was he? And then it came to her that he very well might be. Carl was the only one who had, by some miracle, escaped the life that had been laid out for him, through luck and his own talent. Thanks to her aunt and uncle, Carl wore a tuxedo tonight and lived in a grand apartment in Østerbro.

A pause, a few raindrop-like plinks, and then a crash. She jumped an inch in her seat. The woman next to her also started, and then smiled at Nik, but Uncle Jens never moved a muscle. She'd been far away, not listening with any understanding to the music, when the thunderclap of drums and cymbals woke her. It was the symphony's storm, which blew and rained hard before subsiding, into the last movement, "The Shepherds' Song, Happy and Thankful Feelings after the Storm." Now came the strings again, pulsing together.

She saw again the girl acrobat with black hair from earlier today, twirling her parasol as she stood in the middle of the wire high over their heads. Remembered how she didn't fall, how she ran those last few feet over to the second platform, where the boy was holding out his hands to her.

When the symphony was over Uncle Jens roused himself from his stillness to clap like mad. They waited for Carl outside the Tivoli Concert Hall, lit up like a fairytale palace. The humid evening was soft as feathers around her neck and shoulders and the music from "The Shepherds' Song" continued to sound in her ears.

In the hackney cab traveling away from the hall, she and her uncle sat opposite Carl. Nik rested her head back against the seat. She and Carl couldn't even touch hands here, but that only seemed to increase how close they were, knees almost touching. His kisses from earlier today were imprinted on her neck and lips and made her press her lips together a little, remembering the feel of the scratchy green box hedge at her back. Her skin still felt swollen from the music and her limbs were terribly heavy, especially her legs, in a seductive way, as if she were on the verge of falling asleep.

Outside the open cab window was the city. She caught glimpses of carriages and barouches, of ladies in satin capes and men with top hats in the other cab windows. All that was ugly and hurried about Copenhagen in the daylight disappeared now in blue shadows. The dusty, dank smells of the day had become something else at eleven o'clock. The night air was sweet and the trees, half illuminated by the golden lamps, rustled in the wind.

Uncle Jens and Carl were talking about the extended coda of the *Pastoral Symphony*, its length and complexity and how it took up the themes again and kept playing with them. The last movement didn't want to end, as if Beethoven had been reluctant to part with it.

"I long to begin a symphony," said Carl. "I don't play something like this tonight without thinking what I could do, how I would shape it and explore it. I have music in my head all the time."

"But you will compose symphonies," said Uncle Jens. "Of course you will."

Would it really be so awful to live with Uncle Jens and Aunt Marie for the first year or two, until Carl found a regular position as a violinist? Or perhaps, if they married, Uncle Jens would see fit to set them up in their own small apartment? That seemed quite likely. An apartment with a piano and a painting studio. Or perhaps she and Carl could travel for a year if he were to be awarded a state travel stipend. As a married woman she could do what she liked; she would have more freedom, not less. She could walk around in Paris by herself to all the museums and galleries. She could walk around in Rome and Florence. That luxurious emotion, from the last movement of the symphony, of being on the verge of life, swept her again.

Another carriage pulled up to Slagelsegade at almost the same time and a servant riding on top alighted to open the door.

"The Siamese princes," Carl whispered to Nik.

What a disappointment they were! She had expected colorful brocades and embroidered silk caps and slippers. Instead they were in evening dress. One was rather plump and the other had a wispy beard. Their eyes were only the slightest bit slanted, their skin pale gold under the gas lamps.

But they smiled and bowed to Uncle Jens quite graciously and Nik dropped a little curtsy.

"Your Excellencies," said Uncle Jens, lifting his hat and allowing the princes and their servant to enter the apartment building first.

"*God morgen!*" they said in unison, and went inside.

21.

NIK WOKE FEELING AS IF AN IRON WERE PRESSING DOWN on her body below the waist. Blood dripped down her legs and had made a mess of the sheets and her nightgown. She was cramping so badly that sweat poured from her armpits and her hair and forehead were damp.

She had to ring for Westberg but then asked her to call Hanne, rather than confide in Westberg herself.

Hanne brought back rags and warm water and went out again to call Aunt Marie away from the breakfast table.

"My dear," said her aunt briskly. "Don't worry a thing about the sheets. It has happened to all of us at one time or another. A young girl's system takes a while to sort itself out sometimes."

"It's early," Nik said, as her aunt helped her to a chair and Hanne began changing the bed. She began to sniffle. "Now my visit is spoiled."

"Emilie, you've been wearing yourself out. Anyone can see that. But Copenhagen is not going anywhere. There will be other visits. Many other visits, I hope." Aunt Marie helped Nik out of her bloodstained nightgown and began to bathe her with a cloth and warm soapy water, as if Nik were a child. It was comforting that her aunt seemed more the practical, calm woman Nik remembered from childhood than the frivolous and dissatisfied matron of recent years.

"Now Hanne is going to bring you breakfast in bed and I'll come in again shortly to visit with you before we go to church. Maj will be back soon and she can read to you. It's just as well she was away last night, I suppose. You'll have a lovely quiet day and by tomorrow you'll be feeling much better."

Uncle Jens and Aunt Marie always went to church at eleven, and although Carl tried to find ways to escape it, he often ended up going too. But today Nik knew that Carl had left early. He was to play at a private concert at an estate some miles from the city and he and his musician friends had gone by train. She was glad he wasn't here to ask her aunt questions or wish to come in to visit her. She wouldn't want him to see her in a heap of bloody bedclothes. How did married women manage?

She had tea and toast spread with English marmalade and a boiled egg. Hanne brought her a hot water bottle wrapped in soft flannel. The velvet drapes remained closed, though it was possible to see a line of dull yellow light around the edges; somehow the drapes themselves seemed of a different texture with daylight outside, softer and plusher, like green moss on stones. Nik watched the light for some time; the cramps were painful but eventually she fell back asleep.

She wasn't sure what time it was when she heard voices from somewhere in the apartment, louder than usual. One of them was surely Maj's. Groggy, she pulled herself up to a sitting position as her sister burst into the room, followed by Eva. Pale and agitated in the green gloom of the room, they had the appearance of noisy ghosts.

"Oh Emilie," said Eva. "The most terrible accident has taken place."

A wave of nausea swept Nik: Papa? Mama?

Carl.

Maj pulled at Eva's arm. "Wait, dearest. Let's have some light in here at least. Hanne said you were feeling poorly this morning." She shoved open the drapes. Eva's face was revealed to be not pale at all, but shiny red with weeping. Maj was like a little statue, still and shocked.

"What happened?" said Nik. It felt like her voice came from somewhere else than her mouth.

"At Leopold's Hotel. Late last night . . . Ingeborg found her this morning . . . Oh my God, my God," said Eva, throwing herself on the bed next to Nik.

"It was Victoria Benedictsson," said Maj. "She took her life last night. Three doors down from us. Just three rooms away."

"I knocked on her door," moaned Eva, with her swollen face in a pillow. "I tried to show her some friendliness. But I didn't try hard enough. I didn't push her to leave Copenhagen. When Ingeborg told me of her unhappiness with Georg Brandes, I treated it as a *weakness* of hers, something she would get over eventually. I watched her suffer and never held out a hand, not so much as a little finger. *None* of us helped her."

"You tried, my dearest, you tried to help her," said Maj. She stroked Eva's back. "When a woman is as unhappy as that . . ."

"But to slit her throat. While we slept so peacefully just down the corridor. No, it can't be. It can't be."

For the first two days after Victoria Benedictsson's suicide, the newspapers printed nothing. Only *Politiken*, whose editor was Edvard Brandes, ran a small obituary, saying that Mrs. Benedictsson had died after a long illness. Then the story burst out on July 24, in *Aftenbladet* and *Social Demokraten* under the headline "Swedish Woman Writer Has Cut Her Throat."

They reported that sometime after midnight on July 22, the well-known Swedish author Victoria Benedictsson, thirty-eight years old, undressed herself and took a mirror in her left hand and a barber's razor in her right. She made four finger-long cuts at the side of her neck. She was found in the morning by the maid Ingeborg Larsen, who immediately alerted the hotel's owner, Mr. Leopold. He called the doctor and the police. He also sent messages to two of Mrs. Benedictsson's friends, Axel Lundgård and Georg Brandes. She had left letters for both of them.

The two newspapers questioned why the obituary in *Politiken* claimed Victoria Benedictsson's death had been the result of a long illness. Was there some attempt by the Brandes brothers to keep the cause of death unknown? Mrs. Benedictsson's friend Axel Lundgård wrote to the newspapers the next day and said that *he* hadn't tried to keep it quiet.

According to Maj and Eva, who had it directly from Ingeborg Larsen, Mr. Axel Lundgård and Mr. Georg Brandes had arrived at Leopold's Hotel at almost the same time, along with the police. Mr. Lundgård read his letter immediately and showed it to the police. Mr. Brandes, on the other hand, refused to hand over his letter. He said it was of no importance, it was merely raving. Mr. Lundgård had then raised his voice to Mr. Brandes, saying that Victoria had expected only Axel to be called to the hotel. Victoria had asked in her letter to Axel that he make a copy of her letter to Brandes before giving it to him. She feared that Brandes would destroy it and she wanted Axel to read it and know what Brandes had done to her. Brandes raised his voice in return. She was a madwoman. She was not going to ruin him. He could be blamed for nothing.

It was when the police were carrying the corpse on a stretcher down the corridor that Maj and Eva had opened the door. Victoria Benedictsson's body was covered with a blood-smeared sheet; her long dark hair hung in strands out from under one end. Mr. Leopold tried to get the girls to go back into their room, but Eva made him tell her the basic facts. He begged the girls not to say anything yet to their friends or the press.

They'd gone into Victoria Benedictsson's room and found poor Ingeborg Larsen, charged by Mr. Leopold with the task of cleaning the bed and rug immediately, down on her hands and knees with a basin of hot water and carbolic soap, scrubbing and sobbing. Victoria had removed her nightgown before slitting her throat, so that Ingeborg wouldn't have the task of taking off her blood-soaked clothing.

Georg Brandes had gone, taking his letter with him, while Axel Lundgård, in shock, sat in Mrs. Benedictsson's armchair by the window, beginning to read her journals as Ingeborg scrubbed the carpet. Victoria Benedictsson had left her literary estate to Mr. Lundgård and given him the task of organizing her manuscripts and journals for publication.

Eva said she could not continue at Leopold's Hotel after that, and Aunt Marie, when she returned from church that morning, said of course not. Eva's trunk was sent for and she was installed in the room Maj and Nik had shared, for the two distraught girls declared they could not be separated. Nik was moved into a small dark room next to Hanne. Overnight, the tragedy changed life at Slagelsegade. Aunt Marie, originally welcoming, turned against Eva by the next day. She said that the sight of Eva weeping in her drawing room was distressing. Who was Mrs. Benedictsson to Miss Sandström, when it came down to it? The Swedish writer was, by all accounts, a dissolute woman. This according to Aunt Marie's French milliner, who stopped by on Monday to deliver two round black and white striped hatboxes with the *chapeaux* she'd created for Nik and Maj.

Mademoiselle Clarisse had been living long enough in Copenhagen to recall all manner of Parisian depravity and to have renounced it for more sober Lutheran living while still enjoying good gossip. According to her, Mrs. Benedictsson had left an elderly and respectable husband in Sweden—a retired postmaster—to travel to Copenhagen and live in a hotel and receive visits from a married man, the Jewish Darwinist and reprobate Georg Brandes. They had been intimate and he had scorned her. Hence the shocking suicide, right *there*, in Leopold's Hotel.

It didn't matter that Eva had immediately left the hotel. The damage was done, and the fact that Aunt Marie's own niece had been forced to be a witness to such depravity was all Miss Sandström's doing. Aunt Marie would never have allowed Maj to stay in the hotel had she known what sorts of things went on there. The fact that Miss Sandström moaned and wept because she hadn't visited the Swedish writer *more* often in her hotel room was a sign that Eva had already started down the road to depravity herself. Who knew what Miss Sandström had been up to at Leopold's Hotel, what visitors *she* had received in the anonymous secrecy of a public hotel?

Aunt Marie did not accuse Eva directly, but she poured out her anger and misgivings to Nik when she came in to kiss her niece good-night. Nik was helpless to respond; she knew nothing about Mrs. Benedictsson's life, only that she had been terribly unhappy and in love with a man who didn't love her back.

As for Carl, he seemed to find Eva's presence in the drawing room quite disturbing. For Eva was a young woman impossible to ignore. Perhaps she didn't mean to strike poses that drew every eye or declaim in her strong velvety voice that Mr. Brandes should be arrested and charged with murder, but the effect was the same as if she were acting a part in a Wagnerian opera at Bayreuth, said Carl.

"How the devil am I going to compose with all this drama going on?" he complained to Nik when he caught her in the hallway sometime on Monday. He'd tried to embrace her, but she'd stopped him. She was still bleeding heavily and cramping; she feared he could smell her menses. She did not want to be crushed to his chest and have her mouth smeared open with kisses. The thought made her feel ill.

Carl had been gone much of that Sunday. He'd returned home around four in the afternoon, flushed with champagne and cash in his pocket, to the awful news about Leopold's Hotel and to Eva's tragic presence.

"Many people are blaming Georg Brandes," Carl said. "But that seems to me quite unfair. The woman was obviously not well. You saw her that afternoon in the Café à Porta. She was soaking wet, just stood there, and then fell to the floor, making a scene. She seemed quite mad. Brandes can't be held responsible for her feelings about him. He has supported women's emancipation—and that's made him a target for women of all kinds, who see in him someone who *understands* them. Is it a man's fault that women run after him and make themselves miserable?"

"Yes," said Nik. "If he encourages a woman without loving her." She pulled away from him. "If he *torments* her. Yes, he's responsible."

"Nik, my darling," he said impatiently. "Don't be angry with me. What are Brandes and his dead mistress to *us*? We have so little time as it is; we mustn't quarrel. You and Maj leave on Friday. Will we ever have more than a moment together in a dim hallway, looking over our shoulders to make sure we're not watched? We were so happy on Saturday, don't you remember?"

She did remember; she remembered the kisses, the promises, and the magic of Beethoven's symphony, how happy she'd felt and how right. But everything now seemed chaotic and confusing, and Carl was part of that confusion. Would he never stop pushing and pulling at her, as if she were a rag doll he could amuse himself with?

On the Tuesday that the newspapers came out with the truth about Victoria Benedictsson's death, Aunt Marie suggested to Uncle Jens that they visit the Exposition together and spend a few hours in Machine Land—which showed how desperate she had become to get away from Slagelsegade, she who usually preferred to lie on the sofa with her feet up, eating cakes.

It was about three in the afternoon, stuffy in the apartment. Nik was in her uncle's usual chair by the window reading a book, while Maj sat with some sewing on her aunt's sofa. They had not said anything for some time. Carl had departed an hour ago. He wasn't in the orchestra at Tivoli tonight but was to attend a chamber music concert with Margrethe and Vilhelm Rosenberg and afterwards take coffee with them in a café.

He'd begged Nik to come, but she had declined on grounds of tiredness. This was true, but Carl took it as a snub, even though

Aunt Marie gave him an embarrassingly meaningful look and said, "This young lady needs to *rest* for a day or two."

Eva had gone out earlier to meet friends of her parents at the Hotel d'Angleterre, a long-standing date to which Maj could not be invited at the last minute. But she should have been back some time ago and it was clear Maj was growing agitated.

Finally Eva arrived, all in a rush as usual. She dropped dramatically on the sofa next to Maj and took both her hands and kissed her. In the last day or two Eva seemed to have become more physically attached to Maj. There was hardly a moment when she wasn't putting an arm around her friend's waist and drawing her close or stroking her arm or hair. She seemed to need the closeness and reassurance. Maj's own touches were more tentative but they grew in frequency as well. Watching them from her chair by the window, Nik thought that if Carl were to come into a room and stroke her like that, her aunt and uncle would be shocked.

"I wasn't able to stop myself," she said to Maj. "Even though I never *imagined* darkening the doorstep of Leopold's Hotel ever *again*. But I was so *near* the place; it *drew* me like a magnet. During the meal I began to think there might be letters for me at the hotel. I couldn't recall if I'd reminded the desk clerk to send them on to Slagelsegade."

In the front hall she met Ingeborg Larsen, who told her that Mr. Axel Lundgård was upstairs. He had, in fact, been there often the last two days, organizing the journals and other papers that Mrs. Benedictsson had left.

Eva decided to go upstairs and talk with him. She found him red-eyed, with a fat journal on his lap, in Victoria Benedictsson's old chair. There was still a stain on the carpet, which would have to be replaced, and the room still smelled of carbolic soap. Mr. Lundgård rose when she came in and gave her the armchair, while he pulled forward a smaller one. This was how Victoria and Brandes used to sit, Mr. Lundgård said. Victoria liked to be by the window, he said, so that the light came from behind her and helped soften her face and shield her expression. But Brandes always pulled his chair close to hers so that he could stare into her eyes and caress her face, if he felt so inclined that day.

"That's what Mr. Lundgård said. It was all in the journals. He told me he knew there was something between Victoria and Brandes—of course he knew—but he had thought it was a simple case of infatuation, a kind of *hero* worship on her part, borne of loneliness in her marriage. It wasn't that her husband was such a bad man, just that he was an ordinary man, and much older than Victoria. All her life she had longed for love, yet the *physical* side of love repulsed her. She had only known the demands of her husband. What she wanted was an intelligent man who would talk with her and hold her in his arms."

Eva spoke in a low voice as if Maj were her only listener, but Nik in her chair nearby could not help but hear.

"Yes, she made herself *available*, you could say. She leapt at the chance to know the great Brandes, but she didn't mean to begin an affair. Brandes was the one to pursue *her*, in his cold, calculating way. He decided he would seduce her, even though he so clearly did not find her attractive and told her so. For months she resisted, but she kept being drawn back to Copenhagen, and staying for weeks longer than she meant to, just for the chance of seeing his face and hearing his voice, of that *promise* of intimacy with someone who *understood* her as a writer and a woman. Days would go by and he'd never come, and then he'd arrive when she least expected it, in evening dress, on his way to a dinner somewhere or a concert, and he would press his case and pour out his heart. How *miserable* he was in his marriage, how Victoria understood him, why must she play with him, couldn't she see that he wanted her? But all he wanted was to break and bend her, said Mr. Lundgård. Once he had managed to seduce her, he tried to shame her with the knowledge he now had about her. She was not so *superior* after all; she was merely a woman, like any other woman, who could be conquered and then *discarded*."

"Why didn't she leave?" said Maj. "Why stay to be tormented like that? Why write it all down in a journal and kill yourself?"

"Do you know, Victoria was not the *first* woman to kill herself after Brandes seduced her? The first one was Adda Ravnkilde, five years ago. Mr. Lundgård said she was also a writer, but very young. She came from the provinces to make a name for herself in the literary world. She had prepared for her career by reading Darwin and John Stuart Mill and she'd written several short novels. She brought them herself to the *great* Brandes to look at and became his pupil. She was only twenty-one. Immediately after one of his lectures, she went home, drank poison, and slit her wrists. And then Brandes had the *gall* to see to having her first novel published and to write an introduction praising her. Oh, it's all too *horribly morbid*. What kind of a country is Denmark that such things can happen?"

Victoria Benedictsson's funeral was set for Thursday, July 26. Her body had been taken on Sunday to the morgue at St. Johanne's Foundation, where all suicides, accidental deaths, victims of murders, and people who had died without identification were conveyed until they could be buried. It was Mr. Lundgård who told Eva about the funeral, and that it was to be small. The husband, from whom Mrs. Benedictsson was long estranged, was not coming, nor her daughter, but a stepdaughter would be there representing the family.

"We must go to the funeral tomorrow," said Eva to Maj and Nik. It was Wednesday morning and Nik had come into the bedroom Eva and Maj were sharing to finish dressing. Westberg had begun to pack some of their things away in the large trunks to be sent on to the station early Friday morning.

Eva and Maj were still in bed, sitting up, drinking coffee, and engaged in some kind of debate which they did not halt just because Nik came in. Eva's straw-blond hair fell abundant and remarkably straight and long over her embroidered cotton gown, while Maj looked as she often did in the morning, milky and damp, tousled curls pulled out of her braid and her eyes, without spectacles, a little blurry. She did not have on her nightgown but had already half dressed in her corset and chemise, and then had evidently gotten back into bed with an India shawl over her shoulders.

In spite of herself, Nik kept glancing at them in the mirror. They seemed so close, so . . . wound into each other . . . It reminded her in a strange way of Mama and Papa, back when she'd been a little girl and had occasionally snuggled in bed with them—not in the morning, because they were such early risers, but before they went to sleep when they sometimes read by candlelight.

"I don't know, Eva," said Maj. "If it's just the family—and it's being held at a chapel next to the *morgue*—do you think it's the right thing to do? It's not as though we actually knew her well."

"It's not a private event," said Eva. "Victoria Benedictsson should have people there who admire her writing and what she accomplished. I fear no one will come besides Axel Lundgård and her stepdaughter and Ingeborg Larsen. Many women are furious at Brandes and the rumors that he and his brother tried to bury the story. But they're also furious at Victoria. How *could* an intelligent woman, a *feminist*, destroy herself for the love of such a horrid man? Ragnhild Goldschmidt told me that no one from the Danish Women's League plans to attend the funeral. That makes it even more important for us to be there. You must come, Maj."

"I'll go with you," said Maj. "Of course I will. Her novel *Money* meant so much to me." She looked at her sister, who had hastily dressed and had her hand on the door knob. "And Nik as well. We don't want you to go alone."

"But we have a whole day planned with Uncle Jens and Aunt Marie and Carl," said Nik. "We leave for Selde on Friday, and tomorrow at noon we're to go on our picnic. Aunt Marie has been planning it for ages."

"The service is early in the morning, at nine," said Eva. "And the chapel at St. Johanne's Foundation is only a ten-minute walk from here. So we can go and bear witness and then you can go off to have your wonderful day with your uncle and aunt."

"But you'll come with us on the picnic, won't you, Eva?" Maj's voice rose with a little panic. "Aunt Marie said you were welcome. You won't leave me to spend the entire day with them? Our last day in Copenhagen?"

"I don't know how I'll feel after the funeral," said Eva, tossing her straight hair and looking tragic. "To be honest, everything seems difficult at the moment. And with your aunt so set against me, I don't know if I *could* spend the whole day with her."

"Dearest, Aunt Marie certainly is not set against you. She said you are welcome to stay on here after Nik and I leave on Friday. But of course I'm still hoping that you'll come with us to Selde, or at least as far as Odense. Don't you want to see all our friends there? You've often said you did."

"Oh, I thought everything in Copenhagen would be so much better," said Eva, beginning to tear up. "When I arrived in June I was so *glad* to be here, to share what I could of America, to see you again. I didn't think I'd miss my parents so much or that Denmark would seem so *backwards* and narrow and hateful to me. I can't imagine staying on in the city after you're gone, Maj. But how can I follow you to Selde? What if your parents are like your aunt and uncle?"

"They're not at all like Aunt Marie. They'll make you welcome. We can swim and go riding. Ask Nik—it's so lovely there by the Limfjord in August." She stroked Eva's shoulder, then added quickly, "But of course if you wish to stay for a while in Odense, that would be wonderful too. I won't go on to Selde then, I'll stay there with you. Who knows, perhaps you'll even decide that you like dear old Odense just a little again and want to get your teaching degree there."

"I won't change my mind about going to America, Maj," said Eva slowly. "I feel so tired of Denmark. I want to be *gone*. There's a ship leaving August 1. The sister ship to the *Geiser*, the *Thingvalla*.

I have half a mind to go to the steamship office today and buy a ticket."

"So soon? You want to leave Denmark so *soon*? Without even going to Odense and seeing some of our friends?" Now it was Maj who looked suddenly teary. "Don't you care anything about me?"

That morning Maj and Eva went out for a walk and some last-minute shopping. Their absence was a relief to Aunt Marie, who could barely stand up, she claimed, after the exertions of the Exposition yesterday.

"It will take a complete day of quiet and rest to summon my strength for tomorrow," she said to Carl and Nik from the sofa. "However, I am determined to take my family out for one last glorious view of Copenhagen. It may be raining, very likely it *will* be raining, but that should not deter us. We will huddle together in our carriage and be merry in spite of the weather." Where exactly they were to go was not much of a surprise; Aunt Marie had been talking about the quaint fishing village of Dragør for some time. It had an excellent restaurant if the weather was too damp for a picnic.

Nik was being given her last piano lesson by Carl. A simple Bach fugue, transposed to the piano. He wanted her to pay more attention to holding a note, to not lifting her finger too quickly from the keyboard. He had tried to explain the reason for this several times, but it didn't come easily to Nik. How long should a note carry before it was replaced by a new note? How could she keep up the forward motion, the tempo, if she had to remember the notes she'd just played? Carl heard all the notes, it seemed, the ones still echoing and the ones to come; they were all connected in his composer's mind.

"Do you remember what I used to tell you in Selde, Nik, when we first met and I began to teach you—notes by themselves are just bits and pieces. But if you hum them or sing them, they run together. They continue. All compositions are organized with just this in mind: creating a continuous surface of sound—the notes and the sounds between the notes. The melody. Sometimes this melody rushes forward, like dancing at a ball or riding a horse, and sometimes the melody seems to almost stop, suspended. The main thing you must remember when playing is that the melodic line takes place in time. You mustn't break the melody. I often think to myself when trying to compose that if my music is to have any value at all, it is because I try to create a certain current, a certain motion forward. If that's broken, none of it is any good. Do you understand?"

"I don't understand tempo with my head, not like you," she said softly. "But perhaps I can understand it with my body. I *feel* how time rushes forward and slows or seems to stop. I can feel that in music too."

"Of course you do, my darling girl. Oh Nik," he whispered. "Isn't there a way we can have just one or two hours together somehow, just the two of us? Things seem to have gone so wrong since last Saturday. And now we'll soon be parted, for as long as another year." He put his hand on her left hand, which was resting on the keyboard. "Play the bass again, Nik," he said in a normal voice, and then, as she obediently moved her fingers under his, he whispered, "I can bear the separation if I feel that we're of one mind and heart when you go. But to part on awkward terms, no! That is too hard-hearted of you."

"I am not hard-hearted," she protested in a whisper. "I don't want to part with you on bad terms. I don't want to part with you at all."

"Then help me find a way to be with you, my darling. Just an hour before you leave. But an hour alone somewhere."

"What are the dear children whispering about, Jens?" called Aunt Marie to her husband, who sat dozing in his armchair by the window with a newspaper in front of him.

"Eh?" Uncle Jens jerked fully awake. "Can we not hear some real music instead of this infernal droning bass fugue? I feel like I'm in church."

Nik and Carl couldn't help laughing. After that, the piano lesson went much better. Carl praised her mightily and stroked her fingers as she played. She had promised, under her breath, to meet him outside St. Johanne's chapel tomorrow at half past nine in the morning.

Carl went out at eleven to teach a music lesson, and sometime later Eva and Maj returned with unexpected news.

They had been to the offices of the Thingvalla Line near Larsen's Plads and had purchased tickets on the *Thingvalla*, set to leave Copenhagen on August 1 for Christiania and then New York. Not just a one-way ticket for Eva, but a ticket as well for Maj. Also one-way. Maj's face when she told her aunt and uncle was a mix of defiant and supplicating. She knew how much distress she would cause her family—but the ticket was bought, the deed was done. She had long been of a mind to see America and this was a perfect opportunity. They would be each other's traveling companions and Maj would stay with Eva's family in Brooklyn.

"The ticket may be bought, young lady," said Aunt Marie, "but the deed is hardly done, and in fact it will *not* be done. I couldn't face your mother if I let you sail off to America just because you feel like it today."

"Maj, where would you get the money to pay for a steamship ticket?" asked Uncle Jens.

"I . . . I am in Eva's debt. And I have thought about it for a long time, Aunt," said Maj. "Nik knows. She's heard me talking about America for weeks."

Nik didn't say anything. When was the decision made? In the short time before breakfast, or there, at the steamship office, standing in line? Maj was a stranger these days; she clung to Eva as if Eva were her family and all the rest of them were mere hindrances to her happiness.

"Dear friends," said Eva persuasively. "Blame me if you will for what must seem like a rash act, yet, please, don't be hasty in your judgment. There is *no* financial outlay for your niece in this, Mr. Nielsen. I drew funds from my father's bank account for this purpose. He won't mind at all, he has plenty. I think, on the contrary, that both my parents would feel greatly *relieved* to know that I'm traveling with a companion and that I am homeward bound. I know this is terribly sudden, but you must think of this as a great *opportunity* for your niece."

Uncle Jens interrupted Aunt Marie, who had roused herself from the sofa and was actually standing, so great was her anger. "Marie, sit down a moment. Let's have a rational discussion. Maj," he turned to her. "This is not something to be undertaken lightly, young lady. This is a foreign country we're talking about. It's the Atlantic Ocean, not the Kattegat. You can't just go there and return in a month. If you leave now you'll miss the whole of the school year and won't be certified as a teacher. Your parents have given up a great deal to make sure you have an education. Don't you think you owe them the respect of finishing at Odense Seminary?"

"Yes, Uncle," said Maj, and, "I know, Uncle."

"Isn't it possible that you could wait and go next year? It's not the idea of America that is in itself so disturbing, not at all. Why, in fact, as you know, I have stock in the Thingvalla Line and have long been curious about taking the steamship across the ocean and back. Perhaps next year you and I could go together. How about that, eh? Can you wait just a year for your old uncle?"

"But, Uncle, I want to go now," said Maj, in a small but firm voice. "I have decided."

"A young girl can't just *decide* things," said Aunt Marie with violence. "And Jens, what is this about a trip to America next year? You will certainly do no such thing. Why are you encouraging Maj and making this sound at all reasonable?"

"But Mrs. Nielsen," said Eva, "If you would only consider the matter quietly— "

"Consider it quietly? Consider telegraphing my sister in Selde and saying I have allowed her daughter to sail off across the ocean with an unknown Swedish girl, to who knows what sorts of temptations and depravities?"

Eva stood with her mouth slightly open, half ready to laugh and half to cry. But what had Eva been thinking, wondered Nik. That she could simply sweep Maj up in her plans and carry her off to America just because they were *friends*?

"We already have the tickets," Eva said finally. "I can assure you, women traveling by steamship is perfectly *respectable*. We have a cabin of our own in first class."

"I don't care if you bought a hundred tickets," snapped Aunt Marie. "You can march right back and return them, Miss Sandström. You've done our family no favor by buying Maj a ticket. As if we couldn't afford a mere steamship ticket. You've created dissension from the moment you arrived here. Look at Maj, she's steaming like a loaf of bread."

"Am I to live my own life?" Maj interrupted. "And if I am, then when does that begin? I thought it would have begun long before this. Yet here I am, twenty years old, and still my relatives are telling me what to do. I won't have it. I'm going."

"We will send a telegram to your father, my dear," said Uncle Jens. "I will endeavor as best I can to explain your point of view. But I hope you'll agree that we must abide by his decision. You are not a child, but until you marry you are still legally under your father's care. Will you allow me to send him a telegram? If he says yes, then you may go to America with my blessing."

Aunt Marie still looked mightily put out, but even she had to accept that it was ultimately Papa who had the right to decide his daughter's future.

22.

BY EARLY THURSDAY, NO TELEGRAM HAD YET ARRIVED from Papa. Eva, Maj, and Nik went out immediately after a breakfast that none of them really touched, without knowing what the day would bring. Maj told their uncle and aunt they were walking one last time around the lakes and would be back well in time for the departure to Dragør at noon. The packing for Selde was to continue while they were gone. Maj had tried to hold out her clothes from the big trunk, but Westberg, on instructions from Aunt Marie, continued folding. Carl wasn't up yet; he had played in the Tivoli Orchestra last night.

It was foggy and misting when they crossed busy Østerbrogade to Sortedam Dossering. Out in the lake, the white swans were barely visible. Eva and Maj walked arm in arm under a single large umbrella, and Nik trailed behind. She wasn't sure why they wanted her along or what she should expect. She had been to only one other significant funeral before, her grandmother's, and that was remote in time. Her father had looked somber; her mother had wept. The pastor said a few words, and then Grandmother went into the churchyard earth and was buried and everyone wore black for a while. Of course people were always dying in Selde and the surrounding district, but few of the dead were well-known to Nik.

Eva wore her blue striped skirt and bodice, with a black armband and a black ribbon around the rim of her hat. Maj had on her dark blue traveling dress and a black armband as well. The umbrella hid them from time to time, but she could hear the murmur of their voices: Eva's distraught; Maj's comforting.

Nik had always seen Eva as brave and confident. Unlike Maj, she was never quarrelsome or bad-tempered, but persuasive and encouraging. But now she wondered if Eva were the more fragile and excitable of the two, driven along by impulse as much as principle. Surely it was more reasonable to finish one's education in Odense. But Eva was willful—in the matter of America as in going to this funeral and dragging Maj and Nik with her.

Maj was a tugboat with a small steam engine, well-suited to small loads and most weathers. Eva was a private yacht in full sail, tacking this way and that, beautiful in the breeze. Her ship rode high in the water and had a shallow keel. In storms she was in danger of capsizing. But somehow this yacht had hold of her sister, and if Papa agreed, would sail off with her to New York and never bring her back.

St. Johanne's Foundation was a complex of brick buildings that took up an entire city block, with one side to Sortedam Dossering and the other facing Blegdamsvej. There was a hospital and a receiving ward for abandoned or ill-treated children, before they were sent to an orphanage or foster care. On the main door to the workhouse was a sign: "Poverty Is Not a Crime."

The three of them went into the small brick chapel and found fewer than ten people there already. A sober Axel Lundgård stood with the maid, Ingeborg Larsen, and a young woman who must have been Mrs. Benedictsson's stepdaughter, with her husband, who had come from Sweden for the service. Eva went immediately over to the group and shook everyone's hand before beginning to cry and spontaneously hugging the stepdaughter. The group all stood around the open casket, which was draped with black cloth and wreaths of white roses.

Maj and Nik hung back. It was not Maj's nature to show much outward grief, even if she had felt strongly about the death of Victoria Benedictsson, and Nik saw her sister was uncertain how to behave in this situation. Never in her life had Maj gone uninvited to the funeral of someone she didn't know personally. Yet it wouldn't have occurred to her either to refuse Eva's wish. Was that always the way it was? One of a pair bent and bowed?

"Eva was right," said Maj finally to Nik, under her breath. "No one from the Danish Women's League has come to pay their respects. They must feel, as I do, that Mrs. Benedictsson failed us in some way."

"How can a single unhappy woman fail an entire movement?" Nik kept her voice low too. They were still standing just inside the chapel door.

"Mrs. Benedictsson's suicide may have put a stop to her immediate suffering, but time would have done that as well. You can live through anything. Her self-murder only reinforces the notion that a woman, once shamed, doesn't have a life worth living. Eva finds it in her heart to pity the woman. I find it harder."

"But what's so shameful about being in love?" said Nik uncertainly. "Where is the shame to *her*? It's Dr. Brandes who should be ashamed of himself." She stopped abruptly. For the chapel door opened again, and Georg Brandes and a man who resembled him and must be his brother, Edvard, came inside, wearing tall hats, black frock coats, and armbands. Georg Brandes glanced briefly at Nik and Maj and lifted his hat mechanically. He recognized them, but must have wondered what they did here. His deep brown eyes met Nik's. She thought she'd never seen a person in so much pain.

The group around the casket stepped back to let the two come closer, but no one said a word to them, not even Axel Lundgård, who had been a friend. Eva turned her back on them with a furious look. It seemed astonishing to Nik that Georg Brandes would have the nerve to come to Mrs. Benedictsson's funeral, given that he was the reason she'd killed herself. He must be doing it for appearance's sake, and yet Nik saw his shoulders shudder violently as he looked into the casket and away. Nik did not want to go up and pay her respects to the dead woman. In a few minutes she would have to leave to meet Carl. She had not mentioned this yet to her sister.

The chapel smelled damp and cold. It had no organ and only

a blue and red stained glass window above the altar, which cast a faint purple haze over the lime-washed bare walls. A door to the side must connect with the morgue. Mrs. Benedictsson would have been lying there for four days among the suicides and murder victims. How could anyone look in the casket at her? How could Eva?

In his white ruff and black gown, the pastor came up to the altar and everyone seated themselves. There were no pews in this chapel, only rows of hard chairs, and Maj and Nik took a seat near the door. Eva came back to join them and clutched Maj's hand. She began to shake with emotion. "That *he* should have the bad taste to come to the service. *He* of all people."

"I admire you for all you did for her," whispered Maj, and she took Eva's hand. "Anyone can see you tried to help her." She said nothing about the Danish Women's League or her own true feelings. The pastor began to speak in flat voice about God and his infinite wisdom. There was to be no extolling of Mrs. Benedictsson's literary gifts or any pity for her death. The pastor must think the woman in Hell by now.

Nik hardly paid attention after the first few sentences. She was preoccupied by Georg Brandes, whose face she could see in profile. It was an intelligent face, with sensuous lips and a prominent nose, but it was dragged down now by misery. His dark hair waved up from the center part and she could see his eyebrows were the same glossy brown, like a stoat's. She feared him turning and looking at her; his gaze was too penetrating, too hypnotic. Once she'd seen an illustration of a turbaned Indian man in a loincloth sitting cross-legged on the ground and playing a flute while an enormous cobra uncoiled itself to almost a standing position in front of him. She had asked Papa if she could find such a figure, a Swami, for her toy circus; she'd been nine and perfectly serious, but he couldn't help laughing.

Georg Brandes made her think of that Swami, mesmerizing the cobra. She imagined Brandes staring into her eyes, and then crushing her to his lips. A wave of nausea and cramping passed through her body. Victoria Benedictsson's lips must be cold white now, like the roses on her casket. She had lost most of her blood through the gashes in the neck. What would it feel like to slash at your throat so methodically, with a mirror in front of you? To feel your life's blood drain out? Did she feel the vengeful satisfaction of finally punishing the man who had scorned her? Brandes could never have guessed she would kill herself and broadcast it to the world.

Why were men and women so different? Why did they want such different things and fear such different things? Why was it a woman's shame that a man took advantage of her weakness, if it was even weakness at all? Didn't a girl, a woman, have the same feelings as a man? Why shouldn't she act on them? But if she did, she was a fallen woman, she was a prostitute, she was an outcast. She was, as Brandes had said about Mrs. Benedictsson to Mr. Lundgård, a madwoman.

Georg Brandes was evil—he had sent his mistress to Hell and would follow her there, in spite of the fact that perhaps he didn't believe in the Lutheran Hell, being a Jew. And yet, how sorrowful he looked; she couldn't help pitying him. His shoulders hunched and his head drooped; his brother had to put an arm around him to comfort him.

The pastor went on, droning about God's will and human frailty, but Nik couldn't feel God's presence in the chapel. She only felt weak and rippled by cramps. Sometimes she had a last violent surge at the end of her menses that soaked her rags through. With a sudden movement she was out of her chair and opening the door to the outside, where she leaned her face against the brick of the chapel. It was raining harder now, but still in that soft summer way, white and foggy.

Maj came out to find her. She held Nik's umbrella over both of them. "Are you ill? What's wrong, Nik?"

"I couldn't breathe in there. And my cramps started up again. I'm bleeding. I can't go back. But I'm fine, you don't need to worry."

"I can't just leave you here." Maj showed no great eagerness to go inside again either. "I should take you back to Slagelsegade."

"Eva needs you. More than I do. Really, I'm fine. I don't really think I'm bleeding that much, it just felt like it for a minute. Maj—to be honest, I told Carl to meet me here. For one last walk. I've hardly been able to talk more than a few minutes with him for days and this will be the last time I'll see him for months, even a year! Please, please understand. We won't be long."

"But Uncle and Aunt . . . they'll be worried." Maj looked at her and then away. Nik could see she was thinking that this would give her time alone with Eva.

"Carl will think of something to tell them."

"All right," she said finally. "But if for some reason he doesn't arrive here soon, please come back inside. I don't want you wandering around outside the morgue and hospital. And if he does come, please walk back in the direction of Slagelsegade and don't dither about. I'm in enough trouble with Aunt as it is. I can't just misplace my sister too."

Nik nodded without agreeing and watched Maj slip through the door. She had no intention of waiting here. She was sure that Carl had overslept and would not find her here and she did not plan to ever go back inside that chapel again. She crossed the street to the park alongside the lake. She did not quite have her bearings, but she wasn't alarmed. She knew perfectly well that if she simply returned in the direction they'd come earlier she would find herself back at Slagelsegade. There would be no chance of seeing Carl alone—but it was his fault, not hers.

She began to follow a path between the trees. The umbrella shielded her from the rain and the lake was beautiful in the mist, with its ducks and cormorants. How refreshing to be on her own for once, out of the apartment and feeling the weather.

A man's voice at her shoulder in the rain startled her. He was saying something—what?

"How much to lie with you, girl?"

She lashed out blindly at him with her umbrella and shouted, "Leave me alone! Monster!" But as soon as he backed away—she could see his face clearly; he was more discomfited than alarmed and ready to try again—anger was replaced by fear. Everything was strange and white in the day-lit misty rain. She quickened her step. No one else was around. Nik began running along the path. She was almost at the far end of the lake, near Østerbrogade, when she saw him.

Carl. Walking hurriedly along the path with his light athletic step. He had no umbrella and his jacket was up to his ears, his spiky hair dripping. How dear his face was, how welcome. She called to him with a shaking but strong voice.

"Nik! My darling!" He dashed up to her. "Aunt Marie said she'd wake me for breakfast but she didn't, and I found I was late. I feared I wouldn't be able to see you alone for an instant, that I wouldn't be able to tell you how much I . . . Oh Nik," he said. "What are you doing here? You've been running. You're out of breath. I would have met you at the chapel. Maj shouldn't have allowed you to just leave."

And she was just as glad to see him, as relieved. She didn't tell him about the man who had hissed at her. She let him believe that Maj had in some way abandoned her. For she *had* been abandoned. Maj had not been a good sister to her; her friendship with Eva was too consuming. Nik was through with Eva, and it was comforting to be with Carl. She was no longer cramping; the pain and nausea seemed to have been scared out of her. She only felt cleansed and light.

"Shall we walk for a little?" asked Carl gently. "I have in mind to show you something."

Arm in arm under their umbrella, quite like proper sweethearts, they walked around the end of the lake and into a neighborhood of terraced houses, built in the English style, with small gardens to the back. Nothing in Copenhagen that Nik had seen looked quite like this village of short streets, lined with pale ochre brick houses, each with dormer rooms above the second story. Carl told her the quarter was called "Potato Rows," for the regularity of the streets and the color of the buildings. In the white rain, the lighted windows cast a glow into the street.

"Some families let out their dormer rooms to students and artists," said Carl, as they turned up Voldmeistergade. He put his arm around her waist. "I lived on this street, in one of those rooms, when I first came to Copenhagen from Odense. Imagine me, a boy of eighteen, with a little cash in my pocket from my generous patrons, living alone in a room at the top of this house, reading Plato and Shakespeare and playing my violin in the evenings, with a candle at the window and a bit of bread and cheese on the table that I shared with a resident mouse."

Carl had stopped in front of one of the houses and from under their umbrella they looked up to one of the lighted dormer windows.

"It's like a doll's house," said Nik. "I like to think of you up there with your violin and books."

"A musician friend of mine lives in the same room now," said Carl. "He lives there with his new wife. The quarters are a bit cramped, but they're happy." Carl's hand tightened on her waist. "The garret might not do for *us*, dear Nik. After Ibsen, perhaps we should be wary of living in a doll's house? But downstairs, wouldn't it be snug and comfy? You wouldn't rather live with your aunt and uncle at Slagelsegade?"

"I would rather live here," said Nik. "I think I could be happy here. We could be happy. Nora never had such a nice doll's house as this."

"You may think of it as a doll's house if you like. For me the rooms look just the right size. I never had much room growing up; I hardly know how all of my family squeezed into the little two-room cottage we rented. I remember we slept three or four to a bed. As I grew up the older boys went out to apprentice or abroad. The girls died of consumption. We were on poor relief—I don't think I've ever told you that." His arm tightened on hers. "We had so little money sometimes that Mother took us gleaning in the fields for sheaves of wheat. Finally my mother and father managed to get a larger cottage; that's the one I think of as home. But I only lived there about a year before I joined the regiment in Odense. Since then, dear Nik, I've had no real home. I've been in barracks or in rented rooms, at the mercy of my betters."

"No one is your better, Carl," Nik said quietly. "And you will always have a home with my family—and with me. Just think, when you come home from conducting one of your many symphonies at the Royal Theater, here I'll be, waiting for you."

He kissed her cheek, a soft, husbandly kiss. "At heart I'm the most domestic soul you could imagine. Once I have a wife and children, you'll see, I'll be perfectly content and won't go around complaining half as much as I do now, yearning for fame and fortune. There's nothing that would please me more than to come home from a concert and find my dearest Emilie waiting for me and a child or two sleeping soundly."

Two silhouettes crossed the lighted dormer window, like paper cut-outs against the gold, and for an instant Nik imagined that the figures were familiar, Nik and Carl, married, in their own home, two little figures playing house with tiny doll babies tucked up in their beds.

By luck, Carl and Nik walked into the apartment only five minutes after Maj and Eva had returned, and things were in such an uproar that their later arrival was hardly noticed. A telegram had finally come from Papa. It said in no uncertain terms that Maj did not have his blessing to travel to America and that they were expecting her in Selde in a few days. The message was curt, in the way of telegrams. If there had been any wavering, Maj might have gone ahead. Now she bowed her head and accepted it.

Eva burst into tears again and announced that she could not endure another day in Slagelsegade. She would pack her bags and move to Ragnhild Goldschmidt's for the duration of her stay in Copenhagen. She was leaving right now, no one should try to stop her. Maj said she would go with her, to get her settled. By this time Maj was crying too, not the abundant dramatic weeping of Eva but small painful tears.

Aunt Marie, in a horrid humor, said that in that case, if Maj wanted to spend the day with Miss Sandström, the excursion to Dragør was off, and she went into her bedroom and slammed the door. Uncle Jens gave Hanne instructions to cancel the hired carriage and unpack the picnic basket. Apologizing for his wife's bad manners to Eva, he said he nevertheless would ask Miss Sandström for the favor of giving him Maj's steamship ticket, which he would undertake to get reimbursed. As he was a stockholder in the company, there should be no problem. He would have the money deposited back into Mr. Sandström's account. Polite as he was, everyone understood that he meant to have no further surprises and did not quite trust Maj to follow her father's decision.

Opening her bag, Eva took the ticket out and gave it to him. She was calm and cold. "Come, Maj," she said. "Let's go immediately. I'll send for my things later. Mr. Nielsen, good-bye and thank you for your hospitality. Please *thank* your wife for her *kindness*. Carl, farewell. Emilie, good-bye for now and good luck. I expect to hear great things of you from your sister. And you are always welcome in Brooklyn!"

She embraced Nik, and for just an instant Nik felt such a strong sense of loss that it was as if Maj herself were leaving. Then the two girls were gone.

"A tragedy has been averted," said Uncle Jens, settling into his chair with the newspaper.

"And the diva has left the stage," said Carl, sitting at the Bechstein and beginning to play Mozart.

But Nik already missed Eva and stood by the window looking at Eva and Maj walking down the street, arms wrapped around each other as if they would never let go.

23.

THE FIRST MORNING NIK WAS BACK IN SELDE, IN HER own room, her own bed, she lay for a while without getting up. She'd lost the habit of rising at dawn, but she also wanted to savor the birdsong in the beech trees and the dry wooden creak of carts on the Skive road. She watched the rosy light on the yellow and white wallpaper and breathed in the cool morning air, sweet with hay, from her wide-open windows. The smell of yeasty cardamom rolls came up from the kitchen and she was surprised at how hungry she was.

Now that they were safely home, all that was difficult about the visit began to recede. Nik was left with some sense of triumph. She had made a momentous journey out into the world and had returned to the blanketing soft safety of home to tell about it.

Yesterday when they finally arrived, Mama sighed, "Sweet girls, how I've missed you. Yes, I know you have seen and done so much, but summer hasn't been summer here without you. Maj, my dearest, how glad we are to have you among us, where you belong."

Papa said, "Had enough of big-city living, have you, Nik?" and "Maj, you'll realize that it was all for the best to wait to make such a big decision. Finish your schooling and then we'll see. America is not going anywhere—that, we know." He folded her into his arms, trying to erase the memory of the strongly worded telegram, and after a moment, Maj hugged him back. He was *Papa*, after all.

Mama wanted an inventory of the rooms at Slagelsegade and more details of the shops and cafés they'd frequented. She admired the *chapeaux* in their black and white striped hatboxes with Mlle Clarisse's elegant label. Papa couldn't hear enough about the Nordic Exposition. How he envied his girls for having seen such marvels as Machine Land, the aquarium and fisheries buildings, the replicas of churches, the giant Tuborg beer bottle.

But the more they all talked about Copenhagen, at breakfast, at dinner, in the parlor with guests, the more Nik realized how much she couldn't tell. How many stories had to be rearranged. Nothing could be said about Victoria Benedictsson and Georg Brandes, the suicide and the morgue—that was a given. The Rosenbergs must not be mentioned, certainly not that Carl and Nik had gone there alone in a hackney cab and passed prostitutes soliciting in the side streets. Eva's lecture at the Women's Reading Room was recounted, but Nik couldn't tell the story of discovering the art shop that same day or lingering at Larsen's Plads to see the *Geiser* boarding its passengers. They could not even talk about the *Thingvalla* and the great upset at the end of the visit to their uncle and aunt. Aunt Marie had written Mama with *her* version; that would have to stand.

Nik did tell her parents about visiting the Misses Mundt and Luplau in their studio, but in her description they were respectable spinsters, not two women who lived together, one of whom had cropped hair and smoked cigars. Nik mentioned only that she'd discussed her plan of becoming an artist with the ladies. "What plan?" said Papa, but he didn't discourage it. "Is that why you have some tubes of paint and pencils among your things?" asked Mama. "I hope you'll now get serious about mastering an accomplishment or two."

Carl, of course, came up often, but it was always musical, well-behaved Carl, playing gratefully on the Bechstein at Slagelsegade or in concert at Tivoli. No mention could be made of Carl's feverish kisses and gropings in dark hallways and hackney cabs. In the way that Nik and Maj told their stories, you'd think that Carl had always had a score in front of him, intent only on getting ahead as a musician and composer. Nothing could be said about the day alone at the Exposition, about the labyrinth and its windings; nothing about the moment they stood in front of the doll's house in the

Potato Rows and imagined their future as husband and wife.

Nik put Carl's letters in her new metal chest, and she wore the key under her dress on a chain around her neck. And sometimes when the key moved against her skin, she remembered all that she was hiding, and she felt quite grown-up.

"How glad I am to see you again, Emilie! I've been bored to within an inch of madness these last weeks, especially since the doctor has confined me completely to bed. I can hardly see my legs over this great lump—sometimes I wonder if I even *have* legs anymore or if they work. Who could have imagined it took so long to produce a child?"

Mette put her knitting to the side and embraced Nik warmly. She wore a white robe trimmed with white lace, like a bride, but her complexion was coarser from pregnancy than Nik recalled, with red splotches among the freckles on her forehead and cheeks. Her feet, propped up on a pillow, were red and swollen, like Aunt Marie's, in too-small slippers.

"Sit down beside me. I'll ring for coffee. I'm dying for news of dear old Copenhagen. How much I miss it! Tell me everything you did, don't skimp on the descriptions! The French art exhibition, the ballet, the theater—I want to hear all about them. And you wrote that you were taken to see Emilie Mundt and Marie Luplau. I've only seen their paintings, never met them properly. Tell me everything about their studio and what they said to you about studying drawing with them."

"There's so much to tell about them. And everything else," said Nik, perching next to Mette on a chair. "Where to start?" But then it all poured out, from the meeting with the Misses Mundt and Luplau to her visit to the art shop to the paintings and sculptures in the French Pavilion. She talked and talked and the story in the middle of the story was Miss Mundt telling her that she could be an artist and that she could study with them if she came back to

Copenhagen. It was her choice to make. Yet everything was connected to Carl and what his plans were and how she would manage to persuade her parents to allow her to marry perhaps as soon as seventeen. If she was married, she could do what she wanted and live in Copenhagen and take art classes. Even though Miss Mundt had said she should not marry too early or perhaps at all. And what did Mette think?

Mette listened with avid and occasionally amused eyes, asked a question here and there, and finally said, "You went away a little girl and you come back a woman of experience, Emilie. I envy you being able to walk through Kongens Nytorv. You had nothing to be afraid of on your own—I walked there many times by myself. I know Petersen's art shop on Nikolaj Plads. I bought sketchbooks there, paints and brushes. Of course you must study with the Misses Mundt and Luplau. Of course you must go to art school!

"And as for Carl . . ." She stopped and took up her knitting again. Would Mette rebuke her for being in love at her age, or would she understand? She'd loved a young man once; the boy who went to the West Indies and never came back. "And as for Carl," Mette repeated with a smile, "how lucky you are to have a young man in love with you, a man who's not only a fine musician but who knows and admires all forms of art."

"He told me I should study sculpture not painting. He likes sculpture better."

"Sculpture." Mette sighed and adjusted herself awkwardly as the baby kicked. "Oh, to be loved by a young man who has an opinion about sculpture . . . Seventeen is young to be married, of course. But married women have certain freedoms. And certainly you could think about sculpture if it interests you."

"It doesn't," said Nik, the memory of those freezing white bodies in the French Pavilion merging for the briefest of moments with the white roses draped over the casket in the damp, cold chapel.

"And you had oysters at the Hotel d'Angleterre and chocolate torte at the Café à Porta. How elegant! I envy you—the doctor has me drinking so much milk I'm beginning to feel like one of Henrik's Holsteins. Never mind. I shall get to Copenhagen again. When I lived there I didn't have the money to enjoy myself. My head was down, studying to earn a living. But when you're married I shall come to visit you and stay at the Hotel d'Angleterre and we'll eat plates of oysters. We'll do whatever we like, go to art exhibits and the ballet every day."

They continued talking about Copenhagen until the city grew as burnished in Nik's mind as a golden painting. She forgot the smoky fug and dirty streets and feelings of claustrophobia in the rooms of Slagelsegade. She remembered Tivoli's pleasure palaces and the ornate buildings around Kongens Nytorv. She saw herself with a brush and palette in the studio of the Misses Mundt and Luplau. She saw herself walking confidently by Carl's side or sitting in the audience as he played. Margrethe Rosenberg would have no cause to patronize her. Her aunt and uncle wouldn't be able to keep her locked up like a fancy doll. Every day would be like the day she went to the Misses Mundt and Luplau or the day she walked through Nikolaj Plads. The idea of such freedom dazzled her.

Nik wasn't sure why, but the lethargy that had plagued her before the trip to Copenhagen was now gone. Within a week she was swept back into the familiar summer activities: swimming, horseback riding, picnics, and excursions to Fur with the Strandgaards. They did not go to Scotland this year but made the most of the dry sunny days of August to collect butterflies and beetles, to experiment with different flowers and vegetables in their garden, and to fossilize like mad. Joachim and Sophie had made great finds in July on Fur: fish skeletons, birds, and insects had all been pried out of the moler and cementstone at Knudeklinterne. They were eager to find more fossils before the short summer ended and they were all back at school. Mette might consider Nik a woman of experience now, but she was still a girl in the presence of the Strandgaards. They were all interested in the Nordic Exposition, of course, but after hearing about it once or twice, they were satisfied. Harald Strandgaard had never taken his children to Copenhagen, but they were, to a one, sure that it could be no finer a city than Edinburgh. None of them had questions about Carl. None of them bothered much about concerts or the ballet. And none of them knew or cared anything about the Café à Porta or the Hotel d'Angleterre.

With her skirts hiked up and her feet bare, Nik hardly minded that she had to wear a corset. If her braid slipped out of its coil to her shoulders, no one said anything, and if she got sunburnt or scraped her elbow, that was fine too. Sophie was a mass of bruises and scabs. Her skin was tanned as a boy's, even her legs, and her ginger hair was white with salt crystals. She was bony and fast, leaping over the rocks like a cat. Her eyes were sharp as a marsh hawk's. She sparred with Joachim and her father, confident in her ability to name the world correctly.

She couldn't really be a friend to Nik; she was only twelve years old. Nevertheless, of all the Strandgaards, Sophie was the one Nik was most curious about. Would she change as she became older? She didn't give a pin about love and marriage. She was opinionated and frank; she didn't care what anyone thought. She reminded Nik of what she herself had been like, as recently as the beginning of last summer, on the day she'd arrived back at home from her godparents' to meet the mysterious musical foster son from Copenhagen.

With the Strandgaards Nik sometimes forgot about Carl. Joachim was a friend again. He had a sweetheart—a girl in Jebjerg. She was the foreman's daughter at Joachim's grandparents' farm. Tom and Sophie teased him a little about Kristine and he seemed pleased. Nik was happy for him—and relieved. She didn't want to admit it but male attention, even from someone you loved, could be wearing. No one *looked* at her now, with longing or frustration. No one squeezed her waist or nibbled at her neck.

A married woman might be free, but a girl scrambling over the rocks on Fur Island—shouting, "I found something"—was far more free than Mrs. Carl Nielsen could ever be.

On August 1, the day the *Thingvalla* sailed from Copenhagen, Maj stayed in her room and didn't eat breakfast. She came down, composed, for coffee in the afternoon. Within a day or two she received the last letter Eva sent from Copenhagen. And then came an envelope posted from Christiania where the *Thingvalla* stopped to take on more passengers before beginning her passage across the Atlantic to Newfoundland and then down the coast of North America to New York.

Maj didn't share the letters but kept them in a pocket in her apron and read them frequently. Withdrawn when they first returned to Selde, she had recovered a little of her customary poise and took to saying at the dinner table and to visitors that she was looking forward to returning to Odense and finishing her last year at the teachers' college. Nik thought that away from Eva, Maj seemed more herself. But by her bed Maj kept an English grammar book, and occasionally Nik encountered her in the far reaches of the orchard where she was practicing speaking American to the apple trees.

Nik had her own letters. Carl wrote to her twice a week through August; most of the letters recalled the good times they'd had and how much he cared for her. She must never doubt his undying affection and his hopes and plans for the future. She was his darling and his treasure and the next year would go by quickly and then they would have the summer together. Aunt Marie had promised a good long visit to Selde, and he would try to get away from Tivoli so as to have July and early August free. He would be auditioning for the Royal Theater orchestra next August and was sure to find a position, for Maestro Svendsen looked on him favorably. And now he must tell her about being almost finished with his Suite for Strings and how Maestro had been exceedingly pleased with what he heard; he said the waltz movement was particularly fine. There had been one rehearsal and Carl was making some last changes to the "finale." What a remarkable thing to hear notes that you had only heard in your head come to life through instruments played by real musicians. And Nik must be sure to practice, now that she had had lessons from the great Mr. Carl Nielsen in Copenhagen; she must not forget what he told her about tempo and holding the notes. She must do exercises to strengthen her fingers and let Maj listen to her as she played and let Maj correct her, for Maj had a good ear, even if she lacked Nik's real feeling for music.

They were lovely letters, but seemed to come from another world, the strange city world and what passed for amusement there. He wrote them late at night when he came in from playing at Tivoli and had taken a glass of champagne and was fired up with dreams. Nik did not share his instructions to her with Maj; it was the last thing she wanted, to have Maj listen to her and correct her. Besides, there was no time to practice; she was too busy picnicking and swimming and revisiting all the dear old places at home, the moors and woods, the Strandgaards' house and garden, the squire's estate. She could imagine Carl and Copenhagen, but as the days went on her own presence in those memories grew fainter.

Two or three times she did get out her new watercolors from their wooden box. She took a glass of water up to her room and a plate for a small palette. She squeezed out color onto the plate, dipped her brush into the water, and made bands of vivid Rose Madder and Prussian Blue and Gamboge on the page. It made her happy to see these colors, but she wasn't sure what to do with them, what to make of them. Her skills as an illustrator were still the same as they'd been before she went to Copenhagen. She was not a young lady of great accomplishments and her sketches of trees and country roads were amateurish and unsatisfying. Besides, nothing in the world she looked at out her window was such a bright red or bold blue as the colors on the thick paper of her sketchbook. She would have to thin and tame the colors if she were to dab them in between the pencil lines, and she was reluctant to do that.

One day in the middle of August, Papa came into the garden, where Nik and Maj and Mama were taking coffee in the afternoon, holding the Skive newspaper. "There has been an accident at sea," he said.

"At sea?" Mama said, putting down her china cup. "Has a ship gone down with some of your timber?"

"No," said Papa, looking at Maj, who was half out of her wicker chair. "A collision between two steamships near Newfoundland. One was the *Thingvalla* sailing from Christiania to New York and the other the *Geiser*, returning from New York. It happened August 14."

"It can't be," said Maj. She tore the newspaper from her father's hands and read, but the news was unclear. Both ships had been damaged and passengers drowned. But only one, the *Geiser*, had gone down.

Eva had been on the *Thingvalla*. But that ship too had been rammed and was disabled, in danger of sinking. The article was brief. News had come by telegraph to Copenhagen and then out to the newspapers of the country. The article printed no passenger lists but said, only, "At least 100 passengers are feared lost."

The same thought seemed to race across Mama's face as Papa's: Thank God Maj was not on the ship.

But Maj had only one thought: Eva.

An hour later Nik found her sister diagonal across the quilted white cover of her bed. In Maj's hand was a balled-up handkerchief. You would have thought she was in a dead faint except for the small tremors left from stronger sobs. Nik had wanted to come up sooner, but Mama had said, "Let her be. Let her cry. It's likely that her friend was saved, but Maj doesn't know that yet."

How strange to hear Eva referred to as just a friend—Mama didn't know her, didn't know what a force Eva was, what a glowing bright presence in the world. Mama had never seen Maj's face when Eva came into a room, had never felt the brilliance of her smile, of her velvety Swedish voice saying "Nonsense," laughing at all obstacles. Eva had taken Nik to see the Misses Mundt and Luplau. She had spoken confidently before crowds. She had rushed to Victoria Benedictsson's side at the Café à Porta and stood up to Georg Brandes. She'd bought Maj a ticket to America, just because she wanted Maj with her all the time.

Most of all, Eva had made Maj happy.

Nik crept over to the bed and touched her sister's back, which set off a round of muffled sobs. Maj twisted her head away. Nik put a blanket over her sister and held her hand. Maj finally said, in a quilted mumble.

"If only Victoria Benedictsson hadn't killed herself. We could at least have had a happy last week together. Now even the memory of Leopold's Hotel is all mixed up with that. Three doors away, a woman was slitting her throat."

Nik didn't understand what she was talking about. What did Leopold's Hotel have to do with anything?

"I know Eva was upset about all that, with Mrs. Benedictsson. But Maj . . ."

"I should have been on the ship with her. She *wanted* me with her; she *begged* me to come. Why didn't they let me go with her? Why was I a coward? If Eva has drowned, I don't want to live either. I'll never forgive myself."

"We must wait and see," said Nik helplessly. She remembered standing at Larsen's Plads in July and watching the *Geiser*'s passengers getting ready to board. All of them had made it to New York. It was the passengers on the homeward voyage who hadn't lived to see their friends or families again. Like Eva, they'd believed that steamships were safe, that it was nothing anymore to cross the deep cold Atlantic.

"If she's alive, if she has managed to survive and gets to New

York, I must go to her. I must." Maj sat up. Her face was creased from the quilt and streaked with red. Nik had never seen her like this before. She wanted to say, "You know Mama and Papa will never let you go, not after this," but she was frightened at her sister's determination. She stroked Maj's blond curls around her hot forehead, as if she were a younger sister with influenza. "Now, now," she said. "Let's wait and see."

Papa rode to Roslev and sent telegrams to Uncle Jens and to shipping companies in Denmark and Norway, asking for more information if they had it, particularly about the passengers who survived and what might have happened to them. Meanwhile the newspaper in Skive printed more about the disaster in the following days, some of it taken from the Halifax *Morning Herald* and some from *The New York Times*. The collision had happened around four in the morning off Sable Island. The *Thingvalla* blamed the *Geiser* for being on the wrong course, but Captain Møller of the *Geiser* said their course was true. The *Thingvalla* rammed the *Geiser*, which went down rapidly. About forty people were taken from the freezing waters onto the *Thingvalla*, which already had over four hundred passengers and had suffered great damage to the bow, though the watertight compartment held. Passengers from both ships had then been transferred to a passing ocean liner from Germany, the S/S *Wieland*, en route to New York.

On August 18 a cablegram from New York came for Maj from Eva's father: "Eva safe and well. Bengt Sandström."

Maj kissed the cablegram and put it in her pocket. Eventually a long letter arrived and Maj read parts of the dramatic story to the family:

> I was awakened in my berth by a loud crash and thump, then machinery roaring and bells and whistles. I was sharing my cabin with another lady. We quickly dressed, fearing the

worst, and climbed up on deck. Another ship was very near to us. People said it was the *Geiser*. It was about four o'clock and a calm morning and rather clear. How was it possible that our ship had rammed another ship or been rammed, especially one of the same line?

The damage to the *Geiser* was plain to see. The iron hull was smashed amidships and water was pouring in over the rails. People were on deck, frantically looking for lifeboats and having trouble with them. Fathers, mothers, babies in their arms. We could see them well, and didn't know why we weren't moving to help them. Instead we had reversed engines and seemed to be steaming away.

Within ten minutes the *Geiser* went down with a huge sucking noise and every person on its deck or already in the sea vanished into a watery vortex. Most of them never came up, but we began to see heads and bodies, some swimming, some in cork life vests, some clinging to wreckage. And still we were steaming away. People all around me were shouting—it was hard to make sense of it. Something to do with our propellers, which would endanger the survivors if we came too close. A fog meanwhile began to settle in.

It seemed like forever before our lifeboats were lowered and began picking up the survivors. Of course our ship was in danger as well; the bow had almost been sheared away. The crew was dragging timber and iron struts down to the bulkhead to try to shore up the damage. I went down to the ship's hospital to see what I could do to help. There was only one surviving woman passenger, a Mrs. Lind from Sweden. She could hardly speak, her face was white, her eyes staring like two black coins. She kept saying the names of her two little ones, who had been drowned, Ida and Charlie. No one could do anything for her. I fed warm soup to the survivors and helped bandage their wounds. Most of them were half frozen, but when they came into our ship and warmed up the wounds began to bleed heavily.

In the afternoon, we saw another ship on the horizon, a German liner, the *Wieland*. They were asked to transport us all to New York, because the *Thingvalla* had to be repaired and the captain had decided to make for Halifax. The *Wieland* was already full, of Polish Jews, mostly, yet they took us on, nearly five hundred of us, with many crew members. We weren't allowed to take our luggage; it is to be sent to us with another ship. Never was a voyage so long as that horrible trip to New York. We had little to eat or drink, had to sleep without blankets, and nothing in the way of privacy, and worst of all, we had the memories of what we had seen. I did not let Mrs. Lind out of my sight; I was afraid she might slip overboard or do herself some harm. But when we arrived in New York, or rather Hoboken, I lost track of her. Papa and Mama and my dear brothers were waiting for me. Never could I have imagined being so happy to see them, nor to be taken home and petted.

"What else does she write?" asked Nik. "Is she coming back to Denmark? Will you go to America?"

"She says that she has nightmares," said Maj quietly. "Captain Møller of the *Geiser* was a friend of her father's and was the reason her father let her come to Denmark in June and travel alone. She dreams about Mrs. Lind, who lost her babies. She dreams of the babies sinking down and down into the water. She says . . . she says the Atlantic Ocean is not the same to her now. She fears it."

"But then, she won't come back here, if she's afraid to cross the ocean."

"She'll never come back to Denmark," said Maj, still in the same quiet voice. "But that's all right. She's alive. It just means that I'll be going to America next summer, when I finish my schooling. I will learn English this winter. I'm not afraid of the Atlantic. I won't let her forget me."

As if Eva could forget Maj. But Maj could forget her own family when she talked like this. She no longer belonged to them.

Carl's Suite for Strings was a triumph.

He wrote the day after in high excitement that the applause for the second movement was so great that Maestro Dahl took the unusual step of repeating it, to even more applause. And Dahl had dragged him from the string section to the conductor's podium and made him take a bow. His first bow in front of an audience wildly cheering and clapping.

All his friends had been there, Aunt and Uncle of course and all the Rosenbergs. Margrethe had brought a Miss Brodersen, an art student. Carl was sorry his parents weren't there to see him. Just the Rosenbergs and Nielsens. If his mother and father and Nik had been there, his joy would have been complete.

At the end of August Maj had returned to Odense. Her letters were infrequent and often perfunctory, but in October she wrote Nik, describing a visit from Carl to Odense.

> He came to conduct the Suite for Strings. It was a tremendous success here. How amazing it was to see our Carl at Odense Town Hall, conducting! And so beautifully. The crowd quite roared with pleasure to hear their native son. Uncle Jens and Aunt Marie had brought him and were there, pleased as punch. They were all staying at Uncle Hans's and Ottilie was quite beside herself, the silly goose, to be in the presence of someone so famous. We all met his parents; they are quite respectable and his mother has the kindest face. One sees where Carl gets his genuine kindness. He had heard of the tragedy at sea and sat with me for an hour and talked about Eva. He said how glad he was that she had escaped harm. We talked about you too, Nik. I take back all the foolish things I ever said about him, my dear.

> He loves you truly. When it comes down to it, love is all that really matters, no matter what unexpected shape it takes or whether others disapprove. Two people who really love each other should never be parted.

Nik put this letter, along with Carl's, in her strongbox. All his triumphs reflected on her; she must look forward to the day she would sit in the audience as he conducted and be congratulated by everyone.

Mette's baby had strands of colorless hair and a large jolly face. He looked just like Henrik, and they named him little Hans, after the old squire. But that was the only thing that happened of note in Selde that fall and winter, and Nik, for her part, was glad. Life slowed and thickened. All the young Strandgaards went back to school. Last year it had been strange not to return to school with them, but this year it felt more normal. She was not clever, she thought, not like Sophie. She preferred to dream and help Mama around the house, to read and write letters to Carl. The letters she wrote were not like his; they concerned only the doings of the house, the inn, and the district. Still, he seemed overjoyed every time he heard from her.

That Christmas he sent her a gold locket in the shape of a heart, which Mama allowed her to wear in public. And they talked about Nik returning to Copenhagen at Easter for a few weeks. Aunt Marie had invited her especially, making note that Nik was an easier child in every way than dear stubborn Maj.

As often in the winter, the family sat together in the evening: Papa re-read his political journals and a travel book or two and Mama continued with Dickens. Nik kept meaning to read *Money*, now that she was sixteen; instead she started on Plato's *Republic*. Carl had sent her a copy.

But alone in her room she got out her toy circus. She strung up a tightrope using part of the old telephone cord and turned Flor the Ballerina into an acrobat. Flor walked the tightrope, almost falling, but never falling, always making that last little leap, over to the side where Jacques stood with his hands out, waiting for her.

AUTHOR'S NOTE

Fossil Island IS THE FIRST OF TWO NOVELS BASED ON THE life of the painter and ethnographer Emilie Demant Hatt, called Nik by her family. Her story continues in the sequel, *The Former World.* At the end of that novel, you'll find more about my sources in the writings of Carl Nielsen and Emilie Demant Hatt, their letters, and the historical times they lived in. Information can also be found on the website www.emiliedemanthatt.com.

I'm grateful to those who read this novel in manuscript—Katherine Hanson, Betsy Howell, Rose Katz, and Michele Whitehead, and to Kyra Freestar for her brilliant copyediting. I'd also like to thank friends in Denmark, particularly Lis Bruselius, Mette Dyrberg, John Fellow, and Henrik Gutzon Larsen, all of whom, with patience and kindness, have given me insight into Danish history, literature, art, and music. Lis was also generous enough to read *Fossil Island* with Danish eyes and to suggest corrections.

I spent a memorable day driving around the countryside near Selde with Knud Erik Jakobsen of the local history archives in Salling and Fjends. I also thank Marianne Jørgensen, one of the owners of Kjeldgaard, a manor house near Selde, for her hospitality. I thank John Brinch Bertelsen, director of Fur Museum, which has a fine collection of fossils from the area, and Karen Klitgaard, who gave me a tour of Fur's fossil coastlines. I'd also like to thank the staff of the retreat residence at Ørslev Kloster.

ABOUT THE AUTHOR

BARBARA SJOHOLM IS THE AUTHOR OF MANY WORKS OF fiction and nonfiction, including *The Palace of the Snow Queen: Winter Travels in Lapland* and *Blue Windows: A Christian Science Childhood.* Her essays and travel journalism have appeared in *The New York Times*, *Smithsonian*, *Slate*, *American Scholar*, *Harvard Review*, *Feminist Studies*, and *Scandinavian Studies*. She has translated several books from Norwegian and Danish, including *With the Lapps in the High Mountains: A Woman among the Sami 1907–1908*, Emilie Demant Hatt's narrative of her travels in Lapland. She is currently working on a book about Demant Hatt's career as an ethnographer and artist.

Read *The Former World*, the sequel to *Fossil Island*

Two sisters look for independence and love in late nineteenth century Denmark

Cedar Street Editions
ISBN: 978-0-9883567-5-7
Also available as an e-book,
ISBN: 978-0-9883567-3-3

The story of the two sisters, Nik and Maj, begun in *Fossil Island,* continues in this equally engaging sequel. Now sixteen, Nik resumes her relationship with the passionate musician Carl Nielsen, who returns once more for a summer visit in 1889 to her provincial village. But their bonds are strained by social convention and Nik's own stirrings of ambition to study art. Now twenty-one, Maj finds a teaching job, but her mother hasn't given up the idea her eldest daughter will marry and forget about her close friend Eva Sandström. Taking place over the course of two dramatic years, the sisters' lives will be utterly changed by love, heartbreak, illness, and death. A vivid portrait of two stubborn daughters who love their family, but yearn for freedom on their own terms, *The Former World* recreates a time when women's lives and Danish society were in transition. Whether it's Nik learning to cycle or Maj dreaming of working in Brooklyn as a teacher, Nik and Maj are memorable characters in a setting both distant in time yet familiar.

Praise for *Fossil Island*

"*Fossil Island* reads as well as any Jane Austen novel, but its political themes and social commentary really matter to the 21st-century reader. This novel not only offers an insightful, engaging view of personal manners, social mores and romantic love, but also it deals with the politics of manners, mores, and love. In particular it illuminates the social history of women of the time, including lesbians and other women who wanted to live independent lives. *Fossil Island* brought to mind the wonderful and internationally acclaimed historical novels of Sarah Waters. *Fossil Island,* like Waters's books, made me gasp out loud at its plot turns. The characters are so richly drawn, so compellingly human and difficult and funny and likable, and their interactions so humanly complicated, so impossible and so tender, that I think any fiction reader or history lover will read this, as I did, with avid enthusiasm."

— Gillian Kendall, author of *How I Became a Human Being*

"Barbara Sjoholm transports us to Denmark in the 1880s, a time when traditional customs and ideas were giving way to new technology and modern thinking, and enchants us with the story of a girl's first love. *Fossil Island* captures beautifully the conflicting worlds the young lovers Carl and Nik move between: the harmony and lazy rhythms of village life on Jutland's Limfjord, the dissonance and hectic tempos of Copenhagen. *Fossil Island* is a book to savor — you won't want to put it down, you won't want it to end."

— Katherine Hanson, editor of *An Everyday Story: Norwegian Women's Fiction*

With the Lapps in the High Mountains: A Woman among the Sami, 1907–1908

By Emilie Demant Hatt, translated by Barbara Sjoholm

University of Wisconsin Press
ISBN: 978-0-299-29234-8

With the Lapps in the High Mountains is an entrancing true account, a classic of travel literature, and a work that deserves wider recognition as an early contribution to ethnographic writing. Published in 1913 and available here in its first English translation, *With the Lapps* is the narrative of Emilie Demant Hatt's nine-month stay in the tent of a Sami family in northern Sweden in 1907–8 and her participation in a dramatic reindeer migration over snow-packed mountains to Norway with another Sami community in 1908. A single woman in her thirties, Demant Hatt immersed herself in the Sami language and culture. She writes vividly of daily life, women's work, children's play, and the care of reindeer herds in Lapland a century ago. This English-language edition also includes photographs by Demant Hatt, an introduction by translator Barbara Sjoholm, and a foreword by Hugh Beach, author of *A Year in Lapland: Guest of the Reindeer Herders.*

"Barbara Sjoholm's graceful and sensitive translation of Emilie Demant Hatt's classic ethnographic memoir opens to an English-language readership a Sápmi of a century ago, when herding Sami were born, grew up, and died in a life shaped by the seasonal migration of their reindeer and their culture's age-old traditions for effective life in Scandinavia's far north. It is a land and culture gripped in change, and Demant Hatt chronicles the issues and injustices that face the Sami of her day, while exploring continuities in tradition and worldview that seem to stretch back into time immemorial. Demant Hatt's insightful observations of daily life, jovial narrative style, and at times impassioned pleas for the culture she had come to love make her *With the Lapps in the High Mountains* an essential source for anyone interested in the culture of Sami people or in the shaping of a female ethnographic voice in the history of anthropology."

—Thomas A. DuBois, translator of Johan Turi's *An Account of the Sámi*

“Emilie Demant Hatt’s *With the Lapps in the High Mountains* is an important and significant contribution to the history of anthropology and ethnography. Weaving artful description and personal narrative, Demant Hatt recounts a story that, until now, has been largely unknown to English-speaking anthropologists and ethnographers. Many perhaps know of her collaboration with Johan Turi, but this work sheds further light on Demant Hatt’s role as an observant participant involved in the daily lives of Sami people. Thanks to Barbara Sjoholm’s careful and skillful translation, Demant Hatt’s work is fortunately now available to a much larger audience.”

—Luke Eric Lassiter, author of *The Chicago Guide to Collaborative Ethnography*

The Palace of the Snow Queen: Winter Travels in Lapland

By Barbara Sjoholm

Counterpoint Press
ISBN: 978-1-59376-159-2

A frequent traveler to Scandinavia, Barbara Sjoholm set off one winter to explore a region that had long intrigued her. *The Palace of the Snow Queen* is the result of Sjoholm's travels in Lapland, starting with her visit to Kiruna, Sweden, to observe the construction of the Icehotel. Over the course of three winters in the North, she met ice artists and snow architects, reindeer herders, and Sami writers and activists. Throughout *The Palace of the Snow Queen,* Sjoholm provides a deeply moving look at the people of Kiruna and the Sami's struggle to maintain their grazing lands and migration routes in the face of tourism, while focusing on the various political and ideological changes occurring within this icy region. Ultimately, Sjoholm contemplates the tensions between contemporary tourism and traditional culture, and delivers a powerful travel narrative of this comparatively little-known region of Europe.

"*The Palace of the Snow Queen* is an exquisite book. I would recommend it to anyone interested in Lapland in particular, or travel in general."

—Vendela Vida, author of *Let the Northern Lights Erase Your Name*

"A captivating homage to the frozen far North and the Sami."

—*Booklist*

"There are not many books I read in a weekend, pausing only to eat and sleep. This is one of them. *The Palace of the Snow Queen* is a spectacular book, not to be missed by anyone fascinated with the North, or anyone who enjoys reflections on culture, art, and history."

—Bookslut

"*The Palace of the Snow Queen* is the coldest I've ever been reading a book, but it was worth it."

—*The Seattle Times*

CPSIA information can be obtained
at www.ICGtesting.com
Printed in the USA
FSOW01n1002071215
14274FS

9 780988 356740